The Caves of Balhok
The third book of
Seeds of Balhok

By

Rick AW Smith

COPYRIGHT

The Caves from Balhok, Book 3 of Seeds of Balhok, by Rick A.W. Smith
© 2018 by Rick A.W. Smith. All rights reserved.

No part of this book may be reproduced in any written, electronic, recording, or photocopying without written permission of the publisher or author. The exception would be in the case of brief quotations embodied in the critical articles or reviews and pages where permission is specifically granted by the publisher or author.

Although every precaution has been taken to verify the accuracy of the information contained herein, the author and publisher assume no responsibility for any errors or omissions. No liability is assumed for damages that may result from the use of information contained within.

Cover Design: Blake E Davis.
Map Design: Joel Ray Pellerin

Publisher: Kindle Direct Publishing Amazon.com Inc., CreateSpace, a DBA of On-Demand Publishing, LLC
Copyright registration number TXu 2-064-340

ISBN: 9781982984731

10 9 8 7 6 5 4 3 2 1 v2

1. Fantasy

First Edition
Printed in USA

Dedication

To my grandchildren. Now that the Trilogy is finished, I realize it's for them.

Contents

Dedication	4
Planets	7
Races	7
Cities and Villages of Storlenia (country north of the Southland Mountains)	8
Cities and Villages of Shaksbah (country south of the Southland Mountains)	8
The Guilds of Storlenia	9
Major Characters in "The Caves of Balhok"	10
Preamble	12
Chapter 1 - A League of three unconscious men	1
Chapter 2 - A trip to Harleem	6
Chapter 3 - The three missions	12
Chapter 4 - The blanket of secrecy	18
Chapter 5 - The Canticle of Goldenrod	25
Chapter 6 - A report from Ankoletia	27
Chapter 7 - *Secrets* of the 'Dagger of Truth'	29
Chapter 8 - The Green lady's compromise	34
Chapter 9 - The *Buzz*	44
Chapter 10 - The Pit of Pain	52
Chapter 11 - Ranoof's history	60
Chapter 12 - Two minds are better than one	66
Chapter 13 - The celebration of Bra-ten	73
Chapter 14 - The Medallion of Authority	81
Chapter 15 - A new name in Kel-eetan	88
Chapter 16 - The messenger from Harleem	93
Chapter 17 - The power of Mercy	100
Chapter 18 - The Next Quorum Leader	103
Chapter 19 - One too many mistakes	108
Chapter 20 - The Master Spy	112
Chapter 21 - Yaneek's decision	114
Chapter 22 - Yaneek's confidante	120
Chapter 23 - The Great Escape	125
Chapter 24 - The Harvest of Loyalties	130
Chapter 25 - Biskin and the two towers	133
Chapter 26 - The breach of permission	138
Chapter 27 - The Hypocrite	141
Chapter 28 - The shift in power	145
Chapter 29 - A halo of soft light	146

Chapter	30	-	The cage of deceit	153
Chapter	31	-	Wagons roll	156
Chapter	32	-	Zephra's genetics	159
Chapter	33	-	The missing bricks	163
Chapter	34	-	The shifting sands of honour	172
Chapter	35	-	The return of the five	182
Chapter	36	-	The grasslands of death	188
Chapter	37	-	The wedged wall of death	193
Chapter	38	-	The Oath of Life	199
Chapter	39	-	The slope of death	205
Chapter	40	-	The Ledge of death	212
Chapter	41	-	What is your name?	216
Chapter	42	-	Water water everywhere	219
Chapter	43	-	The abandoned mine shafts	225
Chapter	44	-	The Mines of Death	233
Chapter	45	-	The chain of remarkable events	239
Chapter	46	-	The Etchings of Knowledge	246
Chapter	47	-	More than flesh and blood	254
Chapter	48	-	The Cocoon Transporter	262
Chapter	49	-	Lost in space	268
Chapter	50	-	So many Caves	274
Chapter	51	-	Back from the dead	278
Chapter	52	-	The return of the Old Woman	285
Chapter	53	-	The best laid plans	295
Chapter	54	-	Prisons within prisons	299
Chapter	55	-	The Offer	306
Chapter	56	-	The Blanket of White Light	311
ABOUT THE AUTHOR				319

Planets

A planet of Seers, called 'Balhok', located in the Middle of the Galaxy.

Planet Harleem, populated by a predatory race, located on the far side of the Galaxy.

Ankoletia, a planet in the same Galaxy as Balhok and Harleem, inhabited by two races, Storlenians in the north and Shaksbali in the south.

Races

The Seers of Balhok

The Plunderers of Harleem

Storlenians, living in the northern hemisphere of Ankoletia (otherwise known as the country of Storlenia)

Shaksbali, living in the southern hemisphere of Ankoletia (otherwise known as the country of Shaksbah)

> The El-Bhat, living in the far southern reaches of Shaksbah, are a warrior group feared by the other Shaksbali. Their way of life is to plunder. They are known as Brothers of the Silk and are ruled by The Quorum.
>
> The Sherilin, an ancient and extinct Shaksbali tribe, lived on the eastern plains of Shaksbah before the Great War. They found the first Waterless well and the Dagger of Truth, which draws its power from the Green Necklace of Harleem.

Cities and Villages of Storlenia (country north of the Southland Mountains)

Arborville, home of the Tracking Guild that produces Olleti, north of Seven Oaks.
Border Pass, Tracker fortress in the Southland Mountains
Borit Betoon, Redemption Guild that contains ancient relics
Breckenden, home town of Benekee
Crestal Mountains, area famous for its crystal. Along its borders lay the villages that spawned the Trackers.
Cross Rivers, town of Shu-len and his son Haybin, Blacksmiths
Lithgate Wilderness, location of Urshen's cabin
Pechora, residence of Petin (Guild Master of Pechora's Planning and Development Guild)
Port Airiken, on the western coast
Port Aqabah, on the eastern coast
Qar-ana, Main headquarters of Planning and Development Guild of all Storlenia
Tinker Village, established by Braddock, close to Arborville

Cities and Villages of Shaksbah (country south of the Southland Mountains)

Chitouf, Ac-user village close to the Southland Mountains that contains the El-Bhat gold.
District of Denlen, southern Shaksbah, where the El-Bhat live
Kel-eetan, capital of Shaksbah
Mines of Tenleth, Gold mines operated by the El-Bhat for the government of Shaksbah
Toobor, city located in South Bounty District, populated by immigrant Storlenians

The Guilds of Storlenia

    Accounting Guild
    Astronomy Guild
    Blacksmith Guild
    Communication Guild
    Financial Guild
    Hospital Guild
    Hunting Guild
    Mechanical Guild
    Medical Guild
    Planning and Development Guild
    Precious Metals Guild
    Redemption Guild
    Roads and River Management Guild
    Sea Shipping Guild
    Sporting Guild
    Tracking Guild
    Transportation Guild

Major Characters in "The Caves of Balhok"

Aram-Dentee II, previously the Butler, now the new Assistant to Axion, the unseated Head Guild Master of the Planning and Development Guild of Qar-ana

Axion, self-exiled Head Guild Master of the Planning and Development Guild at Qar-ana, the Capital city of Storlenia

Arl-Sheen, member of the El-Bhat Quorum, second to Shanteef in authority

Benekee, a young Guild Brother who can tap the power of the Shards from afar

Bernado, Head Master of the Tracking Guild of Pechora. After finding the Necklace, he moved to Qar-ana

Biskin, Tracker from Arborville with a Gift for smelling trouble. His Gift has led him to find and protect Protas

Braddock, Tinker Leader in charge of building Tinker Village, and Zephra's father

Craslin, Guild Master of the Planning and Development Guild at Qar-ana, the Capital city of Storlenia

Esch-Terra, Leader of the Shaksbali Government, resides in Kel-eetan, capital of Shaksbah

Far-fel, Specialist Tracker that was held captive by the Necklace until he found Urshen's Amulet at Pechora Tracking Guild

Finn, Gatherer of the Specialist Trackers

Fre-steel, Tracker that defected to the El-Bhat at Border Pass, now works for Bernado

Jokta, long-time Tracker friend of Axion

Kareen-hys-Tebeel-del-Harleem, from the planet Harleem. Assigned to extract slaves, gold and genetic material from the planet Ankoletia

Mishri, previously the El-Bhat Band Leader at Pechora Tracking Guild, now returned to the Quorum as Shanteef's most trusted Band Leader

Nusdek, leader of the Militia Guard at Qar-ana

Ou-Leesen, El-Bhat Leader, his Advisor is Stek

Protas/Robe Man, Friend of Urshen and adopted brother to Ee-lath

Ranoof, Tracker who helped train the Militia. Carried Zephra's completed Amulet to Braddock.
Shanteef, El-Bhat Quorum Leader, rules from The Keep in southern Shaksbah
Stek, Tracker, working as an Advisor to Ou-Leesen
Urshen, first Seer in over a thousand years, carries an Amulet that is the Key to the knowledge and power of the Garden

Yaneek, sister to Benekee, living at the Planning Guild with Zephra her friend
Zephra, a Tinker Wagon Mechanic, daughter of Braddock

Preamble

Previously …

As a young lad of fifteen, Benekee had a disquieting dream, showing him how he will discover Shards and eventually, through the power of these Shards, be able to convince Yaneek, his sister, to believe. But Benekee is raised as an unbeliever and eventually has forgotten his dream. Four years later, at the Redemption Guild of Borit Betoon, he watched lifeless Shards glow before his unbelieving eyes … the result of Zephra using her White Bauble. After a trip to Qar-ana, he believed that the Shards had adopted him, realized he no longer needed the Redemption Guild, and headed home with the Shards to live with his sister Yaneek.

Meanwhile, Urshen gathered the victorious Leaders at Border Pass to discuss the need for a Tinker Guild. Urshen and Zephra renewed their love but needs pulled them in different directions as she headed for Arborville to help build the Tinker Guild and Urshen left with the Trackers to recruit the Blacksmith Haybin. As they prepared to leave Cross Rivers with Haybin, Urshen and Toulee discovered that Stek was still hypnotised with instructions to assist the El-Bhat. Urshen immediately dispatched a Half-Circle including Deema, Toulee and four others, hoping that they would find Stek in the Lithgate Wilderness. One night, as the Half-Circle headed north, Peloree, a Tracker, was killed by El-Bhat, but his need for assistance triggered the expansion of the powers of this half of the Circle.

While a confused and determined Stek arrived at Pechora to enlist the help of Bernado to help him find the Cave, the Half-Circle continued north. They practised their new ability to see what each other could see, and read each other's thoughts, allowing them to successfully destroy an El-Bhat group that were pursuing them.

Back at Arborville, Urshen proposed to Zephra by the river at the new Tinker Village.

Sometime earlier, Mitrock headed towards Mantel with Protas, Bru-ell and Biskin to find a safe place for Urshen's family to stay. As they headed for Pechora Tracking Guild, with Benson and his family, Jalek headed for a Redemption Guild to acquire a Robe.

At Pechora, things didn't look right for Protas, so he convinced

Benton to use the Medallion given to him by Mitrock, to answer the question ... if they should stay or not. The answer propelled Protas, Bru-ell and the Benton family out the door, but it was too late for Mitrock who had found Pechinin in the prison cells below. They were both killed by El-Bhat.

After Protas escaped, he found Jalek's horse and decided he had to find him.

At Breckenden, Benekee understood that he needed to reassemble the Shards, and was asked by Yaneek to find a job. At the Mechanical Guild, Benekee used one of the Shards to pass the test for apprenticeship and was enthusiastically hired by Beelstop; an old but talented inventor.

Meanwhile, in the Lithgate Wilderness, Benton's Family and Bru-ell met Stek. Unaware of his divided loyalties, they showed Stek where the Cave was and they all worked to improve the security of the path to the Cave.

The story then returned to the few El-Bhat that escaped the carnage at Border Pass and followed them as they headed south to advise the Quorum of the disaster. Ou-Leesen volunteered to be the messenger of their failure and thus accepted his predetermined death. However, Shanteef, the Quorum Leader was impressed by his warrior heart and quick mind. Instead of killing him, he bonded with him and gave him the Dagger of Truth, and the assignment to build a Pass to allow the El-Bhat to move their gold into Storlenia, to buy the power of the Guilds.

Before he left, they met at the Mines of Tenleth where Ou-Leesen had serious concerns, regarding the Storlenian women and children who had been shackled as slaves to work the Mines. In the luxurious Keep, Ou-Leesen learned about the Dagger of Truth and the Sherilin who first found it at the bottom of a Waterless Well. Once Ou-Leesen left, Shanteef sent the Advisor to assist Ou-Leesen as promised ... but as an Assassin.

The Half-Circle led by Deema, decided to head west, to throw any additional pursuers off their trail. Convinced that they were successful, they abandoned their wagon and headed north. They came across a village of death, and spent months assisting the villagers. Finally, they headed east, and then descended south down the Lithgate Wilderness valley until they found Bru-ell and Benton's family in an abandoned cabin. Unfortunately, they discovered that

Stek had headed south, and he knew the location of the Cave.

Unknown to them, Stek had advised Bernado of his success in finding the Cave. Satisfied, Bernado sent him to find Shanteef, the Quorum Leader, by way of Ou-Leesen pass. His orders were to give Shanteef the location of the Cave.

Back at Arborville, Biskin informed Urshen that Pechinin and Mitrock are dead. Urshen had hoped to receive guidance from Pechinin on what to do next. Instead, he falls on the wisdom of Braddock who told him to go find Protas. With the remaining six Trackers, led by Tallin, they headed north for the Pechora Tracking Guild, where they are drugged by Bernado. Ranoof, never one to drink wine, escaped to an abandoned barn.

Back at Breckenden, Benekee was accused of being crazy by his sister Yaneek, because of his belief in the Shards. He desperately wanted her to believe. Then he had a dream in which the Old Woman with long white hair, told him of their family bloodline and how this has given Benekee significant access to the power of the Shards. Meanwhile, Benekee and Beelstop built the Brass Sling and with Yaneek, took it to the Hunting Guild. After a very successful demonstration, the threesome left, elated with their success. But were soon held up on the road by three men sent by Craslin to find the Shards. These three men stole both the Brass Sling and a fake copy of the Shards.

Using the power of the Shards, Benekee, Yaneek and Beelstop escaped and then headed to Arborville, the place where Benekee knows he will find the missing shard.

Back at Pechora, while Protas searched for Jalek, he spotted Ranoof escaping from the Tracking Guild and followed him to a barn. But unfortunately, Jalek had also spotted Protas and Ranoof. He told Bernado, who sent men to capture them both.

Ranoof was already on his way to Qar-ana but Protas was caught by Bernado's men and then sent to the Quorum as a gift.

Jalek discovered that Protas was the only person who knew where his horse could be. He followed the group south and rescued Protas. As the two members of the Redemption Guild spared with words, Jalek decided to leave Hunger behind, convinced that Ranoof had sent his horse back to Pechora.

Protas headed south to avoid re-capture and spotted a Mountain Cat stalking a small herd of sheep, attended by a village boy.

He killed the cat, saved the boy, and collapsed from loss of blood. The villagers of Chitouf nursed Protas's scarred body back to health, but before he had a chance to fully recover, Ou-Leesen appeared and challenged the villagers as to why Protas was still alive.

Because Protas and Ee-lath are bonded for as long as they live, Ou-Leesen reluctantly let him live and took the bonded pair with him.

Back in Qar-ana, Craslin, Axion's Assistant, now with the Brass Sling, convinced the Head Guild Master Axion, to build the Militia Guard, due to the threatening advance of the El-Bhat into Storlenia. As soon as Ranoof appeared, he was conscripted to train the Militia Guard. But by this time, Craslin's ambitions had become traitorous. He hired a Butler, by the name of Aram-Dentee, to assassinate Axion, the Head Guild Master.

Axion managed to escape with an old Tracker friend called Jokta, but the Butler followed them, intent on finishing his mission.

By now, Benekee, Yaneek and Beelstop are in Arborville. After a brief stay, Benekee, Yaneek and Zephra left to find Urshen, assuming he would counsel them as to who should possess the completed Amulet of Shards. They followed Urshen's trail and ended up in the Tracking Guild of Pechora. While they talked to Bernado, who afterwards sent them to Qar-ana, Urshen tapped the power of her Amulet, connecting Urshen with the Half-Circle that is with him. Eventually Urshen used this connection, to draw on the combined strength of the Half-Circle, to fight the power of the Necklace, used by Bernado.

Meanwhile, in the far eastern mountains of Storlenia, Far-fel, a Specialist Tracker, was given the assignment to kill the Silent Reaper. In due course, he found him in the town of Pirtelin, but unknown to Far-fel, the Silent Reaper wore a Necklace that gave him enormous power.

Far-fel managed to kill the Silent Reaper but not before he lost much of his 'life' into the Necklace, which he must use to get his life back.

At this point, a flashback in the story covers the history of the Necklace, which was originally planted at the bottom of a Waterless Well, by the people from the planet Harleem. It was their intent, through the Necklace, to eventually enslave the people of Ankoletia.

Because Far-fel must use the Necklace to get his life back, he became a slave to the green stone, and was led to the Pechora

Tracking Guild. There he was healed by Urshen's Amulet and escaped with his life. He decided he must return and steal the Amulet.

As Far-fel left with the Amulet, Urshen felt the Amulet leave. At the same time, Bernado was awakened in the middle of the night and instructed in the use and power of the Necklace. Eventually, Fre-steel observed the dark power of the Necklace which inspired him to leave for the Mines of Tenleth, to free the women and children.

Back at Qar-ana, Craslin took control of the government. Fascinated by Zephra, he decided that she must eventually be his wife. To keep her there, he insisted that she stay to inspect the wagons that he had purchased. While living at the Planning and Development Guild, Zephra met Ranoof, and asked him to take the Shards and her White Bauble to her father, but as one complete talisman.

Ranoof sent the tall black horse with the white stockings back to Pechora as a false lead and then headed south, until he found a Jeweller who reassembled the Shards and White Bauble into a complete piece, which produced an enormous flash of light.

In the meantime, Craslin found out from Yaneek, that Benekee was the one who had designed the Brass Sling. He decided to enlist Benekee in his efforts to improve this weapon, but before he could release him from his prison cell, Benekee was beaten and left for dead by the three men who stole his fake Shards.

This unfortunate turn of events prompted Craslin to invite the Healers into his Guild to heal Benekee. Craslin worked at the side of the Healers to save Benekee. First, because of the Brass Sling, and second, by trying to save Benekee, he hoped to strengthen his relationship with Zephra.

While Benekee was being treated, he had a very important dream. He met the Old Woman with the long white hair and discovered that he had the remarkable ability to pull power from the Garden without having to touch the Amulet because the Garden trusted him. After careful consideration, he used this power to heal himself on the inside but left the healing on the outside to progress naturally, to keep his secret.

Back at Pechora, Bernado used the second Medallion, to find out about Urshen's Crystal Amulet. Urshen barely succeeded against the Green Power with the aid of his Half-Circle … and the completed Amulet held by Ranoof. But unfortunately, pulling the power through Ranoof, who was not bonded to the combined White Bauble and Shards, broke the link of the Circle, including the Half-Circle protecting

Urshen's family at the abandoned cabin, in Lithgate Wilderness.

At Arborville, Biskin was sent east to help search for other Shaksbali spies inside the Tracking Guilds. Before he returned to Arborville, he felt the need to search for Protas, and headed southeast towards Ou-Leesen pass. By a twist of fate, he saved the life of Ou-Leesen, which resulted in Protas becoming the new Advisor. Then Stek walked into the El-Bhat camp on his way to deliver the location of the Cave to the Quorum. Ou-Leesen ordered him to stay with him instead. When Biskin mentioned that Mitrock was dead, Stek was released from his mental chains.

With Ou-Leesen Pass finished, Protas was sent to Chitouf to load up eight wagons of gold, disguised as bricks. Then Ou-Leesen and twenty of his El-Bhat warriors, along with Protas, Biskin, Stek and the boy Ee-lath, headed for Aqabah, a port city. On the way, Protas recognized the landscape, from Urshen's description, of the location of another Cave. This was one of several Cave locations that Urshen had carefully described to Protas after Urshen almost drowned.

On the way to the Cave, he rescued a dog that he named Sausage who helped him find the Cave. Protas left the Cave with an Amulet, hidden in the dog's collar.

In Qar-ana, Stek and Biskin negotiated with Craslin for the shipping rights from Shaksbah to ports Aqabah and Airiken. While Craslin considered how he would use the gold, Bernado, the Head Guild Master of the Tracking Guild in Pechora, is visited by Kareen-del-Harleem. This Visitor instructed him to go to Qar-ana, where Craslin had acquired gold, a superior weapon and would soon have an army sufficiently large to conquer all Ankoletia.

Having arrived in Qar-ana, Bernado is invited by Craslin to join him as they work together to rule the planet. Meanwhile, Craslin is determined to find the rest of the Quorum's gold and steal it.

While intrigue increased in Qar-ana, Axion and Jokta made their way to the Crestal Mountains where they found Finn, the Gatherer of the Specialist Trackers. Eventually Far-fel joined the gathered Specialists and told them about the Necklace and the Amulet and the power that threatened all Ankoletia. With direction from the Amulet, the Specialists travelled to Arborville where the Tinkers had set up a new Guild.

Finn, Far-fel, Axion and Jokta travelled together. On their way, they stopped at an Inn for stew, but it was poisoned by the Butler who was still determined to assassinate Axion. Far-fel used the Amulet to determine that the Butler was in the kitchen and soon Finn and Aram-Dentee were in a death struggle ... until the Butler saw the Amulet glow. He agreed to make an oath to join them while holding the Amulet.

He collapsed, still holding the talisman and when he finally awoke in three days, the Amulet had affected a significant change in the Butler.

After this event, Jokta left for Qar-ana to keep his eyes and ears open, while the rest headed for Arborville to meet up with the Tinkers.

As the group met with Braddock, they informed him of Craslin's takeover of power, the infestation of El-Bhat at the Pechora Tracking Guild and about the dark power of the Necklace.

While Far-fel showed Braddock his Amulet, Ranoof appeared with Benekee's Amulet (now completed with Zephra's White Bauble) and placed the glowing Amulet on the table. Instinctively Far-fel picked it up while holding his own and then collapsed.

Meanwhile, Yaneek met Protas in the Planning Guild, thinking he was Benekee in a Robe. She is fascinated by this man and Protas welcomes the idea of having a visitor in prison. Because of the spies, they whisper to each other ... as they both fall in love.

Across the Southland Mountains, Ou-Leesen and his small group arrived at Chitouf to pick up more gold. But it was gone! The houses ... the villagers ... the gold.

Back in Qar-ana, Bernado visited Protas and extended an offer of immunity to his crimes if he will work for Bernado. Protas agreed. Then Bernado rushed back to Pechora and brought Urshen to Qar-ana, intent on studying Urshen before he handed him over to Kareen-del-Harleem. Bernado was convinced that the only way to defeat a Colossus was to know his secrets, and he was sure that Urshen was a key to help unlock those secrets!

For the first time in many months, Protas and Urshen find themselves together again ... in a prison cell ... guarded by the Necklace!

Chapter 1 - A League of three unconscious men

Previously, Far-fel, along with Finn and his Specialist Trackers, arrived at the Tinker Guild in Arborville, as instructed by the Amulet. While Far-fel showed Braddock his crystal talisman, Ranoof suddenly appeared with Benekee's Amulet (now completed with Zephra's White Bauble) and placed the glowing Amulet on the table. Instinctively Far-fel picked it up while holding his own ... and then collapsed.

A circle of men, expanded with the arrival of Axion and Aram-Dentee II, had gathered around the unconscious body of Far-fel as the rest of the men looked on in bewilderment.

  Trackers and Tinkers were by nature extremely independent, but the combined experience with Amulets was extremely limited and gave reason to pause, as Axion, Finn, Braddock, Ranoof and Aram Dentee II looked at each other, hoping that someone might have a clue of what to do.

  Finn had used the blade of his knife to check if Far-fel was still breathing ... so they knew he was alive. But beyond that, it was complicated. He was still holding *two* Amulets ... one in each hand ... that had glowed only moments earlier ... and then he fainted.

  Were they allowed to touch him? Would he lay there for three days like Aram-Dentee? If they disturbed him would they interrupt an important communication with the Amulets?
  Every one of them expressed valid concerns but no one had a clue of what they should do next.

  "Aram," Finn finally began, "I wonder if you remember anything from your experience of holding Far-fel's Amulet while you were unconscious at the Inn?"

Aram-Dentee II looked down at the kneeling Specialist Tracker as he reflected on his experience. There were memories for sure. Memories of darkness and pain ... memories of things not of his world. So mostly, not anything that Finn was fishing for. "Well ... I remember a flash of light," he finally offered.

"Yeah ... me too," Ranoof added.

"I think it's up to you two," Finn said, as he led the way for the rest of the group ... away from Far-fel.

Standing alone with Far-fel on the floor, the two men stared at each other, hoping the other would have the answers that everyone was expecting.

"Tell me what was going on when you saw this flash of Light," Aram suggested.

"I ... I was sleeping, holding the Amulet for safe keeping," Ranoof began. "Then I heard a voice. It was Tallin, shouting for me to help them. As soon as I recognized Tallin's voice, I was linked to him, Urshen and five other Trackers. We were all falling towards a sea of darkness and ... and that's when I saw a burst of Light." Ranoof offered for Aram's consideration.

"What do you mean linked?" Aram saw a glimmer of understanding.

"I was inside their mind ... all of them. I could feel the terror and the pain, see what they were seeing. Actually ..." Ranoof amended, "it was Urshen that was having this weird experience. All of us Trackers were inside *his* mind. So ... 'linked' to Urshen through the power of the Amulet."

"Hmm ... why these particular Trackers?"

"At Border Pass, Urshen needed us to help defeat the El-Bhat. Our Tracker blood helped increase the range of his Amulet."

"Blood?" Aram encouraged more detail.

"Through our cut hands, we formed a Circle of blood."

"Ahh ... I am beginning to see a path forward," the ex-Butler mused to himself.

"You think *we* should link through our blood?" Ranoof guessed.

"Yes."

Ranoof pulled out his Tracker knife and made a cut. "Ready?" he asked as he extended the knife towards Aram.

Finn stepped forward. "Wait. Didn't you say the Amulet's power was controlled by Urshen ... while you were connected?"

Ranoof was nodding yes ... but slowly.

"Okay," Ranoof began, "so you are concerned that we might release a power that could kill everyone from here to the Front Gate?"

Finn shrugged, "Maybe."

"The question is reasonable," Aram-Dentee II agreed, "but you have helped me remember something from *my* experience that was important." His eyes went back to Ranoof. "The blood *is* the key. You see when Far-fel wrapped his hands around mine, while the Light of the Amulet was coursing through my body, trying to help me see a part of me that was worthy of renewal, I was lost. Faced with the enormity of my own darkness, I had fled into a corner, seeking desperately to escape the Light that surrounded me... until I felt the taste of blood on my tongue. Perhaps it was from the struggle with Finn." He looked at the Gatherer with a playful grin.

"But ... the taste of my own blood made me think of my bloodline, particularly my mother's father. And he ... was a Tracker ... just like the man who held me with hope," Aram looked down at Far-fel, "as I struggled to let go of the talisman."

The ex-Butler already knew he was ready to take the risk to help the Tracker at his feet.

Aram extended his hand to Ranoof. "Yes, let's try."

The two men clasped bloodied hands and then they each used their free hand to grasp one of Far-fel's hands ... completing the Circle of *two* Amulets!

There was an immediate burst of blinding Light.

When everyone could see again, Ranoof and Aram-Dentee II, were both on the floor with Far-fel.

"Now what?" a frustrated Braddock asked Finn who was frowning in disbelief.

"We wait," Finn retorted, only because he didn't know what to say.

"Perhaps there is something that we can discuss while we wait," Axion suggested.

"Finally," Braddock exclaimed as he waved the decision makers towards his large planning table.

"But first," Axion advised, "we need to have the Arborville Tracking Guild Master, here in this room.

Finn waved a command to a couple of his Specialists who swiftly left on the errand.

A short time later, as The Commander entered the room, he looked directly at Axion. "You were recognized by a few of my men, as you entered our town. For a dead man, you look remarkably fit."

"You're right, there's a story," Axion offered as he glanced at the unconscious Aram five paces away.

"My Assistant Craslin, hired a Butler to assassinate me. As soon as I discovered this, I left Qar-ana. Usually not my first impulse, but I had no idea at this point how far the corruption had spread.

"I knew my own Guild was affected, and reports of infiltrated Tracking Guilds here in Arborville and elsewhere, suggested that I head for the Specialists. Now that the picture has been illuminated somewhat, I am sure the Tracking Guild in Qar-ana is unaffected.

"However ... although they are unaffected by the intrigue, they have become ineffective because the Militia Guild has replaced them temporarily ... due to a document that I signed. And knowing Craslin's ambition, the Militia probably number over a thousand.

"Before Craslin makes his move, we need to return to Qar-ana to advise the Tracking Guild of our countries' dilemma. Perhaps there is still time for the Tracking Guilds of northern Storlenia, to gather and crush this Militia and displace Craslin."

The Commander listened respectfully but he knew things were different. More than anyone had imagined.

"It's time I shared intelligence that I have been receiving from Qar-ana," the Head Guild Master of the Tracking Guild interjected. "Ever since I received word that Axion was replaced by Craslin ... and that Craslin initiated the 'Executive Command' which gave him *full* powers, I have been in close communication with the Tracking Guild Master of Qar-ana."

All eyes in the room moved from the three men on the floor to The Commander, anxious to hear what news he was about to share.

"This Militia Guild that you speak of, as you have suggested, *has* exceeded a thousand." Axion was listening intently, waiting for The Commander to continue. "In fact, their numbers exceed fifty thousand!"

Murmurs of shock continued for a moment until The Commander raised a hand to signify he wished to continue.

"And ... they have over a thousand War Wagons."

"But that's impossible ... isn't it?" a wide-eyed Braddock suggested.

"It's not only possible ... since they have commissioned the entire Transportation and Blacksmith Guilds ... but they also seem to have a treasury that is unlimited." The Commander was panning the group of men at the table, hoping that someone would have something to add that would explain the sudden wealth that *also* seemed impossible.

"It must be El-Bhat gold," Braddock finally suggested. "Protas told me a story some time ago, of El-Bhat gold that made its way into the hands of Petin ... a Tracking Head Guild Master at Pechora. I didn't believe it then, but ..." he looked at The Commander with an apologetic look.

"Unfortunately ... I think you're right," The Commander conceded. "And that's not all ... there's more. This new Militia Guild have a new War Weapon that must be seen to be believed. It has replaced catapults on all their War Wagons! Far more effective and no one seems to know where this *impossible* design has come from." Now The Commander was staring back at Braddock.

Braddock started shaking his head. "As far as I know, Urshen never mentioned anything about a new weapon. His efforts only went as far as the wagons we are all familiar with."

"*Whatever* is behind the success of Qar-ana's Militia," Finn observed, "it clearly has enough power to defy all of the Tracking Guilds combined. Furthermore, it's obvious that we cannot simply walk into Qar-ana and remove Craslin from his seat of power. So why were we brought *here*? By Far-fel's Amulet."

The question had barely escaped the Gatherer's lips when a moan was heard from the three bodies lying on the floor.

Chapter 2 - A trip to Harleem

Ranoof heard a great rushing Wind as he fell through a dark space. It reminded him of the terror at Border Pass.
But what he felt ... was soft, like feathers, as he gently settled on his feet.

He opened his eyes. Standing only a few feet away was Aram-Dentee II. They were both at the base of steps that led up to a small circular platform. A man was standing on that platform, looking upwards in deep concentration. Above him was a pillar of Light that seemed to reach for the stars above.

Suddenly the man turned to look down at Ranoof and his companion. As he walked down the steps, Ranoof recognized him as Far-fel. On the bottom step, he paused as he studied their faces.

Ranoof was the first to speak. "We have come to rescue you."

The Specialist Tracker grinned, "Come. There is something I want to show you." They followed him to the platform. "You are about to see things that are meant only for eyes that have been touched by the Amulet. To understand what you are about to see, I must explain a few things.

"There is a race of people that live on a different world than ours. Their ambition is to conquer us, but they cannot, unless we allow it. This is because of the Worlds of Balhok. Many other worlds are observed by the people of Balhok and Harleem.

"The people of Balhok, are friendly and supportive to all that is good in us. The Caves have been planted for this purpose.

"The people of Harleem have planted Waterless Wells ... to seduce us. They want us to partake of their dark powers ... to drink deeply from the Well of this power. But in return, they will take our gold, the strength of our bodies ... *and* they have an insatiable need for slaves.

"If we stay within the Crystal Garden of Balhok, we are protected. But if we leave that Garden, and enter the dark forests of Harleem, we must manage our own affairs.

"And that, is not a good place to be. On their own, most worlds would crumble under the deceit and seduction of the dark power of Harleem and eventually become slaves to the immense population of their planet.

"You have been called to this place, as I have, to be instructed more carefully in what must be done to keep our people from leaving the Garden.

"Now ... look upward and learn about the possibilities that lie ahead."

As Ranoof looked upward, he was instantly flying above strange forests. He occasionally caught glimpses of large herds of animals he had never seen before. This was not Ankoletia.

Suddenly the three men were standing atop a large building, looking down upon a vast crowd, facing a high and large platform.

A man wearing a gold Necklace spoke to the people from this platform. The more he said, the stronger was the Green Light that swirled from his Gold Necklace and tumbled down amongst the crowd. He spoke of the wealth that had suddenly saturated their society … all because of the generosity of Harleem. And of the greater wealth that awaited them once they arrived on the planet of Harleem.

"We must never forget that 'Harleem' means *Paradise in the Sky*," the man reminded the people. "For the people of Harleem, there is no sickness, there is no death … they live forever." Eventually he led the people in the chant, "Harleem is Paradise."

The man waited for everyone to join in the chant before he continued with the words that would make him Emperor over his race.

"Are you ready … as I am … to give up this world for a life on Harleem?" Without waiting for their reply, he began to chant "Harleem is my choice!"

Soon everyone had joined him in the hypnotic chant.

Then he touched the sixth Medallion of the Necklace.

Strengthened by the Green Light, the chant turned into a frenzy of jubilation. Then as one, the people began to march towards the forest, where the Green Light guided them up the metal ramps into immense star ships.

The size of the star ship was unbelievable and yet, to Ranoof's astonishment, it began to lift off the ground once the crowds were settled inside.

The threesome watched until the ships disappeared into the night sky. Then in a blink, they found themselves on one of the star ships.

They watched as the people were told that they would be tested for body strength and then classified. Those that tested high for 'genetic suitability' would be referred to as *the chosen*. Holographic images showed to the crowds the privileges that would be bestowed on *them*. Luxurious compartments, fine food and the honours of Harleem were among the abundant rewards that fell to these *chosen*.

The effectiveness of the propaganda was proven as the 'classified' crowds were separated, parents from children, men from their wives, as *the chosen* were led away. Their grief was substantial, but it was not in the parting. It was, in not being chosen!

The scene switched again as the ships landed on Harleem. Masses of soldiers were waiting to escort the people into crowded pens, or as in the case of *the chosen,* into beautiful flying shuttles that carried them into buildings they called labs.

Ranoof and his two companions watched in horror as *the chosen* were strapped into long chairs or tables as tests were conducted, to verify their genetic strength and suitability. If they passed, tubes were inserted into their bodies as fluids and genetic material were extracted. This continued for weeks until their bodies could no longer be kept alive.

Those that were taken to the pens were outfitted with metal devices on their wrists and ankles. The unquestioned obedience of millions of slaves was secured within the day. The punishment administered by these devices, was both swift and excruciating.

High above the pens, in an elaborate building of glass and polished steel, the three companions stared across the skyline of the city of Lanc-biller-wun, the capital of Harleem. It was massive, impressive beyond belief, and it looked like it housed the entire population of Storlenia ... maybe more.
Everywhere, machines flew above while other machines travelled on the surface, carrying the millions of inhabitants of Lanc-biller-wun that regulated the power of Harleem.

"Our only hope is the Caves of Balhok," Far-fel said as he stared towards a distant horizon, searching for a boundary of the capital city. But there was none. The limitless extent of Harleem's capital, seemed to reflect its insatiable appetite. An appetite that had turned its attention to the world of Ankoletia.

"Well, now we know ..." he began as he turned to his two companions, but they were not there ... and he was no longer on Harleem. Instead, he was standing on a high ledge that overlooked a mountain chain, that stretched north and south for hundreds of leagues. 'I'm in Shaksbah,' he decided as he surveyed the far valleys that flowed beyond the foothills of the mountain range.

He studied the landscape for a while, committing it to memory. Somehow, he knew that this place would be important in the future struggle to defeat Harleem.

Satisfied, he was ready to begin the descent to the foothills, but there was something familiar about The Ledge. He turned to look behind ... and there, carved into the mountain side was an immense Quartz Door. He walked to where the Key ledge should be. It was there ... and he knew that one day, he must insert an Amulet into that hole.

Ranoof was thinking about Far-fel's comment regarding their only hope, when suddenly he found himself on a dusty road on a hot and windy day. He looked around for something familiar. There was nothing. He decided he was either still on Harleem ... or in Shaksbah, far past the Southland mountain range. His first guess was Shaksbah.

His hopes were to meet a fellow traveller, who could tell him something about where he was. So, he braced himself against the fierce wind and waited at the roadside.

Eventually he could see someone walking towards him, his head covered in the traditional desert garb of the Shaksbali, who lived in the far southern reaches of Denlen. He was bent into the wind, head down, fighting the elements every step of the way.

As the man got closer, Ranoof stood and then merged step for step as the two walked together. The only sound that could be heard above the howling of the wind, was the crunching of their boots against the rock-hard path.

Eventually, Ranoof touched the man's shoulder, bringing him to a stop. "I'm not sure where you're going, but I'm convinced that wherever it is, we should travel together."

The Traveller's eyes stared at Ranoof between the bands of cloth that protected his face from the sand and wind. For a moment, Ranoof thought he was going to start walking again without responding. But then, as though something changed the Traveller's mind, he started, "I am on my way to the Mines of Tenleth ... to rescue women and children that work there as slaves."

The words were muffled from the fabric, a bit difficult to hear above the wind, so Ranoof leaned his ear closer to the man. The words were repeated.

"Perhaps you could use another good short sword," Ranoof offered, as his hand drifted to the hilt of his weapon.

"Certainly," was the quick reply, "but are you sure you want to fight at my side," the stranger added, as he began to unwrap his face.

His face was browned and leathered by the desert sun, but Ranoof would have recognized Fre-steel, anywhere! Fre-steel … the traitor of Border Pass … the Tracker that had betrayed his vows to help the El-Bhat kill Tinkers and Trackers in the Butcher Block!

Ranoof unconsciously took a step backward in horror. 'Why him?' Ranoof questioned the Amulet that had brought him to this place. The thought had barely formed, before Ranoof was caught up by a terrific wind, that carried him high in the sky and then allowed him to plummet to his death below!

--------- <> ---------

Aram-Dentee II had been trained to appreciate the finer things in life, especially things related to the time before the Great War, when culture, wealth and technology had reached a pinnacle in Storlenia.

As he looked across the vast and luxuriant city of Lanc-biller-wun he couldn't help but wonder what treasures of culture and refinement were part of everyday life.

Part of Aram understood the mix of refinement and the violence that was required to maintain that lifestyle. It wasn't that long ago that he was of a similar mind. But understanding was not the same as agreement.

He quickly gave his head a little shake … as though he could shake that sentimentality out of his mind. These were dangerous thoughts.

He turned to Far-Fel, the Tracker that had introduced him to the power of the Amulet. But he wasn't there!

And Aram was no longer in the tall tower of steel and glass.

Instead, he was standing in a small darkened room. By the smell, he knew that this room was seldom used. The air was stale and musty.

By the scarcity of light, he could see the only door to the room. Barely big enough to allow him to leave.

He took a step towards the source of the light. A small crack in the wall.

He immediately recognized the purpose of the room. To spy!

Looking through the crack he could see two people talking.

One was a Tracking Guild Master. The other ... was from Harleem!

He placed his ear close to the crack and listened carefully. He knew that the Amulet had brought him here for a very definite purpose.

"... your enemies gather in a place you call Arborville. They have been in communication with supporters here in Qar-ana. Their combined efforts could be a threat to your ambitions to become Emperor. But be assured, I am watching your enemies and will return with further instructions."

"I understand," was the reply.

As the room on the other side of the wall went silent, Aram traded his ear for his eye. The man from Harleem was gone. He watched the Guild Master for a while as he walked to a desk and began to write.

'So, I am in Qar-ana,' thought Aram, 'and ... as impossible as it seems ... this Tracking Guild Master has become a traitor!' Things were only getting worse in Qar-ana, the 'City of Power'.

Aram was perfectly aware of the coup he helped support to replace Axion with Craslin. But these developments ...

He pushed himself away from the crack and headed for the small doorway a few steps away. He was anxious to see what else he could discover as he explored the secret hallways that were on the other side of that small door.

He opened the door and silently stepped into the darkness beyond ... as he fell through windless space.

Chapter 3 - The three missions

Simultaneously all three unconscious men awoke abruptly, suppressing a gasp of horror.

As they became aware of their return to the Hall of Braddock, all eyes in the room were upon them. Everyone's head tilted slightly towards the three men, expectant, waiting to hear what they had experienced after the Amulet took them all into a world of unconsciousness.

No words were spoken, instead, the three on the floor looked at each other.

Eventually they stood, their gaze fixed, waiting for someone to speak.

Far-fel spoke first.

"When you left the tower of steel and glass ... did you learn something before coming back here?"

The other two nodded yes ... slowly. "I know what I have to do," Far-fel spoke with confidence, inviting a response from his comrades.

Ranoof and Aram offered an acknowledging nod, confirmation that they too had a similar experience.

"I shall leave within the hour," Aram stated, as he surveyed the room, "and I shall take no one with me."

"I wish to speak with The Commander ... before I leave," Ranoof added, as he looked towards the Head Tracker of Arborville.

Far-fel was hefting the two Amulets as he listened to his two fellow dream-travellers commit themselves to the tasks assigned them.

"Perhaps one of you would like to take this Amulet to assist you in your quest?" Far-fel said as he held up the Amulet brought by Ranoof. He looked at Ranoof, indicating that he had earned first right by bringing it to Arborville.

"Never been inside a Cave," Ranoof replied, and then looked at Aram to see if he wished to accept the offer.

He was shaking his head no, as he said, "Neither have I."

"Besides," Ranoof added, "the Amulet belongs to either Benekee or Zephra ... depending on how you look at it."

The men in the room began to stir, as it appeared that the business between the three was finished.

"Welcome back," Braddock began, intent on finding out what had happened to the unconscious three. "Mind telling us what happened while we waited for you to ..." Braddock ended with a flourish of his hand.

Far-fel, still holding both Amulets accepted the role of spokesman as his two fellow travellers looked his way.

"I was taken to a ... place of instruction, by the Amulet, after I touched Ranoof's glowing talisman. Shortly after my instruction had begun, I was joined by Ranoof and Aram. We were shown a dangerous future, one already lived by many other worlds like ours."

Everyone in the room expressed their amazement as they looked around at each other. Satisfied that Far-fel's words were equally mysterious to all, eyes turned back to him.

"Out there," he continued, "among the stars, floats a world with the ability to plunder an entire world in a day. The name of this world is Harleem. Fortunately, they are lorded over by the worlds of Balhok and are only allowed to plunder if given permission by the people of the target world."

"Why would any people ... of any world ... be willing to give up their freedom to a plundering race?" someone in the room asked.

Far-fel looked at the two Amulets as he held them higher for all to see and said, "Greed for power and fair promises."

Now everyone was looking at the two talismans with cautious concern.

"Have we made a mistake," Finn spoke for everyone, "by our anxiety to possess and use the power of these crystal stones?"

"For some it would be a mistake," Far-fel agreed. "You see ... *intent* is the key. These talismans were placed on our world to protect us from the designs of Harleem, but they can only be used to build our race, not to tear it down and enslave it. These Amulets teach us that ultimately, the only security against the immense power of Harleem, is the enlightenment that convinces men to abandon the works of darkness.

"Before coming here," Far-fel continued as he looked at Braddock and The Commander, "I held in my possession a talisman from Harleem. A gold Necklace and a companion green stone. These artefacts of seduction are from Harleem and their purpose is not to enlighten, but to enslave ... by offering *us* power beyond belief."

"Where are these artefacts now?" a curious Braddock asked.

"The Tracking Guild at Pechora."

The Commander's brows were furrowed in angry concentration as he thought about the reported deaths of Mitrock and Pechinin.

"Things have certainly gotten complicated," Finn inserted. "The enemy includes El-Bhat that have invaded us through the Guilds, the Emperor of Harleem that has the potential to enslave us all, and our own corrupt government that has at its disposal an unwitting assembly of Militia … fifty thousand strong. This begs the question … what enlightenment did the three of you receive while you were … gone?"

"I will leave immediately for Qar-ana to work as a spy. I will work alone and send gathered information to this Tinker Village," Aram was quick to reply.

Finn nodded, pleased with Aram's decision. He knew that if anyone could extract needed intelligence from the halls of power at Qar-ana, it was the ex-Butler.

"There is a Master Cave, located in Shaksbah," Far-fel was the next to speak, "somewhere in the mountains east of Kel-eetan. It is important that I find this Cave."

"Are you also going alone?" Finn asked, beginning to wonder why his small team of Specialists were directed to follow Far-fel to the Tinker Village.

The Specialist Tracker played the dream over in his mind. Of course, he was alone as he stood before the Quartz Door, but what did that really mean. One thing he did know … opening the door of that large Cave was important if their race was to avoid slavery.

"I want every Specialist Tracker to accompany me," he said, dropping the Amulet in his leather pouch.

Satisfied, Finn looked at The Commander, "I bet you're curious about what your Tracker has to say?"

But The Commander had never taken his eyes off Ranoof, as he waited for the Tracker to take his turn.

Satisfied that he had what he wanted, Finn cast a nod towards Far-fel, indicating that he wanted to get going.

"I must find … Fre-steel," Ranoof explained.

"Easy enough," The Commander replied. "My men spotted him a few days ago on a road headed south. Not sure what you're supposed to get out of him, because he hasn't said a word since we picked him up and threw him in prison … waiting to be tried and executed."

"He's made a decision that's important … to the Cave." Ranoof looked down at his boots as he remembered how he had judged Fre-steel harshly in his dream … and how he felt the displeasure of the Cave.

Looking up he continued, "I want to see him right away. And if I am successful, we will follow Fre-steel south to the Mines of Tenleth."

"We?" The Commander asked.

"I will need as many Trackers as you can spare."

"Why the Mines of Tenleth?" Braddock asked, interested in both the reason and an opportunity for the Tinkers to get involved.

"In my dream, Fre-steel was on his way to rescue the Storlenian women and children that work there as slaves."

"Bound to be heavily guarded," Braddock commented, "if these are the Mines I think they are. Maybe you could use a Tinker or two?"

"Yeah, a Tinker or two," Ranoof grinned as he looked at The Commander.

--------- <> ---------

Finn was already at the door ready to leave but then hesitated. He realized he needed to hear about Ranoof's mission. After all, all three men had been instructed by the Cave and those details ought to be considered carefully. It was probably the *only* way to defeat Harleem, the El-Bhat and the corrupt officials of Qar-ana.

When Ranoof was finished, Finn's mind was made up. With a loud voice, he called for everyone's attention.

"Before I leave with my men ... could I offer some final advice for us all?"

Everyone turned to listen to the mysterious Gatherer of the Specialist Trackers.

"Before coming to Arborville," Finn started slowly, "I felt overwhelmed by the enormity of the enemy and curious as to why Far-fel's Amulet would direct us to come here. Now I see that our enemies are even stronger than we had first estimated ... but also, that the Amulet has been generous in directing our efforts. Maybe because we came here as instructed.

"Which brings me to the point I wish to make. Is it possible that the *only* way to confront and defeat the enemy, are these three missions? And if that is true, may I suggest that we consider a few adjustments.

"First, that Axion and five of my Specialists accompany Aram Dentee II. Axion's experience and knowledge of Qar-ana could be invaluable, and maybe even critical to Aram's success. And to ensure that the intelligence gained, reaches us, my five men will act as couriers, between Qar-ana and this Tinker Village. The two other missions would do well to assign men, to connect them with Braddock. This way, we will all be informed of what is happening and what needs to happen as things unfold.

"Second, that Aram take the second Amulet with him, and try to find either Benekee or Zephra. Very little is known about the use of these Amulets and placing this one in the hands of those who have used its power, would probably serve us well.

"Third, that every available Tinker and Tracker accompany The Commander on their journey south. The Mines of Tenleth have always been the foundation of Shaksbah's strength, and that strength seems to have drifted into the hands of the El-Bhat. Freeing the slaves could be only part of the reason for going there. And by 'every available' I mean that we send out a call to Tinkers and Trackers everywhere, to come to Arborville, and form a wave of reinforcements. This could very well be a war to the last man."

"Agreed," was Braddock's terse reply.
"Agreed," The Commander followed.
"Are you ready to go back to Qar-ana?" Aram looked at Axion.
"You know I am," the ex-Guild Master said, his expression stern with resolve.

"Then it's settled. Anything else before we leave?" Finn asked.
"Yes," The Commander offered. "Before we leave with Ranoof, we will need to gather in the Trackers from all over Storlenia. I could use another fifteen trusted men."
"What do you have in mind," Finn asked.
"Your Specialist Trackers, along with my men, will deliver messages to Tracking Guilds within a one hundred League perimeter of Arborville. These delivered instructions will then be relayed to Tracking Guilds further out by trusted Trackers of these Guilds of first contact.

"I suspect that this will delay your departure by at least a few weeks."
Finn looked at Far-fel who nodded in agreement. "Consider it done. We will come by in the morning to pick up the papers."

Ranoof entered the doorway and waited while the iron-clad oak door clanged shut. Even in the dim light, he recognized the eyes of *the Traveller*. In his 'dream' those eyes stared at Ranoof between bands of cloth that protected his face from the sand and wind. Eyes that were hardened from the determination of a desperate man.

The dress was different, but those eyes were the same.
"Can we talk?" Ranoof asked softly.

With a nod in the affirmative, Ranoof sat down on a cot, opposite Fre-steel. He decided that he may as well get down to business. After all, there was a reason the Cave took him in the dream to southern Shaksbah where he met Fre-steel. And he wasn't surprised that Fre-steel was willing to listen to him when he wouldn't talk to anyone else.

"I remember you from Border Pass …" Ranoof began, his eyes matching the intensity that shot back at him. "But I am here because I have had a dream. In this dream, you were heading south into the far reaches of Shaksbah. In my dream, I was … supposed to go with you. You said that you were on your way to the Mines of Tenleth, to rescue women and children that work there as slaves."

Fre-steel's tightened jaw began to relax at the mention of the dream and the women and children.

"The Trackers I am with believe that your mission is extremely important, and we wish to accompany you and assist in this honourable undertaking. In fact, a very large group of Tinkers are assembling as we speak. They want to join their forces with ours.

"Have you been to the Mines of Tenleth before?"

"Yes," Fre-steel replied with encouragement. "There will be difficulties and challenges. Especially on the last leg of the journey."

"We have War Wagons. Will they be able to make it to our destination?"

"If modified," was the terse reply.

"I suggest you have a look at our wagons, they are … different. They are made by the Tinkers. I assume you are willing to be our guide and leader on this expedition?"

Fre-steel nodded yes.

"Then let us begin," Ranoof said. He stood, offering the hand of friendship to someone he never thought he could.

Chapter 4 - The blanket of secrecy

Previously, Urshen had been transferred from a Tracking prison cell in Pechora to a Home prison cell in Qar-ana. Bernado wanted to surround himself with clever and useful men. And Urshen ... 'the young man who defeated the second Medallion', qualified.

With both hands gripping the iron bars on the door, Protas was grinning at Urshen, waiting for a response.
For over a day, he had waited for him to awake from his obvious drugged condition.
    And now, they were together again. What remarkable luck!

    Urshen was still sitting on his cot, rubbing his eyes.
    He shook his head. He could still feel remnants of the powerful drug that Bernado must have given him.
    Urshen let out a mournful sigh, as he studied the barred windows and doors.

    Finally, he allowed his eyes to return to Protas, as he rehearsed again the invitation to re-engage in the battle. *'They should have never put us together in the same place ... it will be their ruin.'*

    "Okay," was all he said as he grabbed his blanket and walked towards the barred door separating their rooms. Without a word Urshen shoved part of his blanket between two bars.
    "Time to talk?" Protas guessed.
    "Cover yourself with the blanket and I'll do the same."

    Within moments they were nose-to-nose under the darkness of the cloth cover, both eager to hear what happened since they last saw each other.
    "You first," Protas encouraged.
    "Okay ... there must be spies watching us ... this is probably our last opportunity to do this. For now, tell me what I need to know ... things they mustn't know. Oh yeah ... thanks for saving Zephra at the forest."
    "Speaking of Zephra ... I saw her a few days ago."

"Is she okay?" There was a pause. "Where did you see her? She was supposed to be in Arborville ... helping to build the Guild."

"I saw her *here* ... in Qar-ana. She looked fine."

"Did you talk?"

"Couldn't, I was being escorted by two guards and she was looking at me from the balcony above ... in the Planning and Development Guild."

Urshen finally saw through Protas's guarded responses. "What aren't you telling me?"

"She wasn't wearing the White Bauble. She was dressed in a fine Storlenian dress. And when I looked up, she had been watching me ... but it was like she no longer knew me ... or no longer cared."

"I don't know how, but we need to get out of here," Urshen responded, anxious for Zephra.

"I know *how* ... I've just been waiting for a reason. When do you want to leave?" There was a pause, as Urshen thought of the months he had unsuccessfully schemed to get out of Pechora's prison cells.

"How," Urshen began, "do you do ... what you do?"

"Well, it's not just me ... there's this dog."

"A dog?" Urshen asked. It was the last thing he had expected to hear. "Are you okay?" he queried, suspecting that Protas wasn't the same man he used to be.

"Yeah ... I've been through a lot ... but yes, I'm okay. I'll explain the dog later. But like I said, I can get us out whenever we are ready ... because of this dog."

"Okay ... I believe you," he replied, but he wasn't sure yet if he did. "Now tell me about my family, I heard you were recruited with Bru-ell to protect them." Urshen could hear Protas take a slow deep breath.

"Yes ... we were ... and you have probably guessed ... it was interesting seeing your father and Pateese again."

Urshen smiled.

"We wasted no time in taking your family to the Pechora Tracking Guild ... for safe keeping."

There was a pause so Urshen jumped in, "You can skip the surprise you found ... I just spent several months in a Pechora prison cell."

"Okay. Your father was given this Medallion by Mitrock. A very interesting artefact. It can give a yes or no answer to any question. It was how we knew to run, moments after we arrived. Mitrock and Pechinin are dead."

"I heard."

"Anyway, I got separated from the rest but the horse I stole for my get-away, belonged to Jalek … so I decided to scratch that itch once and for all. But before I could find him, I found Ranoof, one of *your* men."

Urshen should have been surprised, but he *was* talking to Protas. "Good to hear he got away okay. Do you know where he is?"

"Last we talked he was heading for Qar-ana. And shortly after that, I was re-captured and sent to the Quorum as a gift from Bernado."

"Don't ever drink his wine," Urshen interjected. "How did you escape the Quorum?"

"On my way, I was rescued by Jalek. He thought I still had his horse. He's very attached to horses … lucky for me. It saved my life."

"So … is he …?"

"I don't think we ever have to worry about him again. Then I headed south into Shaksbah to avoid another re-capture and that's where I met Ee-lath, my brother, facing a Mountain Cat."

The after-effects of the drug made him wonder if he heard that right. "You have a brother … living in Shaksbah?"

"We *became* brothers because I saved his life … and that's when I was confronted by Ou-Leesen, the leader of the El-Bhat who escaped Border Pass. With his leadership, the Shaksbali have built a new mountain pass wide enough to take War Wagons through."

Urshen had heard that some of the El-Bhat had managed to escape the 'Wind' of Border Pass. "Have they started moving wagons into Storlenia?"

"Yes … but only eight … full of gold. Ou-Leesen used them to purchase shipping rights to Port Airiken and Port Aqabah and six shipping vessels."

Urshen was shocked at how much progress the El-Bhat had made since their defeat at Border Pass … and surprised that Protas had managed to acquire so much intelligence on the activities of the El-Bhat. "How did you find out about all of this?"

"Easy … I was Ou-Leesen's Advisor."

"Sorry," there was a long pause, "I thought you just said that you are working for the El-Bhat."

"Let's just say, I'm a dual citizen now … because of my brother Ee-lath … and my life is *complicated*. But I wouldn't call them El-Bhat. Ou-Leesen has plans that will eventually give the Quorum a huge headache."

Urshen was struggling to catch up with everything Protas was telling him … and he knew the Guards could walk in at any moment. "Who was the gold given to?"

"Craslin, the Head Guild Master of the Planning and Development Guild here in Qar-ana."

"You're sure?" Urshen asked louder than he intended.

"I helped unload the gold ... along with Biskin and Stek, two Trackers."

Stek! Protas had met Stek! "Where is Stek now?" Urshen asked, concerned that the double agent he had help create, was running with a group of El-Bhat ... that Protas was convinced were sympathetic to Storlenians.

"While we were unloading the gold, I was taken into custody by Bernado ... I assume Stek headed back to the Pass with Ou-Leesen."

Urshen hesitated as he considered his next question. "Did Stek seem confused?"

"Oh yeah, until he was told by Biskin that Mitrock was dead ... and then he was ready to run like a rabbit. But he stayed. So, tell me about what *you* have been doing."

Urshen's head was still spinning from everything Protas had mentioned. He wanted to ask him more questions ... there were *so many* contradictions. But the Guards could burst in at any moment, so he began with his own story.

"After our success at Border Pass, all of the Tinkers went to Arborville to start a Guild. After I proposed to Zephra, I headed to Pechora ... to find you." Suddenly Urshen could hear footsteps. "If you really know how to get out of here ... we need to do it quickly!" he whispered urgently. They both headed for their cots.

Two Guards entered Urshen's room and positioned themselves on either side of the door.

They waited. After a while, he could hear more footsteps. When Bernado entered the room, he was wearing the Golden Necklace ... with the small green stone.

He hadn't worn his Necklace in front of Urshen since his failed interrogation. It was time to make a change ... and observe Urshen's reaction. He was nervous. Good.

"It appears that you don't appreciate having a blanket to keep you warm. You think to use it as you please. Guards remove it."

Protas was watching from his room, curious as to why Bernado was wearing a gold Necklace, something he had never worn before. And the workmanship … it was like nothing he had ever seen.

"Any further acts of disrespect and you will lose your cot," Bernado added once the Guards had the blanket. "But after that … I will not be so generous."

He touched the Necklace's chain.

Then he turned his head towards Protas. "Am I clear?"

Protas nodded with enthusiasm, anxious to prevent any escalation of hostility towards him or Urshen. They needed to stay together.

--------- <> ---------

Satisfied that he had what he came for, Bernado left. He expected another visit from Kareen soon and he wanted the Alien to find Urshen exactly according to his instructions … healthy and alive.

If he had to, he would punish Protas for Urshen's mischief. He must insure he had the one candidate that Kareen asked ….

He stopped mid-stride. "I wonder …" he whispered to himself, as he contemplated a possible replacement for the Tracker who stole Urshen's Amulet.

--------- <> ---------

Before the echoes of the slamming door had died, Protas was already considering the bizarre encounter.

He had many questions.

Why was Bernado suddenly wearing a strange-looking golden Necklace?

Where did it come from?

And what power did it hold over Urshen? He obviously recognized it.

And … now that he thought about it, why didn't Bernado send Urshen to the Quorum, like he did Protas … instead of bringing him here to Qar-ana?

Which brought him to the most important question of all. Why … would Bernado bother with the blanket?

It was such a meaningless punishment considering that he had sent Protas to the Quorum, as a toy for their amusement, and wasn't surprised when he saw the deep scars that covered his body. He fully expected Protas to die at the hands of the malicious El-Bhat.

So ... something very important had changed, at least for Urshen.

He looked over at his friend who was still staring at the door.

Protas walked back to the iron barred door. He would continue their conversation ... in code.

"I don't envy you ... having to sleep without a blanket tonight."

Urshen turned to Protas, eyes intense with recent memories of the Necklace. There was a moment of silence while he considered why his friend was willing to engage in conversation so quickly after Bernado's threats. Then Protas gave a little nod of encouragement. 'Ahh,' Urshen realized, 'He's talking in code!'

"You're right ... I'm not looking forward to it. By morning I will wish I was somewhere else."

Protas gave a knowing nod, as he thought, 'So, he wants to get out of here tonight. Perhaps it's because of the Necklace.'

"That's quite the impressive necklace around Bernado's neck. I have never seen him wear it before," Protas explained.

"Yeah, it's beautiful. He found it in a diamond bed," Urshen added.

Protas grinned acknowledgment as he thought, 'So it's a talisman of power.'

"Does it make you feel uncomfortable when he wears it?" Protas continued.

"Yeah, there's too much ... shiny gold."

'It's very powerful,' Protas concluded. "Uncomfortable enough that you actually had to leave the room?" Protas chuckled.

"No, I was really tempted though."

'Okay ... so Urshen was *almost* defeated.' "You should have worn the silver bracelet I gave you ... you wouldn't have felt so ... uncomfortable," Protas suggested.

"Yes, it would have helped me fit in ... but someone stole it before the big party. But I was with friends, so at least I wasn't alone."

'So', reflected Protas, 'no Amulet, someone else has it, and somehow others were able to help Urshen stand against the Necklace.'

"Do your friends live around ..."

The door opened before Protas could finish.

Two Guards came in and removed Urshen's thin bed.

"But we were just chatting about ..." Protas began.

The door slammed and now Urshen was without a bed.

"Sorry," whispered Protas, grinning his mischievous grin. The 'sorry' was for the spies. He already had a plan, and it meant that Urshen wouldn't be sleeping here tonight anyway.

--------- <> ---------

At the sound of the whistle, Urshen was immediately alert, his head turned towards Protas's cell. He slowly got up and walked over to the barred door that separated their rooms.

Protas returned to the window and whistled again. He always knew he could leave this prison anytime he wanted to ... with the help of Sausage. What he didn't know was *when* he should leave.

But when Urshen walked in, he was sure that, *that* time was coming soon. And then when Bernado came strutting in with a dark talisman ... well, that was all the encouragement that Protas needed. As Urshen suggested in code it would be tonight.

He figured the Fates had brought them together for a reason and he wasn't going to wait for Bernado's capricious strategy to separate them.

A soft bark, along with Protas's dangling arm, and soon he was pulling the Amulet between the bars into the cell.

Urshen grabbed the iron bars with both hands, as he watched Protas approach the door that separated them ... with a *Crystal Amulet*! He couldn't believe it!

Protas muttered a few words as he held the talisman close to the lock and soon the door swung open. As he walked past a startled Urshen, he whispered, "I know ... I'll explain later."

Within moments, the Guards were asleep, two more doors were open and Urshen was following a Robed Man ... with a dog, into the night.

Chapter 5 - The Canticle of Goldenrod

Lanc-biller-wun, Capital city of the World of Harleem

Many centuries earlier

In the Military Academy for boys, the Canticle of Goldenrod was recited first thing every morning ... and always led by one of the young boys.

> Goldenrod
> Our Gift to the worlds in space
> Their people watched over by the eyes of our People
>
> Goldenrod
> Planted by the hands of our People
> Secure in the sacred box of Aldereen
>
> Goldenrod
> Protected by the Dagger of Hope
> It waits for the One of Courage
>
> Brought to the surface of the Well
> Pu-el-la, the Lady of Harleem
> Appears and brings to their world
> The power of the Green Light
> As Goldenrod is touched
> By the One of Courage
>
> Through space, a shaft of Green Light
> Is sent to the ears of our People,
> A message of Celebration,
> Now the six Medallions will awaken
> - Six Servants of Goldenrod -
> Because of the One of Courage
>
> Medallions of Goldenrod, our Gift to the worlds:
> The first, a blessing of Immortal Life to the One of Courage
> The second, to know the Thoughts of his enemies
> Third, to subject the Enemies will, to the One of Courage

Fourth, to find Possessions and Servants for the One of Courage
Fifth, to find the source of the Dark Power
Sixth, to bring the people of the Discovered World to Harleem

We trust the power of Goldenrod
It will assist the One of Courage
To teach his people the ways of Harleem
To bring them safely to the world of Harleem
Servants of Goldenrod
Servants of Harleem

As Kareen-hys-Tebeel-del-Harleem walked from the front of the class to his place, he was sure that one day he would travel to another world … to plant the Waterless Wells.

Chapter 6 - A report from Ankoletia

Back to the present, on Harleem.

The Commander General skimmed across the pink clouds of Lanc-biller-wun, until the Government Buildings were in sight. After a quick descent, the General was taken to the Throne Room.

Once seated comfortably, he waved a hand to the attendant, "Bring him in."

As usual, a messenger came rushing forward to the person on the Throne ... but there was nothing *usual* about the message. It was why the General was notified in the middle of the night.

After the man kissed the circle of gold on the floor, and prostrated himself, he spoke. "Most Holy One, we have another report – from the planet called Ankoletia."

"You may rise," the Harleem General commanded.

The man obeyed ... but he also looked the General in the eyes ... the message was that important.

"Give me the report," he said as he leaned forward.

"There is enough gold to fill this room ten times."

The General was previously led to believe the gold was pure, but this estimate seemed to suggest that it wasn't. "Is the gold refined?" he probed the messenger.

"Yes, moulded into bricks ... and the Mines are still in operation ... no depletion is evident."

The Commander General straightened as he contemplated the almost unbelievable report. Finally, he said, "Marvellous!"

And then added, "How much is Kareen-hys-Tebeel-del-Harleem skimming?"

The question was threatening, so the messenger stopped to kiss the Gold Disc again, hoping to protect himself from the words he was about to speak. "Your spy has found a secret partition in Kareen's personal cabin, large enough to hold several hundred bricks of gold ... and he has plans to smuggle two genetic candidates."

"Previous reports suggested good genetic material ... how good is it?" the General leaned forward again.

"Class six," he said with excitement.

The General stared at the messenger with a look that challenged the accuracy of the report.

"Class six," he repeated. "I asked him to send the raw data through your secure channel ... it checks at class six."

The General frowned. "We are NOT allowed to *screen* at this stage of involvement," he responded in irritation.

The man allowed himself a guarded grin as he said, "No screening ... random sample."

The Harleem Commander rubbed his chin as he contemplated what he wanted to do next. "I want to be notified the moment the *'Trade Contract'* is signed. You have done well," he added.

The messenger bowed in appreciation, and before he could turn to kiss the Gold Disc, the General extended his hand ... offering the Golden Ring towards him. The man approached the Throne, his eyes fastened on the Ring. "In humility, I kiss the Ring of Aldereen," he whispered.

The messenger left with his eyes to the floor.

Many messengers were employed by the government, but now the General would always know where to find this one ... his genetic signature was recorded by his Ring.

Chapter 7 - *Secrets* of the 'Dagger of Truth'

The Quorum's Keep, Country of Shaksbah, World of Ankoletia
Sometime before Ou-Leesen transferred the gold to Qar-ana

Shanteef, leader of the El-Bhat Quorum and Protector of the largest unregistered accumulation of gold in all Ankoletia, was not about to send only one man, to watch over Ou-Leesen … and his gold.

But it wasn't just about the gold … he wanted the Dagger of Truth back in his possession, just as soon as Ou-Leesen had finished 'Ou-Leesen Pass'. It was why he sent the Advisor … to ensure that Ou-Leesen was removed at the appropriate time.

And to make sure all his interests would be protected, even if the Advisor failed, he sent *several* spies who posed as common labourers, to watch Ou-Leesen and the Advisor, and on a regular basis they took turns returning, to keep Shanteef informed.

In the security of the Keep, the Quorum Leader nodded for the spy to proceed.
"The news I bring is as bitter as the waters of Porsha," the spy said, to prepare Shanteef.
"Your Advisor is dead. Against your orders, he tried to kill Ou-Leesen." The spy looked down at the carpet he sat upon, unwilling to look the Quorum Leader in the eye as he prepared to share the next piece of intelligence.

"A Storlenian has replaced him. They have dismantled one of the houses in Chitouf. Wagons carrying these bricks have left Ou-Leesen Pass … taking the gold into Storlenia."

"Where is it being sent?" Shanteef asked, his voice calm, considering the news.

The spy was expecting more of a response, perhaps even the end of his life. Optimistic, his gaze floated upwards until their eyes met again. "I don't know … it was knowledge he kept to himself."

Satisfied, he dismissed the spy, and sent for his most trusted El-Bhat ... someone who had recently returned from Pechora with critical intelligence.

As he waited, Shanteef considered the plan he had put into motion ten years earlier and how recent events were accelerating his developments at dizzying speed. Within a year, he expected to see the El-Bhat in control of all Ankoletia ... and *he*, as leader of the El-Bhat, would be the ruler of everyone who walked under the sky above.

Without a noise, Mishri entered the room, kissed his ring and sat on the carpet. Since arriving at the Keep, he had waited for this moment. He had been advised, regarding Ou-Leesen, the rogue El-Bhat leader and his secretive plans to move the gold. And now there would be a plan of *action*!

"The gold has begun to move," Shanteef began, "one entire house. We don't know its destination or for what advantage Ou-Leesen hopes to gain. But I am sure of one thing. Ou-Leesen will return for more."

Mishri released his knife from his scabbard and laid it in front of him, a gesture that he was ready to give his life, in obedience to the instructions that were about to follow.

"Ou-Leesen has ignored the Quorum's requests. For this he must die. But not by your men. No ... your assignment is to bring the gold to me.

"When Ou-Leesen stares at the empty plains of Chitouf, he will be capable of only one thing. He will ride hard until he arrives at the Keep. And then I will use the Dagger of Truth to silence his lies.

"Our gold is in peril," Shanteef continued, "gather the El-Bhat ... all of them ... and with haste, travel to Chitouf. Then bring the gold to the Keep."

Mishri returned his knife to his scabbard, not totally satisfied. He would have preferred that the honour of killing Ou-Leesen was offered to him. He bowed in submission as he left, knowing that he would return with news that Ou-Leesen was dead.

Shanteef watched as thousands of War Wagons headed north. Soon they would break up into smaller groups, to avoid detection by the Shaksbali government.

Moving the gold to the Keep would mark a new era for the El-Bhat. No longer would they have to hide the gold they had successfully skimmed from the Government Mines of Tenleth.

Because soon there would no longer be skimming. Soon, the gold would never again flow to the rich merchants and government officials of Kel-eetan.

There were two Jewels of Shaksbah … the Tenleth Mines and Kel-eetan. And he must have them both!

But he would take Kel-eetan first.

He would pick a feast day, when the Government troops were mostly drunk. Then with El-Bhat speed, his men would storm into the seat of government power.

Then … he would fortify the Keep with the slaves he would gather from northern Shaksbah. It would become the strongest fortress anywhere in the world.

And because large quantities of gold would flow through the passes to buy Guild power in northern Storlenia, he would insist on controlling the passes. And that control … would be the beginning.

He turned and began walking back to the Keep, as his thoughts turned to his mistress of power … the Dagger of Truth. He wondered how many times Ou-Leesen had used it.

He smiled wickedly, as he thought of how easy it always was, to pass on the Knife of power … and then bring it back … to replenish his aging body.

Ou-Leesen and others like him always saw the gift as a token of great respect, marvelling that they could be deserving of the emblem of authority, passed on by the Leader of the Quorum himself.

But the real reason he was so willing to allow this talisman of power out of his grip, was hidden in his next step … showing them the power of the Knife. He began by showing them how it could cut *anything* and finally he would reveal that with the Knife, they could *learn* anything from anyone. All they had to do was to press the blade against the forehead of the victim.

As usual, it didn't take long before his victim became drunk with the prospects of their future.

But what they always learned … too late … was how demanding his mistress of power really was. With every use of the Knife, the jewel in the pommel would glow, the sign that it was pulling another bit of life out of the one holding it.

It was a hard lesson for Shanteef to learn. But then he understood why the original Leader of the Sherilin, was found dead with the Dagger of Truth lying beside him. Such power *and* such demands on the user! 'There must be a way', he had thought, 'to entice the mistress of this power to reveal to me her secrets!'

Then one day, he decided to speak to the Dagger. Sitting in the privacy of the Keep, he expressed his concerns and his willingness to enter into an agreement. He believed that the Dagger wished to be used, and he was eager to be true to that need, but he wanted to know how he could overcome the debilitating effect of using the Knife.

That night he had a dream. He was alone, in a large room that reminded him of the Keep, but much more elaborate. There was a gold disc on the floor, encased in pink marble. And out of that disc, rose a swirling mist of Green Light ... which formed into the most beautiful woman he had ever seen. She spoke to him, *"You have called me, what is it you want?"*

"Tell me of the secrets of the Dagger of Truth. How can I use it ... *without dying*?"

She nodded in response to his request and then pulled from her robe the Dagger of Truth. Holding it aloft, she began her instruction. *"A man's life force will always be the payment for using the Dagger. To retrieve the life force, you must use the Necklace."* She turned her gaze from the Dagger to Shanteef. *"But since you do not have it ... I will tell you of another way."*

The Green Lady paused as she lovingly touched the beautiful green stone encased in the pommel.

"Fortunately, all payments of the life force are stored within the emerald stone ... and can be retrieved by the *last* person to use the blade." She looked at Shanteef, her expression one of anticipation ... for his next question.

"So," Shanteef began, "if I give the Knife to another to use, then his life force will *also* be in the Dagger's jewelled pommel." Shanteef grinned wickedly at the lady. "And ... if I successfully retrieve the life force ... I will be stronger than I was before I ever touched the Dagger of Truth!"

She nodded in approval of his reasoning.

"And to retrieve this life force ... I only need to use the Dagger ... by killing the wielder of the Knife or the Assassin who brings me the Dagger of Truth?"

She laughed. *"It is so easy."*

She placed the Knife back inside her robe. After sharing one last instruction with Shanteef, she disappeared.

Immediately he awoke.

He finally understood the simple secrets to the Dagger of Truth. If he was careful, he could live forever. He smiled as he thought of the necessity to pass the Knife on to others. It was the perfect arrangement. No one would ever suspect that the Knife was the source of his long life *and* invincibility ... because he was so willing to give it to others as a token of friendship and esteem!

Yes ... he was willing to give it away ... but he hated the long separation from his mistress of power. Especially when she was so far away.

Thoughts of uncertainty of what might happen to the Knife, or the person he had given it to, often plagued him. But he had learned that these concerns were frivolous. The Dagger of Truth and the Mistress that watched over it were very powerful. They made sure that it always returned to him, the rightful owner.

A dark chuckle escaped his lips as he considered the last recipient of the Dagger. He had told Mishri that he knew Ou-Leesen would come to the Keep because of the gold. But the truth was different.
Ou-Leesen would come, because of the insatiable desire the Dagger would plant in his mind, to return to Shanteef *with* the Dagger of Truth!

Chapter 8 - The Green lady's compromise

Several weeks later,

Ou-Leesen pulled Ee-lath close as they stood on the hill, staring at the stretching landscape where Chitouf used to be. It was hard to believe that *everything* was gone. And ... he had no idea where to look for the rest of his men.

He had spent many hours during the lonely trek across the foreign lands of Storlenia thinking about what he might do with the rest of the gold. Opportunities multiplied as he remembered how much could be accomplished with only one dismantled brick house.
And in the middle of those opportunities, was the weight of knowing the location of two Caves. At some point, he would have to use some of the wealth to bury the two Caves.
Perhaps he would buy up large tracts of land around the two ports that soon would move goods and men from Shaksbah into Storlenia.
Perhaps he would buy a thousand of those new wagons that Protas had told him about ... and convert them into War Wagons.
But now, all those plans were only shattered dreams. The gold was gone.

And what should he tell Ee-lath. Protas was probably in a prison cell somewhere in Storlenia, and Ee-lath's family was ...
"Where do you think your family have gone to?" he said quietly, not really expecting the boy to respond.
"They will be with the bricks," he responded in a matter of fact tone. "Our village has always been with the bricks."
"Of course, they are," Ou-Leesen offered encouragement. "And although the Quorum could have moved the gold anywhere, I think I know where it is," he added as his hand rested on the pommel of the Dagger of Truth.
"Come Ee-lath, we must continue our journey if we are to find your family."

Not far away, in the foothills, Mishri's scout was watching a cloud of dust trailing behind Ou-Leesen as he led twenty warriors, a young boy ... and a cursed Tracker as they headed south.

'So Mishri was right about Ou-Leesen,' the Scout thought to himself. He watched for a while as he wagged his head in unbelief. "A Tracker!" he whispered, as he silently disappeared into the brush. Soon he would meet up with Mishri who anxiously awaited news about Ou-Leesen.

--------- <> ---------

The stars were bright before Ou-Leesen stopped for camp. He wanted the cover of darkness for at least two hours as they wandered among the low-lying hills, to ensure they were lost to whoever would be watching for his return. And there would be no fire for the entire journey.

His plan was to head south to the Shaksbah Mountains, then continue along the eastern foothills to the end of that mountain range. Then, head directly west to the Keep.

The men dismantled their horses under the light of the rising moon, and soon gathered around Ou-Leesen to share their meagre rations.

Quietly Ou-Leesen began the conversation. "Advisor ... tell me about those machines that we saw as we unloaded the bricks."

Stek knew what really intrigued Ou-Leesen. It was when one of those machines fired a brass ball as a warning shot ... and the significant damage it created to the side of the wagon. Stek reached into his pocket and pulled out the brass ball that he had picked up when no one was looking. It wasn't that big, but it probably came close to doing as much damage as the large steel balls that were attached to Tinker lariats ... the kind that were thrown by two Tinkers.

He held up the brass ball until the moonlight glittered off its surface. "Not particularly big, but I've never seen so much damage come from something so small. I'm afraid I can't tell you much about these machines ... never seen them before. But what I can tell you is that something is terribly wrong."

"You've never seen these machines before?" a surprised Ou-Leesen asked.

"Nope ... and that's my greatest concern. I should know where these machines come from ... but I don't. And I should know *who* has been developing such a powerful weapon. Development of weapons *always* includes the Tracking Guild. But not this time!"

"How is this possible?" The El-Bhat leader asked, surprised at Stek's response.

"Well ..." Stek eventually responded, "*that* is a very good question, especially as I think back to the problem of infiltration, that the Tracking Guild recently faced. I could hardly believe my ears when Biskin told me about his assignment to purge our southern Tracking Guilds of Shaksbah infiltrators. But this ..." his words trailed off, as he examined the brass ball again.

"You see," he eventually continued, "what the El-Bhat accomplished was a complete surprise, but nonetheless, the logic was clear. It was the result of a very clever and well executed plan, that involved Storlenian immigrants, that only a hand-full of our diplomats even knew about. And ... it was sure to be short-lived as normal procedures and policies came to bear on that situation.

"But this new situation suggests that we are facing an *internal* problem of a magnitude that could affect everyone ... in both Storlenia *and* Shaksbah."

No one said anything for a while as Stek's spoken concern hovered above the small group. Finally, Ou-Leesen began, "The El-Bhat had always considered that we were free from invasion by our northern neighbours ... for many reasons," he added as he thought about how similar Trackers were to the Sherilin. "But you are suggesting that *this* could all change."

"The Trackers will keep the borders safe for a while," Stek advised Ou-Leesen, "but I am afraid that our Tracking Guilds are no longer in control of the peace." He shook his head. "Never thought I would hear myself saying that. Does this change *your* plans to find the Quorum?"

Ou-Leesen grunted at the suggestion that he was still in control. "Advisor, I'm afraid that I no longer know who is leading this Band of El-Bhat. I used to believe that it was me ... but since I have been given this Knife ..."

The warrior rose as he pulled out the Dagger of Truth. "Advisor ... let me show you what I mean." The El-Bhat held the blade in front of him as he spoke, the moonlight glittering off its ornate and polished surface. "Where should I go?" he demanded.

Immediately, shimmering Green Light erupted from the green pommel. The light transformed into a million green stars drifting on the night breeze. They floated southwest ... directly towards the Keep.

Eventually the travelling cloud of shimmering lights could no longer be seen. Pointing the blade in the direction of the vanishing Green Lights, Ou-Leesen commented, "The stars in the night sky above, confirm that the

Dagger wants me to travel to the Keep. So, tell me Advisor ... why do I really want to go to the Keep?"

--------- <> ---------

A couple of days later, Stek rode up beside Ou-Leesen to share a concern. "We are being watched and followed ... probably since we left the abandoned village of Chitouf."

The El-Bhat never took his eyes from the landscape in front as he spoke. "I know ... the Dagger tells me things it wants me to understand. It is me they want. Tonight, when the moon is high, you will take my men onward for another twenty leagues ... but I will stay and watch."

--------- <> ---------

As they left the wilderness landscape behind, it became necessary for Mishri and his spies to follow much closer than before. It would be easy to lose someone in the forests and hills that now spread before them as far as he could see.

He nodded to the spies as their prey disappeared into a valley. Soon he wouldn't have to worry about losing Ou-Leesen, because tonight he would kill him ... and then he would return the Dagger of Truth to Shanteef.

True ... the Dagger was only a symbol of authority, but in his mind, his old friend Shanteef was wrong to allow Ou-Leesen to continue to possess it, once he was a confirmed traitor. And why Shanteef would allow this deserter to walk into the Keep was equally foolish.

So ... to solve these problems, he would kill Ou-Leesen. He would say that Ou-Leesen and his Band caught up with them, and, in the ensuing struggle, the traitor died.

As Mishri and his men entered the forest, dusk had already settled over the land. He hadn't ridden far into the darkened forest when he pulled up on his reins. His El-Bhat sense told him that something wasn't quite right ... there was unseen danger ahead.

"My instincts tell me we are close to Ou-Leesen," he shared with his spies. "In fact, he might be waiting for us. Ride low in the saddle," he instructed one of the spies as he sent him ahead. Mishri followed immediately behind with the other spy covering his back.

They had travelled a couple of leagues when the familiar whistling sound of an arrow could be heard. Almost instantly, a loud thud told Mishri that the first spy lay dead on the forest floor.

He quickly pulled his horse to a stop as he slid to the ground. While rushing to a large tree, he managed a quick glance to memorize the position of the arrow in the dead El-Bhat.

Now he knew where Ou-Leesen was when he shot the arrow. As soon as the other spy was by his side, they moved speedily through the trees, occasionally stopping to listen for movement.

The third time they stopped, Mishri heard what he needed to know. After a hushed conversation, they crept forward, carefully moving further apart the closer they got.

--------- <> ---------

Once Ou-Leesen spotted the other El-Bhat, the exchange of arrows began in earnest as he retreated, to avoid being caught in their pincer-style movement.

He was lucky with the first El-Bhat, who now lay dead on the forest floor. But now he must be wary, or he would never live to confront Shanteef, the only thing that mattered anymore.

He had hoped to even up the odds before the arrows ran out, but unfortunately, he was fighting El-Bhat … and they knew exactly what he was about to do before he did it! It was like fighting two of himself. He managed to save one last arrow as he madly dashed through the dark forest, trying to exhaust their supply.

Suddenly everything went quiet. He listened carefully for a while, but the silence continued so he began to crawl on his belly … carefully and silently … towards his pursuers.

He had only moved about twenty paces when the forest erupted, as the remaining two warriors came crashing through the bush.

He leapt to his feet and released his last arrow to the closest dark shadow. He heard a grunt, suggesting that he was at least partially successful.

But there was no time to confirm that one El-Bhat was down … he could hear the other black warrior step into the space of death, as he swung his sword to cut his victim in half.

With the speed of a snake, Ou-Leesen whipped his bow around, just in time to block the deadly blade. But the seasoned hard wood was no match for the razor-sharp steel that cut through the bow and continued in its swing to find flesh and bone.

Ou-Leesen leaned backwards as he pushed his bow against the arc of the sword, to minimize the force of the blade that he knew would draw blood. The fierce thrust of his bow and his lightning quick movement away from the sword, saved his life, but he grunted as his flesh burned hot from the wound.

Falling backwards into a roll, Ou-Leesen came up with his sword in his hand. And not a moment too soon as both El-Bhat rushed him. Apparently, his last arrow was not as successful as he had hoped.

Frantically he swung his sabre back and forth between the two advancing warriors, looking for an opening that would give him back the advantage.

But it wasn't to be ... because one of the El-Bhat held two sword-breakers ... that he used with expert skill.

Ou-Leesen immediately changed his swordplay, hoping to frustrate the efforts to break his sword.

Soon, the ring of breaking steel could be heard and Ou-Leesen and his opponents knew that it was all over.

The second El-Bhat dropped his sword-breakers as he pulled out his own sword and waited for Mishri to finish the kill.

The El-Bhat Leader stopped himself mid-swing as he heard the blade snap. He wanted Ou-Leesen to suffer a traitor's death. He would cut off his head, the greatest shame to an El-Bhat warrior.

"Will you run ... *traitor* ... or will you kneel and accept your fate?" Mishri growled at the dark figure that stood before him. The El-Bhat Spy moved carefully behind Ou-Leesen to cover a possible retreat.

Ou-Leesen calmly dropped his broken sword to the forest floor as he stared into the green eyes that burned brightly with contempt. He neither ran nor dropped to his knees as he studied those eyes ... eyes that belonged to a Warrior of Blood.

That realization stirred something deep within Ou-Leesen. Standing there in the moonlight, wounded and defenceless against his executioners, he suddenly knew with certainty that he was a Warrior of Peace ... and that he would live to challenge Shanteef for all his evil deeds.

"My fight is not with you, it's with Shanteef," Ou-Leesen quietly responded to Mishri's question.

"So ... you are not only a traitor, you are a coward," Mishri bellowed angrily, as he continued to hold his sword to his side. He hated what Ou-Leesen had become. It was a contemptible descent into the dark pit where warriors abandoned everything that made them El-Bhat.

Now that Ou-Leesen stood before him, a defeated coward and traitor, Mishri could hardly believe that such a thing was possible. It was an insult to every El-Bhat that had died ... serving the Quorum. In anger, he shouted a final warning at the lost warrior, "Kneel and accept your punishment!"

The longer Ou-Leesen stood in defiance, the closer the spy crept up behind him. Mishri was very clear from the beginning about how the traitor would die, and who would carry out the execution.

But the Spy had been warned of Ou-Leesen's renowned skill, making him wary of Ou-Leesen's continued defiance. Finally, he decided that the risk was too great ... the Spy raised his sword.

Ou-Leesen kept his eyes on Mishri but his ears were on the El-Bhat that had positioned himself behind him. And when he heard a raised sword, his warrior instincts pulled the Dagger of Truth from its Scabbard as fast as he turned to meet the descending blade.

The Spy was determined to end the conflict as he pulled his blade down hard against the puny Dagger that was raised in defence.

He had expected to feel some resistance from the knife as his sword crashed past the pitiful attempt, seeking Ou-Leesen's flesh. But there was no resistance at all ... as though the knife blade was made of air!

Before he could raise his sword again, the pommel of the Dagger crashed into his skull. The bewildered Spy sunk in agony to his knees, his head swimming in pain.

Knowing he was only moments from death, he feebly raised his sword ... but the blade was hardly as long as his hand. With eyes wide, he fell, face-first, never to rise again.

--------- <> ---------

Mishri's repeated command to kneel had barely finished leaving his lips when the scene before him exploded into chaos. In barely the blink of an eye, Ou-Leesen had turned towards the remaining Spy as a sword came rushing down from above.

Mishri should have heard the clanking sound as metal blades crashed into each other. But there was no sound … only the grunt of the Spy as he crumpled to his knees … as his sword blade fell to the ground … severed from the hilt.

Mishri was still holding his sword at his side when Ou-Leesen turned to face him. 'Impossible' was the word that floated across his mind … the word that held him motionless, staring in disbelief.

But Mishri's training soon overcame the unbelievable, as his instincts moved him to action. If the Dagger could cut his blade like paper, then he would have to sacrifice his sword … while he plunged his dagger into Ou-Leesen's heart.

--------- <> ---------

As the Spy fell to his knees, Ou-Leesen had already turned to face his last opponent, raising his Dagger against the blade, that he was sure was already cutting an arc towards his flesh.

But Mishri was frozen to the spot … in the same position that he left him only moments before. "It doesn't have to end this way …" Ou-Leesen hurriedly began, as he began to lower his Dagger.

--------- <> ---------

But those words broke the spell, as the seasoned El-Bhat Leader swung his sword into an arc that fell directly against Ou-Leesen's head … as he slipped his left hand to his dagger, which he plunged into the traitor's chest.

--------- <> ---------

Ou-Leesen's speed easily matched the descending blade, confident that the Dagger of Truth would again save his life. But this time there was a difference. His opponent was *expecting* his blade to fail. And was already plunging a dagger directly towards his heart!

With arms holding the Dagger of Truth high against the sword, Ou-Leesen managed to turn his chest away from Mishri's dagger ... a little. He couldn't avoid the dagger, but the thrust missed his heart.

Ou-Leesen clenched his teeth, fighting against the pain, as he staggered backwards. His free hand gripped the silk that covered the wound, already wet with blood ... as he feebly held the Dagger against another attack.

But by now, his head was beginning to spin. He had already lost too much blood from his other wound and now his lungs were quickly filling from his chest wound. He didn't even notice that he had closed his eyes as he fought to remain standing.

--------- <> ---------

Mishri needed no other invitation.

In a swift and graceful motion, the El-Bhat leader stepped forward, grabbing the traitor's hair, intent on plunging his blood drenched dagger into his neck.

His resolve had not changed ... he would sever Ou-Leesen's head from his body. With hands trembling with rage, the El-Bhat prepared for the final thrust as he pulled the dagger back.

--------- <> ---------

Controlled by an unbidden reflex, Ou-Leesen thrust the Knife upwards, catching Mishri under the chin as the blade sunk deep into the El-Bhat's brain, his expression of rage frozen on his face. But Ou-Leesen never saw that look ... his eyes were still closed,

--------- <> ---------

In the instant the Dagger entered Mishri's body, Light flared from the emerald stone that was seated in the pommel of the hilt. It encircled the two El-Bhat, frozen in their death struggle.

His eyes were still closed but with his mind's eye, Ou-Leesen could see a strikingly beautiful Green Lady to the side. She was studying him, watching, waiting for him to respond to her presence ... he could feel it. She was anxious to teach him.

But *he* was not anxious to learn. The Dagger and this Green Witch was an abomination, and he was disgusted that he carelessly used the dark blade in his defence. With blade still sunken deeply into Mishri's body, Ou-Leesen staggered again ... his life was quickly slipping away.

--------- <> ---------

Her seductive smile instantly transformed to a frown. She needed him to set aside his stubbornness and accept her offer to assist him. But there wasn't time ... she couldn't wait.

Reluctantly she touched the Dagger of Truth as the life-force of Mishri rushed into the body of Ou-Leesen.

Chapter 9 - The *Buzz*

The sun had started his ascent by the time the El-Bhat warrior stirred. Ou-Leesen could smell dead leaves and felt the wetness of dew on his skin. His eyes opened to fragments of blue sky that filtered through heavy branches above. His mind searched for recent memories.

He could see the flight of arrows and remembered crawling through dense deadfall. In the darkness, he saw the rush of blades ... that drew his blood.

He sat up, remembering everything. He looked around. The two bodies still lay where they had fallen. The Green Lady was gone.

His black silk garment was crusted with copious amounts of blood ... but there was no pain. His hand drifted to his two wounds. Curious. His skin was unbroken!

As he stood, he noticed that the Dagger of Truth was back in the Scabbard. He stared at the Knife as the emerald stone sparkled in the sunlight.

There was much more to this Knife than he had first thought. It was not just a dark talisman, it was 'owned' by some dark force ... a *very* powerful force! And now he suspected that *he* was linked to that force. It was certainly why he was still alive.

When he first left Chitouf, he knew that he was no longer a free man. He was influenced by this Dagger in ways that were not easily recognizable. But now he wondered how far this power had cast a cloak of possession over Ou-Leesen. 'Does it own me?' he wondered to himself.

He knew what he wanted to do ... he wanted to throw it away. But would it be that simple? He remembered the Green Lady, and her beckoning power that could have easily seduced him, if he didn't already loathe the Dagger.

He searched the clearing to see if he was alone. Which really meant that he wanted to know if *she* was watching.

She wasn't there ... but what did that mean? Still uncertain, but determined, his hand drifted to the Scabbard. He felt nothing, so he slid his fingers to the hilt and touched it. Nothing. Slowly he pulled it from the leather Scabbard ... and then tossed it into the trees.

He stared off towards the Keep as he considered his journey … and his objective to cleanse the leadership of the Quorum.

'No,' he decided, 'that can wait.' He needed to test something.

He spotted Mishri's dagger and bow. He cleaned the blade and placed it in the Scabbard. Then he found the third El-Bhat and gathered whatever useful items that he could. In the process, he recognized two of them. They were among the Chitouf men working on the pass!

"So … besides the Assassin, Shanteef had sent his spies," Ou-Leesen muttered to himself.

He found his horse where he had left him, and then spent the rest of the morning crafting arrows. He would need to eat.

For the rest of the day, he hunted as he moved north, back the way he had come. He needed to reassure himself, that he had the power to decide what *he* would do.

By nightfall, he was far north of the three dead bodies he had left behind. He cooked the rabbit as he contemplated what he would do the following day. It appeared that his power of decision had returned. He could do what he wanted.

With that comfortable thought, he extinguished the fire, and rode on to find a safe place to sleep.

Ou-Leesen spent a restless night, as he tried to escape dreams of death and blood and the Dagger.

Finally, he awoke to the howl of a wild animal and decided it was time to move on. But first he would have a small meal of the meat he had saved from the night before.

He pulled the sack from his saddle bag, unwrapped the meat and reached for his knife. But the knife never made it to the meat.

Ou-Leesen's gaze drifted to his hand. Under those fingers, he could feel the ornate hilt and the bulbous green emerald that capped the end of it. Slowly he retracted his hand and stared at the impossible. He thought of his dreams. And he knew for sure, that ridding himself of the Dagger, would take more thought, than simply discarding it.

He put the meat away and mounted the horse.

He gripped the reins fiercely, as he allowed the fire within him, to beat back the resignation that threatened to overcome him … as he headed south!

--------- <> ---------

A member of Kareen's team was watching the holograph image as Ou-Leesen decided to head south again. He smiled to himself, pleased that he would be able to report this unexpected success in 'guiding' the Dagger back to its original owner. Ou-Leesen was not only strong willed but an unusually uncooperative subject.

Previously, he was on the edge of his seat as he watched Ou-Leesen throw away the Dagger, anxious to see what he would do with the Scabbard, the Technician's last hope.

With a sigh of relief, he sat back as he watched Ou-Leesen place a common knife into it. Then he chuckled as he watched the subject ride in the opposite direction. "So, you think it's as easy as that?" he said to the Hologram, knowing what his next move would be.

The following day, the Technician had gathered a couple of his team members to watch the warrior as he awoke. Everyone was silent as Ou-Leesen walked to his horse, unsuspecting that he was about to see the impossible.

Then he reached for his knife ... and froze ... unaware that laughter echoed through the control room of a ship, many leagues above him.

"You shouldn't be paid for this," one of his teammates joked, "it's too easy!"

"Maybe," he retorted. "But with dirt for brains ... they will make good slaves."

The comment reminded everyone, that with so much gold, good genetic material, and lots and lots of slaves, their bonuses would be bigger than anything they had imagined.

"Just don't mess up," he reminded the Technician, "now that Shanteef has the gold, he *must* have the Dagger."

"Or *we* could end up as slaves!" another Technician added.

"Don't worry ... the Subject will soon be dead and the Dagger back with the previous owner ... as planned," the Technician argued, as his teammates left the room.

But his protest of triumph was false. The Subject's will was *not* captured by the Green Lady. She had to interrupt the linking process to save the Subject's life. He sighed in anguish as he considered the unlikelihood of this happening! He had *never* heard of this ever happening before!

The only thing to do was to prepare for the next step.

To keep the Subject from his warrior friends as he propelled him into the jaws of the Keep.

Stek had instructions to keep moving towards the Keep as fast as horses and the heat would permit. And if Ou-Leesen didn't join them, he was to rotate the warriors as spies that would watch their rear.

They were headed to the end of the Shaksbah Mountain chain and then west towards the plains of Denlen. Towards their destination ... the Keep.

Stek wasn't completely surprised on the first morning when Ou-Leesen hadn't showed.

Previously, as they left Chitouf, Stek had caught glimpses of at least two Spies ... which probably meant there were more in the party that followed.

Stek had advised Ou-Leesen to take a few of his men with him. But for some strange reason, the Band Leader was inflexible on that point.

For leagues Ou-Leesen could feel the itch in his brain ... like he was forgetting something. Finally, he reined up his horse, to think and look around. The horse pranced at the tight rein that held him ready.

As he moved in a circle, his free hand brushed the pommel of the Dagger. It was like scratching an itch ... that begged for more.

He stopped the horse and stared down at the Knife. Now the itch was relentless ... like starting to scratch an itch, and not finishing the job. He didn't think he could continue riding all day and the next, without sorting out this itch.

He thought some more, and then reluctantly laid his hand on the pommel. It was a message ... there were others ahead ... lying in wait ... it was an ambush. And it was clear in what direction he was to continue if he wished to avoid the trap.

By the end of that day, Stek's thoughts were no longer occupied by the prospect of whether Ou-Leesen was dead or not. Instead, his attention was directed to the elegant Dagger with the emerald pommel that Protas had told him about. '*It can cut rock as easily as my knife can cut soft cheese*,' were the surprising words that Protas had shared.

Strange that he hadn't picked up on it before, but now that the Dagger was leagues away, he realized that he could no longer feel *the buzz*.

'Well ... to be exact,' he thought to himself, '*the buzz* is still there ... but it's become very, very quiet.'

And by the end of the second day he realized that *the buzz* had increased slightly, as though the Dagger of Truth was getting closer. 'Is it Ou-Leesen?' he mused to himself, 'or someone who now carries the Knife while the El-Bhat Leader lay dead, leagues behind them?'

That night, Stek lay perfectly still, with eyes closed, searching for the location of *the buzz* ... and its movement. It didn't take long before he had located the rider's current location ... back in the forest where they had left Ou-Leesen.

His imagination created a map of the terrain they had already passed through, allowing him to track this rider, as he travelled through the night, determined to continue until the Rider stopped.

But the silence of the night and the heat of the day pulled his weary body into the imaginary world that he had created.

Standing on the top of a low rolling hill, as stars shined brightly overhead, he watched as a single rider pushed his horse through the dark landscape.

As Stek watched the scene below him, he wondered who the El-Bhat was that flew through the night. Suddenly his Tracker instincts drove him to action ... this was an El-Bhat!

He raced down the hill, determined to intercept the horse and dislodge the man in the black silk garment.

He flew like the wind, down the hill and across the plain. His trajectory was perfect, as he leapt high in the air, knocking the rider off his horse.

Tumbling into a roll, he ended up on top of the rider, thrusting his short knife hard into the chest of the black warrior.

In horror, the man looked into Stek's eyes as he gasped the Tracker's name.

Stek bolted upright, with Ou-Leesen's face etched on his mind. He looked around. Everyone was asleep except for the posted Guards who looked his way.

He paused to consider the dream that had awakened him. 'Either Ou-Leesen is on his way … or he is dead and those that killed him are riding hard to catch up.'

He quickly packed his belongings and gathered the men.

"We are being followed," he began, as the Scouts expressed surprise at the middle-of-the-night announcement. "It could be Ou-Leesen … or not. We leave immediately. There will be no Scouts that protect our rear. We ride hard and won't stop until daylight."

Once the sun was up, Stek began looking for a place that would afford an ambush. He wanted to be prepared for the outcome if it wasn't Ou-Leesen … and rid himself of the threat that was behind them.

--------- <> ---------

Approaching another hill, Ou-Leesen directed his horse into the forest as he continued forward. He wanted to have the advantage of surveying the next valley from the secrecy of the trees.

Moving to the forest's edge, the broad valley stretched before him, all the way to the Shaksbah Mountains. His eyes told him that the way was clear, but the temptation to check with the Dagger was strong.

Earlier, as he rode through the day, his blood encrusted silk robe constantly reminded him that without the Dagger, he would no longer be alive. And now he depended on it to guide him past dangers along his route to the Keep.

It was a disquieting thought … relying on this powerful dark associate … that he didn't trust. For now, he would keep his hands on the reins, and his eyes away from the Dagger.

The plains before him made him think of his men. Were they already at the Mountains … or behind him, waiting for a Leader who would never show, because of the Dagger?

"It doesn't matter!" He muttered angrily to himself. Soon the Dagger would silence Shanteef's lying lips.

With the reassurance of his resolve, he nudged his horse forward. He would let the Green Witch lead him safely to the Keep … because he knew that, no matter what else, death would be waiting to take Shanteef, once he arrived. His Sherilin blood had told him so.

As the forest fell further behind, he thought back to the day that he had stood before Shanteef and the Quorum, defending the actions of himself and his men, as Warriors, devoid of shame. Successful in his defence, the Quorum Leader then passed the Dagger of Truth to Ou-Leesen.

And later, in the privacy of the Keep, he stared in unbelief as his Leader used the Knife to cut a brass jug like it was a piece of fruit.

At the time, Ou-Leesen had assumed he was being instructed in the Knife's power. But he wasn't. He was being *tempted* … to use its power. Shanteef wanted him to use it over and over again. Why … he wasn't completely sure. But the advantage certainly fell to Shanteef.

Leagues later, the Warrior of Peace grunted. 'My pride has made me stupid,' Ou-Leesen chastened himself. 'I believed that he gave me the Dagger because he saw me as a great warrior.'

He grunted again … he wasn't finished with the self-rebuke. 'And my pride blinded my eyes. I could not see the Assassin … and yet he lived and spoke like an Assassin!'

His anger against his pride continued to rise as he thought of the spies, sent from Shanteef. El-Bhat who tracked him with Mishri.

Since the moment he had looked into their dead faces, he searched his memories … and sure enough, the clues were there! They behaved differently from the workers from Chitouf … but he was blind.

He reined in his horse as he neared the mountain foothills. It had been a hard road to travel, learning of his blindness. But now he could see.

When it came to power ... he knew he was nothing. The Green Witch taught him that.

When it came to value ... he knew he was everything. The Sherilin blood that ran through his veins taught him that. Blood that he would soon sacrifice to kill Shanteef.

--------- <> ---------

Stek's trail was easy to follow, and yet after waiting for several hours, no one entered the carefully planned ambush. In fact, the distance between him and *the buzz* remained relatively constant ... as though the pursuers had stopped.

And so, he waited some more, until eventually *the buzz* began to fade. It was moving further away.

Puzzled, he closed his eyes and returned to the map he created the night before and saw his mistake. The constant distance between him and the Dagger was because it was moving in an arc, to avoid them! And now the Knife was far ahead of them.

He gathered his men quickly. "We have been fooled. Whoever was following, is now ahead of us." He looked at the Scouts. "Move ahead with as much speed as we dare."

Chapter 10 - The Pit of Pain

Ou-Leesen and his weary horse looked down at the Keep from the low-lying plateau to the east. He knew exactly what he needed to do. He had spent days thinking about it.

He remembered clearly from his previous visit, that the Keep was heavily guarded with El-Bhat. That swept the perimeter and interior constantly. He would never make it to Shanteef alive ... unless of course, the Quorum Leader wanted him to.

But then again, all events pointed to one conclusion. The Dagger of Truth was on its return journey to its original owner.

'From the beginning,' Ou-Leesen thought, 'Shanteef knew that the Knife would come back to him like a loyal horse.'

Thinking back, it was strange that the Quorum Leader would let it go in the first place. But the circumstances back at the forest, when Mishri died ... and *he* didn't, suggested that it wasn't so strange after all.

Perhaps Shanteef was using the Dagger of Power like a fishing net. Casting it into the unknown deep, knowing it would eventually come back ... full of power that only Shanteef could extract ... by plunging the blade into **Ou-Leesen**.

Except that this time, Shanteef would be the victim, of the Knife.

Ou-Leesen nudged his horse forward. The sun wouldn't set for another hour, giving him time to arrive at the large front doors, where the Guards would recognize him.

He had no doubt that he would be allowed to enter the 'palace of corruption' without a question ... because of Shanteef's instructions.

His eyes narrowed as he thought about the deceitful cunning of the Quorum Leader. Ironic because those same instructions allowed him to enter as a Warrior of Peace.

The task demanded it.

The Guards nodded briefly at Ou-Leesen as he entered the beautifully carved doors. As he walked down the familiar halls, an unwelcome thought crept into his mind.

Words without being words; challenged his desire to kill the Quorum Leader.

He slowed as he considered the tremor of doubt that this new experience introduced to his mind.

After all, Shanteef had been the honoured and beloved leader of the El-Bhat for as long as he could remember.

'Yes ... and how long was that ... really?' he challenged the doubt, as he thought of receiving Mishri's life force.

'Sometimes Leaders do what they must do, for the benefit of the greater community,' another wordless thought plummeted into the ocean of his thoughts.

The invading thoughts continued for some time until Ou-Leesen had to stop. The doubts were so convincing that he couldn't walk and think at the same time.

'Leaders ... should always honour the Sherilin blood', was his eventual rebuff.

'How can you be so sure that you have a complete understanding of his motives?' the wordless voice disputed.

Ou-Leesen leaned against the wall as he rubbed his temples, desperate to clear the fog that grew stronger with every new doubt.

Before he could find a satisfactory answer to the latest doubt, another thought followed.

'Do not all men have weaknesses that they humbly struggle against?'

Ou-Leesen gave up trying to reason against the invasive suggestions. He didn't seem to have the power. It made him wonder, how he could have believed so strongly in his quest to kill Shanteef.

He opened his eyes, his head hanging in misery ... and saw a soft glow coming from the pommel of the Dagger of Truth.

Again! The Green Lady had never left!

Angrily he pushed himself away from the wall. 'Well ... there is only one thing to do,' Ou-Leesen thought, as he clenched his teeth together. 'Keep walking!'

Another set of Guards were standing outside the Quorum Room, where he last met with Shanteef. But these Guards didn't look so ... indifferent. The nod of permission to enter, was the same, but there was a look in their eyes, that told Ou-Leesen that he was entering a place of death and darkness.

As he entered the room, Shanteef was sitting on the same gold-embroidered cushion as he was on their last encounter. There was the same bowl of fruit and chilled drinks.

But his expression was different ... as he glanced at the Dagger.

Shanteef motioned for Ou-Leesen to take his usual place on the thick carpet.

The relaxed atmosphere felt odd. Ou-Leesen looked around the room. Nothing seemed out of place. And yet, here he was ... the guest of the man he was about to kill.

He looked at Shanteef's eyes. Should he kill him before he took his next breath?

'No', he decided. A Warrior of Peace was never in a hurry, to administer justice. A man's last words were sacred, even for someone like Shanteef. Ou-Leesen sat down.

"You look like you have ridden hard for many days ... won't you refresh yourself with a cold drink?" the Quorum Leader suggested as he waved a hand in the direction of the pitcher.

Ou-Leesen ignored the comment. He trusted nothing about the man sitting across from him.

Since his guest refused to respond, Shanteef had no choice but to encourage him. It was part of his plan ... to put this warrior at ease. So, he took the pitcher himself, poured a drink and emptied his goblet.

Ou-Leesen countered by pouring himself a drink, but it remained sitting to his side.

Finally, Shanteef began the dialogue. "I have received word that you have moved some of the gold into Storlenia. For what purpose have you done this?"

Without hesitation Ou-Leesen answered. "I have purchased the shipping rights to two ports, one on the east coast and one on the west ... as well as several merchant ships."

Shanteef was surprised at such a bold move. If it was true, the strategy would advance the El-Bhat plan in significant ways.

He poured himself another drink as he considered what Ou-Leesen had offered in response to his question.

"Well done ... but we have no contacts on either coast," he stated matter-of-factly. "How did you manage such an impossible task?"

"It was easy. I had the assistance of two Trackers."

Again, the unflinching answer came without hesitation. And again, Shanteef was tempted to pour himself another drink as he considered such a reply.

Instead, he offered a thin smile as he countered, "I am aware of two Trackers that have come to our side. Perhaps they are the same. What were their names?"

"Stek and Biskin."

As Ou-Leesen continued to share the truthful details of his rebellion, he noticed that he felt no fear. Instead, what he felt was the strength of his conviction returning. Now it was his turn to offer a guarded smile to Shanteef ... for he realized that he would know when it was time to execute Shanteef. For now, let the Quorum Leader continue with his sham interview.

Shanteef's eyebrow raised at the mention of the name Stek. Mishri had told Shanteef about his conversation with Bernado ... about a very resourceful Tracker that had been recruited by Retlin. But the intelligence was known to only a few high-ranking El-Bhat. And the fact that Ou-Leesen had pulled Stek into his service was indeed impressive. And ... the more Ou-Leesen shared with Shanteef, the more the Quorum Leader was convinced that everything he said was true!

"I have heard of Stek," Shanteef commented as his glance returned to the Dagger at Ou-Leesen's side. "But not of Biskin." The Quorum Leader was beginning to wonder if Ou-Leesen's accomplishments were because he had discovered previously unknown secrets of the Dagger of Truth.

And *that* possibility sent the old El-Bhat into a state of anxiety as he considered that the Dagger might have found a new home.

Things were not going as well as Shanteef had hoped. The interview was supposed to convince Ou-Leesen to give the Dagger back to Shanteef ... because of guilt, and shame. It was time to take a different approach.

"It appears that you have indeed, exceeded my expectations ... and that is hard to do."

Ou-Leesen refused to embrace the praise. His face was like stone as the two men continued to stare at each other.

Undaunted, Shanteef pressed forward. "What you have done ... acquiring two ports inside Storlenia, and adding another Tracker to our cause, is an accomplishment of *three* lifetimes. But now it is time to return the Dagger of Truth ... to me."

And once he had the blade, he intended to extract the secrets of Ou-Leesen's accomplishments as the Green Power filled his mind with treasures of knowledge.

Ou-Leesen knew that the moment had finally come, and it was Shanteef that had unwittingly signed his own death warrant. If he had let the Dagger go, perhaps things could have been different. But now that path was closed.

He leaned forward as he delivered the message that he had ridden days to deliver. "I did not come here to return the Dagger of Truth … I came here to remove you from your position as the undisputed Leader of the El-Bhat."
Surprisingly, the words flowed on a current of peace. The rage he had felt so many times, was gone. He had *become* a Warrior of Peace.

"You presume too much!" an angry Quorum Leader shouted as he jumped to his feet and unsheathed the sword hanging on the wall.
Ou-Leesen slowly rose to his feet with Dagger in hand.
Facing the Dagger of Truth seemed to change whatever Shanteef was about to do as he backed towards an exit. Suddenly he turned and rushed from the room.
Ou-Leesen dashed after him, determined to cut him down with the dark blade.
But as he stepped onto the carpet that Shanteef had subtly avoided … it gave way to his weight.

The floor of the dark pit rushed up to slam into Ou-Leesen's feet. He cried out as the sharp spikes cut into flesh and bone. Trembling with pain he looked up at the edge of the floor. It was above him by at least three paces. He would have to use the Dagger at least six times to free himself.
He began cutting footholds into the side of the rock pit, determined that Shanteef would not escape so easily from his blade.
With each step, the Dagger glowed more brightly as Ou-Leesen's life began to slip away, trapped inside the green pommel.

Standing by the open doorway with sword in hand, Shanteef watched as the green glow approached the top of the spiked prison. His greatest concern was whether Ou-Leesen had enough life force to make it out of the pit. That anxiety forced him to walk closer to the pit, ready to assist him out.

--------- <> ---------

Reaching the top, an exhausted and trembling Ou-Leesen, pulled himself out of the pit, his feet burning with pain.

--------- <> ---------

High above the activities of the Keep, a concerned Technician was desperately working the controls to send a message to Shanteef. The Quorum Leader *must not* follow the normal instructions to extract the life force and knowledge from Ou-Leesen!

The Technician had considered advising the others several times of his unique problem, but he was convinced that he could sort it out himself ... and thereby avoid Kareen's wrath.

As far as he knew, it had never happened before ... that *the Subject's will was not captured by the Green Lady*. He was horrified when he saw her interrupt the linking process to save the Subject's life.

He watched anxiously as Shanteef wove words of guilt to encourage Ou-Leesen to pass the Dagger of Truth back to the original owner. But that wasn't working!

And now he watched in horror as Ou-Leesen dug himself out of the hidden pit with the Dagger.

He wasn't sure what would happen if the determined warrior used the power of the Dagger until all his life force was extracted and collapsed dead into the pit.

But of greater concern was his uncertainty of the outcome if Shanteef plunged the Dagger of Truth into Ou-Leesen.

'Do not use the Dagger of Truth against the warrior' was the hurried message he sent to Shanteef as the old man approached a weary Ou-Leesen who had just pulled himself out of the pit.

--------- <> ---------

With sword held aloft, Shanteef circled the struggling Ou-Leesen as he slowly climbed out of the *pit of pain*. The sword was for effect … he never intended on using it. He must kill Ou-Leesen with the Dagger of Truth!

--------- <> ---------

Ou-Leesen had never felt so weary as he threw his free arm over the edge and painfully pushed against his bleeding and torn foot. Finally, with chest secure against the floor, he raised his head to look for Shanteef.

--------- <> ---------

Kareen's Technician adjusted the hologram to get a clear view of the Quorum Leader as he took two quick steps and plunged his sword into Ou-Leesen's arm, opening his hand like a flower. Shanteef quickly extracted the Dagger in triumph.

Touching it, triggered the message from above that immediately flowed into his mind. The aging El-Bhat could feel a swirl of words at the back of his mind, but his desire to plunge the Dagger into Ou-Leesen fuelled his entire concentration.

"No, no, no!" the Technician wailed at the hologram, "You mustn't use the Knife against the warrior!" His hands flew to his controls to measure a response. The reading showed almost zero adaptation. The El-Bhat was nearly unreachable.

He looked behind to see if anyone had entered the control room. He was about to contradict protocol and exceed the strength of the Dagger-to-mind connection. A very serious offence. But if he lost Shanteef and control of the Dagger, his life was over anyway.
Good … he was alone. With trembling hands, he slid the control knob upwards … as high as it would go.

--------- <> ---------

Shanteef fell to his knees as he raised the Dagger above the half-dead body of Ou-Leesen. "Now we will see what secrets you hold!"

Anxious hands thrust the blade towards the warrior's back.

Like a roaring Desert Lion, the words *'Do not use the Dagger ...'* thundered inside his head.

But the words were too late as the Knife slid with ease through flesh and bone.

Shanteef's agonized features, froze, as a burst of Green Light flashed from the emerald pommel of the Dagger of Truth.

And the life force of Shanteef poured into Ou-Leesen ... along with the secrets of his mind.

Chapter 11 - Ranoof's history

Previously, while Ranoof slept in the forest, holding the now completed Amulet, the power of the Circle of Blood, called out to him as Urshen and his fellow Tracker prisoners, struggled against the Black Wind. Ranoof answered the call, but the pull of power from an Amulet that wasn't his to hold, was too much for Ranoof and he collapsed.

In the quiet of the forest, a Hunter heard a cry. It was a man in distress. He followed the sound until he found a Tracker, crying out from his nightmare. The Hunter shook him awake.

'A day earlier'

    The explosion of Light, left Ranoof tumbling through the silence of dark space, for a long time, as he connected with scenes from his past, that flowed unbidden across the landscape of his mind.

    He saw the first time his father took him hunting, in the great Woods of Lartenelle, far from their home.

    One morning he awoke to find his father gone. Perhaps he would return soon with fish from the nearby lake. But after a few hours, he decided his father must be in trouble. He would find him.

    He immediately left camp with his bow, his sling and his knives. He set traps for food as he followed his father's tracks.

    The signs led him to the water's edge … and then they stopped. He stripped and dove into the lake multiple times as he searched for a body in the dark depths close to the steeply dipping shore.

    Eventually he knew he had to go for help. His father had disappeared, and he had done everything he could to find him.

    He returned to his traps. He would need food for the long journey home.

On the second day, he came across a fellow traveller and immediately told him his story. The man seemed sympathetic and suggested that he go back with the boy to help him find his father. Eventually, he asked Ranoof if he had any food. "I have certain skills," he added, to encourage the boy.

When the evening meal of roasted rabbit was finished, the man retired to a large tree trunk, where he consumed an entire bottle of wine. Ranoof was curious to know more about the man, but the more he drank, the more the mood of his travelling companion turned sour.

As the man tipped the bottle for the last time, he paused briefly as though considering the boy's question. Through bleary eyes he suddenly barked at the boy, "Shut up and go to sleep!"

In the morning when Ranoof awoke, all his food and weapons were gone. He could have easily tracked him. Ironically the man had no skills after all. But the young boy was helpless without his weapons and could only go home, hoping to beg food on the way.

He tied up his blanket and turned to the trail ... where he saw his father watching him. Ranoof was both pleased and confused. But only for a moment. Then he understood and walked with purpose towards his father.
"What did you learn?" were his father's first words.
The boy was quick to respond. "I will NEVER drink wine!"

Ranoof's tumble through dark space suddenly connected to another memory about wine ... and treachery, and escape, and an Amulet under a cloth and a flash of Light.

The next memory took him to a place of darkness and fear, where his friends called to him, desperate for his help. Feeling the anguish of their plight, he cried, 'I must help them', and immediately there was a flash of Light that broke both the chains of Darkness and the link that connected the Trackers to Urshen.

'Back to the present'
As Ranoof heard the words, "You must awake ... it's only a dream!" a crack of light appeared above him.

The Hunter shook him again before his eyelids began to flutter towards wakefulness. Ranoof sat up, rubbed his eyes with his free hand, while the Hunter noticed he clung to something in the other.

"What's in your hand?" the Hunter asked, trying to encourage Ranoof to speak. But instead of speaking, Ranoof was anxious to stand and be on his way. But before he took two steps, he fainted.

--------- <> ---------

"Enough is enough," the Hunter's wife mumbled to herself as she carried a pail of cold water into the spare room. With a strong arm, she sent the water flying onto the sleeping Tracker.

Sputtering and gasping, Ranoof was awake immediately. He wiped the water from his eyes. He found himself staring into a face that would make a bear run the other way.

He was in a small bed, in a small room with a small window … completely unaware of what to say to the large woman glaring at him.

So, she spoke first. "You've been lying there long enough; expecting someone to spoon feed you broth. Time to pay your way. Husband …" she bellowed, and almost without a pause, Ranoof could hear footsteps enter the house and continue down the hallway, to the place where Ranoof slept.

"He's awake," she scowled, "and now he's yours," she directed as she carried the pail out of the room. As soon as she was out of ear shot, Ranoof addressed the man. "Sorry to be any trouble … but where am I and who are you?"

The man closed the door and began telling him the story of how he had found him.

"I was hunting along my trap trails when I heard you cry out. I found you lying alone, as though you were having a nightmare. You were clutching a crystal talisman. You tried to stand and feinted, so I brought you here. I thought you must be on your way to dispose of the terrible talisman, so I put it in the kitchen cupboard.

"Then when the missus woke in the middle of the night, to make herself a cup of tea, the talisman came to life. She could see a blinding light escaping from the cracks of the cupboard. She was frightened and called me. The Light was gone when I arrived, so together we watched the cupboard all night until the morning. The talisman never did glow again that night. But after the sleepless experience, we agreed that I should throw the terrible talisman into the nearby lake."

Ranoof's eyebrows floated upwards as he considered what the Hunter had done. "Well ... that's quite a story. You probably have many questions ... but unfortunately the last thing I remember, was lying down in the forest for a night's sleep ... where you found me."

"What were you doing with the terrible talisman?" The Hunter was still curious.

"I was taking it to someone who could examine it more closely," Ranoof said carefully as he stared at the Hunter. "Perhaps you could take me to the place where you disposed of the terrible talisman. I will need to give a proper report," Ranoof carefully added.

"All right," the Hunter agreed, knowing his wife was anxious to see the Tracker on his way.

Later that day, they were both sitting in the boat. "About here is where I dropped it," the Hunter indicated, holding the oars, ready to head back to shore.

Ranoof looked over the edge and dipped his hand into the water. "Looks deep. Most likely no light down there. Perfect place to keep others from ever finding it," he congratulated the Hunter. 'And me as well,' he acknowledged to himself.

Ranoof was beginning to feel the despair of an impossible task. He rubbed his closed eyes with his wet hands, as he considered what he might do.

To buy a few moments more, he added, "The water is very cold, must be good fishing ..." but he stopped mid-sentence. He felt something, as he returned his hand to the water. He looked at the Hunter.

"Fishing is great," the Hunter agreed. But Ranoof had already made up his mind.

He stood and dove into the lake.

He swam down to the bottom, but all he found was complete darkness and lungs pleading for air. He pushed himself off the bottom and swam to the surface. He treaded water as the small boat raced for the shore. He knew the Hunter would be back, probably with his bow.

Ranoof was puzzled. He knew the Amulet was below. He had felt the need to retrieve it. And he had seen the glowing Amulet as soon as he entered the water, but then it winked out. Wasn't he supposed to find the Amulet? He knew he had to find it before the Hunter returned or he would be dead ... with or without it.

He treaded more slowly, calming his mind, and thought about what had happened. He first felt the Amulet's presence when he dipped his hands into the water, felt it again as he wet his eyes ... and as soon as he entered the water he saw its light. But then everything went dark.

How was he supposed to figure this out ... he wasn't a Seer like Urshen!

While wishing Urshen was there, an image of being on the Plateau at Border Pass crossed his mind, and how they gathered and closed their eyes to ...

He grinned as he plunged back into the inky waters. But with his eyes closed.

Surfacing he saw the Hunter re-enter his boat. As the oars plunged back into the water, Ranoof placed the Amulet around his neck for safe keeping and swam for the opposite side of the lake.

Scrambling out of the water, he hurried behind the nearest tree as the first of the Hunter's arrows whizzed past him. Luckily for him the Hunter had the disadvantage of having to balance himself in an unsteady boat ... or he might already be dead.

As Ranoof hurried deeper into the forest he occasionally looked back, but as expected, the Hunter was reluctant to pursue a Tracker through a forest. Eventually the Hunter turned the boat around and headed back to his wife, probably with a tale that Ranoof was gone for good ... with the talisman still safely at the bottom of the lake.

Deep in the forest, as Ranoof rested, he decided that he needed to travel as a common labourer for the rest of his trip. After escaping from the Pechora Tracking Guild, he had been fortunate in Qar-ana to be under the protection of Craslin, but everything had changed in the last few days.

Before Craslin realized he was gone, he had hoped to get half way to Arborville, but his extended stay at the Hunter's Cabin, changed all that.

Now, he would be a fugitive sought after by Trackers from Pechora, Craslin's Militia and friends of the Hunter. Getting to Arborville would be more difficult than he had expected ... if he made it at all.

And now, he was hungry and very weak. Arborville would have to wait a bit longer while he set up trap lines to gather food for the trip.

And … he was no longer comfortable with the Amulet under his vest. He looked around the forest for a suitable hiding place. Once hidden, he turned his efforts to finding food.

For the rest of his journey, Ranoof repeated his strategy of hiding the Amulet while he found food and then, with sufficient supplies for travelling, moving the Amulet south to its next hiding place.

Eventually Ranoof found himself at the Arborville Tinker's Village and headed for the Planning Building where he knew he would find Zephra's father.

His steps quickened as he pulled out the Amulet in anticipation of finally placing it into the hands of Braddock. And to his surprise, the talisman was already glowing softly.

He began to run, and by the time he burst through the door, the crystal was glowing fiercely!

Chapter 12 - Two minds are better than one

The El-Bhat Guards glanced anxiously at each other as the sounds from the other side of the door suggested that they quickly enter the Quorum Room. But they had been instructed to remain outside until Shanteef opened the doors. And his instructions were *always* to be obeyed exactly as given!

--------- <> ---------

About a half day's journey from the Keep, Stek and the warriors who followed him, were suddenly surrounded by a large contingent of El-Bhat. They were stripped of their weapons and supplies before the journey resumed.

--------- <> ---------

When Ou-Leesen awoke, his legs were still dangling over the edge of the *Pit of Pain*. Carefully he pulled himself up the rest of the way and then stood to survey the room.

By his feet, was the Dagger of Truth. Slightly further away, was the dead body of a very, very old man ... who wore the garment of the Quorum Leader. Everything else, was as it was before he lost consciousness.

He remembered the Guards on the other side of the door ... but there was something else he remembered about those Guards. He remembered the instructions that *he* gave them before he arrived. 'Strange', Ou-Leesen thought. He was recalling a memory that was really *Shanteef's* memory ... he could hear *his* voice speaking to the Guards!

He looked down at the Dagger, lying lifeless on the tiled floor. There was no doubt that it was the Green Power that gave him the knowledge about the Guards ... but that knowledge was also a memory!

'But how ... and what happened here?' he asked himself as he looked at the blood-stained floor and the shrivelled old body that he knew must be Shanteef.

Suddenly the answer came as other memories flooded into his mind.
He could remember watching anxiously as *he* watched Ou-Leesen climb out of the pit.

'I am looking through Shanteef's eyes,' he quickly realized, as the memory continued to move forward in time.

In the memory, *he* rushed forward to circle Ou-Leesen and then *he* thrust the sword into his arm. The hand opened instantly and then *he* felt the familiar touch of the Dagger as *he* snatched it away from Ou-Leesen. He could feel the pleasure as *he* raised the Dagger above *his* head to sink it into Ou-Leesen's body, anxious to have *his* youth restored and to gain the precious memories of the El-Bhat warrior ... especially memories that might involve the location of a Cave and new discoveries regarding the power of the Blade.

He followed the arc of the blade as it plummeted towards Ou-Leesen's back.

Then he heard a thunderous voice telling him that *he* mustn't use the Dagger, just an instant before the Knife easily sank into flesh and bone. But Shanteef was so drunk with the excitement of the moment, that he paid no heed to those words.

And ... before everything went black, *he* remembered a promise made by the Green Lady ... a promise of immortality if *he* could find and destroy another Cave.

'Two Caves,' Ou-Leesen thought to himself, 'I actually know where *two* Caves are!'

Ou-Leesen's brow furrowed as he thought about how things would have been different if Shanteef had been successful and was alive with Ou-Leesen's memories.

"But you're not!" he angrily whispered to himself. Instead, he had Shanteef's memories ... and *he* was the one alive.

Ou-Leesen looked back at the doors, with Guards on the other side, waiting for Shanteef to emerge from their meeting. His plans hadn't gone past this point ... he had expected to die. Maybe if he searched Shanteef's memories ...

Satisfied that he had a reasonable plan in place, he removed the Leader's garment, pushed the dead body into the pit, replaced the carpet, placed the Dagger of Truth back into the Scabbard, and tied it to his waist as he headed for the 'unknown' on the other side of the large gold-gilded doors.

Two surprised Guards turned to look at Ou-Leesen as he left the Quorum Room ... dressed in the garment of the Quorum Leader.

Suspiciously they raised their swords, as they looked at each other, wondering what to do.

"Shanteef will soon march on Kel-eetan," Ou-Leesen began, raising his hand, as a sign to resume their guard position. "The Capital of Shaksbah will fall and the leadership of our nation will be transferred to the Keep.

"Our great Leader has honoured me with the task of preparing our forces, while he seeks the support of our ancestors. He is in his room ... and is not to be disturbed!" Ou-Leesen added.

The Guards eyed Ou-Leesen suspiciously. They had always received instructions from the Quorum Leader himself.

Ou-Leesen was not deterred. Boldly he continued. "I have received instructions that you are to come with me," he advised as he extended the pommel of the Dagger to the first Guard, while speaking the words "El-beka-noota."

Immediately the Guard dropped to his knees as he kissed the green emerald stone, and repeated the words, "El-beka-noota."

The only El-Bhat that were aware of this ritual, were the personal Guards to the Quorum Leader. Shanteef must have shown Ou-Leesen the ritual ... and therefore it must be obeyed.

As he extended the ritual to the Guards, memories from the dead Quorum Leader flowed unbidden to Ou-Leesen's consciousness ... about a very important door to the El-Bhat kingdom. All the El-Bhat under Shanteef's command had been trained to follow instructions from his Personal Guards. And with those guards at his side, the rest of the Keep would fall into place.

As Stek swayed in the saddle under the searing heat of the Shaksbah sun, with no water, he figured that the only reason he was still alive, was the impossibility of El-Bhat being led by a Storlenian. This was something their leaders would want to understand.

Stek was amused by the thought that his leadership was the most significant aspect of his being there in Shaksbah. Understanding his relationship to Ou-Leesen, who was probably now dead, was nothing compared to the other knowledge he carried inside his head.

Nothing … because if the El-Bhat had smuggled Olleti into Shaksbah … well then, his knowledge of Tracker intelligence, the two ports that Ou-Leesen had purchased … and the whereabouts of a Cave, would tumble off his tongue. He couldn't let that happen … so he began thinking of a plan to take his own life.

Like a ritual, the El-Bhat stopped on the flat plateau overlooking the Keep. It was the pride of the El-Bhat warriors, and someday it would be the new capital of all Shaksbah … Shanteef had reassured them that this would be so.

Every warrior lined up along that ridge, and with drawn swords, shouted, "El-lukten coureese bin swofet!" Meaning, 'The Glory and power of the World!'

The swords were barely back in their scabbards when Stek collapsed from off his horse. It was part of his plan. If they thought he was unconscious, slung over a horse, then plucking a knife from an unsuspecting El-Bhat would be easy. A quick slash of his jugular and his life would be over before they could stop the bleeding.

Two El-Bhat jumped down and roughly slung Stek over the saddle, amused, that of all their prisoners, the first to collapse was the Tracker.

As the troop of warriors descended to the Gates of the Keep, Stek took an occasional quick look as his head swung idly from side to side. He would continue to gather intelligence until the moment he was sure that all was lost.

An El-Bhat was sent ahead to inform the Guards of the prisoners. It was customary for Shanteef to meet them inside the Gates and examine the prisoners. Then he would decide their fate.

Once the El-Bhat were inside the wall of the Keep, everyone dispersed. Only the Leader of the Band would escort the prisoners forward to meet Shanteef.

--------- <> ---------

Ou-Leesen was resting by the Pool of Peace, an area surrounded by the inner walls of the Keep. He wanted to be by himself. It was important that he continue to probe Shanteef's knowledge. What he had learned so far was that recalling *his* memories was not spontaneous … probably because he didn't know what Shanteef knew, so he had to ask questions.

Of course, his priority was to know what happened to the sixteen men he left behind at Ou-Leesen Pass. The vivid memory surfaced immediately.

With clenched fists and bowed head, he struggled against the pain of their death.

Eventually his head came up. He also needed to know where the gold was hidden. Those gold bricks still played a significant role in his plans. 'Interesting he thought.'

Needing a rest from the memories, he scanned the columns and gardens for his Personal Guards. They were good men and now they belonged to him. He knew they would always be close by … but out of sight.

He was curious about the Personal Guard, and how Shanteef managed to keep his secrets for so long. He knew from *his* last instructions to the Guards, that *he* was keeping the Guards in the dark regarding the Dagger.

Immediately the unspoken question was answered by another flood of memories. It was horrifying.

The Quorum Leader would regularly replace them with new Guards, but only after he extracted their Life Force! A convenient arrangement to protect the secrets of the Dagger of Truth *and* he had a ready supply of young warriors to keep himself from aging.

The memories of a long line of Guards continued to surface until Ou-Leesen was sickened by the bloodshed. 'Stop,' he cried within himself, burying his face in his hands.

Before he could ask another question, a messenger could be heard approaching the courtyard looking for the Personal Guard.

"Tell Shanteef that the El-Bhat prisoners have arrived," the messenger said and then left as quickly as he came.

The Personal Guard nodded and shortly stood before Ou-Leesen.

"Your Holiness, the El-Bhat that rode with you are here … as prisoners."

As Ou-Leesen stood, he quickly searched *his* memories to find that Shanteef never left anything to chance. Yes, he knew that Ou-Leesen would be drawn to the Keep by the Green Power, but it wouldn't hurt to add his own influence to make sure that destiny was following a straight path.

So, he sent out a large Band of El-Bhat, to search the land between Chitouf and the Keep, for Ou-Leesen and his men. All were condemned to die a traitor's death. And their heads would be placed on top of spikes around the perimeter of the Keep.

"Yes, Shanteef had instructed me that they might be here soon. I will take care of it." His memories also advised him that Shanteef always met any prisoners brought to the Keep.

--------- <> ---------

All eyes immediately dropped to the ground, to honour the Quorum Leader, as the large doors of the Keep opened. No one saw that it was not Shanteef that emerged, but instead, a relatively unknown warrior with no important claim to rank or achievement, that walked through those doors.

Ou-Leesen, escorted by his Personal Guards, walked past the Leader of the Band ... straight to the first of his warriors. He grabbed his long hair and pulled his head upward until their eyes met. There was a brief look of bewilderment ... and then Ou-Leesen repeated the action with the next warrior.

He did not speak a word until he had repeated the ritual with every prisoner ... except the unconscious man slung over his horse.
He saved Stek for last. And before he walked to his horse, he whispered to the Leader of the Band. "Is he dead?"
"No. He collapsed back at the Plateau."
This was good news for Ou-Leesen. His plans had expanded significantly ... he would need his Advisor.

--------- <> ---------

From the moment the horse stopped, Stek remained perfectly still. No one must suspect that he was alert and conscious. He listened carefully to the movement of the man who had come to inspect the prisoners ... most likely Shanteef.

It was obvious that he was left for last, and now he could hear the El-Bhat approach his horse. He slowed until he came to a stop. Through partially opened eyes, Stek could see the embroidered robe that fell to the man's feet. It was Shanteef, and he had positioned himself foolishly close, considering Stek's training.

With the swiftness of a Desert Snake, he grabbed the man's Knife and twisted him to the ground. He raised the Dagger, intent on killing Shanteef before he took his own life.

Instinctively, Ou-Leesen's men reacted with the speed of El-Bhat training, to save their much-loved Leader. But Stek was too fast.

As Ou-Leesen hit the ground, he shouted "Stek!" as the Knife arced upwards.

But Stek heard nothing ... neither the shout nor the commotion of the El-Bhat warriors. Despite this, the Knife was frozen in place at the zenith of the arc. Because Stek remembered his night-dream as he thrust a Knife into Ou-Leesen's chest.

A heart-beat later the El-Bhat had dragged Stek off their Leader ... and returned the Dagger of Truth to Ou-Leesen.

The new Leader of the Quorum dusted himself off and then, while looking at the Tracker, he instructed the Leader of the Band. "Bring him to the Quorum Room. I want to know why he hesitated with the Knife. The rest of the *prisoners* are to be fed and rested."

Chapter 13 - The celebration of Bra-ten

"Perhaps ... you would like a cold drink?" Ou-Leesen waved his hand to the cold goblet, already sweating with condensation. "I was told that you were the first prisoner to collapse. This doesn't say much for Tracker training."

Stek returned the grin, quickly accepted the offer and drank heartily until he had emptied the goblet. With eyes closed tight against the pain, he said, "I think I drank that too fast!"

Returning the emptied goblet, he looked at Ou-Leesen and stared for a long time at the new Quorum Leader. "Back at Qar-ana, as we prepared to leave, I told Biskin that I wanted to stay with you ... because *destiny seems to follow you around.*"

Stek wagged his head as he continued, "But I never imagined that I would find you here ... as the New Leader of the entire El-Bhat nation.

"I assume that you fulfilled your quest and that Shanteef is dead?"

Ou-Leesen nodded 'yes' as he oddly glanced towards the carpet that lay on the other side of the room.

"When he died, I knew that he had lived for several hundred years ..."

Ou-Leesen laid the Dagger between them, "... because of the power of this talisman."

"I don't understand how someone in a position of leadership wouldn't eventually ..." Stek began to question.

"Most of the El-Bhat never saw Shanteef, only the Quorum and a few others. And even they, must have believed that Shanteef was kept alive by dead leaders of the past.

"You see there was a legend that a Leader would come among our people who would live far beyond the normal life span ... because he was supported by the Great Ones from the Life Beyond. And this Leader would place our people on the Throne of Power and then the El-Bhat would rule all of Ankoletia."

Ou-Leesen paused as though he was questioning an idea. Then his eyes returned to Stek as he added, "I now know that Shanteef planted this Legend among our people generations ago, sometime after he came into possession of the Dagger. He was very clever."

Stek looked down at the Dagger, as he thought about what Ou-Leesen had just said. Without looking up, he queried, "You told me before that you feared the power of the Dagger and its influence upon you. Is that how you know things of the past ... and why you sit in the seat of authority?"

"I see that my Advisor is back," Ou-Leesen responded with enthusiasm to Stek's question.

The Tracker looked up, gratified to know that the old Ou-Leesen was still in charge of his life. "Okay ... so the struggle continues ... but how is all *this* possible?" Stek questioned as he waved his hand in an attitude of encompassing the Keep.

Ou-Leesen picked up the Dagger and held it in his two hands as he began his story.

"If you can tell me *how*, you will be the wisest Advisor that ever lived. All I know is that after I stayed behind to deal with the spies who followed us, I was seriously wounded, and Mishri was still alive.

"Then the Green Lady appeared, wanting me to embrace the power of the Dagger. But I wouldn't. I remember Mishri grabbing my hair as I staggered to stay standing. He wanted desperately to cut off my head ... a traitor's death.

"I expected to feel the sharpness of his blade cut through my flesh ... but before he could, my blade took his life."

Ou-Leesen paused before he continued. "I don't know how.

"The next morning, I awoke with my garments covered in dried blood ... but there was no sign of my wounds. I was healed. No scars ... only three dead El-Bhat, and the Dagger of Truth in my scabbard.

"I threw the cursed thing away and headed north to Chitouf. I wanted to see if I could start over, freed from the influence of the Green Power. But as I readied to leave the next morning, the Dagger was back in my scabbard. A persuasive reminder that I can never be free of this talisman of darkness. So, I headed south to find you and my warriors."

"We waited ... I could feel the Dagger's power travelling towards us," Stek interjected. "But whoever had the Dagger, circled around us. I assumed it wasn't you."

"The Dagger deceived me. It wanted to bring me here without my warriors ... so that killing me would be easy. I should be dead ... Shanteef plunged this Knife into my back. But, just like with Mishri, when I came to, I was alive, and he was dead.

"And there was something else ... it was the reason I knew he had lived for hundreds of years. His dead body was shrivelled by age, until he was no longer recognizable as Shanteef.

"Advisor *how* is all this possible?"

Stek held out his hands, wanting Ou-Leesen to give him the Dagger. Then he closed his eyes as he thought about the ornate blade with the emerald pommel.

Immediately he could hear the buzz as he slid down a steep enclosed tunnel. He rocked back and forth as his descent followed twists and turns until he left the tunnel and plunged into a pool of water.

It wasn't deep; the water came up to his chest. He stood up and looked around. There was a green mist bubbling off the surface of the pool and soft green lights reflected off walls of gold. Suddenly he realized that he didn't know where he was, nor did he have any memory of ... anything!

He thought he could see a door on one of the walls. He moved towards it, intent on finding out what was on the other side. It was a door, and as soon as he touched it, it opened wide. He walked through.

The next room was slightly brighter with the same green light, and there was deep luxurious carpet on the floor. Stek paused, concerned that he was getting the floor wet ... but he was already dry.

When he looked up, there was a beautiful woman standing behind a table. On the table was a gold cradle that held an extremely ornate dagger with an emerald pommel. The woman was smiling at him, with a tease that beckoned him to come forward.

He had never seen a woman so fascinatingly beautiful before, and she wanted him to ... well he wasn't sure.

He was caught in his hesitation, so she spoke, "Stek ... I know you have a question. Come to me and I will answer it." The way she held her head … it made him feel that she was <u>very</u> important.

His lack of knowledge was extremely annoying. How was he supposed to decide anything if he couldn't remember who he was, or what happened to bring him to this place. Was he supposed to know this lady? And what was the importance of the ornate dagger that sat on the gold cradle?

"Who are you?" he finally asked.

"Some call me the Green Lady, others the Queen of Gold's Power," she responded. "But my real name is Pu-el-tal, the Lady of Harleem."

The words were soft … her voice purred with seduction. Everything about her made his heart pound in his chest. He felt compelled to move forward, but every time he considered this decision, he felt afraid. And the sensation of fear seemed foreign to Stek.

"Your question involves this Dagger … doesn't it?" She prompted as she looked down at the table.

Stek's eyes followed hers … to the elegant blade. 'There is something about this Knife …' he decided after studying it for a few moments.

"Yes," he finally said. Then he took a hesitant step. Now he couldn't take his eyes off the Dagger … as he took his second step.

"Very few are privileged to see the Dagger of Truth," she said, encouraging him to continue forward. "And some, like you, are invited to hold it. Stek, can you feel its power? How it beckons to you and only you. All of this can be yours. All you have to do is kiss the Green Emerald," she spoke with excitement.

Those hypnotic steps took Stek to the edge of the table where he removed the Dagger from the cradle.

"Well done," the Green Lady encouraged him. *"Now ... kiss the Emerald and the power is yours."*

The Emerald glowed fiercely as Stek raised the green stone to his lips.

--------- <> ---------

Ou-Leesen watched intently as Stek took the Dagger of Truth and closed his eyes. The El-Bhat leaned forward as the Tracker began to mumble a few words. He thought he heard the word 'kiss'.

Stek would occasionally jerk his head as though he was caught in a nightmare. But then again, he was more resourceful than anyone he knew ... except for maybe Protas. So, he decided to let him ride out the experience. But quickly changed his mind as Green Light burst from the Emerald, lighting the entire room, as Stek raised the green pommel to his lips.

Using both hands, Ou-Leesen knocked the Dagger out of Stek's hands. He watched as the Knife skidded across the tiled floor. He monitored the unresponsive emerald for a few moments then turned his attention back to the Tracker, who lay lifeless on the floor.

There was a knock as Ou-Leesen was deciding what to do. He rushed to the door and opened it to find his Personal Guards standing with more cold water.

As the one Guard looked over Ou-Leesen's shoulder at the collapsed body on the floor, Ou-Leesen remarked, "Perfect timing," took the water and closed the door.

Pressing the goblet to Stek's lips, he encouraged the unconscious Tracker to drink. Soon he was sputtering and coughing as he mechanically pushed the drink away.

"Are you all right?" A concerned Ou-Leesen questioned.

The wetness on his lips felt good, so Stek reached for the goblet and began to drink.

"Slowly," Ou-Leesen cautioned.

Refreshed, the Tracker set the goblet aside. "Yes, I'm fine." His eyes found the Knife against the far wall. "Thanks to you," Stek added, guessing what Ou-Leesen had done.

"I think I know why you've had those unexpected experiences with the Dagger," the Tracker offered.

"I'm listening."

"You refused to kiss the Emerald."

Ou-Leesen's knitted eyebrows told Stek he needed more explanation.

"As soon as I closed my eyes I fell into a strange place without any memory. A Green Lady stood behind a table. On top of the table was your Dagger resting in a gold cradle. She encouraged me to pick it up and kiss the green pommel. And then this power would be mine. I was about to complete her instructions when the Knife was ripped from my grasp.

"The last thing I remember was the sound of her wailing in agony. Somehow, I understood her grief to mean that not only had she lost a slave to her power, but I had been rescued by 'The One' who has access to the power by right."

Ou-Leesen was more bewildered than ever.

"By right? But I have never laid claim to this power. My Sherilin blood is repulsed by it. Advisor you must be mistaken."

Stek shrugged his shoulders, a witness that he didn't understand the contradiction either. "Maybe we don't need to know 'how' for now. Somehow you qualify for protection by the power you hate. Not the best situation to be in, but at least you're still alive."

Ou-Leesen was listening intently so Stek continued. "You only wanted to remove Shanteef, but life has handed you a people to rule. What will you do next?"

"I think ... *more* than I thought possible."

"Remove the entire quorum?" Stek queried.

"More."

"Do you have a plan?"

"I do ... and I don't. You see, I'm no longer one person. Now I am two ... and both must be considered. Shanteef's memories are like buried gold. I know the answers to all my questions reside inside my head ... I only need to ask the right questions. So, Advisor, what should I ask?"

"What was the relationship between Shanteef and the Quorum?" Stek suggested.

There was a brief pause and then Ou-Leesen began.

"They supported him because he promised them much."

"What about the Government of Shaksbah?" Stek continued.

Another pause. "An uneasy alliance. They saw the El-Bhat as a thorn in their foot. Shanteef tried to gain support, but his usual resource, the *stolen* government gold, of course, couldn't be used. And the rulers of Kel-eetan see the Quorum as uneducated and unrefined."

"Those in government positions, do they rule *for* the people?"

"They are slow to keep their promises ... if at all. They have tried to cheat on our wages. But we are warriors. My warrior half wants to punish them ... severely, but Shanteef's memories remind me that they have skills."

Stek nodded, his expression betrayed an anxiety to say something.

"Advisor, tell me what you are thinking."

Realizing that the warrior could decide for himself if the comment was worthwhile, he shared his thought. "Recently ... I discovered a cure for the many weaknesses of judgment ... two days on a horse with no food or water. Makes a man see things different."

--------- <> ---------

The El-Bhat servant paused in his grooming of the horses as the outer gates opened. He was about to return to his work when he saw the escorted prisoners ... they were El-Bhat!

'The Quorum will want to know about this,' he thought.

He walked to the other side of the horse where we could see and hear better. He went back to work as he memorized details from occasional glances. Everyone dispersed except for the Band Leader and twenty prisoners. He knew it wouldn't take long for Shanteef to walk out, the part he was most interested in. The moment those doors opened, and it wasn't Shanteef, he began to saddle up the horse. Soon he would be whispering into Arl-Sheen's ear.

--------- <> ---------

"So ... you're final plan?" Stek prodded the El-Bhat.

"I'll ask the Personal Guards to select a group of El-Bhat to visit the towns of Denlen. They will have a week to organize one hundred Bands of warriors. They will gather as a group, fifty leagues north of Kel-eetan ... and wait. The Government will be very concerned about five thousand El-Bhat so close to the Capital city.

"They will send troops to march north in response to their posturing.

"Meanwhile, my men and my personal guards will enter Kel-eetan under disguise, on the day of *Bra-ten*."

Ou-Leesen placed the Robe of Shanteef inside the gold and glass case, where it always hung when not being used.

"You've chosen this day for a purpose?"

"Actually, for two purposes. *Bra-ten* celebrates the leadership of Shaksbah. It's only fitting that the Government fall on this day.

"Secondly, everyone who pretends to hold power will be there."

"How can you be sure they will step down?"

"Resistance will be cut down with the El-Bhat sword. The rest will agree quickly ... lives accustomed to soft pillows create faint hearts."

Chapter 14 - The Medallion of Authority

As the El-Bhat began their ascent up the massive stairs of the Government Palace, they shed their common clothing, revealing the recognizable black silk garments.
At the top, they paused to tie their red silk headbands. Then they entered behind Ou-Leesen.

Stek was at the rear. When they entered the Great Hall, he slipped into the shadows.

Ou-Leesen walked to the front of the assembly and cut off the head of the statue of the current Government Head. The Dagger slid through the marble with ease. The head tumbled down the steps and rolled down the aisle as the government officials watched in horror.

The Government Head stood calmly and walked to the aisle where the head came to a stop. He looked down at the severed bust as he spoke to the El-Bhat warrior with the blade that could cut marble.

"Didn't think it did me justice anyway," he quipped as he pushed the head under the long table with his foot.

Ou-Leesen expected a different response from the Government Official. He looked around to see if he had missed anything when they walked into the hall.

Nothing ... only his twenty men positioned up and down the long banquet table. He noticed that Stek was nowhere to be seen.

Ou-Leesen decided to ignore the arrogant attitude of the Government Head.

"Today ... *Bra-ten* will take on a new meaning for all of Shaksbah. All of you are released from your posts. You will be taken to the city prisons until you have your new assignments. If you serve well, you will live. Today, history will re-write the celebration of *Bra-ten* as our rebirth ... a step into the light of freedom."

"Whoever you are ... and whatever your rank," the current Head responded as he scanned Ou-Leesen's men, "I doubt that twenty men are sufficient to enforce your claims."

The demeanour of the Government Officials had changed as they watched the exchange between the El-Bhat warrior and the smooth

Government Head. Ou-Leesen could see that he was losing the tactical advantage he had gained by using the Dagger.

Perhaps it was time for another head to roll.

Without further hesitation, he descended the steps and began to walk briskly towards his verbal opponent.

Esch-Terra, the Government Head, showed signs of dwindling confidence as this unknown warrior quickly descended the steps.

His eyes searched the exits for the expected volley of troops. If they didn't arrive *very* soon, his head was sure to join the marble imitation under the table.

He cringed as the Dagger was brought up to his neck … his eyes following the emerald pommel. It seemed to glow softly. Or was it the effect of the sunlight coming from the windows high above the Banquet tables.

Regardless, he expected his life to be over before his took his next breath.

But instead, the Dagger hesitated at the chain he wore around his neck.

Perhaps because he held his ground. Either way, he had a feeling that if he locked eyes with this warrior, his life would *be* over. So, he kept his eyes on the emerald pommel.

With a deft movement, Ou-Leesen hooked his blade under the chain. In a flash of inspiration, he saw that what he needed most, to turn the advantage back to his favour, was not to kill … but to take the *Medallion of Authority* that hung from the Government Head's neck.

It was obviously the sceptre of power that commanded respect and loyalty from the people of Shaksbah.

Ou-Leesen had barely placed the chain around his own neck when suddenly, the far doors burst open.

From the moment that Stek ascended the steps outside of the Government Palace, he knew his place was somewhere other than at the side of Ou-Leesen. As soon as they crossed the threshold of the Great Hall, he slipped away into the shadows … until he found an exit door to the hallways where the current of activity swept Servants and Guards along as they performed their duties.

Leaving the Great Hall, he expected to have to blend in with the throngs of people that would be busily engaged in attending to the Banquet. Instead, he found the exact opposite.

There was no one in sight! No noise. No sign whatever of anyone scurrying about. This was very strange for a palace of this size. And ... who was waiting on the demands of the celebratory banquet?

Silently he headed for the end of the hallway, intent on finding where everyone was. As he turned the next corner to another empty hallway, a feeling of dread covered him like a cloak. Something was wrong with Ou-Leesen's plan!

He was about to turn back and warn the invading Band of El-Bhat, when he heard footsteps hurrying down a hallway, somewhere ahead.

As silently as he could, he rushed forward, determined to catch up before the *ghost* disappeared behind a closed door.

Luckily those footsteps were met by others as Stek approached another hallway. He slowed and stopped short of the corner. He listened.

The exchange between the men was hurried and anxious. From the words that Stek could catch, it was clear that *the time had arrived.* They were to alert the Palace Guards immediately.

It was too late to warn Ou-Leesen. Stek's only option was to blend in with the other Palace Servants.

He quickly retraced his steps to the last door he had passed and slipped inside.

--------- <> ---------

The chain had barely slipped over the warrior's head when a hundred El-Bhat rushed into the Banquet Hall, positioning themselves around the perimeter of the room. Esch-Terra was as surprised as Ou-Leesen.

Ou-Leesen forgot about the Government Head as he scanned the flood of El-Bhat warriors pouring through the Banquet Hall door.

--------- <> ---------

Esch-Terra saw his opportunity and headed for a clear exit. He knew he had to find the Government Troops and keep them away from the Hall.

He had been advised by the Quorum, of the planned Government takeover during the *Bra-ten* celebration. And they had agreed that the

Government forces would be allowed to crush the small group of El-Bhat that would enter the Hall, while the Quorum directed the large El-Bhat force assembling north of Kel-eetan to stand down.

But Esch-Terra was nobody's fool. He conversed with the Quorum as though he trusted their every move but planned for the worst. And this second wave of El-Bhat was a clear sign that the Quorum was following a different plan than the one proposed. Of course. And why he had prepared a much larger force than suggested ... carefully hidden from view.

But this much change required a definite change in *his* plans.

First, he would let the El-Bhat destroy each other ... then his forces would move in to finish off the survivors. He continued his race towards the Troops, they must be warned in time.

For the last five years, Esch-Terra's Government forces had multiplied significantly in response to the flow of gold from the treasury. His Generals had scoured the towns and villages with promises of good wages and superior training. Weapons of fine steel were supplied in abundance, along with War wagons, horses and catapults. His best kept secret was the size of his troops which numbered in the tens of thousands. Sufficient to defeat the El-Bhat.

During a rushed conversation with his Generals, a message was constructed and sent north to the amassed group of El-Bhat, telling them that the Government had fallen. He watched until the carrier birds were out of sight. Soon these El-Bhat would march in haste towards Kel-eetan ... but they would never make it.

With the loss of this El-Bhat army and the two most senior Quorum Leaders, El-Bhat everywhere would begin to fall until they became an extinct race. Except of course, for the children. They would work the Mines. Esch-Terra loved the irony.

He would send his troops to the Tenleth Mines as soon as Kel-eetan was secure.

The mines had been managed by the Quorum for centuries. Only the El-Bhat were willing to endure the abominable work conditions year after year. He had visited the Mines once. The heat and filth were suffocating. He swore he would never go back.

Soon he would have to find a new source of mine managers. Slaves would be fuelled from the prisons ... and of course the children of the massacred El-Bhat! He loved repeating that thought. The El-Bhat had been such a contemptible people.

--------- <> ---------

A pair of Tracker eyes peered down upon the Banquet Hall through the servant's viewing port. A large group of El-Bhat arranged themselves around the outside of the Hall, hemming in Ou-Leesen and his small Band of trusted followers. As the last of the unexpected El-Bhat warriors rushed into the Hall, a member of the Quorum, wearing a robe of authority, entered.

--------- <> ---------

In his peripheral vision, Ou-Leesen noted that the Government Head beat a hasty retreat for the exit, while a member of the Quorum entered the room behind the swarm of warriors.

--------- <> ---------

With hands on his hips and a wicked smile, the Quorum member glared at the man holding the Dagger of Truth. He was here today, to take the impressive Dagger and kill this arrogant leader along with his twenty followers.

His eyes were drawn to the Dagger of Truth … held by Ou-Leesen like a sceptre of power. He had forgotten how intricate and stunning the Dagger was. The more his eyes studied it, the more his lust for this talisman swelled within him.

--------- <> ---------

Standing a pace behind the Quorum member, Ou-Leesen recognized a servant from the Keep. 'So … you have found the body of Shanteef … and that is why you're here,' he thought as he returned the glare.

With a hand signal, he commanded his men to stay where they stood while he slowly walked towards the Quorum member. He didn't get far before the *other* El-Bhat began to form a wall of protection.

He stopped, and the wall dispersed. Lifting high the Dagger of Truth, Ou-Leesen spoke to every El-Bhat in the room.

"Shanteef is dead … and the power of this blade makes *me* … the new leader of the El-Bhat nation. We are here today to transfer leadership of the Shaksbali people to those who still believe in the ways of the Sherilin and …"

"*We*," the Quorum member interrupted, "are here today to punish you for murdering Shanteef and to return the Dagger of Truth to the Quorum."

Perhaps it was the sound of his voice … but something suggested that he knew this man. Ou-Leesen immediately searched Shanteef's memories. 'I know you, don't I?' he thought, opening the doorway to memories of the man standing before him.

In only a few heartbeats, those memories raced across the landscape of his consciousness until he knew everything about Arl-Sheen that Shanteef knew.

"Your name is Arl-Sheen," Ou-Leesen began, his voice strong and clear. "Shanteef gave you the name 'the compassionate one' after the slaughter of the innocents. Because of your willingness to assist the parents to find those responsible for the massacre of their children.

"But the truth is … Shanteef needed workers at the Mines of Tenleth. He ordered you to kill the children, so their parents would unwittingly follow you … to a lifetime of slavery at the Mines."

Arl-Sheen grunted. "Of course, a condemned murderer will say such things … about his executioner," the Quorum member shouted back at Ou-Leesen.

"Sometimes … words *can* be deceitful," Ou-Leesen agreed. "But scars never lie … do they … *compassionate one*?" Those last words were spit out with contempt.

Arl-Sheen's wicked smile slowly faded as brows furrowed and rage burned behind his eyes.

"I see you remember the day you complained to Shanteef about the knife wound you received to your left shoulder … after a suspecting parent challenged you with his blade. Of course, my deception can now be proven to all here in this room … by simply showing us your left shoulder."

The room went extremely quiet as the Quorum member considered, how this arrogant leader of twenty, could know, what only he and Shanteef knew. 'But of course … the Dagger', he surmised, as his eyes returned to the blade, still held aloft for all to see.

'I never knew that the Dagger could bestow such power on someone', he continued his soliloquy of thought. And now he knew more than anything in this world, that he wanted the power, of the Dagger of Truth, for himself!

"If Shanteef were still alive," Arl-Sheen began, sweeping the room with his eyes, "he would tell everyone here, that my scar was a souvenir from the day I saved Shanteef from an Assassin's blade. But enough of exchanging words with the Son of a Dog."

The Quorum Leader extended his hand to Ou-Leesen. "Give me ... the Dagger of Truth!"

The El-Bhat closest to Ou-Leesen drew their swords, ready to enforce Arl-Sheen's command.

Ou-Leesen looked at the blade as he considered the words of the Quorum Leader. The truth, in fact, was that he wanted more than anything to give the accursed blade to Arl-Sheen. But this was not the act of a Sherilin. He must find a better way to ultimately destroy this blade, without bringing more dark power into the world.

Ou-Leesen closed his eyes as though considering Arl-Sheen's command. But he wasn't ... he was thinking about what to do.

The spy, who stood in Arl-Sheen's shadow, had changed everything and because of him -

They knew Shanteef was dead

He and his men were seriously outnumbered

The large gathering of El-Bhat, north of Kel-eetan, were probably no longer under his command

And he was about to lose the Dagger of Truth ... the talisman he hoped to use to unite the people of Shaksbah.

Chapter 15 - A new name in Kel-eetan

The door swished open as another Technician entered the room. "Everything okay? I heard you shouting ... thought I would check," he added as he studied the hologram of the Green Lady.

"Not now," he urgently whispered, "this is critical ... please leave!"

As soon as he had left, the Technician at the controls, opened the connection between the Green Lady and Ou-Leesen.

Now that Shanteef was dead, he had decided, that his best hope lay in persuading this warrior to accept the Green Power. Since his last failure with Shanteef, he had been busy adjusting the holographic program to better suit this new victim. A *net* that would appeal to his view of the world!

Ou-Leesen reminded the Technician of Bellaroos, reported to have completely resisted the Green Lady on a previous mission to Ankoletia, over a hundred Ankoletian years ago. On that occasion, the Technician's predecessor had successfully managed to get the resistant victim, to pass the Necklace on to someone else. Who was *much* more receptive to the Green Lady.

A good strategy, but first, he wanted to try one more time to seduce the warrior. It would be redemptive.

But if that failed, his next target was Arl-Sheen, the acting Quorum Leader and a willing subject.

His hands carefully guided his controls to bring the Green Lady into Ou-Leesen's consciousness. The warrior was in a tight spot, and if ever he needed Her power, it was now!

--------- <> ---------

"Ou-Leesen," she whispered, *"the power is yours."*

With eyes still closed, he could see the Green Lady, her smile hesitant but hopeful. The tone of her voice was less seductive than before. Instead, he could hear pleading in her words.

"You can save your people from tyranny ... but only if you use my power," she begged him.

In his mind, the warrior turned his head towards the image of rare beauty. It was true that he wanted to use the talisman to gather all El-Bhat under Sherilin rule. But it was one thing to hold high the Dagger that his people recognized as symbolic of their heritage, and quite another to embrace its dark powers.

'I love my people ... but I think that you do not!' he responded to her carefully placed words.

"*Perhaps it is your pride that makes you think you have the skills, to accomplish what no other man can.*" The graceful lines of her perfect eyebrows were stern. "*But with <u>my</u> power,* " she continued softly, "*all of your dreams can be fulfilled. You can free your people.*"

The Green Lady could see Ou-Leesen's hesitation. A good sign. And in response to this encouragement, green trails of a million sparkling lights enveloped not only her, but Ou-Leesen ... and Arl-Sheen, standing off to the side.

As Ou-Leesen's attention shifted from *her* eyes, filled with hopeful pleading, to Arl-Sheen, one of Shanteef's memory exploded into view. A pronounced prophecy, that in the future, the heir of the Green Lady's Power would be Arl-Sheen.

Arl-Sheen held the young man hostage as Shanteef plunged the Dagger into the heart of his intended victim. Before his eyes, as the young man slid to the floor, dead, Shanteef was enveloped and lifted above the marble floor by a green mist ... that eventually unveiled a much younger version of Shanteef.

Arl-Sheen was awe struck as he stumbled backwards into the wall.

Shanteef breathed deeply as he felt the youthfulness of his body.

He looked at his accomplice and with a firm voice encouraged his loyalty with the words, "Someday this power will be yours. But to have this power I must <u>wilfully</u> give you the Dagger of Truth."

Previously fearful, but now elated, Arl-Sheen wrapped his long arms around Shanteef, excited that one day he would be the heir of this immortal Gift.

In pity, Ou-Leesen looked past the embrace of the two Quorum members, to the image of the dead young man, lying on the floor, ripped from life, ripped from his family and his dreams.

If the Green Lady thought to make him jealous for her power, she did not understand the heart of Ou-Leesen! With clenched fists, he shouted at the image in his mind, 'The power will NEVER be mine!'

--------- <> ---------

"Nooo ... this can't be happening!" The Technician moaned as the hologram wavered, threatening to break the connection with Ou-Leesen. He quickly switched the controls of the Green Lady from auto to manual, hoping to have her say something that would deter the warrior from his angry determination to abandon the power that was supposed to be his.

"Ou-Leesen I promise you ..." she hastily interjected, but it was too late. The Technician could see the Dagger leave the warrior's hand and fly towards Arl-Sheen.

--------- <> ---------

Anxious to leave the world of green mist, Ou-Leesen opened his eyes ... and with words that reflected his bitterness, he cried, "You want the Dagger ... you can have the Dagger," and with a flick of the wrist, the emerald pommel could be seen hurtling end over end.

--------- <> ---------

Surprised by the sudden fling of the Knife, Arl-Sheen failed to catch the one thing he wanted most.

The blade was not thrown particularly hard. To the observers, it should have been a shallow cut. But the blade sunk to the hilt, as though his body was warm butter.

With a hard gasp, Arl-Sheen grabbed the hilt with both hands and pulled it out. The Dagger of Truth was now his.

His eyes glowed green for a moment, in response to his willingness to embrace the power ... but the power was borrowed, it wasn't his. He looked over at Ou-Leesen who was watching him with disgust. And then Arl-Sheen sank to the floor, as the borrowed Green Light flowed out of his eyes and circled the room until it enveloped Ou-Leesen.

All eyes turned from the collapsed body of the Acting Quorum Leader, to Ou-Leesen, who sank to one knee from the burden of the new memories that flowed through his mind.

--------- <> ---------

Eventually the Warrior Leader stood and slowly looked around the room, returning his gaze to all who had fastened their eyes upon him. His eyes finally settled on the dead body of Arl-Sheen ... and the spy who already held the Dagger of Truth.
"The Dagger of Truth is returned to the Quorum," the spy shouted desperately and yet triumphantly, to the assembly as he held it high.

Ou-Leesen heard the wrongness of those words as they echoed around the large room. He knew that something had changed. The Dagger now belonged to him! The Green Lady was gone ... forever.
He extended his hand towards the blade, beckoning it to return to its master.
Immediately the spy found his hand empty and to his utter surprise, the Dagger was now in the outstretched hand of Ou-Leesen! He lowered his arm and stepped backwards, hoping to disappear into the crowd of El-Bhat who were already beginning to drop to one knee in recognition of the new Leader of the El-Bhat nation.

As the Bands of El-Bhat knelt as one, with swords held high in support of the unknown warrior, Ou-Leesen realized several things –

His small Band of twenty had dodged the arrow of certain death and now stood as a Band of Sherilin warriors, ready to lead the El-Bhat nation.

The Spy had also knelt with the others, in support of Ou-Leesen.

The Government Leaders were also kneeling, hesitantly at first, but what they had seen could not be denied ... and they had never seen anything like it. Power that was beyond everything they could imagine.

And finally ... he was no longer Ou-Leesen, the unknown warrior who failed at Border Pass. He needed a new name.

"Many of you do not know me. From this moment ... EVERYONE ... will refer to me as *Ou-Leesen-el-Bra-ten.*"

Still holding the Dagger of Truth, he knew there was something else that he needed to take care of. He walked over to the Spy. "You may rise."

He placed the blade against the forehead of a very nervous Spy. "Where are your loyalties?" he asked, knowing the Truth would flow into his mind.

"To you ... and only you," the Spy said with confidence.

"Perhaps ... this is what you wish was possible ... at this moment." He removed the blade from his forehead. "But you are who you are. A Spy and a traitor. If we let you go today, you will soon be on the road that leads to the rest of the Quorum. Kill him," Ou-Leesen-el-Bra-ten commanded the El-Bhat who knelt nearby.

Turning to the Government Officials he commanded, "If any of you doubt your loyalty to Ou-Leesen-el-Bra-ten ... step forward." No one did.

His hand on the emerald pommel told him that he need search no further. To a man, everyone in the Hall was ready to obey Ou-Leesen-el-Bra-ten, the holder of the Dagger of Truth.

Chapter 16 - The messenger from Harleem

Stek was wagging his head in surprise ... again! He couldn't believe how destiny carved a path forward for Ou-Leesen ... through solid rock!

He had been watching the entire scenario from the servant's viewing port as the Quorum member entered the Banquet Hall, ready to seize the Dagger of Truth and execute Ou-Leesen and his twenty men.

They were seriously outnumbered ... they had been betrayed ... and then Ou-Leesen threw away the Dagger, their only hope of rescue.

And now everyone in the Hall were kneeling in obedience to the unknown warrior, otherwise known as ... Ou-Leesen-el-Bra-ten!

'Everyone except the Palace Guards,' Stek reminded himself, as he hurried away from the viewing port.

Suddenly a side exit burst open as Ou-Leesen-el-Bra-ten was placing the Dagger in his Scabbard. "The Palace Guards will be here soon," a servant shouted to the men in the Hall.

Ou-Leesen-el-Bra-ten recognized the voice and grinned. His Advisor had been watching his back!

Ou-Leesen-el-Bra-ten quickly turned to the Government men. "Who here can tell me how many Guards there are and how soon they will be upon us?"

One of the men stepped forward, and with confidence replied, "I can. Besides the Palace Guards, there are at least several hundred Government troops. Judging from when Esch-Terra left the room, and where the troops were hidden, we probably have enough time to make it to the Front Gates."

Ou-Leesen-el-Bra-ten rested his hand on the pommel as he listened carefully to the report. "The Dagger tells me there are over a thousand troops. Is this possible?"

"Very possible. Esch-Terra handled these matters exclusively, due to the unreliable promises of the Quorum. No offence intended," he added with a slight bow of his head.

"Advisor," Ou-Leesen-el-Bra-ten asked Stek, who was now standing by his side, looking ridiculous in his undersized servant's garb, "what shall we do?"

Stek turned to the Government Official who had just spoken, "what would *you* do if your life depended on escaping these troops?" As he spoke he began ripping off his disguise, revealing his Tracker clothing underneath. He wanted the man to know that he would personally hold the man accountable for the quality of his advice.

"I would use the Government Tunnels to get outside the city and then ..." he shrugged, indicating that, that was a far as his strategy could take them.

"You lead, and we will follow," Ou-Leesen-el-Bra-ten urged him to action.

--------- <> ---------

Everyone in the room was kneeling when Ou-Leesen-el-Bra-ten announced that they would be escaping the city through the Government Tunnels. The El-Bhat Band Leader, that had accompanied Arl-Sheen, stood with everyone else. But his eyes were on the body of Arl-Sheen, the Quorum Leader that had replaced Shanteef.

As the men in the banquet hall quickly migrated to the exit, the Band Leader secretly checked Arl-Sheen's Robe for important papers that the Quorum would be expecting.

--------- <> ---------

"Advisor ... thanks for watching the back door," Ou-Leesen-el-Bra-ten whispered to Stek as they rested briefly in the tunnels, waiting for the government officials to catch up.

The next time they stopped, Stek had questions that needed answering. "I was watching the Banquet Hall through the servant's viewing port. I saw everything from the time the large Band of El-Bhat and the Quorum member entered the Hall. Want to tell me what really happened?"

"The Green Lady was there ... and again I refused her. I saw in Shanteef's memories that Arl-Sheen knew about the dark power of the Dagger of Truth and wanted it desperately. In my anger, I tossed it to him, glad to be rid of the accursed blade. But it wasn't meant to be."

Stek nodded in the dark. "I saw the Green Lights leave the Quorum Leader, circle the room ... and disappear inside of you. Are you all right?" Stek queried, remembering Ou-Leesen-el-Bra-ten's previous comments about not making his own decisions.

"This was the Dagger transferring his memories to me ... and his life force. I think I could run all day."

"The Dagger seems to obey you," Stek added as he remembered how the blade flew across the room to his waiting hand.

"Yes ... the blade is mine and the Green Lady has lost all power over me."

"How is this possible?" Stek wanted to know.

Ou-Leesen-el-Bra-ten didn't know, so he nudged the Government Official to commence running.

With care, the Warrior followed the rhythm of the Official's footsteps, as they worked their way through the inky black tunnels under the city. Occasionally his thoughts returned to the question of how he was able to wrest the power away from the Green Lady.

By the time they stopped again, he was ready to share an insight with Stek.

"I remembered the first time that I met the Green Lady. She desperately wanted me to receive the Blade of Power ... to embrace it ... but I wouldn't."

Stek was reminded of how quickly he had been seduced to kiss the Emerald pommel. And if not for Ou-Leesen-el-Bra-ten, he wouldn't be having this conversation right now.

"But despite this, the Dagger helped me kill Mishri and restored my life. I think at that point, she was beginning to lose her control over me.

"Then when Shanteef tried to kill me with the Dagger, he couldn't, because the Dagger saw Shanteef as misusing its power ... to kill a legitimate user. So instead, his life force was transferred to me, thus restoring my life. The strange part was that I also received his memories."

"Probably because the blade already had the power to extract memories from others. I saw the result as you place it against the forehead of the Spy," Stek added for clarification.

"Well done Advisor," he said.

"Does this mean," Stek suddenly had an additional insight, "that you now have the memories of Arl-Sheen?"

"Yes ... and I think I see why the Dagger is now mine. Arl-Sheen desired the power of the Dagger but had never used it. I had not only used it several times, but also recently in the Great Dining Hall. My attachment to the Dagger had grown significantly, overpowering the pull from Arl-Sheen."

"Perhaps the blade will make the difference between success and failure after we exit these tunnels." Stek suggested.

"I still need the gold if we are to accomplish everything I want to," Ou-Leesen-el-Bra-ten reminded Stek.

Stek could see how useful those memories were going to be as he added, "You must already know where the gold is?"

Ou-Leesen-el-Bra-ten smiled inwardly at the question. Stek had no idea how much he already knew from the memories of Shanteef and Arl-Sheen.

"The gold was moved by Shanteef, out into the desert," he started. "It sits on top of a large eight-sided plate of steel. The El-Bhat involved were sworn to secrecy."

"That doesn't make sense; the plate of steel would have to be the size of the Government buildings in Kel-eetan," Stek protested.

"It is. The work was not of El-Bhat origin. The instructions to move the gold came from the Green Lady."

"Doesn't sound good … I mean why the Green Lady has an interest in the gold," Stek commented, as they waited by the exit of the Tunnels.

"All is clear," the El-Bhat scout reported.

Ou-Leesen-el-Bra-ten could still hear the Government Officials, herded by a few of his El-Bhat through the tunnels. It would be a while before everyone was at the exit.

The Tunnels exited onto a plateau, with a view that covered the land for a hundred leagues. To the south, the city of Kel-eetan glistened in the afternoon sun like a jewel. The traffic of all roads heading north, and south were easily monitored.

"Come with me," Ou-Leesen-el-Bra-ten directed Stek as they separated themselves from the group.

"I'm impressed with these tunnels," Ou-Leesen-el-Bra-ten began their discussion. "The Government has prepared well. It will not be as easy to displace them as I thought."

"I expected to see troops heading north." Stek commented. "It wouldn't take long for the Government to find out that we escaped through these tunnels."

Ou-Leesen-el-Bra-ten rested his hand on the Emerald Pommel as he chatted with Stek. Now he had two Advisors. 'Never has an El-Bhat leader been so gifted,' he thought to himself. 'But will it be enough?' he wondered.

"They are no longer interested in us," he shared with Stek. "Their attention has been directed to the many Bands of El-Bhat, waiting north of us. They intend to slaughter them all."

"We must hurry then," Stek boldly suggested, as he considered the Government Officials that would slow them down.

"It is already too late for that," Ou-Leesen-el-Bra-ten clarified. "Birds carrying messages, falsely signed 'by me', have already been released to the El-Bhat, advising them that the Shaksbali government has fallen, and they must all march quickly to Kel-eetan.

"But they will never make it to the Capital. Other troops with catapults are already on the move to join the Government forces. The El-Bhat will suffer huge losses."

"Perhaps you can send a message … through the Dagger?" Stek wondered.

Ou-Leesen-el-Bra-ten scanned the area. "Your advice is good, but I need to be alone for a while. I will be over there."

Soon the El-Bhat warrior was out of sight, so Stek returned to the others.

Sitting alone, holding the Dagger and desperate to find a solution, he whispered, "I need to send a message to the El-Bhat north of here. I need a messenger."

--------- <> ---------

"Son of Balhok," the Technician screamed at the hologram. "This should have been impossible," he added as he pounded the Command Console with both fists.

"Easy with the equipment. If I decide to let you live, you will need a fully functioning Queen of Gold's Power Console," a voice said from behind. The Technician knew the voice … it was Kareen-hys-Tebeel-del-Harleem!

"Your Holiness … how, how can I help you?"

"Give me a full report on the *only* functioning Dagger of Hope."

The time had come. The Technician had played his last card … and lost.

"I should have told you before," he said with bowed head. When he looked up to break the silence, Kareen's face was expressionless, a signal that he better get on with it. "Due to circumstance and exceptional will … for an *off-planet* ... a warrior of the El-Bhat community has managed to gain control of the Dagger of Hope. I have tried ..."

Kareen raised a hand to indicate that the report was over. "I wish to visit this warrior myself. Advise me as soon as an opportunity surfaces."

--------- <> ---------

As silent as streaming sunlight, Kareen-hys-Tebeel-del-Harleem appeared behind Ou-Leesen-el-Bra-ten.

He was aware of the subject's aversion to the Green Light. Once he was sure the green glow of the transporter had disappeared, he spoke. "You have summoned me. What is it you want?"

Ou-Leesen-el-Bra-ten turned to see a man dressed in clothing he had never seen before. He was tall, with very fair skin, long hair and a warrior's face. He didn't look like a messenger.

"How did I summon you?" Ou-Leesen-el-Bra-ten asked suspiciously. It was only hours earlier that he finally freed himself from the Green Lady.

"Through the Dagger of Hope, you are holding."

It didn't add up, but Ou-Leesen-el-Bra-ten, with hand on the pommel, felt the truth of his response. He would dig a bit deeper. "Do you know the Green Lady?"

"Yes."

The warrior's eyes narrowed, and his posture shifted from relaxed to ready.

"But it is my belief that she will never bother you again. What is it you want?"

Again, the confirmation of spoken truth. Ou-Leesen-el-Bra-ten was reluctant to engage another unknown in his quest for a Sherilin-style Government. Especially so soon after winning the victory over the Green lady.

But five thousand El-Bhat would die if he didn't do something very soon. It seemed that this Visitor was his best choice ... to be his messenger.

"I have two Personal Guards, positioned north of here ... about fifty leagues." Ou-Leesen-el-Bra-ten paused to gauge his Visitor's response. His subtle nod seemed to suggest that he knew them, or would have no problem finding them, so he continued. "I need to get a message to them. Can you do this?"

"As easily as I came to you."

Ou-Leesen-el-Bra-ten shared the message with the Visitor.

'We have been betrayed. Move the El-Bhat warriors to the Tenleth Mines with haste. I will meet you there. From Ou-Leesen-el-Bra-ten, the possessor of the Dagger of Truth.'

"That's all I want," Ou-Leesen-el-Bra-ten added, expecting the Visitor to leave. When the Visitor didn't leave, Ou-Leesen-el-Bra-ten insightfully asked, "What is it *you* want?"

"One hundred gold bricks."

'If you know about the Dagger, then of course you know about the *bricks*,' thought Ou-Leesen-el-Bra-ten. "You will have to wait for payment," the warrior finally said. "I have what you want but it is far away."

"All I need, is your word that I can have the gold."

"You have my word ... but how do you know the gold is mine to give?" A curious Ou-Leesen-el-Bra-ten added.

"Because you wear the *Medallion of Authority*," the Visitor answered, as though he was stating the obvious.

Ou-Leesen-el-Bra-ten's hand instinctively rose to touch the Medallion that only hours earlier was worn around the neck of Esch-Terra. 'Strange that this Visitor would honor our nation's scepter of power,' Ou-Leesen-el-Bra-ten mused to himself. So many things about this new Visitor that he needed to understand. But for now, his priority was to rescue the doomed El-Bhat, who awaited his command.

"You must hurry ... this message must be delivered quickly."

"Consider it done."

Kareen-hys-Tebeel-del-Harleem turned and walked away until he was out of sight. Then he disappeared into a mist of green ... the light that the warrior must never see.

Chapter 17 - The power of Mercy

At the flick of thought, having delivered the message, Kareen-del-Harleem left the two Personal Guards to return to his ship.

As usual, his technique was flawless. Everything he said; everything he did; was according to The Protocol.

His offer was genuine; an assistance to save lives; at the request of a local authority. Payment was agreed to, without any coercion or undue persuasion.

He was born to this work.

As he exited the Transport Globe, he was surprised to see The Technician assigned to Ou-Leesen ... waiting.

He was waiting ... but in obvious distress, head bowed, afraid to look Kareen in the eyes.

The way the Transport Operator kept looking at the Technician told him that this was an opportunity for *mercy*.

Mercy ... scoffed at by his peers ... considered a plague to the warrior mind. But he knew different. Yes, *mercy* could be authority's destruction if it was used carelessly ... but when used at the right moment, it could purchase what other efforts could not. Loyalty for example, and a silent tongue!

He smiled to himself as he remembered back to Military school and his assignment to submit a paper on 'the dangers of mercy'. He hated the assignment. The obvious always bored him. So out of spite, he took the opposite view.

He researched carefully and even experimented with the possibilities of using mercy effectively as a warrior, in his personal life. He was surprised at what he discovered.

But the paper was never taken seriously. The instructor gave him a mediocre score, and his peers thought it was a clever response to a boring assignment. Everyone in the class got a good laugh out of the effort. But Kareen knew better. He had discovered a power that was overlooked by the Military Academy. One that he used carefully from time to time.

He stopped in front of The Technician and waited patiently for the man to speak ... or at least to look at him.

Finally, words came, spoken in misery to the feet that stood before him. "I was very worried for your safety. This warrior ... Ou-Leesen ... has accomplished the impossible. He can use the Dagger of Hope against us ... to know if we are speaking the truth." The Technician began to shake uncontrollably.

Kareen placed an understanding hand on his shoulder and kept it there until the shaking stopped.

"I thank you for your concern," Kareen began, "but you shouldn't be worried about your failure to trap this warrior. In fact, it is something that I have been meaning to discuss with you. Follow me to my room."

In the room, Kareen poured the man a drink and invited him to sit.

He turned on his personal security box against listening devices. Then he looked the man straight in the eye.

"I chose you to accompany me on this mission because of your reputation as a superior Technician. And you haven't disappointed me. I'm not so sure that any of your peers could have done any better regarding the assignment of Ou-Leesen-el-Bra-ten.

"Yes ... he has renamed himself. He is on a determined path to lead the entire race of the southern hemisphere ... and perhaps all Ankoletia.

"His warrior instincts are exceptional ... he is constantly wary and clear in thought. I am not surprised that you failed. But know this ... I have already seduced him ... persuaded him to accept a favour for some of his gold. So, you have no need to be concerned. Rather, it couldn't have worked out better. I have discovered his only weakness. He is *too* concerned about his men!" Kareen allowed himself a satisfied grin as he poured himself a drink.

The Technician couldn't believe his luck and was anxious to leave Kareen's private room while the current of favour still flowed in his direction. He stood and bowed in gratitude.

"Before you leave, I have a favour to ask. It is important to close the bargain with Ou-Leesen-el-Bra-ten. This will strengthen our relationship of trust. We must take the one hundred bars of gold ... soon. But it would be misunderstood by the Commanding General if I were to bring them on this ship before we begin to stock pile gold for Harleem." Kareen walked to his port window and stared into space, creating an opportunity for The Technician to consider his Master's situation.

"But *you* could transfer them," Kareen continued, "recorded as a *test of permission?*" Kareen looked back at his guest, waiting for The Technician's agreement.

"Of ... of course," he stammered in gratitude for an opportunity to return the unexpected kindness Kareen extended to him.

"You will need a place to secure these bars. Here is the key to my personal storage box."

The Technician gladly took the electronic device and returned immediately to the Control Room. He would not disappoint Kareen-hys-Tebeel-del-Harleem.

As the muffled sound of footsteps faded, Kareen returned to the port and stared down at the surface of Ankoletia.

He was amused at the attitude of off-worlders like Ou-Leesen-el-Bra-ten. They never understood that *permission* was everything.

Back home, the Leaders of Harleem were annoyed that they were always held prisoner to the rules of permission ... enforced by the worlds of Balhok.

But Kareen-hys-Tebeel-del-Harleem didn't care. Why should he. It had been his experience that it was never that difficult to get the required *permission* anyway.

Like the one hundred gold bars. It was so easy! And now, even if everything else went wrong, those gold bars were his insurance that he would never have to leave Harleem again.

By the time they reached the first oasis, the El-Bhat Band Leader and his second-in-command, slipped away from Ou-Leesen-el-Bra-ten's men, and headed for the Keep with the precious document that was hidden inside Arl-Sheen's Robe.

Chapter 18 - The Next Quorum Leader

Previously, Arl-Sheen's spy waited for Shanteef to exit the Keep, to 'judge' Ou-Leesen's men who had just arrived. But it wasn't Shanteef ... and the prisoners were pardoned. He quickly hurried to Arl-Sheen, with the news that Shanteef was dead!

When the spy first brought the information to Arl-Sheen, about the death of Shanteef, the Quorum rushed to the Keep with as many El-Bhat as they could gather on short notice.

As promised by the spy, they found the body of Shanteef, in the Pit of Pain.

The body was unrecognizable, but the finger rings belonged to Shanteef.

With Shanteef dead and hundreds of El-Bhat Bands pledging loyalty to Ou-Leesen, the Warrior with the Dagger of Truth, things were going badly for the Quorum.

Arl-Sheen quietly listened to the rumbling disapproval as he considered the opportunity that was his for the taking.

"My most Holy Brethren," he finally interrupted. "Such dire conditions require a bold new strategy. I have a plan." All eyes turned to Arl-Sheen.

"It is time to make an alliance with the Government of Kel-eetan."

Furrowed eyebrows showed discontent, but the silence continued.

"Our spies tell us that Ou-Leesen has gathered almost one hundred El-Bhat Bands, that have gathered north of Kel-eetan. And he plans on walking into the celebration dinner of *Bra-ten* in the Great Dining Hall, where all the Government officials will be gathered.

"With his most loyal, which apparently, number about twenty, he plans on taking over the government. Within hours the thousands of El-Bhat waiting north of the city will crush any resistance and then fall upon the leaderless Capital city."

"And ..." an impatient Quorum member said, anxious to hear the rest.

"And ... the plan is a good one. The city will be celebrating. The decision to march on Kel-eetan was made so recently, even the Government spies will be surprised. And ... most assuredly, on the day of Bra-ten, Ou-Leesen *would* become the new self-appointed leader of Shaksbah ... if we didn't interfere.

"But ... we will interfere. We will advise the government of Ou-Leesen's plans. And we will guarantee them that the gathering of El-Bhat north of Kel-eetan, will be under *our* control and they will never march into the Capital city. All we ask is that Ou-Leesen is executed with his men, for treason. Treason against the El-Bhat nation and the Government of Shaksbah."

"Is there more?" another impatient Quorum member demanded.

"Of course. We cannot allow this very resourceful warrior to succeed. Therefore, *I* will also be there on the day of *Bra-ten*, with two Bands of El-Bhat. And with the help of our spies, we will enter the Great Dining Hall, short moments after Ou-Leesen. And we will kill him and retrieve the Dagger of Truth. It must never fall into the hands of the *unclean* Shaksbali."

"I see an opportunity to finish what Ou-Leesen has started," another Quorum member suggested.

"It is truly tempting ... but the timing is wrong," Arl-Sheen proposed. "We have known for some time, that the Government has opened its Treasury to build its Military. They have never been stronger.

"No ... we will not finish *anything* that Ou-Leesen has started. We will be content to walk away with the Dagger of Truth and the good will of the Government. It has always been Shanteef's plan, to first buy the power of the Guilds of Storlenia, and then, we will be able to crush the government of Shaksbah and own the limitless Mines of Tenleth.

"As we enter the Great Dining Hall, spies will already be on their way to Qar-ana to confirm that we are ready to ship the promised gold for the Leadership of certain Guilds."

"But Ou-Leesen has already sent them wagons of gold," a Quorum member protested.

"Indeed ... but these foolish Storlenians will have spent their gold by now. They will need more ... *much* more."

Heads were nodding in agreement around the circle.

"Luckily, we have an insatiable supply," Arl-Sheen continued, "for their insatiable greed."

"This ... is good," a Quorum member said as he began to pound the pommel of his dagger on the carpet in support of Arl-Sheen's arguments. As soon as the entire Quorum joined him, he carried the Robe of Shanteef and placed it on the shoulders of Arl-Sheen.

"I will leave first thing in the morning," Arl-Sheen promised his Brothers.

"Before you go," one of the Quorum added, "you will advise the Band Leader, that you will be carrying a parchment with the location of Shanteef's Treasures. As you say, this warrior is resourceful and if anything were to happen to you …"

Arl-Sheen nodded in agreement, satisfied that the parchment would never be needed.

And he shared his confidence with the Band Leader.

'But it was needed, and luckily, I have it,' the Band Leader thought to himself, as he boldly walked down the halls of the Keep.

It had been a long journey. He would have preferred to head directly back to the Keep, but he had to be sure of Ou-Leesen-el-Bra-ten's plans. After all, this Warrior was still in possession of the Dagger of Truth … and he knew how to use it!

The Next Quorum Leader would have some difficult decisions to make.

With treasure in hand, the Next Quorum Leader dismissed the Band Leader … and waited until he was alone … then quickly opened the Sealed Parchment.

To his amazement, there were only ten words on the Parchment. Two lines, five words per line.

"Ten words," he angrily muttered to himself, "to guide me in the affairs of an entire nation … in very turbulent times!" He looked at the words again. He shook his head in despair. "What mischief has Arl-Sheen invented this time?"

He rolled up the Parchment as he considered his options. 'Perhaps the Band Leader heard something that might help,' he considered. He would call him back immediately.

He had barely placed his hand on the gold gilded handle, when the doors opened to reveal the returned Band Leader.

"Your Holiness … on our journey to Kel-eetan … Arl-Sheen said … 'Tell the Next Quorum Leader he need only be concerned about the location.'

"We had been drinking … so I dismissed his comment. Arl-Sheen was sometimes like that when he drank too much. He would talk about strange things … your Holiness."

"You did the right thing," the Next Quorum Leader praised the Band Leader.

The doors were closed again.

He unrolled the Parchment.

"So, these ten words describe a *location*," he excitedly said. Now things were beginning to make sense. He paced as he studied the words. And it wasn't long before he was hastily heading for, the *location*.

For the remainder of the night, as he sat beside the opened metal box, he studied the history of Shanteef. Many times, he found himself saying aloud, "Yes, of course!"

So many secrets to absorb in one night. It was frightening. It was shocking. It was exciting to consider that this was to be *his* future.

Then Shanteef's history mentioned a map … of a *second* Cave … that was passed from the previous Quorum Leader to Shanteef.

And how the El-Bhat villagers who discovered the healing ability of the Cave, were all murdered, to bury the secret of this Cave.

He found the leather map and studied it until he was sure of its exact location. He was about to put the map back in the box when a Green Light appeared in the room.

He wasn't totally surprised, it was the Green Lady that was mentioned on the pages of Shanteef's history many times.

He took a deep breath … and held it as he waited for her to begin her instructions.

Shanteef's forehead lifted from the carpet. She was gone. But she left great promises for him to consider.

He returned to Shanteef's history and when dawn had finally arrived, he laid the last of the pages back in the box.

He knew what his priorities were.

First, he must send the El-Bhat of the Keep to the location of the second Cave. He had been warned that Storlenians were already on their way ... to open this Cave. And if they succeeded, it would be the end of the El-Bhat nation.

Second, he must safeguard the Mines of Tenleth ... and the slaves, against Ou-Leesen-el-Bra-ten and the hordes from Storlenia.

As the first rays of the desert sun swept into the room, the Next Quorum Leader stood and went directly to the El-Bhat Leader that brought the message.

He would command him to gather the El-Bhat and hasten to the location of the *second* Cave. A location that only he knew about.

He would promise him that, soon after they arrived, the Storlenians would arrive ... and then his men would crush them ... and know that his words were truth.

The Green Lady had promised him that this would be the beginning of his greatness as the Next Quorum Leader. That for as long as men walked the planet of Ankoletia, they would speak of him as the Greatest Quorum Leader that ever lived!

Chapter 19 - One too many mistakes

Previously, Jokta had help his friend Axion escape from Qar-ana, where his life was in danger from the Butler, hired by Craslin, his Assistant. After meeting with Finn and the other Specialist Trackers, everyone headed to Arborville, following the direction of Far-fel's Amulet. On the way, they met the Butler, at an Inn, and after a life-and-death struggle, Aram-Dentee agreed to accept an invitation from the Amulet, to join Finn and the others.

On the road to Arborville, an anxious Jokta had left Axion and the small group, to return to his wife in Qar-ana. He had been gone many weeks longer, than he had supposed.

And now that he was back, he yearned to know what was happening. Had Finn and his Specialist Trackers made it to Arborville? Had the Tinkers really established a Guild and were they ready to throw themselves into the cause, of purging the corruption within Storlenia? Had Aram-Dentee remained loyal? So many questions.

Jokta had been watching the Planning and Development Guild for a few weeks now; in response to Axion's last words. *'You will be our ears and eyes for what happens in Qar-ana. I am sure Craslin is very busy.'*

One day, he bumped into an old Tracking friend. As they chatted, Jokta found out that a Tracking Guild Master, from out of town, had taken up residence in Qar-ana.

Strange indeed that he wouldn't contact the Guild Master of Qar-ana. But perhaps this Guild Master leaned into the wind ... the same direction as Jokta. It would make sense. Eventually, suspicion regarding the activities at the Planning and Development Guild had to reach the ears of the Trackers.

He decided that he would pay him a visit.

Jokta sat in Bernado's office, waiting for the Aide to fetch him. He was admiring the furnishings. Something a bit unusual for a Tracker's taste ... too opulent.

At that moment Bernado entered with an extended hand and warm smile.

"Surprised by the standard of living?" the Guild Master asked as though reading his mind. Jokta smiled at the insight. They shook hands as Bernado answered his own question. "A gift of Craslin. He loves the finer things. Don't believe we have met before?"

"Jokta, retired Tracker. Heard you were in town. Came by to discuss a concern."

"Have you discussed this concern with the Qar-ana Tracking Guild?"

Jokta simply shook his head 'no'.

"I see. Perhaps I ought to close the door," Bernado suggested. But before his hand touched the doorknob, a servant walked in with a tray of tea.

"Splendid," he said as the servant left and he closed the door.

"So ... what concern do you have?" Bernado said cheerily.

"It might be a common concern between us," Jokta suggested. "Did Craslin ... invite you to Qar-ana?"

"No." Bernado shifted in his chair as though he was about to discuss something uncomfortable. Then he continued, "There are currents of activity at the Planning and Development Guild that are troubling. I felt that I needed to be closer to the view, if you catch my meaning?"

"Now that you are here, do you have specific concerns?" Jokta asked, still not completely comfortable opening up to Bernado.

"Yes," he answered. "The escalation of things since Axion disappeared. Especially the initiative of the Planning and Development Guild to build their own Militia. And the introduction of a new weapon with superior firepower, incomparable to anything available to the Tracking Guild. Perhaps you would like some tea," Bernado offered, as he poured himself some.

Their discussion was going well ... almost too well if he compared past discussions with his old Guild Master. He knew before he walked into Bernado's place that he was breaking protocol and yet Bernado was not concerned about that at all. Either their concerns were *the same*, or Bernado was hiding something.

"Thank you," Jokta said as he accepted the cup. He watched Bernado as he placed the teapot back on the tray ... beside a small green stone. He hadn't noticed it until now. Odd to be on the tray, and yet ... there was an attraction that he couldn't explain. His eyes remained riveted on that stone for a few moments, until he remembered something Far-fel had said to the

Specialists at the Gathering. *'In the middle of the Necklace was a cradle that held a dark green stone, when not being used. Otherwise, the 'owner' of the Necklace would trick his victim into holding the stone …'*

Jokta ripped his gaze away from the stone, only to find Bernado staring at him … his green eyes glowing with excitement. 'So … you're from Pechora,' Jokta realized, wishing he had been more thorough before making his visit.

Weapon-less, except for the cup of tea, Jokta knew his life was hanging by a thread. Without further hesitation, Jokta threw the hot water into Bernado's face and ran.

Reaching the outer door, he opened it, shouting anxiously at the Guard, "The Guild Master needs you right away!" As the Guard ran past, Jokta's foot sent the man sprawling, as he grabbed his long knife. Now at least he had a weapon!

Once outside the front entrance, he hesitated a moment. He remembered that there was a turret mounted with one of those weapons, that had become commonplace at the Planning Guild. So, he *walked* towards the front gate.

He hadn't gone far, when the front door flew open and a Guard shouted, "Shoot him!"

The moment that front door flew open, Jokta was already sprinting down the broad path, dodging and weaving as he listened carefully for the movement of the weapon above. His plan worked for the first and second shots, which got him past the gate.

Now he was sure he would make it. All he had to do was to keep the large trees that lined the boulevard between him, and the weapon in the turret.

Unfortunately, he didn't notice the second weapon that was already following his movements … as he ran ever closer.

The 'Popping' sound that came from ahead, instead of behind, told his trained ears that he had made one too many mistakes today. The brass ball ripped into his shoulder, spinning him off balance, as he tumbled into a roll.

He was immediately on his feet again, positioning himself behind the closest tree. He had learned enough from Far-fel about the green stone that he knew he didn't want to be captured.

He groaned in pain as he removed his jacket to get a better look at the shoulder wound. It was bad, and bleeding hard. It was time to make a choice.

Rip a strip of cloth and stop the bleeding ... or, if he thought his chances of getting caught were high, let his life bleed out. Because his secrets about the Specialist Trackers must die with him.

Chapter 20 - The Master Spy

The spy entered the darkened anteroom from a secret passage. He could see the candlelight seeping under the heavy curtains from the room beyond. He slipped between the drapes into the room where the Guild Master was working late.

As he approached Craslin, the only sound that could be heard was the sputtering of the candles.

A floorboard creaked. Craslin whirled around, momentarily terrified, as the shadowed face emerged into the light.

"This better be important," Craslin angrily barked at the familiar messenger, still struggling to gain his composure.

The spy calmly walked to one of the opulent chairs and sat down before responding.

"You *pay* me to live in the shadows," he said without apology. "It is why I am still alive to deliver my message."

The man was right. The usefulness of spies was lost once they were dead. They both knew this fact only too well.

Recently Craslin had lost three spies. Disappeared without a trace. He suspected that this was the message this spy had come to report. "Is it about the dead spies?"

"Yes," was the terse reply.

"You have done well to come right away." He laid aside his papers. "Please continue."

"Bernado works with a dark art. It is unlike anything I have ever seen."

"Has he used this art to kill my spies?" asked a surprised Craslin.

"Yes ... he has a Golden Necklace and a dark green stone. Together they can extract information from a man, as long as he is holding the green stone."

Craslin was drumming his fingers together in concentration. The spy's brief explanation reminded him of the Redemption Guild's report regarding glowing shards he had spent good money chasing. Deciding what to believe was not always easy when one was chasing a shadow. "Tell me exactly what you saw," the Guild Master continued.

The spy knew that the story was unbelievable even when it was witnessed. But he had already decided ahead of time, what he would tell and what he wouldn't.

"Bernado wore a golden necklace. Then, while placing a green stone in the hand of your spy, he touched one of the Medallions on the Necklace and began to ask questions. The spy then answered the questions without any reservation ... like he had been given the drug that the Trackers use."

Craslin was impressed with the spy's knowledge regarding Olleti. Not too many people knew about the Tracker's secret.

"Then," the messenger continued, "he killed the spy by touching a different Medallion."

"Did you witness both deaths?" Craslin asked, leaning forward in anticipation of the answer.

"Yes ... and both times, the procedure was the same."

"So, he needs the small green stone to work this device."

The spy was nodding in agreement to Craslin's conclusion.

"It appears to be a powerful talisman ... but with a significant weakness," the Guild Master whispered to the shadows.

Craslin signed a note and handed it to the spy. "This will be your reward if you bring me this small stone." Craslin had little doubt that the spy would return with the green stone. He was the best spy he had ever hired. He thought of him as his Master Spy.

--------- <> ---------

Across the street, the spy looked back at the windows of Craslin's office.

'He suspects nothing,' he smiled to himself. His disguise was perfect ... his clothes, his face and hair and even his voice. There was nothing to give him away.

'And now, it's time to fetch a dangerous talisman,' he thought to himself as he looked at the amount of reward, written on the paper ... and smiled.

Chapter 21 - Yaneek's decision

Weeks earlier, before Urshen was brought to Qar-ana.

Craslin realized early on, that Zephra was not one to be bound to, or intimidated by, non-Tinker authority. That was why he gave her permission to enter his office at will. Which she took advantage of constantly.
Like today.

Zephra had come because she had finished inspecting the last of the Tinker War Wagons.
"As usual ... the wagons are flawless," she said, almost irritated that she was forced to check in minute detail every wagon.
"As usual ... I appreciate your thoroughness," Craslin reassured, pleased that his clever idea, kept Zephra in Qar-ana for so long.

Normally Zephra would smile politely and leave ... but she remained, staring at Craslin, as though she had something to say, but wasn't sure how to say it.
Craslin laid his pen down. "Won't you take a chair?"
Besides Urshen, and *he* wasn't really a Stor, Zephra had never asked anything of a Stor before. She bit the corner of her lip as she brushed aside the last bit of prejudice and annoyance towards Stors ... and then sat down.
"I want to learn ... everything. Especially things that *you* know." That last phrase came out real slow, like she was still struggling with her heart. But she managed to say it, and that, she knew, would make the rest easy.
Craslin could hardly believe the words. It was what he'd always imagined in his fantasies. But to actually hear it, was a great surprise! So much so, that he couldn't allow himself to believe it, so he said, "That's ... quite a compliment, but what has brought you to this decision?"
Her eyes went to her hands that fidgeted on her lap. "I know ... that being a Tinker isn't enough." She lifted her eyes to measure his response. They danced with excitement, so she waited for him to respond.
"I propose," Craslin began, "that I organize instruction every morning. There will be books to read for your afternoons, and if you have questions, please come to my office and we will discuss them in the Guild Gardens. How does that sound?" He asked hopefully.
Zephra stood immediately. "More than I'd hoped for," she exclaimed and then headed for the door. Before she left she turned to say, "Thank you."

The moment the door closed, an excited Craslin quickly pulled the silver tassels calling his army of assistants.

--------- <> ---------

'Perhaps he thinks my decision was spontaneous,' Zephra thought to herself, as she walked towards the Gardens. It was where she went to think ... and *celebrate*. And today, was a great day to celebrate.

'I think he would be surprised beyond belief if he knew how much he has influenced my decision.' She grinned as she exited into the Gardens. She knew Craslin was infatuated with her, so the journey was ... difficult ... like a Tinker balancing act. Trying to encourage him to teach her without encouraging him in his fantasy.

But here she was ... in a place she never expected to be ... with privileges beyond her expectations ... and wanting changes that she had never anticipated.

She stopped by the benches to survey her new world, filled with Stors and a culture she used to abhor.

"Hi stranger," a familiar voice was chirping at her side.

She smiled at her best friend ... a Stor.

"You appear to be deep in thought ... what's up?" Yaneek continued.

"I wasn't really thinking ... I was celebrating. Today I asked Craslin to be my Teacher."

Yaneek was nodding like she did when she needed time to process a difficult concept. Finally, she stopped nodding. "You once said that *he was very clever and that you expected to learn a lot from him.* But that was when you were trying to throw off the spies. I never took you serious."

"Yaneek ... I want to learn ... *everything* there is to learn. You see, Tinkers have been given an opportunity that ... well, we never saw it coming. Imagine ... our own Guild and a life of discovery and respect."

"Yeah, that's pretty wonderful. I have to admit, that back in Arborville, I was as surprised as anyone to see the beginnings of both Tinker Village and a Tinker Guild."

"But what most people don't realize, is that Tinkers have never known anything else but being a Tinker. Yes, in Arborville, we have laid the foundation for buildings and homes, but where will the knowledge come from to build the culture, economics and government that will integrate us into a life beside the Storlenians? The prophecy about Urshen was meant to mean more than building wagons. It means embracing everything the Stor culture has to offer. We have been stubborn fools," she admitted as her gaze swept the massive Guild building.

"Interesting to hear a Tinker say this," Yaneek offered.

Zephra sighed. "I remember years ago when I was young, it rained for ten days, and the thought occurred to me then, that our life was meant to be more than travelling in a wagon for our entire lives.

"And I think I can learn a lot from Craslin. He has helped me see how our Tinker world can be so very different. Remember when he introduced me to the Guild Library and the first book he gave me was about Tinkers?"

"Yeah, it seemed a ridiculous place to start with so many books to choose from," Yaneek said, remembering.

"I thought the same … but now I see his wisdom. He wanted me to see my own culture through the eyes of a Stor … so that I might see clearly, what Qar-ana has to offer Tinker society."

Yaneek was never comfortable when Zephra talked about Craslin like that. Besides, there was something else that Zephra needed to consider. "What are you going to do about his romantic ambitions?"

"Manage it. I have no choice. When I return to my father, I no longer want to be a Tinker Wagon Mechanic. My ambitions expand every time Craslin introduces me to new knowledge."

"I think you like the good life," Yaneek teased.

Zephra looked at her friend and slowly nodded. "Yes … you're right. But that good life also includes better medicine, education and limitless opportunities. I never realized before how narrow Tinker life was. So … I will dance with a bear if that's what it takes to get what I want."

"You make it sound easy. But please remember," Yaneek pushed back, "how easily Benekee ended up in a prison cell."

"It's definitely a linchpin situation," Zephra agreed.

"Linchpin?" Yaneek scrunched up her eyebrows.

"Another time and place when I had to pull the linchpin from a wagon … with precision … or everyone in the wagon would have died. Including Protas." She grinned at the memory.

Yaneek's eyes locked onto Zephra's face. "You … said Protas." She was wagging her head in disbelief. "How do you know him?" she asked with enthusiasm.

Zephra's thoughts went back a couple of weeks when she saw Guards removing Protas from the Guild. She didn't even know that he was there … and she was careful not to show any recognition as she stared at him from the balcony above.

"He is Urshen's best friend … and we fought side by side at Lundeen Forest against the El-Bhat. You met him here at the Guild, didn't you?" she suddenly realized.

"I've tried to talk to you about him a couple of times … it's why I came into the Gardens today."

"Talk about what?" Zephra asked as she looked around to check for spies.

"Well … we sort of have this *thing* going. For some time now, I wanted to talk about the fact that he's a criminal … so I wasn't sure … and needed another girl's advice. But now I think I'm past that. Now it's more like … our relationship is complicated."

Maybe it was the way she said it, but Zephra gave up a light-hearted laugh. "Complicated is a good word for *everything* Protas does," she finally said.

There was an uncomfortable silence until Yaneek finally said, "Zephra, I don't have the knowledge you do about what's going on inside these walls, but even to my eyes, it doesn't look right. I have heard the staff say that the Militia Guard will soon be fifty thousand strong!"

Yaneek paused as she sorted her thoughts. "Before we left your father, you said we would know what to do about Benekee's Shards once we found Urshen. He was supposed to be in Pechora, and then we came to Qar-ana and stayed, because Craslin wants to have *you* around.

"So far," Yaneek continued as her voice got louder, "we haven't found Urshen and neither you nor Benekee can wear the Amulets for fear they will be stolen. And quite frankly, I don't know why you insist that we continue to stay here. My desire to stay here crumpled, around the time Benekee almost died!

"And as my best friend," she continued … but in a quiet voice, fearful that others might hear, "I think you have kept me in the dark long enough … don't you agree?"

Zephra took Yaneek's hands in hers. "You are perfect for Protas," she said, wanting to comfort her good friend.

Yaneek looked away from Zephra, as tears began to stream.

"What you say is not enough … I need to know more," she added as her eyes returned to stare into Zephra's golden-flecked orbs. "I told you, I want to be strong like you, responsible like you."

Zephra led Yaneek to a bench where they could talk without being overheard. "I have kept this information from you because I wanted to protect you. But, I could have asked you what you wanted to know. Sorry.

"Apparently Urshen was in Pechora all along," she continued. "Probably still is, held captive under the direction of Bernado, Craslin's new Assistant. I'm sure you've seen him around."

Yaneek nodded contrary. She had no idea who this Bernado was.

"So, the Shards along with my White Bauble were given to a Tracker by the name of Ranoof. He can be trusted. He is one of twelve Trackers who were bonded to Urshen through the power of his Amulet.

"Anyway, Ranoof's mission was to replace Benekee's missing Shard with my Bauble. As you know, that's what Benekee wanted. Shortly after the time that Benekee gave me his Shards, the Tracker left with both Amulets, to deliver the new, completed talisman, to my father.

"Now ... about Protas. I saw him being escorted out of our Guild by Guards some time ago. Not sure where he was taken."

Zephra paused at this point, to allow Yaneek to consider everything she had said before continuing.

Yaneek sat tall and straight as she listened intently to every word. When the pause came, she considered what she wanted to ask. But first there was something she wanted to share with her friend. "Protas was taken to a Tracking Guild prison cell, here in Qar-ana," she informed Zephra. Now it was time for the question. "Why are you so indifferent towards Urshen and Protas ... suffering in prison?"

'Here comes the tricky part', thought Zephra, knowing her friend's concerns were validated by what happened to her brother.

"Urshen and Protas are still very important to me. But there is more at stake here than Protas who saved my life, and Urshen the man I'm going to marry.

"When Ranoof first told me what happened to Urshen, my first instinct was to jump back in the wagon and rush back to Pechora. But by then, I had already started to change. I knew I was no longer the Tinker Wagon Mechanic that my father depended upon.

"It was like I was becoming ... a bird, high in the sky. I could see so much more than just the perimeter around my personal wagon."

There was a long pause as her Tinker mind searched for the words to continue. "I have often thought, 'why were we led *here* to Qar-ana'.

"I believe," she began slowly, "that the Fates, have plucked us from our normal lives to do something important. I know I need to stay here and learn from Craslin.

"Yaneek, I think the time has come, for you to decide, what it is *you* need to do." She smiled warmly, knowing that this probably meant she was about to lose her best friend to a different path.

Yaneek looked down at the bench for a long time before responding.

"I have worried over my younger brother for so long ... it seems strange to let go. But I know I must.

"One day, after his recovery," Yaneek explained, "as we met in the Gallery Room, Benekee said to me, '*Yaneek, I have a feeling everything is going to work out all right. You need to stop worrying about me.*' He was right ... he has always been right ... about everything," she finished softly. "I'm not sure how that's going to work out, without his Shards, but his words rang true, even as I resisted them.

"And as for you ... I will miss your warmth and your strength.

"And then there's Protas," she said slowly as her face brightened. "He intrigues me. I think about him all the time. Why do you think he is in prison?" she suddenly questioned.

"Urshen once told me that Protas wasn't always the man he is now ... that there was a past. So maybe his past has caught up with him. Or maybe he's swept up in the whirlwind of trouble, that plagues our land."

"What do you know about Protas's dog?"

"He has a dog?" Zephra asked as her eyebrows popped upwards in surprise.

Yaneek grinned, "Yes, a very unusual dog."

"Do you want to take my wagon?" Zephra suddenly suggested, knowing that Yaneek would never survive without it. "Best made wagon in the land," she added with a smile.

"Thanks for the offer," she heartedly responded, but then panned the Guild and the Gardens.

"Not sure if you're ready to leave paradise?" Zephra asked.

Yaneek looked back at her friend, as she considered the question. But the eyes that stared back at Yaneek were not full of the sympathy that the question implied. They were hard, a definite reminder of the strength that Yaneek would need, in the days ahead.

"Okay, I will leave as soon as I can."

"Tomorrow?" Zephra pushed her friend.

"Tomorrow," she responded.

Chapter 22 - Yaneek's confidante

Weeks earlier, before Urshen was brought to Qar-ana ... continued.

Hiding in the shadows, the spy watched the two women stand, and embrace each other. It looked final, like one of them was about to leave the Guild. Intelligence that Craslin would pay extra for. He waited, until they had both left the Gardens, before he made his way to the secret entrance to Craslin's office.

--------- <> ---------

The following day, true to her word, Yaneek met Zephra by her wagon. The Tinker wanted to explain a few things prior to her departure.

"Under the seat, there is a false bottom where I keep some money. You will need it. I have stocked the wagon with food, for you and the horses. Should last several weeks."

Yaneek gave Zephra a little smile of appreciation.

"One last thing. There could be occasion to push this wagon as fast as she will go. There isn't a wagon anywhere that can keep up. Even the new War Wagons ... too heavy. Have you ever driven a wagon at full tilt?"

"No." Yaneek cringed as she thought about what was coming next.

"We need to change that. Jump up. You are about to get your first and last lesson."

--------- <> ---------

"You're sure you're not part Tinker?" Zephra quipped as they headed back to the Guild.

"Huh? Oh ... yeah, I was surprised myself at how easy it seemed. Guess it's the wagon," she teased as she grinned playfully at her friend. "Or maybe ... I have the best trainer in the world." And then her thoughts returned to her future as she continued to stare ahead.

"Worried about leaving?" Zephra brought her back to the present as the wagon continued to clack over the cobblestone road.

"No ... I know I need to leave. I'm worried about Protas," she said matter-of-factly. "The last time I went to see him; he was no longer in his prison cell at the Tracking Guild. I was told he was taken away by a Guild Master ... wouldn't say where."

She turned to Zephra as she remembered something she said. "You mentioned Bernado, Craslin's new Assistant. Maybe he would be a good place to start?" she asked hopefully.

"Start? No ... he would be a last resort. Remember when we stopped in Pechora at the Tracking Guild? Well he was the Guild Master who sent us here ... when Urshen was in a prison cell right below us.

"Yaneek, you must be very careful when it comes to Bernado. He cannot be trusted ... I would guess even more than Craslin. My best guess is that Protas has been transferred to the prison cells at Pechora. If I was you, I would try my luck there. Yeah, definitely stay away from Bernado!" Zephra added, hoping Yaneek would take her advice.

--------- <> ---------

Yaneek waited until Zephra was out of sight and then encouraged the horses in the direction of the Mechanical Guild ... where Benekee spent most of his time.

Once inside, she was asked to wait while they looked for her brother.

"Hey sis, get lost?" He joked. She never came to see him at his work.

After finding a private place outside, she began, "I am leaving the Guild. Today."

"What uhh ... what will you do?" Benekee stammered, totally shocked by her announcement.

"I am sort of in a relationship ... and I need to figure things out," she smiled at him.

"Oh ... well that's ... wonderful," he shook his head in surprise, trying to keep up with her news. "Will I be able to see you from time to time?"

"Yes, I plan on staying here in Qar-ana. I just need to leave the Guild."

"Of course. Zephra know about this?"

"She is staying ... for a long time. So, there is no need for you to consider moving on."

Yaneek looked towards the Mechanical Guild as she considered the question she came to ask.

"And ... how is your work coming along?" Some time ago, during his recovery from his violent beating, he had told her that Craslin had hired him to help improve the Brass Sling design. But she knew that he didn't have his Shards anymore ... the secret to his amazing design ability. She had wanted to ask him how he was going to manage the expectations. But Benekee seemed so hopeful, standing there with his cane and bad eye.

So, she put the question aside ... until today.

Benekee couldn't help from grinning. His sister had always worried about him. He wished he could tell her his secrets.

So instead he whispered, "I'm able to do what they," he nodded his head towards the building, "*cannot* do."

She wanted to say, 'But you don't have your Shards! How is this possible?' But instead, she returned his grin. And then through trembling lips she said, "Mom and dad would be proud."

Benekee looked down, not sure if he agreed with his sister.

She held him softly by his shoulders and whispered, "Benekee ... there is something that I discovered in father's journal ... that I have never told you.

"A long time ago, our family were believers ... and then something terrible happened. It was too hard to bear ... so our father's mother chose not to believe. You see, our bloodline was meant to be one of believers. So, mom and dad *would* be proud."

Benekee looked up. A reluctant grin washed over his face. It was almost funny how the roles had switched. "I want to believe your story," he admitted to her.

"Then believe!" She encouraged him.

He kissed her lightly on her cheek. "I will remember these kind words until the day I die. Good luck!"

It was time to say goodbye. Tears wet her blouse as she lifted her hand to his youthful face. It lingered there as she said, "Thank you Benekee for helping me believe."

Then she left.

Days later, Yaneek was sitting in her wagon outside the Planning and Development Guild ... her old home with Zephra. The rising sun had begun to chase away the dew that had gathered on her wagon top, as she sat waiting for Bernado to arrive.

'There you are,' she thought. Yaneek recognized him from their brief encounter in Pechora. Zephra had warned her against trusting Bernado, and she was of a mind to stick with that advice.

She wasn't going to contact him as she had initially thought. What she wanted to do, was to monitor his goings and comings. And then, Yaneek would pay a visit to his home, when she was sure he wouldn't be there. Because her heart told her that Protas was still in Qar-ana. She would start with the place where Bernado lived.

Continuing her vigil, the afternoon found her back in front of the Planning and Development Guild, watching and waiting. Her hood was pulled up against the brisk wind, completing her camouflage. The effort was for both Bernado and Zephra. If her friend saw her, Yaneek was sure she would bolt out of the building, intent on rescuing Yaneek from her folly.

But to her, it wasn't folly. She remembered their trip from Pechora. It was long and this time of the year, there was sure to be plenty of rain. And what if Zephra was wrong? What if Protas was still here in Qar-ana? She wondered if her friend was more intent on keeping her away from Bernado and less concerned about how soon she found Protas. Of course, Yaneek needed to be careful. And of course, there was risk. But she decided that she would take the risk ... after she remembered Protas's dog.

He was no ordinary dog. More intelligent than a dog ought to be and there was something between him and Protas. So ... why not include him in her plan to find Protas.

She leaned over and ruffled his ears. "It shouldn't be much longer now ... Sausage."

It was surprisingly easy to find him. Yaneek simply whistled as she wandered the streets of Qar-ana in her wagon.

Then one day, she looked down to her side and saw him running beside her wagon.

She stopped and jumped down. Sausage was so happy to see her.

After taking a few moments to get reacquainted, Yaneek explained to him, what she intended to accomplish and why she needed him. Suddenly he jumped up into the wagon ... and waited for her to join him. Yaneek laughed. She had to admit, a window of fascination had opened upon her life since she met Protas and his dog.

Soon, they were following a group of wagons as Bernado made his way to his home. He was obviously a very cautious man and very powerful. Today's effort was only to find out where he lived. Then Yaneek would decide what she would do next.

Today, like so many other days, she parked the wagon at least ten minutes away by foot, and always in a different spot. Then she would walk Sausage through the park and along the boulevard that bordered the luxurious home of Bernado. Yaneek was gathering details of the going and coming of those that either served or lived on the premises. And she was hoping to see Protas.

So far, there was no evidence that Protas was in the house. But today, while she was still at the top of the Boulevard, a wagon pulled up in front of Bernado's house.

A prisoner was escorted from the wagon and literally carried by two men inside. Yaneek was too far away to see the face of the prisoner but he had a young athletic build like Protas and dressed in a Tracker outfit.

It was enough encouragement to proceed with the next phase of her plan. If one young man was being held prisoner ... then why not another. Yaneek would wait for a day when she was sure that Bernado was gone to see Craslin, and then walk inside and ask to see Protas.

"Looks like Protas might be inside," she said to Sausage as they walked past the entrance. He barked with enthusiasm. Yaneek smiled, pleased that the dog was probably agreeing with her conclusion.

At the end of the street, she turned around and looked back at the empty wagon as it sat in front.

"We will wait until we are sure Bernado has gone for the day to the Planning and Development Guild. Then we will make our move," she said quietly to the dog.

Chapter 23 - The Great Escape

Back to the present. Protas, now in possession of the Amulet carried by Sausage, has managed to escape Bernado's prison cells, with Urshen, and are now far away, covered by the blackness of night.

"Where is my hostage?" The Alien said for the second time as a sleepy Bernado crawled out of his bed.
"Please allow me to get dressed. I will meet you in my office."
Kareen left.

Soon the Tracker was outfitted, complete with his special long knives. He knew they were useless against Kareen-del-Harleem, but they reminded him of his goal ... to bring down a titan!

The Visitor had never come back to ask about the Tracker who stole the Amulet, the man he wanted as a hostage. It seemed reasonable that this was the hostage he was referring to.
Facing him, in his office, Bernado explained, "The man that previously wore the Golden Necklace, cannot be found. But ... I assume you already know that," Bernado probed.
The Alien ignored his comment, confirming to Bernado that he must be referring to Urshen.
"Your hostage is in my prison cell ... of course," Bernado added with doubt.
Kareen's expression told him he was wrong. Which probably meant that Protas was gone as well.
"So, he has escaped ... and you have come to tell me." Bernado was beginning to feel foolish. Not only had he lost the hostage, but he had lost the green stone that would help him find them. He decided he may as well confess but was immediately interrupted.
"My name is Kareen-hys-Tebeel-del-Harleem, and I am *not* your messenger boy."
Bernado flinched at the rebuke. Kareen's lack of expression always added power to his words.
"It has come to my attention that you have lost the green stone."

"Yes, I have," Bernado admitted with as much courage as he could muster.

"Do you have doubts that I am able to place you on the Emperor's throne?"

"No," Bernado said slowly, as feint wisps of green mist licked at the edges of Kareen's face. It appeared that this was the Alien being angry.

After a moment, the green mist disappeared and Kareen continued.

"That is good. Now ... I will explain how to retrieve Goldenrod's companion.

"Using three fingers from each hand, touch all six medallions. Pu-el-tal, the Green Woman, will appear and grant you your request. Tell her you want the stone to return to the cradle. Do not fail us again," Kareen warned as green mist gathered, and then he was gone.

Bernado wasted no time. He rushed to the room where Goldenrod was stored and followed the Alien's instructions.

The moment the Woman said "granted" a swirling Green Light ruptured from Goldenrod and shot forward through the space that separated it from the green stone, finding its companion and pulling it back to the cradle.

As the stone whisked across the room to fall into the cradle, the trail of dust particles, floating in Green Light, began to disperse. The Woman was gone the instant the stone was back.

Bernado's gaze followed the disappearing trail to the perfectly round hole left in the stone wall.

Under the light of the stars, Sausage led as the two did their best to follow, determined not to fall into Bernado's hands again. If there was a way to evade the ambitious Guild Master, the Amulet-carrying Sausage would find it.

'But if not,' Protas reluctantly considered, 'at least the Amulet will be safe.'

Wrapped in the power of Green Light, Bernado could see the trail of where Urshen had gone. Like a scent to a dog.

But as for Protas, there was no trace. Surely, they must be together.

The experience reminded him of the Specialist Tracker that stole his Amulet. Same thing … no trace.

This suggested to Bernado's quick mind, that Protas had an Amulet.

Which was strange. He had been thoroughly searched and at one point, even stood naked before him, except for his scars. How could he have acquired the Amulet? "Never mind," he said, as the Green Light winked out, "I have a surprise for my uncooperative guests."

--------- <> ---------

"It's glowing," Urshen shouted as quietly as he could, while grabbing Protas's arm.

Protas stopped and shouted to Sausage to do the same.

He moved off the trail into the trees as he grabbed the glowing Amulet from inside his robe.

"Something has triggered a response from this Amulet," Protas whispered to his friend.

"Probably Bernado's talisman," Urshen suggested.

Protas asked his silent question. 'Is Bernado using the Necklace?'

With his answer, he turned to Urshen, "You're right, It's Bernado. Tell me about this Golden Necklace. Why would he be using it right now?"

"To find us," was Urshen's quick reply. "Perhaps we should split up?"

"No," Protas shot back. "I mean … I don't think it's a good idea. I think it's better to stay together."

"Okay," was all Urshen said, trusting his friend's instincts.

Protas held the talisman as he asked to see the topography of the area for many leagues north and east. Satisfied, he turned to his dog.

"Sausage run north until you come to a river, then go east until the forest fades into hills, then head south and listen for my whistle."

Before heading east, Protas used the Amulet to infuse them with energy. "A trick I learned from Zephra," he added as he gave the Amulet back to Sausage.

"Good luck," he shouted, as the dog bounded away into the night.

"If Bernado can track the Amulet, his men should be far from us by morning. We will head straight east until we meet up with Sausage. Then we need to find a road. Sound good?"

Urshen nodded yes.

With fear as their companion, and the stars to guide their way, they continued to run for the rest of the night.

By dawn, they had left the forest, and entered a large meadow. "We will wait here for my dog," an exhausted Protas suggested.

The quiet of the meadow carried the shrill sound of his whistling in all directions.

"Because Sausage is wearing the Amulet, his hearing will be enhanced," Protas advised Urshen. "It shouldn't be long now."

Protas was about to whistle again when a large dog bounded out of the forest, happily racing towards the two escaped convicts.

Leaving the meadow behind, they ran towards a range of rolling hills, silhouetted by the glow from a promised sun.

They were soon past the hills and into sweeping grasslands. "I think Sausage has done it," Protas declared triumphantly, as they stopped for a brief rest.

An exhausted Urshen grinned at his friend, convinced that he was right.

"Another hour and we will make it to a major road where a friendly wagon will take us south," Protas shared his optimism with Urshen. The dog barked, anxious to be gone and soon the threesome was racing across the land once again.

But the hope of freedom was dashed, as they approached the road that Protas had mentioned.

A wide swath of armed, uniformed men, advanced towards them like a steel net.

"Sausage ... leave us!" Protas commanded as he slowly led Urshen towards their inevitable capture.

"Who are they?" Urshen asked incredulously, while panning the wall of a thousand men as they began to close in on them.

"The Planning and Development Guild of Qar-ana have been building a Militia." Protas responded soberly. "And they are trained like Trackers ... but with a difference."

"Difference?" Urshen looked at his friend.

"They have a weapon that fires brass balls with enough force to crack oak wagon timbers."

Urshen was thinking about the advanced technology, that would be required to build such a machine. It reminded him of his efforts to re-design the common wagon. "Who was responsible for this design?" he asked Protas.

"From things I've overheard, it appears to be someone working for Craslin."

The Militia were almost a hundred paces away as Protas stopped and turned to Urshen.

"I see," he responded, reflecting on his friend's question. "New technology like that can only mean one thing. That someone has a talisman of power!"

Urshen was nodding as he watched the Militia surround them. It was odd to see that they carried the weapons of Trackers ... and moved like Trackers.

Both fugitives quickly extended their arms in submission. It occurred to Urshen that soon people everywhere would be doing the same.

Chapter 24 - The Harvest of Loyalties

After opening the door, Bernado was pleased to see that the face standing in the darkened doorway, was the Aide he had sent for.

Today was going to be another turning point on the road of success, as Bernado continued his climb, to become the Emperor of Ankoletia.

The reason ... was that this Aide served in Craslin's inner circle. He was considered untouchable. Loyal to a fault.

Today would be the first time Bernado used the Third Medallion, which allowed him to influence the will of the subject. If it worked, he would have the perfect spy ... and he would use it again.

"Please come in," Bernado said with a smile, and then led him to his office.

"The parcel that I want you to take back is over there."

The man walked towards the table and was about to pick up the box, when Bernado said, "But first ... because of the importance of these items, I wish to review them with you, so there is no doubt what is to be delivered ... and received.

"I will also have you sign this document," Bernardo added as he pointed to the piece of paper lying beside the box.

The servant nodded in agreement, as he watch Bernado open the box.

"This is the first item," Bernado said as he held the Golden Necklace before the spy, allowing him to study it. "Eventually I will be transferred to another location, where I will continue my service to Craslin. And this is the Scepter of Power that I will wear, as I direct the affairs of my new assignment," Bernado clarified as he fastened the Necklace around his neck.

"Beautiful, isn't it?"

The spy was nodding in agreement, as he patiently waited for Bernado to finish his pompous charade.

His eyes went to the paper lying on the table. He even picked up the pen, indicating that he was anxious to be gone.

"Yes, the signature ... but first, there is one other item. Not particularly beautiful, but very important," he said as he lifted the small green stone for the man to see.

Then without warning, he dropped the stone. Instinctively, the courier's quick reflexes caught it.

And just as quick, Bernado touched the Third Medallion.

Bernado was about to leave the Planning and Development Guild, when he saw Craslin on the training field, talking to a young man. Beside them stood a War Wagon, mounted with a large Brass Sling.

Recently, Craslin had let it slip, that he had approved further enhancements on the Brass Sling. And that Bernado would be impressed.
The weapon rarely came up in conversation. Like it was off limits. Confined to Craslin's chamber of secrets.
So, when Bernado saw Craslin, beside a mounted Brass Sling, he headed directly for the Guild Master.

Somewhere in the distance were targets, like what Archers used. He heard Craslin say "Fire."
There was a continuous popping noise as the Brass Sling began firing metal balls, in quick succession at the targets. From the time it took Bernado to take a deep breath, the machine must have fired over twenty. Impressive!

He walked up behind them with the stealth common to a Tracker, but his eyes were on the young man beside Craslin. Why was he there? What interest would Craslin have in showing the operation of this powerful weapon, to this young man? 'Only if ...' he thought to himself.

"Your improvements were successful," Craslin said to the young man. "I think we are done. I am very pleased."
The young man gave a small nod and excused himself.
As he walked passed Bernado, he gave a quick look sideways, as though he was memorizing his features.

The young lad's disfigured face captured Bernado's attention. One thing for sure. There was a story behind the mutilation.

He walked up beside Craslin. "You were right. I am deeply impressed with this improved war weapon of yours."
Craslin responded, "Yes, the design has worked very well."
Bernado turned to watch the young man as he disappeared around a corner. "I assume *he* is the genius behind the design?"
"He has his talents," was all Craslin would admit to.
The Tracker nodded in agreement.

"What you have done with this Brass Sling," Bernado began, "is incredible. But … it might convince Nusdek that the Militia is … invincible. Unfortunately, that kind of thinking could unravel all my strategic training. Make the men overconfident."

"What do you propose?" Craslin asked.

"Once Nusdek has seen this for himself, ask him how this new weapon will affect our campaign. If he uses the word 'invincible', or something like it, send him to me. We will need to talk."

Craslin turned to look at the Brass Sling one more time, as he thought of Bernado's concerns. 'Maybe a concern, but …'

He turned to comment, but Bernado had already left.

Bernado had nothing more to say. Besides, he had planted the seed for Nusdek's visit, the most important element of their short conversation.

For some time, he had schemed for an opportunity to get Craslin to send Nusdek … alone … to see him. And today, Craslin had unwittingly provided him the opportunity!

Nusdek and his Wall, were the last obstacle to Bernado's climb to the throne of Emperor. They were constantly at Craslin's side, and even now, he knew they were following Craslin to his home, as they always did.

But sometime soon, he knew Craslin would send Nusdek to his home. And he would use the Third Medallion to capture Nusdek's loyalties. Then he would 'own' the Militia and the contest between Craslin, and himself, would be over.

Chapter 25 - Biskin and the two towers

With the eyes of an eagle, Biskin watched Bernado's Guards escort a prisoner, dressed like a Tracker, from a wagon, into the large house, where Bernado now lived ... and where Protas was held prisoner.

It had been weeks since Biskin had parted company with Stek and Ou-Leesen, determined to watch over Protas, as the rest of Ou-Leesen's group headed back to Chitouf.

Originally, he had thought to rescue Protas as soon as an opportunity presented itself, but apparently, his Gift was more interested in his continuing vigil. As though there was benefit, to having Protas inside Bernado's world. So, he watched and waited every day.

Then one night, he awoke ... the itch in his head was strong. Something was wrong with Protas ... or something had changed.
He rushed to the house prison and then went straight to the back window ... but Protas was gone!

The next morning, Biskin wandered through the Markets, hoping to hear anything that might give him a hint, about what might have happened the night before. His hunch was right, there were murmurs everywhere about large groups of Militia that marched through the city during the night, heading east.
He decided to sit by the City Gates and wait for the return of the Militia. If they had Protas, he wanted to be there, when they re-entered the city.

By late afternoon, Biskin could see a trail of War Wagons heading from the east. There had to be at least a thousand Militia accompanying those that rode in the wagons.
With heightened interest, he continued to watch the parade, as the throng of armed men entered the city. He was now familiar with the Tracker-trained Militia Guard that had become part of the landscape of Qar-ana's streets.
'But surely, this dispatched group of Craslin's troops, was not just for Protas?' he thought, as the stream of men continued to march past.

Then he spotted Protas coming towards him ... with a Tracker. The other young man looked a lot like the Tracker that was taken into Bernado's house, between two of Bernado's Guards.

'So, *this* is what all the fuss is about?'

He couldn't believe it. No matter how he looked at it, it didn't make sense.

'All of this for Protas and this unknown Tracker!'

He had always believed that somehow Protas was important. The fact that his Gift had always tied him to Protas, told him that.

But, *more than a thousand* Militia?

Leaning against a fence he watched as the two came closer and closer. Then, as soon as Protas was as close as he ever was going to be, Biskin spoke the word "Protas".

It worked.

He was careful not to speak so loudly that it would bring attention to himself, but loud enough that Protas turned his head towards him. There was a brief exchange of acknowledgement as their eyes met.

As the two young men shrank from view, surrounded by well-armed Militia, Biskin's thoughts returned to Protas's companion.

'Maybe it *wasn't* Protas that called out enough Militia to capture an entire village. Maybe Protas was only along for the ride.'

And if that was truly the case, "Who's that with Protas?" he quietly muttered to himself.

On an ordinary day, he would have been disturbed, just to see a Tracker in chains. But of course, these were not ordinary times. He had proved that himself. Imagine what another Tracker would think, if he knew that Biskin, had just spent eight weeks, travelling with a group of El-Bhat, carrying wagon loads of gold into Storlenia, to buy ships and docking rights for the Quorum!

So ... setting aside the fact that he just saw a Tracker walk beside Protas *in chains* ... who could this stranger be? Who could be so important to Craslin and Bernado that they would send over a thousand men to bring him back!

He was important, that was for sure. And the more he thought about *why* this unknown Tracker was so important, the more he saw things in Qar-ana differently.

Sure, he had already learned some things from Stek and Protas as they travelled together.

Things about Bernado, Craslin and the true extent of the El-Bhat infiltration.

But he really hadn't given these things much thought. It wasn't in his nature.

He was a simple man who had been self-trained to follow his Gift, regardless of what was happening in the world around him.

But he had to admit. If he considered current conditions, compared to how things should be ... well maybe it was time to start thinking for himself. Gift or no Gift!

He pushed himself away from the fence and returned to his horse.

His plans had changed.

He was going to rescue Protas *and* that Tracker with him. If this Tracker was that important to Bernado ... then he must get him to Arborville as quickly as possible!

The next day, Biskin was back at his daily surveillance of Bernado's house.

But *now*, things were different.

Before, he was just putting in time as he waited for his Gift to inspire him to action.

Now he was watching with a purpose.

To formulate a rescue plan.

Now he must pay attention to every small detail as he watched the day unfold.

He knew that certain things would turn out to be unique.

But most, would be simple daily routine ... services throughout the day.

The Butcher, the Market Man, the Baker, the Winemaker, and so on.

Then there were certain people and their habits.

People taking their dog for a walk.

Couples taking a stroll along the boulevard in the late afternoon.

The occasional Tracker patrol that checked this street twice a week.

Then there were the sentries by the doors, and those above that manned the weapons.

Brass Slings that could fire a brass ball that could bring down a horse.

And of course, the coming and going of Bernado, and the Militia who watched over him.

A few days later, as the young woman and her dog walked down the boulevard, as was their habit, Biskin's eyes lingered on the dog, longer than usual.

The dog noticed him watching ... and looked back for a moment.

Nothing unusual, but a few moments later, when the woman stopped to look back at Bernado's house, the dog was watching Biskin.

Then they resumed walking ... and the dog was still watching him ... with a studied look. His tongue was not hanging out, like when a dog was idle in his thoughts.

There was a focus. He was studying Biskin!

Finally, the Tracker looked away. He was afraid that the woman would notice the curious attraction of her dog, to the stranger across the street.

He didn't want that. He wanted to appear invisible to everyone on that street.

Later, his curiosity pulled his gaze back to the dog. He was no longer looking his way ... until they stopped at the end of the street, and the dog turned his head, and stared right at Biskin, with that same concentrated look. The dog reminded him of a wolf, tracking his next meal.

Then they crossed the street and headed further away. Biskin stared for a while, wondering what had just happened.

A few days later, as Biskin looked down the boulevard for the young woman and the dog, Bernado's front door burst open and a Tracker with a quick step left the building.

Suddenly he began running, dodging between the trees of the boulevard, as the weapon above the door started to fire brass balls.

Biskin's instincts propelled him into action, as he sprinted towards the escaping Tracker. Meanwhile keeping both eyes on the two Military Towers, that boasted the new weapons.

He had a lot of respect for these new 'mystery weapons' ever since that time when a warning shot, split the oak side-board of their wagon ... while unloading the gold bricks with Protas.

The Tower closest to the front entrance of the Guild, was peppering the trail of the escaping Tracker. Fortunately, the large trees on the boulevard provided the advantage he needed.

Biskin had closed the gap considerably, by the time the Second Tower swung the barrel of the weapon, towards the escaping Tracker. He knew this was trouble. The racing Tracker hadn't noticed the new danger.

Before Biskin could shout a warning, the Tracker was hit and took a tumble behind a tree.

Biskin sent an arrow towards the Tower that took the Guard down, as he simultaneously slid into the safety of the same tree.

"Can you move?" Biskin shouted at the bleeding Tracker, keeping himself and the wounded Tracker out of sight of the Second Tower.

He assumed that he was out of range of the first Tower ... but he was wrong.

'Pop' ... followed by a thud ... could be heard as the brass ball ripped into the bark of the tree and then ricocheted into Biskin's ribs.

He groaned, as the two Trackers quickly moved to the far side of the tree, free from the line of sight of the First Tower.

A quick check told Biskin that his arrow must have done some good. The second and closest Tower was silent.

They were safe for the moment, but it was only a matter of time before Guards came running through the front door in pursuit.

His rib felt cracked. Luckily the tree took the brunt of the potential damage. But his new associate wasn't doing so well. He was bleeding badly.

"Yes, I can move," Jokta finally said through gritted teeth.

"Looks like my arrow bought us some time," Biskin responded, as his knife tore into Jokta's jerkin, cutting a strip of cloth. Next, he gouged out a chunk of bark which he placed against the wound and then used the cloth strip to hold the makeshift compress.

"That should keep you from bleeding to death, until we can find something better. And now ... we need to get moving."

Chapter 26 - The breach of permission

The team were sitting around the Strategy Console, all waiting for Kareen's response to the latest development.
By chance, his Communications Officer had discovered that The Commander General, was planning a trip into their quadrant.

Kareen, his face like stone, listened carefully as he was briefed on the situation.
"Everyone is on 'Alert Status' until further notice," Kareen informed the team.

Back in his cabin, he walked to the port window and stared at the planet below. It had become a potential resource of incredible value. Immense quantities of mined and unmined Gold, Class Six genetic strength and slaves in abundance.
Of *course*, The Commander General was on his way ... to claim the prize for himself!
And of course, that meant that he had to find a reason to displace Kareen-hys-Tebeel-del-Harleem.
And of course, it was expected that Kareen would accept the false accusations, the demotion and possible imprisonment.

He poured himself a drink and sat in the corner, where he faced his personal storage box, where one hundred gold bars were stored ... illegally!
He was sure that the loyalty of the Technician was intact. His act of mercy would have guaranteed that to the man's death.

There must be a spy, planted by The Commander General himself. He would ask the Technician to find the break in security and then restrict the spy's privileges on some minor category. It wouldn't prevent the spy from communicating, but it would stop him from sending messages. Because he would know that he was caught.

That would at least allow Kareen-hys-Tebeel-del-Harleem to work his plan in secret before The Commander General arrived.
And *that* plan would involve sending a message back to Harleem. Regarding a possible *breach of permission*, the thing the aristocracy of Harleem, feared the most.

Of course, the message would only make it to the General ... his spies would see to that.

He smiled at the simplicity of the strategy. The General would do anything to avoid attachment to a blunder of that magnitude.

Yes, that would send The Commander General back to Harleem, to quickly detach himself *and* to craft a report of condemnation of Kareen-hys-Tebeel-del-Harleem's mismanagement of the planet.

But the report would never make its way to the Emperor's office. Because Kareen's next communication would be targeted for only The Commander General before he made it back to Harleem. Proposing that he had found a way to prove that there was, after all, no breach.

And he was prepared to turn over the spoils to The Commander General, if all prosecutions against Kareen, were waived ... and he could retain his modest, personal, plunder. In fact, with the wealth that he would garner from this mission, he was prepared to accept permanent suspension from the military. That would be his negotiating card.

Of course, for the plan to work, the failed *breach of permission*, had to have integrity. It would need to be so close to the real thing, that it would stand up to the scrutiny of the legal people, that The Commander General would hire.

And that had already been worked out ... thanks to a request made by Bernado some time ago. *'But you must have weapons that you can give me that would surpass anything Craslin has built?'*

At the time, he had to deny the request. But since then, the benefits to this planet from Balhok, had escalated, allowing Kareen an opportunity to give additional support, to Bernado.

Kareen returned to the port window and smiled. Soon he would give that support in the form of hand-held 'Brass Sling' weapons.

Kareen would ask his team to include scopes for the hand-held weapons, as a special favour to Bernado. Of course, the scopes would need to be of similar technology, to that being used by the Ankoletians.

But a mistake would be made, and superior scopes would be sent ... inciting a technical *breach of permission*.

But, those superior scopes, would have a different mounting mechanism, and therefore couldn't be attached to the hand-held weapons. Making them useless and thus removing the *breach of permission*!

'Perfect,' thought Kareen. The only thing left to do now, was to increase the size of his personal plunder. After all, how could The Commander General refuse his terms?

Chapter 27 - The Hypocrite

Craslin was in the Guild, having a very pleasant evening meal ... but alone. Earlier today he had received word that Zephra's friend Yaneek had disappeared without a word. Mid meal he laid down his fork.

He wondered if Zephra would also leave him.

He was considered the most powerful man on the planet, by all who served him. But all that power meant nothing when it came to Zephra. It was true that she respected his knowledge and seemed very appreciative to be taught by him. But ...

Suddenly, he had no appetite. He got up and went out onto the balcony as he stared across his dominion, bathed in the early evening sun.

What he was feeling now, was not a surprise. He knew it the moment he laid eyes on Zephra.

Years ago, he had fallen in love with *power*, an exciting mistress indeed. As a companion, power played to all his abilities. It was a perfect arrangement.

Except ... there was something missing. Something he would've never expected or understood ... if he had never met Zephra.

How does one anticipate something like that? An event, so life-changing ... that it could vaporize everything he had worked for, in an instant.

Of course, he didn't accept it at first. How could he? It was terrifying to think that he was wrong about everything. That everything he sought to achieve was for nothing.

At least nothing without Zephra at his side.

He sighed, as he thought back to the time he was an Assistant Head Guild Master. Confident, that someday his skills would place him where Axion was.

He was good with numbers.

Logic was his second nature.

He could see value where others could not.

And he could sift through the intricacies of intrigue, like no one else. Allowing him to overpower his enemies.

But Zephra, was not the enemy. And there was nothing logical about love.

There he said it. The thing he wanted more than anything in the world. He wanted Zephra to love him. It was why he had stayed at Benekee's side for weeks. He would show her that he was capable of loving someone, other than himself. He laughed softly as he remembered playing the part of 'Healer'.

Now *there* was an enigma he wasn't expecting to see.

His plan was to pretend to be someone he wasn't. Someone that would attract Zephra's attention. Maybe even her heart.

But the strange thing was … the more he pretended, the more he enjoyed being someone he wasn't. He thought about that a lot.

And decided that his plan had value, but really … it wasn't working. Romance needed more than a Healer's skill and the compassion that went with it.

On the flip side, he felt he knew Zephra better, and why loyalty was so important to her.

Of course, he didn't want her to stay, just to be loyal to his kindness.

He looked at the Gardens below. His eyes lingered on the bench where *she* usually sat, when she went outside.

What was he going to do if she decided to leave, like Yaneek? He couldn't force her to stay, that wouldn't be love. In fact, he couldn't stand knowing that she hated him because he kept her as a prisoner. Even if she pretended to love him, it would be nothing ... compared to what he desired.

He heard someone clearing their throat. It was Zephra!

He wanted to turn around but couldn't.

He feared that his thoughts would be written on his face. Especially his yearning for her love.

"Did you enjoy the books?" he asked, his gaze fixed on the manicured lawns below.

Zephra turned to look at the books she had laid on the large desk. She did have questions and was hoping that Craslin might be willing to take some time now. But there was something in his voice ... some grief that he wanted to hide. It was why he didn't turn to greet her as he always did.

Then like a flood, her Tinker culture reminded her, of how insensitive she had been to *his* needs. All their time together … it had always been about her. He had insisted that it be that way. And she was perfectly willing to *let it* be that way. Without ever a thought of what was important to him.

She could feel her face turning red. She was glad her father wasn't there.

Up until now, she felt perfectly justified in her actions. After all, he was seeking her love ... and he couldn't have it!

But all that seemed petty and childish right now, as she looked over his shoulders at the only thing in his life, that held any meaning for Craslin. His Guild.

"The books can wait," she finally answered. "Until we finish talking about what *you* want to talk about."

The words caught him mid-breath. He wasn't expecting such ... interest. Could it be that she really could read his thoughts, even with his back turned?

His first inclination was to deny that anything was different, that there was really nothing that he wanted ... or Fates forbid ... *needed* to talk about.

But it didn't matter what he said, she would see through it all as soon as he turned around. And if he didn't turn around ... well, she would know anyway!

It was time to be honest. He didn't have to tell everything, but at least he could be truthful.

"Your friend has apparently left us. Will you leave too?" he said, as he slowly turned around.

Her mouth began to open, but nothing came out. She was disarmed in the face of so much honesty. She tried a couple of times, but her hypocrisy wouldn't let her speak. She was willing to take anything he was willing to give, but she had decided, a long time ago, that she would dance with the bear ... to get what she wanted ... but would give nothing in return.

When her eyes went to the floor, he knew he had his answer. Not surprising, but he had lied to himself so long, he had begun to believe his fantasy. Hope will do that if you believe strong enough.

Despite it all, he still wanted to spare her the discomfort she was feeling.

"You can stay as long as you like. But when you are ready to go ... please let one of my Aides know, and they will assist you in packing, and making sure you have provisions enough for your trip."

He watched her study the floor. Her inability to look him in the eyes was a surprise. She was probably the strongest woman that he knew. Okay, if it was that hard, he would make it even easier.

"Zephra … it has been one of the greatest pleasures of my life, to watch you grow into a woman of knowledge and power. When you return home, the Tinkers will be so surprised," he finished with a warm smile.

Good, she looked up at the mention of the Tinkers. He wanted her to see his smile. A gem of truth, that he was genuinely happy for her.

If she thought his words were hard, well, the smile simply did her in. The tears flowed freely as she held her hand over her mouth, not wanting him to see her trembling lips.

"I uh … I uh," she tried to begin, but she was too overwhelmed with emotion. Her eyes went to the floor again.

"I would like it if we can stay friends. If you have questions, or need a good book to read, you could write," he offered, still determined to relieve her of her discomfort.

Finally, she nodded in appreciation, as she turned and walked through his door, grateful for his kind efforts to bring her misery to an end.

Chapter 28 - The shift in power

Kareen appeared out of thin air as he always did.

"I am going to give you those hand-held weapons that you wanted," he declared.

"I thought that wasn't possible. My request cannot exceed our culture," Bernado reminded him.

"Things have ... moved ... allowing a change. Now, I am able to give you *more*."

Bernado was sure that the *move* that Kareen mentioned, was about balance between the two Alien Powers. Perhaps someone had found another Crystal Amulet. Allowing Kareen to give Bernado *more* and re-establish *balance*.

"But these weapons are to be given to a select few," Kareen continued. "You will give them directions, to a Master Cave located in Shaksbah. There are a group of men that you call Specialist Trackers, that are headed for this location. Their intent is to open the door of this Cave. If they succeed, your ambitions to become Emperor will be crushed. I will be back in a few days, with the weapons. Have the men ready."

'Another piece of valuable information,' Bernado thought to himself. The game had changed. Which meant that the rules had changed for Kareen. Further confirmation that these Aliens from Harleem were controlled by someone else.

More than ever, Bernado was desperate to find the secret that would keep him on the Emperor's Throne forever. The Golden Necklace already guaranteed him immortality. But when the Game was over ... he knew that his life was forfeit ... unless he had a plan.

He wasn't sure yet what that plan would be. But he knew that the day was coming when he would know. And then the Colossus would fall.

A brief bow of the head confirmed Bernado's willingness to follow Kareen's instructions. "Of course," he added reassuringly, as the Alien disappeared, leaving behind the familiar wisps of Green Light.

Chapter 29 - A halo of soft light

Previously, Yaneek saw a prisoner escorted from a wagon into Bernado's House. He was dressed like a Tracker and had a young athletic build like Protas. It was all the encouragement she needed to finally enter the House, to see if Protas was there.

Yaneek and Sausage had barely turned onto the Boulevard when she saw the commotion at Bernado's house. They stopped and watched, as the two wounded Trackers, eventually made good their escape.

As she turned to retrace her steps, Bernado was already outside shouting orders to his Guards.

Yaneek was holding the leash with a fierceness that reflected her terror.

"Sausage, this doesn't look so good. I was hoping that eventually I might just walk in there, when Bernado was away, and at least find out if Protas was a prisoner inside the House."

The dog gave a soft bark as they walked briskly towards her wagon.

She couldn't imagine what had set off the incident with the escaping Trackers, but she had learned that Bernado was willing to kill, to protect whatever was in that House.

They were within fifty paces of the wagon when Sausage slowed in his approach. Yaneek placed a hand on the dog's neck, matching his speed as she stared straight ahead. Suddenly the dog began to growl softly.

She thought it might be a thief, busy looking for things in her wagon. But she felt confident with Sausage at her side. So, she continued, as she picked up the pace. Besides, she didn't want him to find her money. That would change everything.

She was twenty paces from the wagon when a man suddenly jumped down. She had expected that whomever was in the wagon, would run away, as soon as they knew that she was approaching with her dog. That's what a thief would do.

But in fact, he stood there facing her, as though he knew her.

She halted. Uncertain about what to do. She did not want to abandon the wagon. That was for sure. It was her home, her transportation. Everything she owned was in that wagon.

As if sensing her uncertainty, Sausage began to growl and bared his teeth. 'True enough,' she thought, 'I do have another option.'
But then in response, the man opened his cloak, so she could clearly see the weapons he was carrying.
With her one hand still on the neck of Sausage, the other hand flew to her mouth, anxious to suppress a whimper of fear.
"I mean you no harm," the man said in a firm voice. "My assignment is to bring you to the House of Bernado. I suggest you send the dog away."
The stern look confirmed that he would use his weapons if he had to.

While she listened to the man speak, another part of her consciousness recognized a steady flow of warmth, that moved from the dog's neck, into her hand and then travelled upwards until she felt a distinct impression.
She was extremely curious about what had just happened. But circumstances demanded she set aside her curiosity for another time.
"Sausage ... you better go. I will find you later."
The dog looked up at her, as he hesitated.
"Sausage, you must go," she said more firmly.
As the dog bounded away, the man closed his cloak. Then he stepped aside as he invited her to climb into the wagon.

--------- <> ---------

Yaneek noticed that the weapon above, swiveled in their direction, as they walked up to the front door of Bernado's House.

She was escorted inside, and then through a door, at the left.
"Stay here," the spy said with finality.

She almost laughed. Moments earlier, she had witnessed a *Tracker* trying to escape. It didn't look to her like that was a complete success.
'No,' she thought to herself, 'you don't have to worry about me trying to run away.'
She sighed as she realized that she was probably going to be captive for a long time.

She surveyed the room. She saw a large, partially opened window, and several comfortable chairs along one wall. 'This must be where they put visitors who wait to see Bernado.' She sat down and began to think about what was coming next.

'Well, at least I made it inside,' she congratulated herself. 'And sooner or later, I will find out if Protas is here ... or not.'

She closed her eyes and let out a soft sigh as she considered the potential irony, if indeed it turned out to be ... 'or not'.

But that didn't seem right. She had felt something as her hand rested upon the dog.

'Actually,' she corrected herself, 'my hand was mostly on the collar. Interesting ...' she thought. But she knew she would have plenty of time in the long lonely days ahead, to work that out.

For now, what she did know, was the *feeling* that accompanied the warmth. And that was why, she wasn't afraid to go with the man. It felt like she was supposed to do that. And she certainly wasn't worried about the dog. Sausage knew how to take care of himself.

After a while she thought about Zephra's wagon. She walked to the window, hoping to see it. There it was. She wondered how long it would take them to find the money. It probably didn't matter. She most likely had driven the wagon for the last time.

Zephra had made a great sacrifice by giving her the wagon. And already it was gone.

She went back to the chair, as she thought about her good friend. She remembered her last words, *'Yaneek, you must be very careful when it comes to Bernado. He cannot be trusted.'*

And here she sat, inside Bernado's fortress.
Wagon gone, money gone, and Sausage gone.
'Wonder what you would say to me now?'
She could see her friend's face and imagined her saying, "Have courage and be strong."

As she thought about that phrase, her eyes wandered in the direction of where she knew Guards were positioned by the front door. Then she looked upwards, past the ceiling, where more Guards manned the Turrets that wounded the Tracker as he escaped. Then she looked towards the back of the Mansion. She wondered what was back there ... waiting for her.

She couldn't help it, but it made her think of Benekee lying on the floor of his cell, beaten almost to death. Her heartbeat increased, and her hands began to tremble.

She closed her eyes as she thought, 'Zephra, I don't know if I can do this.'

--------- <> ---------

After the spy left his captive in the visiting room, he headed straight for Bernado's office.

"I have the woman I told you about. Her wagon has been moved to the side of the house. The wheels are chained."

As Bernado moved towards the window, the spy remembered something else he wanted to say. "Of course, I checked the wagon thoroughly, and found the usual. But I also found, a wagon that is designed after the War Wagons that Craslin has. And I mean the best ones, the ones he got from the Tinkers."

Bernado was now at the window. He recognized Zephra's wagon.

"Why do you think it's important that this wagon has the same design as the Tinker War Wagon?" He said as he turned to the spy.

The spy shrugged his shoulders in indifference and said, "I'm paid to observe."

Bernado's eyes returned to the wagon. The spy was right. Sometimes the smallest detail could bring forth valuable intelligence.

As his thoughts floated backwards to the first time he was shown the War Wagons at Craslin's Guild, he remembered thinking, 'Why hasn't anyone thought of this before?'

He asked the man, who delivered the wagons, if he would take him for a ride. The design was elegant, and the handling of the wagon was beyond his expectations. On the way back to the Guild, he started in with more questions.

"Where does this design come from?"

"How could one Blacksmith and his son, expand the technology so far forward, in such a short period of time?"

"Has anyone been able to improve upon it?"

Apparently, Shu-len, showed up at the Blacksmith Guild one day with a common Utility Wagon, that he had improved. The Blacksmith was hoping to patent the improvements.

But that was never going to happen. Because the changes were revolutionary, not minor, the only kind that *could* be patented by an individual.

Instead, they immediately formed an Alliance between the Blacksmith and Transportation Guilds. By studying the wagon, along with the advanced metallurgical formulas, as supplied by Shu-len, they could build a duplicate.

As the Blacksmith and Transportation Alliance prepared for wide scale production of the new Utility Wagons, Craslin approached them with a *very* large order for War Wagons.

But there was more to the story. Because the initial shipment of War Wagons, that came from the new Tinker Guild, were indeed *improved* ... compared to Shu-len's model.

Again, a manifestation of genius.

It wasn't that Craslin wasn't satisfied with the one hundred wagons, he had ordered from the Tinkers, but it would have taken forever for the Tinkers to supply the one thousand War Wagons that he wanted. So Craslin went with the 'almost as good' technology offered by the Alliance.

But, strange as it now seemed to Bernado, no one had ever bothered to question the genesis of the wagon design.

It was assumed that Shu-len was the man behind the creation. A reasonable assumption based on what he knew and had accomplished.

But ... how were the Tinkers able to improve on the original design?

The Tinkers were always regarded as mysterious ... their ways not easily understood. So, it was understandable that no one questioned their sudden delivery of an 'improved' wagon. Besides, it was rumoured that the son of Shu-len, was living with the Tinkers. That explained how the Tinkers were able to build the original design ... but not where the improvement came from. And to support that, when pushed by the Alliance, Shu-len was incapable of improving on the original design.

So ... that could mean only one thing.

Someone else was involved!

Someone that assisted both Shu-len and the Tinkers. But who?

And that wasn't a question that was easily answered, because that *someone else*, had been carefully hidden behind a curtain of secrecy.

Bernado sighed in resignation, wishing he knew the secrets of Zephra's wagon.

He remembered clearly the first time he saw it. He had walked to his window to see who had just rolled into the wagon yard of his Tracking Guild.

He had to look twice.

Tinkers *never* associated with anyone. And yet, there it was, in all its colourful glory.

The Tinker wagon, and a young Tinker woman, by the name of Zephra.

She was so naïve. It was so easy to pull information from her.

She had come looking for *'Seven Trackers including a young man ... by the name of Urshen.'*

Soon he had sent her and her two young friends on their way.

Other than finding out that Gaeten was really Urshen, he had considered this a minor event in an otherwise very busy day.

At least that was what he had determined at the time ... based on earlier efforts to extract more information from 'Gaeten'.

The young man had been beaten, subjected to Olleti, and all that he could get out of him, when questioned regarding the Amulet, was ... *I'm less tired and never sick when I wear it.*

Urshen seemed like a *nobody*, who lucked into an Amulet of limited power.

And ... it had always been a mystery why Kareen was so interested in Urshen.

And ... Urshen had lied about his name.

And ... was Zephra just another wandering Tinker ... or was she *sent* by the Tinkers?

'Hmm,' he wondered. 'I think I have missed something extremely important.'

'What if ... Urshen wasn't a nobody? After all, he resisted the second Medallion.'

'What if ... Zephra was looking for a Tinker possession that was lost?'

'What if ... the *someone else*, the genius behind the Tinker's wagon, was right here in my prison cell?' He mused.

'And what if ... this *someone else* ... knew how to use a Crystal Amulet to re-design the common wagon!'

"So ... you are responsible for this *incredible* design," Bernado said to himself.

"Pardon, didn't catch that," the spy said.

"I wish to question the woman," Bernado said without taking his gaze from the wagon.

"Bring her here immediately." Bernado was already rubbing his hands in excitement. Yaneek, another nobody, was somehow part of this inner circle of power, that attracted the interest of Kareen-del-Harleem. He was sure of it!

When Yaneek entered the room, Bernado was already wearing the Golden necklace.

She stared at it for a moment, having never seen anything like it before.

The spy pushed her into a chair and then left the room.

Bernado walked towards her and then suddenly threw a small object as he said, "catch."

She gasped as she caught the stone, and soon she was falling through a dark space.

With his hand on the second Medallion, Bernado closed his eyes as he considered the questions he would ask. As usual, he could see a smoky image held bound by the power of the stone.

But there was also something terrifyingly similar. There was a halo of soft light that surrounded her body. It was the same thing he saw when he tried to question Urshen.

Without any hesitation, he ripped his hand from the Necklace. He heard another sharp gasp as Yaneek was released from the power of the stone.

Instinctively she threw it to the floor.

As if it had a mind of its own, the stone rolled in a semi-circle ... until it stopped at Bernado's feet.

Chapter 30 - The cage of deceit

Bernado watched the rolling stone until it came to a stop. He was tempted to pick it up, but first, he checked the room, to see if Kareen was there. He wasn't. Maybe he was asleep. Or maybe his current failure to use the Necklace against Yaneek, wasn't enough of a reason for this Alien Visitor to take it away.

The trembling inside was mostly gone. The Black Wind was not an experience he wished to repeat. He hated the image of that Halo!

He shouted for a Guard to escort the young woman back to the waiting room. He wasn't ready to place her in a cell ... just yet.

As soon as Yaneek was taken away, he closed his eyes to steady his mind ... and to consider the questions that needed to be answered.

'What was this *Halo* and why did it surround Urshen and Yaneek?'
'Could it have something to do with the Amulet?'
'Did this mean that Yaneek also has an Amulet ... or used one in the past?'
'Could it be that using the Amulet left behind ... a stain, seen as a Halo of light when viewed through the power of the green stone?'
'Is it why Urshen had the power to defend himself against the Black Wind, even though the Amulet was taken from him?'

It must be why Kareen was so interested in Urshen *and* the Specialist Tracker who stole the Amulet away from Bernado. Apparently, if someone uses the Amulet, it makes them 'special'.
And that must mean that the young woman had used an Amulet as well.

These thoughts made him smile. Albeit, a weak smile. It was all he could manage with the Black Wind still on his mind. But it was, nonetheless, a sign of his victory.
He had gained *bargaining power* against his Alien Visitor!
He knew he had just acquired another specimen that Kareen would be desperate to have.
Yaneek.

And Bernado was certain that it didn't stop there.

He was sure he had a 'third specimen' ... Protas!

It was how the two young men escaped their prison cells. They used an Amulet!

Neither of them should have had one, but if he had to guess, his bets were on Protas.

Besides, the Guards had told Bernado that when they found them, there was also a dog.

Bernado took a deep breath as he walked towards Protas's prison cell. If he didn't see the Halo of light he would still question Protas. But he was sure that he would. And that was all he needed to know.

The next day as Bernado left his Mansion, he looked up at the manned Turrets. 'Incredible technology that defies a genesis,' he thought to himself. 'Must be an Amulet in there somewhere.'

But Benekee was a puzzle. He obviously had access to an Amulet. It was the reason he, and he alone, could improve on his original Brass Sling design. But his spies assured him that there was *no* Amulet.

'No Amulet the spies could see,' Bernado agreed. But Benekee, somehow, *had* access to the power. Perhaps the Amulet was somewhere else ... and he had a way of using its power without holding it! It didn't make sense. But it had to be.

'This could very well be an insurmountable problem,' thought Bernado. It would be like containing a prisoner who possessed an Amulet. Not something he savoured thinking about. He preferred to use the Necklace on individuals of lesser ability.

Besides, three hostages were still a remarkable offer. He would have to think carefully about what he wanted before he contacted Kareen. But then ... perhaps the Alien already knew about his three *special* prisoners.

'Hmm,' he considered. If that proved to be the case, he couldn't give up on Benekee. He still might need to play a high card sometime in the future.

But ... how was he supposed to defeat someone like Benekee?

Then one day, while looking out his window at Yaneek's wagon, he realized the answer was in front of him all along. 'Leverage!' he excitedly thought. His sister was his prisoner!

Of course, he had to be *delicate* in a situation like this.

Even though he had the mother bear's cub, it didn't guarantee a smooth road to Benekee's submission.

He must get close to Benekee. Find out all about him.

--------- <> ---------

"Did you ever think that your Brass Sling would be capable of killing so many people so quickly?" Bernado asked him one day, searching for the hidden jewels of his thinking.

Benekee shrugged, unwilling to comment.

To Bernado, the response was unconvincing. He already knew, that the moral integrity of the young man ran deeper than most.

"Have you ever seen your machine kill someone?" Bernado decided to take a more direct approach, hoping to get a response.

"No," was all he would say. But he wouldn't look at the Guild Master. In fact, he looked away, pretending to be interested in something in the distance.

'Right on target!' gloated Bernado. All he needed to do, was to arrange for a mass killing of innocents, and let the news leak back to Benekee. He would be destroyed. Incapable of using his power ever again.

'But then ... that would be messy.' It might even be an issue with Craslin. He needed to find a solution that was *elegant*.

'A smaller group ... perhaps even one? ... If the one was Yaneek.'

He turned and smiled at Benekee, knowing the boy's future was already destined for a cage of deceit.

Chapter 31 - Wagons roll

It was later than usual as the two men sat across from each other, ready to discuss the expansion of the 'Empire'.

"Nusdek feels the Militia Guard is ready. Further delay would work against us. The men are *ready* to march."

"What about my personal Guards?"

"He has expanded the Wall to five thousand. These men are the best we have. I suggested he increase the size from your recommended one thousand ... to protect Qar-ana once the others have moved south. Until we conquer Kel-eetan, we are vulnerable to a counter attack. Best to be prepared."

"What about the War Wagons and ships?"

"War Wagons number twelve hundred, all fitted with the new *rapid-firing* Brass Sling. The *six* Silver Sea Shipping Schooners are finished. The additional ships have been purchased, and crews hired, ready to take our Militia to Shaksbah ... from both Port Airiken and Port Aqabah.

"I have prepared papers, ready for your signature, that show that these vessels now belong to the Planning and Development Guild of Qar-ana." Bernado laid the papers on the desk for signature.

"Excellent," Craslin responded as he signed and sealed the documents. "But what about the men ... how are they to be paid?"

"I have promised them payment of gold before the ships set sail. Again, I need you to sign this paper to release the gold."

Craslin readily signed the paper. When it came to Bernado, one thing he didn't worry about was the gold, which had been minted into gold coins. His spies confirmed that Bernado was above reproach. There was never as much as a coin that went missing. Bernado made sure of that. It was as though he thought the gold belonged to himself.

Passing the paper to Bernado, Craslin said, "Everything is ready then?"

"Yes. Nusdek will lead thirty-five thousand Militia through Border Pass and on to Kel-eetan." That was a lie. Kareen had recently advised Bernado, that Nusdek was to take the best three hundred of the Wall to a destination in the Shaksbali Mountains ... where a Cave was located.

"You will go with them?"

"Of course." That was a lie, his plan was to stay behind and dispose of Craslin.

"Are you still sure we should send five thousand to each port?"

"Yes," he continued. "The objective of the main force is to take the Capital. The two pincer movements coming from the west and eastern shores, will convince the rest of the population, that there is a new Government ruling Shaksbah." That was the truth.

"What about the El-Bhat prisoners, can we use them to collect taxes and manage the flow of goods into Storlenia?" Craslin suggested.

"They have never responded well to control, outside their own Quorum. Besides, they never surrender. I suggest we use the taxes to maintain part of our Militia inside Shaksbah and use the reserves of gold to build the Empire."

Craslin had listened quietly as Bernado laid out the plan of conquest ... and *watched* to understand. Bernado was a brilliant Commanding Officer of the Militia Guard. He had achieved more than Craslin had hoped for and in a shorter time than he thought possible.

He wanted to believe that Regent was enough for the ambitions of Bernado. But his eyes told him something that his ears could not.

His eyes knew that Bernado's plan included killing Craslin, along with the Government Officials of Shaksbah.

It was, after all, not too difficult to see. Craslin had done the same thing to Axion.

It was time to give orders to Nusdek. Orders that would have Bernado disappear once the Militia Guard was on the move.

"A world without El-Bhat," Craslin smiled, "and taxes collected from Shaksbah to run Shaksbah. And a limitless supply of gold to build an Empire, greater than any this world has ever seen."

"The plan is magnificent," Bernado smiled in return.

Bernado was smiling because he never intended on leaving Qar-ana. He would need to stay behind and hold the reins of power once Craslin was dead.

Craslin was smiling because he was finished with Bernado. He would die at Border Pass. It was unfortunate. He would have made a great Regent over Shaksbah. But the man was too ambitious.

--------- <> ---------

Bernado returned to his living quarters, feeling triumphant on many fronts.

Now that he had the loyalty of Nusdek, the Militia was his, and they would leave within the week. So simple.

Then there was the triumph of *using* Craslin. The man was extremely talented, and had moved the position of Emperor within reach, faster than he had ever thought possible. But now his usefulness was over and within days, he would be dead. So simple.

Then there was the anticipated triumph against the Alien Power. Because Bernado understood, that there was a 'Referee', and he knew 'why' Kareen wanted his prisoners!

He could hardly wait to sign the Harvesting Contract ... because he would bargain, and he knew what to ask for!

So simple!

Chapter 32 - Zephra's genetics

Three days later, Craslin was looking out his large windows, at the people gathering and moving towards the Guild entrance. This was where he saw Zephra for the first time.

For the last few days, his Aides informed him that Zephra was either in her room or in the Library. The charade was over for Zephra. She couldn't bear to face Craslin.

But for him, he knew, it would never be over. So … he needed a way to express his love every day. And that way, was to *watch over* her.
This way, even after she left, his spies could keep him informed. He would make sure that she was always safe and wanted for nothing. Her joys would be his joys. Eventually he would enter correspondence with her. Send her books as he promised. It wasn't perfect, but he could survive.

But that plan was about to shatter. On the third day of not seeing Zephra, he was informed that Bernado had come to see him, about a very important matter.
'Good, something to take my mind off Zephra,' he thought.

Bernado walked out onto the balcony and then closed the doors behind Craslin, signifying that this was to be a *very* private meeting.
Craslin lifted an eyebrow, showing his surprise and sending an invitation for Bernado to begin.
"I have a friend, a very powerful friend, that is interested in … certain people. For a long time, I thought that the interest in these people was mostly because they were *clever* … like us.
"But then one day, I realized how wrong I was." Bernado offered a thin smile.
"The truth, was that these people, had access to Crystal Amulets. Do you know, that one of these talismans was once in my possession? Yes, but I couldn't use it. For some reason, it didn't 'like' me. Probably a good thing, considering I probably would have ended up, as another possession of my powerful friend.
"But I digress. Allow me to return to the Crystal Amulets. You see, the Amulet that I tried to use, belonged to Urshen. And then, a Specialist Tracker showed up one day at the doorstep of my Guild, with a very special

Necklace ... of gold. A Necklace with unique powers. But then of course, you know about that.

"Anyway, this Specialist Tracker didn't want the Gold Necklace, but went straight to the Crystal Amulet that I had taken from Urshen. And ever since then, my powerful friend has a burning interest in making this Specialist Tracker, his possession."

Bernado turned and stared out at the Gardens below. "Sometimes the simplest things can evade one's analysis. Like the fact that wearing this Crystal Amulet, increases the value of someone ... immensely! At least to my powerful friend.

"And once I realized this strange fact, I remembered something else that I had long since forgotten. The day that a Tinker woman arrived at my Guild in Pechora, with two of her friends ... wearing something that reminded me of a Crystal Amulet. Although it was much smaller. I guess that's why I never thought about it."

After a short pause, he turned to face Craslin, his hands resting on his long knives. "But now, it's all so very clear. And that's why I've come to see you today. My powerful friend wants ... Zephra."

Craslin glared back at Bernado with eyes of fire.

Ordinarily, he would call for Nusdek. And then this matter ... and his agreement to let Bernado rule Shaksbah ... would be over.

But something had changed!

Bernado no longer acted like he was dependent on Craslin for his power.

He was now making demands ... on behalf of his 'powerful friend'.

And, most importantly, Craslin was *sure* that Nusdek was now on the end of Bernado's leash.

Somehow, he must save Zephra!

Craslin ripped his eyes from Bernado and stared out at the Gardens. He needed a moment to think.

When he turned back, his expression was blank. But he nodded in agreement and asked, "How soon?"

Bernado smiled.

Craslin's response told him that the contest was over. Craslin knew that the Militia belonged to Bernado.

And he was now ... the Emperor.

And as Emperor, his first expression of power, would be gracious. After all, he owed Craslin something.

"You may keep her for two days," Bernado answered, and then left.

--------- <> ---------

Craslin watched Bernado leave the Guild. It felt strange to know that he was at the end ... rather than the beginning.

His life was over. But he still had a chance to save Zephra.

If he was *very* careful.

Careful, because Bernado was using the Gold Necklace again. He had retrieved the small green stone.

"It certainly was not removed by the hand of any mortal," the Master Spy had said on the evening they discovered its disappearance. "No ... there is a dark power in operation here."

The Spy moved a chair to allow better visibility of the hole in the stone wall. He poked his finger into the empty space where once there was a solid piece of rock.

"I assume this hole was not here yesterday," he remarked to Craslin. The Spy turned to receive Craslin's response, who was nodding 'correct'.

Saving Zephra would be no small feat. But if anyone could succeed, it was the Master Spy. He alone had put an end to the long list of Craslin's missing infiltrators. He was the one that came back, every time ... no matter how difficult the mission.

He had sent out word for him to come as quickly as possible.

Suddenly, behind him, there was a soft noise. He knew it was The Spy ... and the noise was only a courtesy.

He turned around.

"Thank you for coming," Craslin said sincerely. "The bag is for you."

The Spy walked towards the desk. The bag was a traditional beggar's bag, big enough to carry food, water and a small blanket. He could see right away that it was full.

The Spy dipped his hand inside the bag and pulled out a few gold coins. "That's a lot of gold," the Spy said, surprised.

"If you think you can get a larger bag out of the building without attracting suspicion ..." Craslin offered, indicating his willingness to give more.

The Master Spy hefted the bag with a grunt.

"No ... there's plenty enough here," he said as he let the bag fall to the table with a thud.

"It's really ... several assignments," Craslin began. "Perhaps you've seen the young lady that lives here in the Guild?"

The Spy nodded in the affirmative.

"Her life is now in extreme danger. Within a couple of days, she will be taken to the House of Bernado, and disappear forever. I'm afraid that whatever is left of her life will be ... unpleasant." Craslin closed his eyes and rubbed his temples as he contemplated what he would say next.

"You see," he started again, "I've grown quite attached to her. But as you know, Bernado has very powerful resources.

"Tomorrow, I plan to have the evening meal with her. But there cannot be any spies to overhear what I will say. This is your first assignment.

"Secondly, after Zephra is taken to the House of Bernado, you must find a way to rescue her and take her somewhere safe. She will probably want to go to Arborville. She is from there.

"You wouldn't know it now, but she's a Tinker and would most likely want to return to the village the Tinkers have built.

"But I wouldn't recommend it. You need to know that Bernado will do everything he can to bring her back. So ... I will leave the rest of the plan up to you. That way, no one will know ... including me," he added softly.

"I have no idea how long you will need to take care of her. But the gold should last a long time," Craslin was back to sounding official. Is everything clear?"

The Spy nodded ... slowly, as if there was something else ... something missing.

"What is it you want to say?" Craslin encouraged.

"Why are you doing this? Knowing Bernado, you'll never survive the week if I am successful."

There was the smallest melancholy grin and then finally Craslin said, "You better take that gold before someone steals it from you."

Without hesitation, the Spy snatched the bag and disappeared like the ghost he was.

Chapter 33 - The missing bricks

Previously, Ou-Leesen-el-Bra-ten summoned a stranger through the power of the Dagger of Truth, to take a message, warning the five thousand El-Bhat, positioned north of Kel-eetan, that they were betrayed and must meet him at the Mines of Tenleth.

In the hollow of sand dunes, sat a large eight-sided, partially buried, metal platform. On top of that platform, piled to twice the height of a man, sat red bricks under the burning hot sun.

Looking down from the crest of one of those dunes, sat Ou-Leesen-el-Bra-ten, his Advisor Stek and half of his twenty trusted followers. The other half remained behind at the last oasis with the government officials and the adopted El-Bhat they had picked up from Arl-Sheen.

The size of the metal platform was as large as a small village. "What can you tell me about this metal platform," Stek asked Ou-Leesen-el-Bra-ten, "it looks foreign, like the Dagger of truth."

The El-Bhat warrior urged his horse down the sandy slope, as he searched the memories of Shanteef.

"This is the work of the Green Lady," he shared with Stek as they arrived at the base of the platform. "The Green Lady and those that she serves have strong appetites ... for certain things. Like gold."

"I have a feeling that you knew, without doubt, that we would find the gold bricks, right here," Stek said as he followed Ou-Leesen-el-Bra-ten around the perimeter of the gold. The El-Bhat warrior gave a look of affirmation to his Advisor.

"Which means that there is another reason why we are here," Stek added as the small group came to a halt.

Around the entire perimeter, the top of the red bricks formed a perfect line against the bright blue sky ... except where Ou-Leesen-el-Bra-ten was now staring.

"This is *why* we're here, isn't it?" Stek looked at the El-Bhat leader. "The missing bricks." Stek's gaze returned to the gaping hole in the wall. "Looks like about a hundred," the Tracker estimated.

"Yes ... it is why we are here." The words were followed by a sigh of resignation. He had assumed that no one knew the whereabouts of the El-Bhat gold. His plan was to take the one hundred bricks with him, and then on the road to Tenleth, he would invite the Visitor, through the Dagger, to return and take his promised gold.

"Do you know who stole the bricks?" Stek asked, anxious to understand Ou-Leesen's concern.

"They were not stolen," the El-Bhat replied. "They were promised ... by me. As payment to send a message to my El-Bhat warriors."

Suddenly Stek saw the connection as he remembered the planned ambush against the thousands of El-Bhat, waiting north of Kel-eetan. "The deal seems fair," Stek challenged the furrowed brow. "A few gold bricks for the lives of many."

"Advisor," the Warrior began as he encouraged his horse forward, "we will need gold to trade with the Merchants at the Oases. Bring enough."

Stek watched for a while as Ou-Leesen-el-Bra-ten and his small band of El-Bhat made their way up the slopes of the sand dunes.

The Tracker reflected on his own question, *'who stole the bricks?'* as he watched them disappear at the top of the dunes. The El-Bhat Leader had decided not to answer Stek, but the Tracker was sure it was important. He would bring it up later when the Warrior was ready to talk.

For now, he had another question that needed to be explored.

He quickly scaled the wall to the gaping hole, created by the missing bricks. He carefully counted the missing bricks. "Interesting", he said to himself, as he filled his saddle bags with bricks and jumped down.

On the way back to the oasis, Stek returned to the unfinished conversation. "What part of the deal disturbs you?"

"My Visitor is in league with the Green Lady. He implied he wasn't, but he has the power to take the gold that I promised, as easily as he can appear to me. This tells me he has the power of the Green Light."

"But you still have the gold," Stek replied.

"I have nothing," Ou-Leesen-el-Bra-ten retorted as he pulled the Dagger of Truth from his scabbard, "as long as I continue to use this."

Stek rode in silence as he considered what Ou-Leesen had shared. When he spoke again, the shimmering image of the oasis, could be seen in the distance, as the group came to a halt.

"At the Capital, you told me that you had cast off the Green Lady for good, and that the Dagger of Truth was now yours. That it would do your bidding. You must now believe that this was an allusion. That you have only traded one master for another."

The El-Bhat warrior was nodding slowly, a sign that his Advisor understood.

"You told me before, that you cannot simply throw it away. What if I carry it for you?" Stek suggested.

"It would be a poor bargain. I am certain that we would both end up trapped by its power. At least this way, I still have my Advisor," Ou-Leesen-el-Bra-ten said, his voice betraying his feelings of hopelessness.

"Yes, you do ... and he wishes to speak," Stek said with determination, reminding him that he was still an Advisor of some worth.

Stek usually waited for Ou-Leesen to invite him to speak. Curious, the El-Bhat looked over at his travelling companion, his bright green eyes set in a face of stone. A witness of his unconquerable spirit.

"If your words are pleasing to me ... I will let you live," the El-Bhat sent him a warrior's grin.

"Then pleasing they will be," Stek reassured him.

"I wish to begin by asking a question. If this Visitor who bargained for one hundred gold bricks is so powerful ... and his lust for gold is equally powerful ... then why didn't he take *more* than one hundred? I counted carefully, and he indeed took *exactly* one hundred bricks ... from an *ocean* of gold bricks."

Ou-Leesen-el-Bra-ten was intrigued by the observation. "Why indeed," the Warrior agreed.

He urged his horse forward as he thought about the apparent absurdity. The others followed.

"We don't know everything about this strange Green Power," Stek continued, "but we know some things ... things that might be quite useful. Here is what I believe we know so far.

"First, it *is* possible to defeat the power of the Green Lady. Granted, you might be the only one in our history to have ever done this, and the power behind the Green Lady was quick to replace her with this Visitor of which you have spoken ... but this only confirms to me that you defeated her!

"Secondly ... we also know that despite their enormous power, they are apparently constrained by some *other* power. It is the only thing that explains why the Visitor was anxious to make a deal with you, and then was honour bound to stay within the details of that agreement. To the last brick."

"In the future, you are never to leave my side," Ou-Leesen-el-Bra-ten ordered his Advisor. He saw his mistake and was determined that the next time he stood before the Visitor, Stek would keep him right.

They were close enough to the oasis that they could smell the water and fragrant Canopy Trees. Soon his loyal men of twenty would gather around, expecting instructions, regarding their journey to the Mines of Tenleth.

But Ou-Leesen-el-Bra-ten was troubled by how events were ripping apart his vision of change.

It was no longer as simple, as replacing the Shaksbali Government with men of his choosing.

He no longer believed that the gold was all he needed to bring about his plans.

And he definitely did not believe that the Dagger of Truth was his to control.

Rather, he believed what Stek had said about the Visitor ... and the *other* power that sat above the Green Lady and forced her followers to submit to constraints.

But how was he to walk the narrow Path of Hope ... between these two forces. Or was the path only an allusion?

Were the people of Ankoletia like children's puppets that danced to the superstitions of belief ... about these two powers?

Were *even* the Sherilin deceived about life and its purposes?

He looked over at Stek and thought about whom his Advisor might say was the *other power*. 'Caves' ... would probably be his reply. But even if Ou-Leesen-el-Bra-ten, the new Leader of the El-Bhat, accepted that reply ... what was the *intent* of the power behind the Caves?

Protas had told him that the Caves had both killed *and* healed Storlenians. These were strange words for the ears of an El-Bhat warrior. He had been taught that Caves were to be feared, as they always killed El-Bhat and favored the Storlenians.

But ever since Border Pass ... that truth had been challenged. At first, he stubbornly refused to think about it. He had to. The implications were terrifying. If the threat from the Caves, considered to be a very sacred part of the El-Bhat teachings, was untrue, then ... what was he supposed to believe?

Yes, in the beginning, it was easier not think about it.

But then he met Protas, and Biskin, and Stek.

Then he began to question the Dagger of Truth, the most sacred talisman of the El-Bhat.

Then he acquired Shanteef's memories which completely shattered whatever honour was left of his El-Bhat traditions.

So now ... he was re-considering the world that surrounded him.

Perhaps the Caves *were* this other power.

But if so ... why were he and his fellow warriors allowed to live, while his comrades fell dead all around them.

Circumstances since then, suggested that he was spared, that he might learn about the corruption that existed among his own people.

Or ... was he simply chosen to be the puppet that these two fickle powers would play with?

Maybe all his plans were like dust in the wind. Maybe there was nothing to be done. Maybe the contest of life would always be between these two giants of supremacy.

He didn't remember riding into the camp, but his reverie was suddenly broken as his men rushed to gather around.

He looked down into their eager faces. Men who had been spared from death at Border Pass like himself. They were ready to follow his commands!

For *them*, he would push through the fog of confusion. For *them*, he would find a way to bring sanity to all the madness that surrounded them.

"Tomorrow we leave for Tenleth. There we will meet the warriors of the El-Bhat nation and we will free the women and children. And this will only be the beginning!"

The men saluted with their swords and shouted "El-lukten coureese bin swofet!" Normally this phrase was invoked at the doorstep of the Keep and meant 'The Glory and power of the World!'

For his men to use this phrase here in the desert, meant that wherever Ou-Leesen-el-Bra-ten was ... there was the glory of the El-Bhat.

As the fires burned low, the Warrior's thoughts turned back to the dilemma of the two powers. He looked across the fire to the Tracker.

"Advisor, do you believe in the Fates?"

Stek stirred from his own thoughts. He too had been considering the path forward. He was a bit surprised by the question. The warrior was normally a very practical man.

"Yes." The single word summarized best the response he wished to give.

"Who are they? Are they above all? And if they are, who are we to them?"

Ou-Leesen-el-Bra-ten was like no other warrior, or Tracker, that Stek had ever met. His mind was curious beyond measure. And even more so when he rode the raging currents of life.

Stek stared into the fire for a while, considering how he might respond to such deep questions.

"In Storlenia," he began, "I have a little house with a wife and three children that give meaning to my life. Without them ... well ... life would be very hard. Perhaps, it is the same with the Fates above. Perhaps they need us like I need my family." Stek looked over at Ou-Leesen-el-Bra-ten, the firelight dancing off his green eyes.

Suddenly the warrior's face burst into a wide grin. "One thing I know ... even the Fates must have Advisors!"

The warrior was more pleased than he ever thought he could be, by Stek's answer. It made him think of his own father who had been dead for some time.

Once when Ou-Leesen was young, he questioned the decision of the Quorum about a matter between two El-Bhat communities. It didn't seem fair.

His father responded, "Son, you worry about *your* affairs, and let the Quorum worry about *theirs.*"

For that moment as the two sat across the fire, Ou-Leesen-el-Bra-ten felt the Path of Hope broaden. In his mind, he could see the two of them walking along that path, side by side.

He might never live to see his dreams fulfilled, but in the meantime, there were things that needed to be done.

The following day, as the small group began their journey to the Mines of Tenleth, Ou-Leesen-el-Bra-ten's thoughts returned to the powers that battled for the things of his world.

Until recently his understanding of those powers was simple. The Dagger of Truth was testament that the El-Bhat were meant to rule the world. The Caves, however, appeared to be friendly to the Storlenians and therefore were to be feared ... and buried whenever possible.

But recent events had taught him that things weren't so simple. It was a very hard lesson for a warrior as proud as Ou-Leesen-el-Bra-ten.

He wished he knew more about the Caves and was tempted to discuss the subject with Stek. But decided against it.

He expected that Stek's view of the Caves, was as singular as Ou-Leesen-el-Bra-ten's view of the Dagger ... before.

But who among his small band of followers knew anything of these matters? Unfortunately, warriors were bred to fight ... not to think. Thinking fell into the domain of the ... Quorum.

'Of course,' he suddenly realized. He had overlooked the obvious. Shanteef's memories!

Knowing what to ask, it didn't take long for an illuminating memory to surface.

To Shanteef the old man's hand felt like parchment. Soon to be his successor, he was the only one in the room ... as the Quorum Leader fought against the grip of death.

"There is one other thing that you need to know," the El-Bhat croaked. "A secret that has been preserved for centuries." He coughed from the exertion. With eyes closed he waited until he had enough strength to finish his story.

"As you know, we buried a Cave many years ago. Shortly afterward, a village, close to the Kel-eetan Mountains, heard about this. So, they sent representatives to let the Quorum know, that their ancestors had been worshiping at the entrance of another Cave, for generations.

"An altar had been built near the door, where twice a year the Light from the Cave bathed the villagers who had come to worship. They brought their sick ... who were healed. And the others lived long healthy lives.

"Up to this point, they kept their discovery a closely guarded secret. But they were horrified that the El-Bhat had buried the 'other' Cave ... and felt they needed to set the record straight!"

Re-living his anger towards the impudent villagers, sent the old El-Bhat into another coughing fit.

After he recovered, he resumed his story. "After giving their report, the then-living Quorum Leader sought guidance from the Dagger of Truth.

"Two instructions were given.

"First, several El-Bhat followed them back to their village and killed them all. And then after these assigned El-Bhat returned, with a leather map of the Cave's location, they were killed."

The old man reached for an ornate metal box at his side and removed a large piece of old leather. "This map shows the location of that Cave.

"Shanteef ... the second instruction warned of a time, when Storlenians would try to open the door of this

Cave. If they succeeded, this would mean death to the El-Bhat nation.

"But you needn't despair. When that time comes, the Dagger of Truth will warn the Keeper of the Dagger of Truth.

"For now, you must guard this map, and this secret, with your life."

Chapter 34 - The shifting sands of honour

The desert that covered the area between the Keep, the hidden El-Bhat gold and the Mines of Tenleth, was littered with oases of varying size. The carefully guarded whereabouts of these 'stations of refuge', were known only to the El-Bhat. It was what gave them undisputed ownership of these *desolate* lands.

Stek grinned at the thought. Ou-Leesen-el-Bra-ten's company of El-Bhat had travelled through bustling stations that were the size of a large town. The trade and commerce, untaxed by the government overlords of Kel-eetan, was amazing. The vast tracts of sand were in a way, an illusion of poverty ... but an illusion only to the 'outsiders' to these lands. The key to wealth, as always, was knowledge. Knowledge of the plentiful locations of these oases that connected a vast realm of industrious merchants.

He spit out some seeds from a pomegranate, something he had never tasted, nor seen before. So delicious, and so suited to the hot climate they travelled through.

Finished, Stek stood up and shook his black silk robe free of the ever-present sand. He had traded his Tracker outfit for the traditional black silk garment, once they had entered the desert.

It was time to find Ou-Leesen-el-Bra-ten. He had been around him long enough to know when something was amiss. Since they left Kel-eetan, these moments of despair had become more frequent. The El-Bhat Leader was certainly carrying a very heavy load.

No surprise ... he was by himself. Sitting under the shade of a Canopy Tree.

"Mind if I join you?"

He didn't even look up. Just a hand gesture, indicating Stek should sit beside him.

"I know we need to talk," Stek began in his usual direct approach. Ou-Leesen insisted on it.

"My guess is that it's something to do with that Dagger," Stek prompted.

Without looking at Stek, the warrior began.

"I wanted to know more about the layout and operation of the Mines of Tenleth before we arrived. This knowledge could save many lives as we fight to free the slaves ... and there are sure to be surprises.

"The Government troops of Kel-eetan ... or the Quorum ... can be counted on for that.

"And so, I have carefully searched the memories of Shanteef ... and even Arl-Sheen."

"Were you successful?" Stek asked.

"Yes ... but the memories revealed much more. Much more."

"I would like to know ..." Stek encouraged Ou-Leesen.

Before he continued, Ou-Leesen-el-Bra-ten scooped up a handful of sand and let it pour through the cracks in his fingers.

"The honour of our people has turned into a myth. Like sand it has slipped away without anyone knowing. Except for the Quorum, and those that have been tutored in their ways. Warriors of Blood ... at a level I had never thought possible."

It was hard for the El-Bhat Leader to continue his grievances against the El-Bhat Quorum and their dark Warriors. "There is no respect for the dead. They simply use an abandoned pit. It is half full.

"The workers are all kept in a prison camp. They never leave the Mines."

Ou-Leesen looked up at the El-Bhat as they moved about, in the late afternoon.

"Our people were given the contract of running the Mines, centuries earlier," Ou-Leesen-el-Bra-ten eventually continued. "No one else wanted the contracts. The working conditions are extremely harsh.

"The Quorum told our people that this was a gift from our dead ancestors. It would bring wealth to our people.

"The truth was far different. True, there were wages for those who worked the Mines but the real 'wealth' was stockpiled by the Quorum as they skimmed gold from the large shipments sent to Kel-eetan. Wealth that was used to build the Keep and the 'brick houses' of Chitouf.

"Even with all this gold, and the magnificence of the Keep, the Quorum wanted more. But how could they do this?" The El-Bhat turned to stare into the eyes of Stek, looking for the strength to continue what he must say.

"Up to that point, the output of the mine was fixed by the number of Government workers on the payroll. So, the Quorum secretly opened another mine shaft, worked by men stolen from prison cells ... and *even* El-Bhat communities." The horror of that last statement was beyond the strength that flowed from his Advisor. In shame, he turned to look away.

With eyes fixed on the sand by his feet, he eventually continued.

"A few years ago, Shanteef devised a plan to infest the Tracking Guild with Storlenians, who had immigrated to Shaksbah centuries before. This was a problem ... the Government of our country had promised security to the immigrants of Toobor. But Shanteef always finds a way. He bribed the Government troops, and then threatened to kill the families of the men, he wanted to send into the Storlenian Tracking Guilds.

"As soon as the men were gone, he sent the women and children to the Mines. It's always ... about the gold."

There was a long pause in the narrative. Stek thought he might add a point of comfort. "What about the El-Bhat that ran the Tenleth Mines? Surely some of them thought as you do," Stek questioned.

Ou-Leesen-el-Bra-ten scooped up another handful of sand, and let it trickle through his fingers again, before he continued.

"Shanteef assigned a special group of El-Bhat to run the Mines. They are called the Black Watch. They are ... to the last man, loyal to Shanteef and his dark ways. Because of this loyalty, and the harsh working conditions, they could use the prisoners to satisfy their foul appetites. And ... when Shanteef visited, he watched."

Ou-Leesen-el-Bra-ten turned his head to look straight into Stek's eyes. They were glowing green ... as though he was using the Dagger of Truth.

"These foul memories ... are harder to bear, than I had ever imagined."

As Stek stared at those glowing green eyes, he wondered. Was the Dagger slowly gaining control of his warrior friend? It reminded him of why he sought out Ou-Leesen in the first place.

"Many things are hard for a warrior," Stek sympathized, "especially when he leads. But I think there is something else ... that is even harder to bear than your memories."

Ou-Leesen-el-Bra-ten's gaze returned to the sand.

He scooped up three more handfuls as Stek waited.

"Advisor, have you ever been on a long journey, sleeping at a different place every night. And then one morning, as you awake, you cannot remember where you are, and it takes a moment to place yourself."

"Yes ... for sure. And once ... I even had a spell of sorts, cast upon my mind, so that I could not remember *who* I was. Well ... at least I was confused about who I was ... until the spell was broken."

"Then you will understand what I am about to say.

"These horrible memories ... sometimes they surface in the middle of the night," Ou-Leesen-el-Bra-ten continued.

"In my sleep, I live through them until the terror of these thoughts wakes me. Then as I sit in the dark ... I feel confused about who I am. It sort of feels like I must be Shanteef or sometimes even Arl-Sheen. But not really. There is something inside that tells me that I am someone else. So, I struggle against these memories until I remember who I am.

"But with every new occurrence, the effort to remember takes longer. My greatest fear is that one day, these memories ... of Shanteef and Arl-Sheen ... will overcome me. And whether I wish it or not ... I will forget who I am. And without knowing it, I will have surrendered to the power of the Dagger."

Ou-Leesen-el-Bra-ten turned to Stek again, the green eyes still glowing fiercely. "Advisor ... this must never happen. You must give me your oath, that you will not, allow this to happen."

The Tracker studied those eyes for a while before he asked the warrior, "What is your name?"

There was a moment of silence before the warrior replied, "Ou-Leesen-el-Bra-ten."

"Good answer ... otherwise you would be dead before you drew your next breath."

The warrior simply nodded. He stood, satisfied with his Advisor's plan.

Stek walked beside Ou-Leesen until they were at the edge of the oasis. They watched as twilight gathered and the sun sank into the ocean of sand.

"Are all of the supplies in yet?" Ou-Leesen-el-Bra-ten asked, anxious to continue their journey.

"Not yet. It's amazing how popular gold has become with these Caravan Merchants. Every time I trade a piece of a bar of gold, I am able to purchase an ever-increasing amount of supplies."

"How many wagons will we have?" The Warrior asked.

"Over one hundred."

Ou-Leesen-el-Bra-ten was pleased. It was worth the wait.

The Warrior had known for some time that it would be folly to show up at the Mines with only swords. Acquired freedom was lost on slaves who had no provisions or wagons to return home with.

The Technician closed the holographic image. He leaned forward, his head in his hands.

'Finally,' he thought as he reviewed his recent successes. He wanted more than anything to please Kareen-hys-Tebeel-del-Harleem ... ever since he was invited into his private quarters.

Never had anyone been so supportive of his work.

When he left his Superior's room that day, the Technician's confidence was restored ... completely. Without hesitation, he immediately went to work transferring the gold. Within hours, those bars were tucked safely away in Kareen's personal storage box.

He had hoped to slip quietly away when he was finished but Kareen-hys-Tebeel-del-Harleem had returned as he was leaving.

"The uh ... those gold bars," he whispered, head bowed, "are where you asked me to put them."

When the Technician looked up to measure the response, Kareen made no attempt to hide his pleasure.

That night, as the Technician lay in his bunk, he worked on a plan that would bring the Dagger back into the game. True, Kareen-hys-Tebeel-del-Harleem had implied that only Kareen's superior skill had brought the warrior to a point of submission.

But he was sure that there must be a way to beat the warrior ... and again please Kareen. With time, he would find it.

The next day, with his head in his hands, the door behind him opened noiselessly.

"What are you doing?" An angry voice challenged the Technician. "You're not supposed to be working the Dagger anymore. Kareen insisted on it!"

"You mean Kareen-hys-Tebeel-del-Harleem," he corrected the intruder, without turning around.

"Yeah, that's what I said wasn't it? Anyway, like I said, what are you doing at the Queen of Gold's Power Console?"

"I'm putting the Dagger back in the game."

"You can't. And you mustn't! Kareen has everything under control. He plans on winning without the Dagger."

"Soon the Dagger will be fully operational. You'll see," the Technician rebuffed his angry intruder.

There was a heavy sigh behind the Technician.

"You lost this game a long time ago ... even before Kareen told you to quit."

"His name ... is Kareen-hys-Tebeel-del-Harleem. And he *didn't* want me to quit. He was testing me ... my persistence, my loyalty. And he will be rewarded. You will *all* see. I am *so* close."

"So close to what? Getting yourself blown out a portal with the garbage?"

The Technician's fingers raced across the Golden Console until the Hologram replayed his latest triumph.

"See there ... he is committed. Soon he will kill the Warrior and the Dagger will be his."

"Who is this guy?" he asked with irritation.

"He is the Warrior's Advisor. He plans to kill the Warrior as soon as the Dagger's power crushes him."

"And what makes you so sure that this Advisor will pick up the Dagger?"

"He will do more than pick it up. He will embrace it. He was about to embrace it when the Warrior ripped it from his hands, weeks ago ... at the place they call the Keep. I was so close," the Technician explained.

His intruder grunted, not convinced.

"Another few days and the power of the Dagger will drive the Warrior mad. And then, Stek will be mine. You will see."

"What I will see," the intruder snapped arrogantly, "is you being thrown into a prison cell. This unsanctioned work of yours could cost us *everything*. And Kareen knows it. And within minutes he will know what you have been doing behind his back."

The Technician could hear the intruder turn and head back towards the door. For the first time, he turned towards the intruder ... and fired his weapon.

The body crumpled to the floor. The door was still unopened.

"What was that you said," the Technician began as he walked towards the dead body, "about being blown out a portal with the garbage?"

As they pulled away from the oasis, Ou-Leesen-el-Bra-ten stopped and from the advantage of his saddle, looked back down the line of over one hundred wagons, loaded with clothes, food and tools for the slaves at the Tenleth Mines.

Then he noticed the onlookers.

Everyone had come to see the El-Bhat warriors and the wagons leave. He grinned. The sight was certainly unique for the lands connected by the oases.

He urged his horse forward. The journey would be long and slow.

--------- <> ---------

Several days later, as they approached one of many oases, El-Bhat riders galloped swiftly down the Train looking for The Warrior.

As they approached, he recognized his Personal Guards. This meant trouble. They were supposed to meet at the Mines of Tenleth.

"Ou-Leesen-el-Bra-ten," one of them began urgently, "We have news that we must discuss in private."

The El-Bhat Leader was nodding in surprise that they knew his new name, but then remembered ... that was how he had signed his note.

At that same moment, Stek reined in his horse. He had followed the El-Bhat riders as they raced by.

"Personal Guards ... Stek ... follow me."

Soon they stood as a group, at the top of a dune.

"What news do you bring?"

The Personal Guard hesitated as he stared at Stek.

"He is my Personal Advisor. Begin."

After a small nod of respect, directed at Stek, the Personal Guard began.

"After we received your warning note, of the planned trap that waited south of us, we thought it unwise to head directly for Tenleth. So, we followed the road north to the Shaksbah Mountains.

"But we hadn't travelled far before our spies returned with a message, that heading towards us was a large group of warriors ... from Storlenia.

"This seemed impossible. Never in our history had Storlenian warriors crossed the Southland Mountains into Shaksbah.

"The men were anxious to engage the enemy and drive them back into their own lands. But the spies also reported War Wagons that stretched for as far as the eye could see."

Ou-Leesen-el-Bra-ten turned to Stek, hoping for a comment that might clarify the strange report. Stek shrugged his shoulders in response.

"Finding ourselves between two armies of considerable strength," the Personal Guard continued, "I felt it wise to leave the road and hide our forces in the foothills nearby and wait for the Storlenian army to pass.

"As the last of the Wagons passed, some of the Band Leaders wanted to attack their rear ... to test their strength.

"I gave permission for four Bands to attack, as the rest of the Band Leaders watched and studied the technique of these troops."

The Personal Guard stopped and looked at his companion for reassurance to continue. The other Guard nodded to go on, so he turned and said, "Of two hundred men, only eleven returned. They have a new weapon that fires these." He extended a hand, full of brass balls.

Ou-Leesen-el-Bra-ten turned to Stek, remembering a conversation they had as they left Chitouf on their way to the Keep. "Do you still have that brass ball?"

Stek retrieved it and flicked it towards the Warrior.

As he looked at the single brass ball, Ou-Leesen-el-Bra-ten knew that his world had just changed again, in ways that he could not yet comprehend.

"So many El-Bhat dead from a small brass ball," the Warrior whispered to himself.

"How many of the enemy were killed?" Stek queried, knowing of the El-Bhat skill with the bow and arrow.

"Very few. These new weapons are able to fire these brass balls in rapid succession."

"Does that complete your report?" The Warrior asked as he dropped the brass balls into the sand.

"No. Our spies followed this army as they marched into Kel-eetan. They estimated that the Government forces were at least twenty thousand strong. But even so, they had no power when compared to the Storlenian force. Within a day, this new army was in control of the city. Almost immediately, they marched eastward … determined to take over the Mines of Tenleth."

"Our only option was to look for you."

"They must already be there," Stek suggested, as he considered the reported events. "Either way, we cannot stand against these new war machines. Unless …" His eyes wandered to the Dagger.

The El-Bhat Warrior looked at Stek for a long time before he placed his hand on the pommel of the Knife. "Perhaps we can do this together."

"Of course … together."

Stek knew what 'together' meant. The journey for Ou-Leesen-el-Bra-ten and himself would end at the Mines. From the day that the El-Bhat Warrior mentioned his ambition for the Mines of Tenleth, his Tracker blood felt the finality of this mission.

He would try to send a message home to his wife and children at the next oasis.

--------- <> ---------

The Technician paused outside the Command Deck as he carefully reviewed his message.

The intelligence he was about to share, was significant … and he was the one to discover it.

Yes … he was ready. With confidence, he entered the room.

"Kareen-hys-Tebeel-del-Harleem … we have another man on the ground."

Kareen turned to face the Technician. "The Warrior no longer has the Dagger?" he asked with surprise.

"We are still monitoring the Warrior … and his Dagger. The man I am referring to is the New Quorum Leader."

"How did he come to have a Dagger of Truth?"

"He has no Dagger. But it doesn't matter. Ever since the visit from the Queen of Gold's Power, I have been able to send messages."

"How is this possible?" He asked with a frown.

"The Balance of Power has recalibrated. Someone on their side is using the Cave's power without an Amulet. So now we …"

"That's not possible!" an irritated Kareen argued.

The Technician immediately looked down. He wanted so much to please his Commander … but now he was angry. Devastated, he turned to leave.

"Wait," Kareen commanded his most loyal Technician. "Explain."

"Buried artefact," he quietly replied.

He looked up, Kareen was patiently waiting for more. "There are nuggets of information that the government doesn't want Technicians to know about. I came across this one during my research … years ago.

"It's possible for an off-worlder to have the power of the Amulet without actually having one in his possession. It's been documented."

"Well done," Kareen replied, as he considered the escalation of access to the Cave's power. Bernado had said nothing about this dangerous new development.

"Who is this person?" He asked.

"I have tried to identify this person, but he is either dead or no longer uses his power."

It wasn't the answer he wanted to hear.

He would have preferred to take care of this loose end.

But at least the 'The Balance of Power' had turned to their favour.

And now they had a New Quorum Leader that could be used to destroy those Storlenians who would try to open the Master Cave!

Chapter 35 - The return of the five

Previously, Axion and Aram Dentee II, along with five Specialist Trackers, headed north to Qar-ana, while the other Specialists helped gather the Trackers for their mission to the Mines of Tenleth. Braddock and the Tinkers had been invited to join the Trackers on this mission.

From the moment that the Tinker Guild was officially recognized by Qar-ana, Braddock knew that the path forward for Tinkers ... as a people ... was to gather to Tinker Village in Arborville. It was their future. If they stayed where they were, they might never embrace the change. But at Tinker Village, the excitement of change was intoxicating.

Until recently he had supposed that the effort to migrate would take at least a year. Perhaps much longer depending on the 'attitude' of the Lead Tinkers, spread out across Storlenia. But when the Specialist Trackers walked through his door only a few weeks earlier all that changed.

He immediately assigned his Tinkers to travel out to the various Tinker Trains across the land ... with an invitation to come ... and to help save their country. It would be tricky. The invitation was coming from Braddock ... the first Lead Tinker to abandon Tinker society in over a thousand years. And he was asking them to help Stors.

If he was in their boots, he probably wouldn't come ... unless there was an incentive. So, he sent one of Urshen's improved wagons to every Tinker Train, as proof of what had been accomplished and what Tinkers could become.

His message said nothing about having to leave Arborville once they got there ... and having to travel into Shaksbah. He knew the limits of Tinkers. His hope was that once they got there, and saw Tinker Village for themselves, they would see the sense of the sacrifice.

Braddock had taken on the most difficult Lead Tinker himself.

Previously, he had smiled every time he thought about Protas, taking all the Tinker women and children, north, to leave them with the most cantankerous Lead Tinker that Braddock had ever met.

But now, the smile was gone and his respect for Protas had grown. Obviously, his memory of this man had softened over time.

He was never so glad to be heading back south ... but his thoughts were on the families that depended on the belligerent Lead Tinker, to make good decisions.

He never expected to ever see anyone from that Tinker Train in Arborville. And maybe never again in this life.

On the third day of his southward trip, Braddock turned around in his wagon, as he often did, carefully watching his back. Behind, he could see five Specialist Trackers running down the road towards him.

The second time he turned around, they were closer than he expected. Now he was curious. They must have something very important, to bring back to Finn, to be pushing themselves so hard.

As they pulled up beside him, he encouraged his horses to keep pace as he hollered, "I think we should talk. Jump in."

One of them did, but the others knew the horses couldn't keep this pace, so they kept running and soon pulled away.

"Good day," the old Tinker began, as he watched the Specialist pull out his knife and begin to sharpen it. He guessed that Specialists were never idle.

"I remember your assignment was to bring messages back to Finn ... *one at a time*. What has changed, that brings all of you hurrying back to Arborville?"

The Specialist never took his eyes off his knife, as he began his report. "When Aram and Axion arrived in Qar-ana, the Trackers had already started to evacuate the city. Slowly ... one family at a time ... heading for different locations. So as not to attract any attention."

"So ... things have already started to disintegrate in the Capital."

"Yup. Started with Jokta, the Tracker who helped Axion escape. Thought he could gather some intelligence from a visiting Guild Master. Bernado ... from Pechora."

"Yeah, I heard of him," Braddock added, "my guess ... the meeting didn't go so well."

"Correct. He was badly wounded but managed to escape with the help of another Tracker."

Braddock gave a low whistle, "Now that would have stirred the pot," he suggested. "I'm curious, how did the Tracking Guild Master of Qar-ana fare through all of this?"

"It was quite a dance ... but it helped that Jokta was retired and was acting on his own. Things died down, but the Guild Master realized that they better get out while they still could."

"That's the message you're bringing to Finn?" Braddock asked, knowing there must be more.

"One of us was about to come back to relay the incident, but then a short time later, we spotted twenty War Wagons heading south, loaded with three hundred of the Militia Guard taken from the group known as The Wall."

"I have heard of the Militia Guard ... but The Wall?"

The Tracker slowed his sharpening as he considered the quickest way to answer the question. "*Specialist* Militia ... assigned to Craslin. And those War Wagons, they are essentially Tinker design ... with a difference. They are all mounted with the Brass Sling. A weapon of extraordinary killing power. Seen them training with it."

"What is their mission?"

"According to Aram, they are heading through Border Pass with papers from Craslin. All he knows is that Nusdek, the Militia Commander, is leading the group. Which means ... it's very important to the Capital."

"So ... this *Wall*, will be in Shaksbah before any of our people. Doesn't sound good. And what about these War Wagons, can they be stopped?"

The Specialist stopped sharpening his knife and looked at Braddock. "About as easy as stopping an avalanche."

Braddock placed a hand on his shoulder. "You better get going if you hope to catch your companions."

As the old Tinker watched the Tracker race down the road, he thought about how things had escalated since their meeting in Arborville, with Finn and The Commander.

Originally, Braddock was assigned to use his office in Tinker Village as a central command, keeping the three missions informed of each other's progress.

Staring into the distance, towards Border Pass, he knew that the Wall were already in Shaksbah. Whatever their mission was, he knew it was critical to the plans of Craslin's Militia. Any way he looked at it, this new information changed everything.

He shuddered as he thought of fifty thousand Militia, with their thousand War Wagons all mounted with the new killing machine.

Would Qar-ana unleash the might of their new Militia Guard upon the world as soon as the Wall was safely beyond Border Pass? He knew that's what he would do.

If he was right, the main body of the Militia would enter Border Pass within the week. Perhaps two if they were lucky.

A few leagues later, he had summarized his thoughts.

As soon as he arrived, everyone must leave Arborville immediately and head for Border Pass.

There would be no central command in Tinker Village.

The mission in Qar-ana, headed by Aram Dentee II, was unfortunately already over. At least he sent valuable intelligence.

The Specialists would be the first to enter Shaksbah, probably go over the mountains rather than through Border Pass. The Wall might already own it.

But the main body of Trackers and Tinkers wouldn't have that choice. They would need to take Border Pass if it was closed. He shuddered at the memory of the last time Tinkers and Trackers huddled under the fire of catapults.

Well, they would just have to find a way.

And then a smaller group would need to be organized from the main body, to stay behind at Border Pass to stop the Militia for as long as they could. Definitely a suicide mission.

By the Fates above, he hoped that the Trackers and his people, had time to prepare Border Pass against the Militia. They would need to hold them until the rest of the Trackers and Tinkers were well on their way to the Mines of Tenleth.

--------- <> ---------

Trackers had been posted on top of tall towers, with telescopes, continually checking the roads that fed into Arborville and the Tinker Village. Anything unusual, was shouted to Trackers at the bottom who immediately reported to the War Council. That meant The Commander and Finn ... and Braddock when he was around.

The War Council had just received the report from Finn's fourteenth Specialist. Fifteen were sent out to the Tracker Guilds, and as soon as the last one arrived, the Specialists would leave for Border Pass.

"The other Specialists are at the south end of Tinker Village," Finn dismissed his Tracker.

Far-fel was sitting in the corner as he watched the second last Specialist leave the Planning Room. He had been waiting for days ... impatiently ... for the last of the Specialists to return. He was anxious to begin his mission.

Of course, the delay was unavoidable. The Commander needed help to bring the Tracker community to Arborville. It was important to Ranoof's mission.

And ... they hadn't received a word yet, from the five other Specialists, assigned to act as messengers from Qar-ana.

Occasionally Far-fel would fidget with his Amulet, hoping to feel something ... anything that clarified their situation. But there was nothing.

Suddenly the door burst open as a Tracker from one of the Towers rushed in. "Five Specialist Trackers have been spotted on the north road ... travelling this way mighty fast."

Finn and Far-fel rushed out the door, followed by The Commander. Finn didn't stop at the Tower, he kept running north. Something was very wrong if all five of his Specialists were returning together.

He didn't wait for The Commander. He was the Gatherer. He wanted to be the one to hear the report from his men ... in private.

The report was brief but extremely important.

The Trackers of Qar-ana were abandoning the city. The disintegration of Storlenian society had begun.

The Wall, the best of the Militia, were already on their way to Border Pass, with War Wagons!

Finn was staring at his boots as his men finished their report. His plans would need to be changed.

"The last Specialist should be here by nightfall," Far-fel offered. "We could leave tonight."

"The Wall ..." Finn was still staring at his boots, "they've come to stop us, haven't they?" His eyes drifted up to Far-fel, waiting for the Specialist with the Amulet to confirm his worst suspicion.

With his hand firmly gripping the talisman, Far-fel nodded an affirmative response.

"All right ... we stay as far away from the Wall as possible. We will travel across terrain that will make it impossible for them to follow us with War Wagons ... and hope that we get to the Cave in time to complete your mission."

Shoulder to shoulder, the seven Specialists began to walk towards the Tower, their stride quick and resolute. By morning they would be well on their way to Border Pass. All were prepared to lay their lives on the altar of commitment. Far-fel *must* complete his mission.

"I will pass on the intelligence to The Commander," Finn said as they arrived at the Tower. "Let the rest of the men know of our change in plans."

Chapter 36 - The grasslands of death

Far-fel began his descent on the east side of the first ring of mountain ranges, as he cast his eyes across the wide valley. He reflected to his dream as he stopped to study the detail. It was ... familiar. But of course, he had seen this valley from a different viewpoint.

He wondered where Aram and Ranoof were at that moment. He hoped the Fates were with them. Somehow ... all three of them needed to succeed if Harleem was to be defeated. That was the clearest and most terrifying part of Far-fel's dream.

To help his friend Ranoof, Far-fel suggested that the group of Specialists could clear the way through Border Pass. But Finn was firm on his original decision.

"We will not engage the enemy until your mission is complete. In fact, we will do everything we can to even avoid the possibility." To Far-fel, it was strange to hear Finn talk with such passion about their mission. It was as though Finn had the dream ... and not Far-fel.

So instead of going through Border Pass, they scaled the mountains to the south, using the moon as their guide and then continued without rest until they were inside Shaksbah.

The rest of the group began to surround him as he pulled out his telescope.

He peered through the glass as he surveyed the valley.

"Aha," he gratefully acknowledged, he had found an important landmark. A large stone at the far end of the meadow ... just like in his dream, as he stood on an outcrop and surveyed the expanse below him.

He turned the telescope towards the mountains ... to where he would have stood when he looked upon that stone.

He knew that up there somewhere, there was a ledge. But he was still too far away. He would have to get closer.

And now that he had identified a landmark, he was determined to make his way there first.

And that meant moving across the valley where they would no longer be hidden by the trees and deep gorges that had kept them concealed from spies.

The other option of continuing down to the ravine, at the bottom of the mountain, and then following the heavily forested foothills, was probably safer. And perhaps quicker. But it would be more difficult to identify the location of The Ledge.

As he hesitated, Finn approached him. "Is it time to armour up?"

"Yes … we are close. I recognize that large rock across the valley. If I can get there, I am sure to spot the Quartz Door."

"So, you prefer the valley?" Finn asked as they stared down at the tall grass meadow, between them and the forest beyond.

There was a subtle tone of doubt in Finn's voice, so Far-fel turned his attention again to the forested foothills to the left.

Of course … if they took that path, it would be more difficult to find The Ledge. But probably safer.

Undecided, he grasped his Amulet as he gazed upon the foothills.

"Better choice?" Finn asked, knowing what Far-fel was attempting to do.

After a lengthy pause, he replied, "I feel nothing."

Finn looked at the Amulet and then his trusted companion.

"I don't understand," he softly protested.

"Neither do I. But for some time now, the power of the Amulet has been fading. It seems the closer we get to the Mountain of Hope, the less assistance we get."

Finn returned his gaze to the valley as he contemplated what Far-fel had said. They stood there for a while until Finn finally broke the silence.

"You would think that this *power* would want to assist us all the way. Since as you say … this mission is extremely important. But … this mission also reminds me of the Gatherer's test."

"Yes …," Far-fel agreed.

Every Specialist that had ever been recruited from the days of the First Gatherer, had to pass the Gatherer's test.

Once a Tracker was identified as Specialist material, a message was sent to the Crystal Mountain area. Sometime later, a messenger would show up with a written invitation, for the recommended Tracker to join the Specialists. The two men would chat about what it would mean to be part of this elite group of Trackers.

Invariably the Tracker would always accept and then the messenger would give the only instructions the recruit would receive. "Follow me and I will lead you to the Gatherer."

Immediately the messenger would bolt out of the building and the test would begin. The recruit had two heartbeats to decide what to take with him as he followed this messenger for hundreds of leagues.

During the first part of the test, the messenger could be seen often, and it was easy to pick up the clues along the trail. But as the test progressed, it became harder and harder to follow. By the time the recruit was close to the Crystal Mountain area, the messenger, who was really Finn, would simply disappear.

It became obvious to the recruit that he was now on his own to finish the test.
The intent of the test, as designed by the First Gatherer, was to see if the recruit had the ability to find the Gatherer, with only the will to succeed.

"So …," Finn prompted for a verdict.
"I prefer the advantage of the rock. I say we travel through the valley."
"Okay, but I say we start over there." He pointed where the grasses were tall enough to come up to their waist.

Far-fel nodded in agreement. He always did when Finn decided.

So, they backtracked up the mountain forest, headed south for a short way and then they came down again.
Before entering the area of the tall grasses, they all quietly suited up with the armour of thin steel and leather, they had brought. Far-fel decided it was time to move the Amulet from his pouch, to behind the protection of his chest armour.
In pairs, they checked each other to make sure the cinches were tight. It was very unusual for Specialists to wear their armour. Everyone knew that this meant the strength of the enemy was great and the risk of contact high.

They also knew that the War Wagons couldn't possibly be there, and without the War Wagons the enemy did not have the advantage of the Brass Sling.
But somehow that logic no longer comforted Finn.

Of course, Far-fel was also acting more cautious than normal ... which seemed to fuel Finn's natural intuition. A Gift that kept his Specialists alive on many an occasion when lives were hanging on an unpredictable thread.

With everyone ready, they moved in single file to the edge of the forest.

For the first hundred paces, Finn led as they crawled through the grass on their bellies. Then he stood as a signal for everyone to run.

The moment they had begun to run, everyone could hear a continuous stream of popping noises coming from the forest behind ... and a staccato of clanking sounds as brass balls collided with their steel armour.

"Compress!" Finn shouted. Immediately the line of Specialists that had begun to stretch out, was quickly shortened, reducing the exposure to those closer to the front.

Unfortunately, those at the end of the line, had to bear the full force of the attack and soon a shout could be heard, "Man down at the rear!"

The armour was never designed to protect perfectly. That was too impractical for the style of fighting used by Specialists. Hence, there was always the chance that a lucky arrow could find a crack to wound the Specialist.

But it wasn't luck that brought down the Specialist at the rear, it was simply ... volume. Listening to the clanging sounds, Finn figured he must have taken at least a hundred hits.

"Leave him," Finn yelled as they dashed forward at full speed.

To the men, it seemed impossible that they had already lost a Specialist. Considering their armor and the distance between them and the forest.

But the popping sounds told Finn that somehow, the enemy was using the Brass Sling!

And the continued clanging sound of brass hitting steel, told Finn that soon he was going to lose another Specialist.

And he did.

Soon after, the popping noises stopped. He knew they were out of range.

Finn stopped and looked back towards the forest, as he quickly assessed the situation.

"They must have developed a portable version of the Brass Sling," Finn concluded.

"Our arrows couldn't begin to compete with them," Far-fel added, as he considered how far they were from the forest's edge.

That was all the dialogue they had time for. A swarm of men began to exit the forest into the grasslands, carrying sticks of brass and steel.

Without wasting another heartbeat, Finn raced headlong into the diminishing grasses of the valley, towards the Mountain of Hope.

His consolation was that they had managed to put enough space between them and the enemy. Temporarily making the Militia's superior weapons useless. And he knew that his men were faster than anyone else alive. All they had to do was to keep running … and hope that all the Wall were behind them!

A couple of times, Far-fel stopped to point his telescope towards the mountain that was most likely to be the Mountain of Hope. He needed to be sure that they were headed in the right direction. An error at this point, and the need to change course, would seriously erode the distance between them and the enemy that followed in close pursuit.

They had to keep running in a straight line.

They were within five hundred paces of the mountain base when Far-fel saw what appeared to be the Quartz Door.

He passed the telescope to Finn and pointed. "That's where The Ledge is. At the back of that ledge is a Quartz Door, that must be opened with my Amulet. Look for a keyhole that has the same shape as the Amulet. That's all you have to do … in case I don't make it."

"I'll do my best to get you there alive," was Finn's reply, as he threw the telescope back to Far-fel and raced ahead.

Chapter 37 - The wedged wall of death

After days of scouting, El-Bhat spies returned to the Bands that filled the lower slope of the Mountain of Despair.
"We have discovered two groups of Storlenian warriors. The first group to arrive is large, several Bands in size. They are not Trackers. We assume they are Government Militia. They have been waiting over there," the spy said as he pointed towards a sister mountain.

"We suspected that they waited for reinforcements before they ascended to the Mountain of Despair. But now we know different. The target of their patience has been a small group of Trackers ... about twenty, who have now arrived. We believe the Militia are here to kill the Trackers."

The Band Leader in charge scanned the valley and asked, "Where are these Trackers?"

"By now ... they would be ... there," the spy answered as he pointed to the edge of the forest, that bordered the eastern boundary of the grasslands.

"If they know about the Government Militia, they will use the grass where it is tallest, to make their way across the valley. They will be here ... soon," the spy clarified.

"And the Government Militia?"

They have split into two groups. One group is following the Trackers and the other is heading for the Cave.

"Tell the spies to move to their battle positions."

The spy hurried upward, signalling the rest of the spies to follow him. They would watch from further up, and if the battle was lost, the spies would return to report. But this was only a formality. Everyone knew that today would be a day of victory.

Next, the Head Band Leader turned to the three other Band Leaders. "Bring all of your men to the forest edge. We will all watch as one of our Bands destroys these Trackers."

The enemy were few. It was almost an embarrassment to send in a full Band of fifty El-Bhat against twenty. But Bands were meant to stay together.

So, three Bands would stay at the forest edge, witness to the one Band, that stood ready to descend on the Trackers, as they moved up the mountain slope.

The Head Band Leader was sure that the only group interested in the Cave, was the Trackers. As strange as it seemed, it appeared that the Militia were only there to stop the Trackers. He would use this to his advantage and try to stay out of their way as best as he could.

"Everyone ... do not engage the Militia unless they approach the Cave entrance."

The Band Leader was pleased. He could already see that today would be a day of victory ... with little loss of life.

After his El-Bhat warriors destroyed the small group of Trackers, they would stay at the Cave, until his spies came back with confirmation that the Militia had returned north to Storlenia.

The Band Leader thought back to the departing commands from the Next Quorum Leader. It was with some surprise that things were turning out exactly as predicted by his instructions.

'The enemy will arrive shortly after you have taken position on the mountain,' he had said, back at the Keep.

And ... he had also predicted that the battle would soon be over and the El-Bhat Bands could leave this accursed mountain and return home. Victors with glory.

'It appears that you *will* be right,' The Band Leader thought to himself.

In the recent past, things hadn't always turned out so well.

Unfortunately, those predicted outcomes, were conjured up by men who spent their days sitting on soft pillows.

'How quickly they forget the Band Leaders, who had no alternative but to use the 'Elbayai shout', when victory was *assured* by the Quorum.'

With everyone in place, the Head Band Leader lifted his scope, towards where the Trackers were supposed to be.

Suddenly he saw them rise out of the grass, and then like mountain cats, they bolted across the grasslands towards the base of the mountain ... as sunlight danced off their bodies.

Surprised at the sight, he quickly steadied his telescope on a tree branch, as he watched the thin line of Trackers race closer to the mountain.

'Ahh ... so they are wearing ... clothing of steel?' he realized to his great surprise.

These men were no ordinary Trackers!

He adjusted his scope to focus on the armour. Soon, as they came into range, he would fire the first arrow. He was busy looking for an opportunity to penetrate the sheaves of steel, when the first Tracker would arrive at the base of the Mountain.

He had barely completed the thought, when he heard clanging and popping sounds. He swung his telescope towards the forest, behind the Trackers.

As he suspected, they were being attacked from the rear. By over two hundred men. They were holding strange weapons ... that reflected sunlight ... like metal sticks.

He moved his telescope back to the Trackers, just in time to see the last Tracker fall dead.

These men with their metal sticks, were now focusing on the next Tracker in line.

As he watched, he could see the metal armor bounce, as metal objects pounded against it in rapid succession. Soon, this Tracker fell as well.

When the clanging stopped, he set aside his telescope to get a clear view of where the Trackers were. He wanted to know the range of the metal sticks.

It was ... far!

He pulled a metal tipped arrow from his quiver, as he watched the Militia begin their race across the grasslands, in pursuit of the Trackers.

If he was right about the Militia, they would halt their pursuit once they saw the El-Bhat destroying the Trackers.

He hoped so. He had no desire to face these new weapons carried by the Militia.

Either way, he needed to drop the Lead Tracker with his first arrow.

--------- <> ---------

The closer they got to the base of the Mountain, the more Finn's eyes were on the treed slope ahead. He was looking for any sign of movement. He wasn't convinced that all the Wall were behind them.

Things could get interesting really fast, if his suspicions were correct.

If a part of the Wall were ahead, their only hope was to get enough of his men into the trees alive.

Then the battle would favour the fighting style of the Specialists ... and maybe ... just maybe they could get Far-fel up to The Ledge!

And soon he would know. Because within fifty paces, they would be in range of the dangerous Brass Sling sticks.

Moments later, he entered the death zone, but there were no popping sounds.

He was a bit surprised but never took his eyes off that treed slope. And his vigilance was soon rewarded as he caught the glint of an arrow tip.

He already knew that it was El-Bhat. With ease, he snatched it from its flight.

"El-Bhat arrows," he shouted, above the pounding of Tracker feet and the clanging of their metal armour.

--------- <> ---------

Neither the Head Band Leader, nor the four Bands at his side ... were expecting the arrow to be caught in mid-air. These Trackers were uncommon warriors.

There was a brief pause as the Head Band Leader considered the event.

Then, without further hesitation, the Head Band Leader stepped out of the forest and shouted, "The rain of death!"

With abandon his men began to send a shower of arrows down upon the eighteen Trackers.

A moment after Finn caught the first arrow, the Storlenian warriors came to a stop.

With impossible precision, the Trackers deflected their arrows with the metal sheaves on their arms.

Within moments the entire El-Bhat force had emptied their quivers and only one Tracker had fallen. Now there were seventeen.

Things were not going as the Head Band Leader had expected.

He could have given the command to stay ground and wait for the Trackers to advance up the slope. But he wasn't so sure that was the best strategy.

He saw an outcome where the Trackers waited for the Militia to arrive at the mountain base ... and then make a diagonal run up the mountain, pulling both the Militia and the El-Bhat against each other. And this was an outcome he preferred to avoid.

No, they would not wait, he would stay to his original plan, and send one of his four Bands down the slope immediately.

--------- <> ---------

With the grace of a Mountain Cat, the Specialists began to face their new enemy ... metal tipped arrows. With speed that matched the descending rain of steel, they fought the onslaught until the last arrow had fallen.

Finn shouted, "Status?"

One of his Trackers responded, "One down."

The men waited for the next command as Finn watched El-Bhat pour out of the trees.

The forest emptied quickly of the black silk warriors. Finn estimated about fifty.

He turned to catch a glimpse, of the Militia racing across the grasslands behind them.

"Advance in formation," he shouted to his men.

The Trackers advanced in a wedged wall formation, as the El-Bhat ran down the mountain side.

Suddenly the wall sprang to life as the Black Silk Warriors crashed into a sea of churning blades.

Using the momentum of the human landslide, the wedge of Trackers took turns opening their wall to allow the dead El-Bhat to slide through.

As more and more silk warriors pounded against that wall, they were, without exception, frustrated by the same skill that defied their arrows.

And one by one, like their arrows, they too were laying on the ground, unable to stop these warriors that fought like Mountain Cats.

--------- <> ---------

The Band Leader had insisted that his warriors stay on high ground at any cost. Better to have the advantage of elevation, when facing highly skilled warriors. The crushing defeats of the El-Bhat Bands at Seven Oaks and Border Pass, taught him a new respect for the age-old enemy north of the Southland Mountains.

But as the Band Leader watched the fifty El-Bhat swords, that sought Tracker flesh at every opportunity, he soon learned that elevation was not enough.

These Trackers could use the tempered steel of their armour as effectively as they did their weapons.

And the speed and force of their cutting steel was almost unbelievable. Tracker blades flew as if they had a life of their own!

In unbelief, the Band Leader watched as the ground behind the advancing wedged wall, became littered with black silk corpses.

Shortly, the wedged wall began sprinting up the slope, despite the river of El-Bhat that had flowed down upon them.

And lying among his men were *two* Trackers.
'Who are these men?' he asked himself.

Still at the forest edge, he glanced quickly towards the grasslands.
Fortunately, the Militia were almost at the bottom of the mountain.
There was still a chance, that the Militia with the steel sticks, would engage these Trackers before they arrived at the Cave above.

With bitter irony, he realized at that moment, that the Next Quorum Leader with such keen insight, forgot to tell him that the battle at the Cave, would be like nothing he had ever seen before.

There would be Trackers with legendary strength and skill.
And other warriors would carry *steel sticks* that would send two of the Trackers to their graves.
And that same feat would cost him fifty warriors!

Chapter 38 - The Oath of Life

Some time earlier, before the Specialist Trackers arrived.

Nusdek was sitting on The Ledge with telescope in hand, searching the valley below and the mountains to the west ... the path that Bernado had insisted the Trackers would take to get to the Cave behind him.

"Do *not* attempt to enter that Cave," Bernado had commanded him prior to leaving Qar-ana.

He would occasionally turn and stare at the Quartz Door, curious to know what lay behind, that was so important. But that was only to break the monotony of waiting. He was a man that followed orders and his allegiance to Bernado was absolute.

He used to follow Craslin ... until Bernado convinced him that the Guild Master had lost his way.

He laid the telescope on his thigh as his thoughts drifted back in time.

It wasn't that long ago that Nusdek was recruited into the Militia by Ranoof, the Tracker in charge of the new and expanding Militia Guard.

He smiled as he thought of Ranoof. The Tracker was good. He had the perfect eye for seeing flaws in their training. And he was expert at offering solutions. Everyone was advancing so fast. It was exhilarating.

Nusdek had considered approaching the Tracking Guild a few years before. His natural talents seemed well matched. But eventually he changed his mind. He didn't like all the rules. What Ranoof offered was perfect. All the benefits of Tracker training without the suffocating harness.

After several weeks of hard training, Ranoof approached Nusdek to ask for assistance to train the new recruits.

'I could sure use some help. Too many to train ... and besides, one day I will need to leave, and someone needs to take my place. You're the obvious choice ... a real natural.'

And then one day, Ranoof just disappeared.

He raised the telescope to his eye and began scanning again. Bernado advised him to expect Trackers ... maybe Tinkers as well. He just hoped Ranoof wasn't in that group. 'It would be a shame to kill him,' he thought to himself.

His scope drifted to the ravine where his three hundred Militia were hiding. He watched for a while to see if he could detect any signs of movement. Nothing.

It was what he expected.

His men were the best of the five thousand that made up the Wall.

And the Wall were the best of the Militia Guard ... a total of fifty thousand men.

And ... they had superior weapons with superior range.

Two days later when he first spotted the Trackers, as they began their descent on the mountain to the west, he couldn't believe what he was seeing.

He followed them as they ran down the mountain slope, occasionally moving his scope to other parts of the mountain, expecting to see other small groups.

But there were none. The Command Centre at Arborville had only sent twenty men!

'This is going to be too easy,' he thought as he began his own race back to his men.

When opportunity provided a clear line-of-sight, he would stop, pull out his scope and for a few moments, watch them descend lower and lower.

Soon they would be at the edge of the ravine, and his men would shred the enemy as hundreds of brass balls ripped through their bodies.

But the only sound that echoed through the forest was the sound of his leather boots as they pounded along the forest trail.

--------- <> ---------

Back on the ship, Kareen was interrupted by the Technician.

"Our team has investigated the 'strength' of the group heading for the Mountain of Despair. We beg you to reconsider destroying these men. As genetic feedstock, they would be ..." the Technician struggled to find the right word.

"Yes, I know," Kareen replied irritably. "But if they succeed in opening the Mountain of Despair, there will be NO feedstock!"

Kareen turned and headed for his room. It seemed to Kareen, that the stakes involved in reaping this planet were increasing every day! More difficult than he had ever imagined.

But the wealth of gold and genetics ... was staggering!

--------- <> ---------

By the time Nusdek entered the ravine, his spies were ready to share intelligence.

"They have headed for the grasslands. Just bad luck. I am sure they are still unaware that we are here."

He motioned his Squad Leaders to gather around him. "I want the first fifty men to come with me. The rest will follow the spies."

If his spies were right, his men would easily catch up and this mission would be over by nightfall.

However, he always covered possibilities. It was why he was the Leader of fifty thousand Militia Guard.

As the spies arrived at the forest edge, the Trackers had disappeared. But not for long. The Squad Leaders spread out and soon saw the waving grasses, evidence of their quarry.

They gave hand signals for the men to enter the grasslands, as two hundred and fifty men converged towards the line of Trackers, that crawled out of sight.

The Squad Leaders were about to give the order to sprint forward, when the small group of Trackers erupted out of the grass and began to race away.

"Fire!" a Squad Leader shouted, determined that the conflict would end, before the Trackers ran another hundred paces.

The men at front, raised their weapons and began to fire as the second wave of men behind them, used their shoulders to steady their aim.

The last Tracker should have fallen instantly, but he kept running ... as the sound of brass balls could be heard bouncing off thin steel plates.

His men kept firing and firing, until the last man eventually crumpled to the ground, out of sight.

--------- <> ---------

'Amazing,' Nusdek thought to himself as he looked out across the valley. He had never seen protective covering like this before.

"But ... you have never felt the force of brass balls in conflict either," he whispered to the enemy below. It was still only a matter of time before these twenty Trackers were dead.

Nusdek and his men continued their way towards the Quartz Door. The next time he had a clear view of the Trackers, they had arrived at the foothills and were waiting.

'They have obviously spotted the El-Bhat,' he realized. His own spies had reported them two days earlier. He had no idea why the Black Silk Warriors had suddenly shown up, but he didn't care. His orders were to keep the Trackers from the Cave of the Mountain of Despair.

However, a curious Nusdek kept his telescope fixed on the remaining eighteen Trackers, as the El-Bhat slipped down the mountain to the forest line, while his own men raced across the grasslands.

'Maybe the Black Silk Warriors will do the job for me,' he thought, as hundreds of arrows fell upon them. But only one Tracker died from the onslaught of metal rain.

Moments later, he could feel his own body tense, as the black wave of men and steel, crashed into the wedge the Trackers had formed.

This was a battle that was destined to be short!

With intense interest, he continued to watch through his scope, as the wedge of men churned through the attackers like War Wagons fitted with rotating blades.

"Impossible." He whispered.

He kept watching.

A short time later, with black silk bodies strewn across the foothill landscape, fifteen Trackers sprinted up the hill as the wedge headed for the trees.

"Impossible." He whispered again.

Before moving up the mountain, he checked his men below.
They were not far from the base of the mountain.

"We must hurry to The Ledge," he shouted to his fifty men.
The engagement had suddenly become complicated.

He could no longer ignore the El-Bhat.

And these Trackers were ... something he had never seen before. On the open plain, with their backs to his men's firearms, the battle was easy ... just slow.

But now that these Trackers with their protective metal sheaves, were into the forested area, on steep slopes, it was ... unpredictable.

His men had never trained for this kind of combat. Their brass ball weapons were never intended for close engagement. True, they were the best of the best when it came to using short swords and knives, but he had already seen what these Trackers did to the El-Bhat.

'The battle will be won at the Cave,' Nusdek realized.

As fast as he could, he led his men up the mountain to the place just above The Ledge. Once there, they would spread out behind trees, ready to kill anyone who dared enter the small area in front of the Cave.

--------- <> ---------

There was a simple ceremony when a Tracker was inducted into the small group of *Specialist* Trackers.

It was the *oath of life*.

It meant that the recruit sacrificed his life *on the day* he was chosen as a Specialist. This meant that his life no longer had value to him. It was already offered and could not be taken back.

It meant that he was free to make choices in his assignments, without regard for his life.

Besides, to a man, they trusted in the Fates above. That their sacrifice was honoured, and there was nothing to do, but to complete their assignments, for the good of the people.

And right now, as Finn raced up the mountain slope with the other Specialists, he was grateful for those oaths. It allowed him to face the enemy with clarity of mind, and an undivided determination to succeed in their goal.

His men had never faced a greater foe. And according to Far-fel, their mission was never more important. They *had* to succeed.

They had just left two more of his men dead, on the battleground. He could feel it and he could hear it. The pounding of the feet to the left and right told him they were down to sixteen. Would sixteen be enough? Surely by the Fates above, it had to be.

As they entered the forest, they parted into smaller groups, using the trees for cover.   Finn was wondering how much time they would have, before the men with the Brass Slings would be in range, when he heard the clang of brass on steel and the softer thud of brass on bark.

'Already,' he groaned.

"Rear Guard … ten men," he shouted as the remaining dashed up the slope with Finn.

'That will slow them down,' he thought as he looked over at Far-fel, the man he had promised to get to the door of the Cave.

Chapter 39 - The slope of death

The Head Band Leader rushed up the mountain to join the remainder of his black silk warriors.
They were well off to the eastern side, below the elevation of the Quartz Door, when the Band Leader could hear the familiar popping sound of the Steel Sticks.
The Militia had engaged!

Through hand signals from his men, he quickly learned that the Trackers had divided into two groups, the one staying behind to frustrate the advance of the Militia, allowing the other group to continue their advance to The Ledge.

The Band Leader hadn't anticipated this new development. What if the Trackers who stayed behind managed to keep the Militia from advancing long enough, for the other group to enter the Cave!
It was time for another change in plans.
As they rushed towards the Cave, he knew that soon his men would use the 'Elbayai shout'.

--------- <> ---------

Nusdek's men were barely into position above The Ledge, when he could hear the firing of the Brass Slings from below.
'Good,' he thought, his *other* men had caught up to the Trackers.
After watching the battle between the El-Bhat and these unusual Trackers, he was convinced that their best offense, was using the Brass Sling weapons.

He rested his scope on a thick branch and scanned back and forth between the trees below.
'With a little luck, the battle might never make it to The Ledge,' he thought to himself.
But it was not to be.
Only moments later, he spotted a small group of Trackers below, advancing quickly towards the Cave.

For the first time, he was seeing their steel armour up close. He was looking for the weakness. There was *always* a weakness that could be exploited.

There wasn't much, he grudgingly admitted, but still, he figured their best chance was the head. He whispered for his assistant to spread the word through the Militia. 'Aim for the head.'

--------- <> ---------

The Squad Leaders stopped at the first Tracker that had fallen. They needed to consult briefly before they charged across the grasslands. They had a decision to make.

His body was badly damaged, blood seeping from everywhere. "Never thought someone could take so much punishment," a Squad Leader commented.

Everyone nodded, but that was not the reason they had stopped. It was to examine his quiver … that was full of arrows. The Head Squad Leader pulled one out and examined it closely.

"Never seen better workmanship," the Head Squad Leader said.

The decision, was about whether to abandon the shields, strapped to their backs, and make better time … or not.

The decision was easy. They would need them, or these Trackers would kill them with ease.

They stopped briefly at the next fallen Tracker. Same result. They shook their heads at the ability of these Trackers to run like a deer while their bodies were being shredded by the brass balls.

'This won't be easy,' the Head Squad Leader thought to himself.

"Let's go," he shouted.

They jogged through the tall grass, falling further and further behind the speeding Trackers.

Long before they arrived at the mountain base, they could see the black wave of warriors descend the slope and crash into the Trackers.

'That should buy us some time,' The Head Squad Leader thought. 'Maybe even stop them completely.'

But as they reached the mountain, it was all over as the remaining Trackers bolted up to the tree line.

Moving up through the battle-scarred slope, the Militia gazed soberly at the first and then the other two Trackers that laid amongst the blanket of dead El-Bhat.

The Head Squad Leader stopped short of the forest edge. He waited until the two hundred and fifty Militia had gathered together. If Trackers could decimate El-Bhat on a wide-open slope, he was concerned about what they were facing as they entered the forest.

But he had thought carefully about what they might do if the Trackers made it into the trees.

He removed his shield and held it in front. Then he held his Brass Sling at waist height.

"This will get you close enough to fight with sword and long knife. Then abandon these weapons and fight in teams of four against a single Tracker. Those that are behind, try to add support to those in the front with your Brass Slings. Move forward."

The ten Trackers that remained close to the tree line, paired up into five groups of two ... to fight an enemy of two hundred and fifty. Greatly outnumbered but also in their element, they hoped to hold off the Militia, until Far-fel could open the door to the Cave.

Ten arrows swished through the air in unison, as the Militia advanced into the trees.

Some of the Militia dropped dead but most were only wounded.

"Don't give them an easy target ... and keep those brass balls firing," the Squad Leader shouted in anger.

The Trackers started moving up slope, trying to keep from being out-flanked.

The size of Militia was slowly dwindling but being outnumbered was not their only problem. The Brass Slings were slowly destroying their armour. Several of the Trackers had already experienced serious wounds.

--------- <> ---------

The Militia eventually realized, that there were only ten Trackers. The other five had gone ahead.

The Squad Leader immediately sent thirty men up the slope on the western side towards The Ledge.

--------- <> ---------

The ten Trackers had only one choice, and that was to spread out further and retreat faster, to keep the flanking Militia from escaping up the slope.

Their arrows began to decimate the flanking thrust, but it came at a cost.

The Militia in the centre thrust were now only twenty paces away … and they were pushing hard, trying to close the remaining gap.

The Trackers sent a quick volley of arrows, desperate to slow the flanking Militia before they abandoned their bows, as they faced the advancing Militia.

Besides, if they didn't put a stop to the weapons below that fired upon them with abandon, they would all soon be dead.

--------- <> ---------

Occasionally, Finn would catch glimpses of black silk as they rushed upwards towards The Ledge.

"You see what I'm seeing," he called to Far-fel.

"More El-Bhat above to the right," Far-fel shouted back. He figured they were close to the Cave, but would they get there, before the black warriors?

He watched Finn as they continued to rush among the trees. He sort of expected Finn to send off the other three Specialists to provide interference, hopefully to allow them to get to the Quartz Door first.

But before that happened, volleys of brass balls could be heard, bouncing off their armor … and they weren't coming from below!

Finn had the advantage of being behind a particularly large tree, as he considered the advancing sounds of men from below, the El-Bhat up to the right and more Militia with Brass Slings above them.

They were in the middle of a log jam … and somehow, he needed to shake a few logs loose if they were ever going to open that Quartz Door.

Desperately he ran from tree to tree as he looked for an advantage, while his Trackers followed.

"I see a way," he finally shouted.

He led to the left as his four men followed.

It didn't take them very long before they came to a cliff, with large trees below.

The opportunity was not something Finn could have seen. But he felt it. And his instinct always led him right.

He jumped.

The first branch hit him too hard. He couldn't hold on, but it slowed him down enough for him to grab the next branch. His men followed.

Soon they were heading up the ravine, hidden below by the large trees.

Finn could still hear muffled sounds of battle. He hoped to hear those sounds until they were above the Militia who guarded The Ledge.

--------- <> ---------

With his scope resting on a branch, Nusdek squeezed the shoulder of the man beside him. Indication for the Militia to start firing.

He had caught glimpses below, of a small group of Trackers, pressing forward through the trees. He thought there might have been as many as five, but it was hard to tell. They moved so swiftly and with such invisibility.

He wanted his men to wait until they were close enough to be a significant target and yet far enough away to ensure they didn't make it, onto The Ledge.

It was time.

The sound of metal on metal rang through the forest, as the Trackers tried to escape from the volley of death, that rained upon them.

And then they simply disappeared.

Shortly after this brief encounter, Nusdek received word that the El-Bhat were moving from the east, intent on getting closer to the Cave.

"Leave them be," he advised his Squad Leader. "Tell the men to reposition further west. I want the black warriors to have opportunity to attack the Trackers."

"What if they attack *us*?"

"We seem to share a common mission of stopping the Trackers. A mystery for sure. But if that remains, I doubt we need to be concerned."

Nusdek watched the Squad Leader slip away with his orders.

He hoped he was right. His spies estimated around a hundred and fifty El-Bhat remaining.

He returned his attention to the battle below. He could no longer hear the popping sounds of the Brass Slings. Now it was only the sounds of swords clashing and men dying.

--------- <> ---------

The Head Squad Leader had left the *central thrust* some time ago, intent on following the *western thrust* past the Trackers.

The forest floor was littered with wounded and dead Militia as he raced upwards. But then he heard the sound he was waiting to hear. Nusdek's men had begun to fire on the five Trackers that were above.

He increased his efforts to reach the Militia ahead.

He wanted to be there to guide their support from the rear.

Shortly after the fire from above commenced, the Trackers headed eastward through the forest.

What remained of the thirty Militia from below, spotted them. Immediately they raised their Brass Slings and fired until the trees obstructed their view. Hurriedly they followed, determined not to lose sight of them.

But as they came to the edge of a deep ravine, those Trackers were gone.

"They must have climbed trees," a Squad Leader shouted.

They quickly retraced their steps, searching above for the invisible Trackers.

They hadn't gone far, when they met the Head Squad Leader and informed him of their dilemma.

"The Ledge is well protected by Nusdek and fifty men," he responded. "For now, we will return to assist the *central thrust*."

They raced down the slope as they followed the cries of death below.

--------- <> ---------

As soon as the ten Trackers had exhausted their supply of arrows, they moved further up-slope, trying to keep the Militia from surrounding them.

But soon, Militia were rushing in from below and above.

The ten Trackers were all still alive but every one of them had sustained multiple wounds and their armor was damaged from the continual barrage of the brass balls.

"Re-group," one of the Trackers shouted, knowing that together they would stand a better chance of still getting to the Cave. It was strange that the Militia from above had returned. Perhaps the other five Trackers were already dead. He hoped not, they would need the Amulet.

In a few heartbeats, all ten were in formation to defend themselves. But the Tracker who shouted the command knew that this *wasn't* a defensive exercise.

"We need to make it to The Ledge," he said quietly.

And then, to the surprise of the Militia above, the Trackers were charging up-slope.

The formidable wedged wall weaved in and out of the trees, cutting down the Militia from above, as the Militia from below raced forward, hoping to gain the advantage of attacking from the rear.

Chapter 40 - The Ledge of death

The El-Bhat Leader was positioned close to the Cave, allowing him to monitor the advance of the Trackers from below.
Between the sounds of battle, and catching occasional glimpses through the trees, he had determined that the smaller group of Trackers had managed to escape towards the western ravine. And the larger group, were now moving upwards.

He looked back at the one hundred and fifty warriors, ready to swarm across The Ledge, if any of the Trackers ever made it past the remaining Militia.

It had become *strangely* apparent that the Militia were El-Bhat allies. Committed to the same mission as his black silk warriors.

He returned his gaze to that wind-swept Ledge. His spies assured him that the western slope above and below, were guarded by the Militia. And his own men covered the eastern slope.

It should be impossible for that small group of skilled warriors, to take The Ledge, against such odds.

Yet ... his instincts told him that he would yet see Trackers on that Ledge, struggling to open the door to the Cave.

He decided to follow his instincts. He sent twenty of his men onto The Ledge, while others waited close by, ready to replace them if required.

Having broken through the descending Militia, eight surviving Trackers raced up the western side, now beyond the Militia and within thirty paces of the Cave, as Brass Slings from above opened fire.

They pushed forward, now aware of the El-Bhat that were positioned in front of the Quartz Door, as Militia continued to pursue them from behind.

Undaunted, they used the pieces of armour that still clung tightly to their arms, to deflect the brass balls as they raced to the Cave, and then crashed into the first line of black warriors.

Hoping beyond hope, that the others who carried the Amulet would soon be there!

---------- <> ----------

The El-Bhat Leader watched in anguish as his warriors fell before the Tracker blades ... but mostly to the Brass Slings firing from above!

It should have been different, but his men were unwittingly allowing the Trackers to use them as shields as they struggled against the dance of death on that crowded Ledge.

---------- <> ----------

The sounds of battle that had diminished to nothing, were beginning to return as Finn and his four Trackers raced towards the forest above the Cave.

Those joyful sounds told Finn that some of his Trackers were still alive, and *that* increased their chances immensely.

Racing down the mountain, they could now see the backs of the Militia, sixty paces ahead.

As they entered the zone of battle, like a human hurricane thirty paces wide, Finn and his men disarmed every man with a quick cut to his arm, as they charged towards the top of the Quartz Door.

---------- <> ----------

Before Nusdek knew what was happening, half of his men were wounded and unable to fight ... and five Trackers had leapt down to The Ledge!

---------- <> ----------

The restricted battlefield, in front of the Quartz Door, had become a *very* crowded place once the remaining eight Trackers from below charged into the El-Bhat defence.

Many of his black warriors died on that small piece of rock ... but others were simply pushed off in the struggle.

It was that image of a falling warrior that taught the El-Bhat Leader how he was going to defeat these invincible Trackers.

---------- <> ----------

With precision, each of the five Trackers from above, landed with a killing stroke.

213

For a moment, there were only a few El-Bhat left, but the Militia from below had arrived and had begun to fire into the melee of warriors.

And more El-Bhat came pouring in from the eastern side to replace their black silk warrior brothers.

While keeping one eye on Far-fel, Finn fought furiously to clear the remaining warriors that blocked access to the Amulet keyhole.

Up to this point, his armour had only been exposed to the occasional shot from the Brass slings, but standing on the western side of The Ledge, as he cleared the space of El-Bhat, he was exposed to the full brunt of those deadly weapons.

In desperation he turned and shouted, "Far-fel, the Amulet!"

Far-fel had never imagined having to insert the Amulet under these conditions. But he knew that Finn was right. If they didn't try now ...

Quickly he cut the bands that held his chest armour in place and grabbed the Amulet.

And held it safely in his hand ... against the flying brass balls.

Finn glanced occasionally in Far-fel's direction, ready to assist him once he had the Amulet ready.

He was ready!

He slipped backwards to protect Far-fel as he took those last few steps towards their goal.

Everything was riding on what happened in the next few heartbeats!

A single brass ball aimed at Far-fel's chest would require an adjustment.

Finn pushed forward against the sleet of brass ... ready to take the Amulet if necessary.

--------- <> ---------

With eagerness, the El-Bhat Leader began sending additional warriors onto The Ledge.

He wasn't going to win this battle in hand to hand combat.

He was going to win it, by sheer force of numbers that would push these invincible Trackers off The Ledge into the waiting jaws of the *metal sticks*.

The Caves of Balhok

But no sooner had his warriors begun to overcrowd the battlefield, when five more Trackers descended from above, instantly killing five more El-Bhat.

It was mayhem as the standing nine Trackers slashed into the onslaught of black silk warriors, expertly using them as shields from the Militia that continued to fire from the west and above.

Then the El-Bhat Leader saw the impossible. One of the Trackers shed his armour and pulled out an Amulet!

Without hesitation, he shouted the words that would bring everything to an end. El-bayai!

Chapter 41 - What is your name?

Previously, five thousand El-Bhat, that had waited north of Kel-eetan, were warned by a message from Ou-Leesen-el-Bra-ten, allowing them to escape. Eventually, they found him, and shared intelligence regarding the Militia force that were heading for the Mines of Tenleth.

The few hundred El-Bhat, following Ou-Leesen-el-Bra-ten, suddenly swelled to five thousand. Once again, his plans would need to be modified.
"How are the men?" Ou-Leesen-el-Bra-ten asked, as he rode among them with his Personal Guards.

"It has been difficult finding you. We have pushed them hard and our food supplies have been exhausted for some time. We have leaned heavily on the El-Bhat villages for support. But it was never enough. It is good to be with you again. Your message of warning has given the men confidence that they are led by the Dagger of Truth."

The El-Bhat Leader had seen enough. The five thousand would not have to wait until the evening meal. "Even the best heart withers away … when the body lacks strength," he told his Personal Guards. "We eat now."
"Tell the Wagon Masters to distribute food until the five thousand are fed."

As the Personal Guards galloped away, he turned to Stek.
"Take my Personal Band and enough gold to replenish our food at the next Oasis. Have the Merchants ready, when we arrive at sunset.
"Tomorrow, and every day after, you will repeat this strategy, until we are at the borders of the Mines of Tenleth."

As Stek and Ou-Leesen's personal Band of twenty rode away, Ou-Leesen-el-Bra-ten stood atop the nearest dune, until they disappeared under the horizon of sand.

He turned to the five thousand, spread amongst the hundred wagons as they filled their weary bodies with much needed food.

The Caves of Balhok

'These are good men' he thought to himself. 'Worthy of the sacrifice they will face at the Mines of Tenleth.'

He looked down at the blade hanging at his side. Stek was right, it was their only hope.

Somehow, he needed to figure out how he was going to use this power, to defeat an enemy that was unbeatable ... and survive the nightmares until they got there.

The following morning, Stek found the El-Bhat Warrior in his tent, sitting on his bedroll.

"Permission to come in?" he said as he entered.

The Warrior looked up, as though he was trying to figure out who had just entered his tent.

Stek went down on one knee, his hand at his scabbard ... ready to take his life.

"Are you well?" the Tracker asked.

There was a pause. "Yes."

"What is your name?"

Another pause. "My name ... is Ou-Leesen-el-Bra-ten."

Stek's hand drifted away from his knife. "Good to hear. We are ready to leave. We will meet you at the next oasis. The food supplies will be ready when the wagons arrive."

The ritual was repeated every morning as the camp was arising. Every day the pause was getting longer.

On the fifth day of the ritual, as Stek entered the tent, Ou-Leesen did not look up.

Stek went down on one knee, his hand at his scabbard ... ready to take his life.

"Are you well?" the Tracker asked.

The head came up, the eyes narrowed, and a scowl began to form.

This was the moment Stek had prepared for.

He immediately left the tent, grabbed the water jug he had left outside, re-entered, and threw it at the face of the Warrior Leader.

On one knee, with one hand holding the water jug, and the other ready at his blade, he asked, "Are you well?"

217

Still sputtering, and gasping for breath, the Warrior shook his head of the excess water and said, glaring, "My name … is Ou-Leesen-el-Bra-ten!"

Stek grinned and said, "Good to hear. We are ready to leave. We will meet you at the next oasis. The food supplies will be ready when the wagons arrive."

That night, as Stek sat down across from the Warrior in Black Silk, he waited for the El-Bhat Leader to begin.

"That was a good trick," the Leader said, as he poured sand through his fingers. "Something a friend would do."

The small fire sputtered cinders into the night air.

"How many more days before we arrive?" the Tracker asked.

"You need to keep me alive for four more days," Ou-Leesen answered.

"Glad we are almost there. It's not so easy to feed a family of five thousand."

The Leader poured some more sand.

"You are right. They are like my children. And it grieves me that I am taking them to their death."

"So … we aren't sure yet how to use the Dagger against our enemies," Stek concluded. "Nothing in those memories?" he pressed.

"The problem with my memories, is that Shanteef never had to face an *unbeatable* enemy. But … perhaps when the time comes … my Advisor will have a solution."

Stek was nodding slowly. "Perhaps …"

The following morning, Stek didn't bother to leave the jug outside or even to ask the question.

He simply walked in and threw the water.

Chapter 42 - Water water everywhere

Previously, Braddock, with his gathered Tinkers, and The Commander with his gathered Trackers, left Arborville, guided by Fre-steel and Ranoof, to the Mines of Tenleth.

Braddock was waiting outside the Border Pass Guard House, as The Commander exited. They walked together, back towards the hundreds of wagons that waited for permission, to take the Trackers and Tinkers to the Mines of Tenleth.

"You were longer than I expected," Braddock commented as he gave a final glance towards the Guards, who stood above, on the Plateau Fortresses on either side. The place held so many tortured memories.

"Yeah, well ... it wasn't as easy as it should have been." The Commander finally replied.

The Tinker took another look at The Commander. "Actually, you don't look so good. What happened in there?"

"Well for starters, they didn't want to let us through."

"Uhh ... wasn't this a formality ... you know, a Tracker Commander signing the Passage Book?"

"I thought so. But remember the three hundred Militia that were sent ahead of us. Well they came with signed papers from the Planning and Development Guild. The instructions were to let them through and to restrict all passage through Border Pass, until further notice from Craslin."

"That doesn't sound good. How did you convince them to go sideways on those orders?"

"Agreed to take Olleti. Not a pleasant experience. But it got the job done."

"What about the 'until further notice' part? Craslin has to be referring to the thousand wagons that will soon arrive."

"The Tracker in charge understands things differently since I took Olleti. His men will drop the boulders off the Plateau Fortresses, plugging the Pass temporarily, and then join us. It won't stop them but will surely buy us some time."

They arrived at the first wagon. The two on the driver's bench, were Fre-steel and Ranoof.

"The Gates are open," The Commander advised, and then continued walking.

Braddock hesitated, as he looked at Fre-steel. "I understand you've been to the Mines of Tenleth before."

Fre-steel nodded in the affirmative.

"You sure you remember how to get there?"

He looked towards the Pass as he said, "In my dreams, the road to Tenleth haunts me ... every night."

Braddock laid a hand on the bench. The look, the words, reminded him of Urshen. "Guess you *can't* forget," the old Tinker said. "Ranoof, keep him alive," he added, and then hurried towards his Tinkers.

--------- <> ---------

They hadn't travelled very far before Ranoof was sure that he was seeing El-Bhat spies.

That night they discussed their situation.

"We need to pick our resting stations carefully," Braddock suggested. "A spot that is easily guarded through the night." Everyone nodded in agreement. If anyone understood wagon security, it was the Tinkers.

"We will rotate the Guards, and they will sleep during the day," The Commander offered.

"And uhh," Ranoof said, as he looked across the fire to his companion, "I suggest that Fre-steel sleep in the middle of the wagon enclosure."

Ever since Braddock told him to keep their guide alive, he couldn't stop thinking about how easily their mission would be scuttled, if Fre-steel was killed.

"Agreed," both Leaders said in unison.

Soon the Guards were assigned, the wagons repositioned, and Ranoof was finally able to get a good night sleep.

As the days continued it seemed odd to Ranoof that there wasn't more of an effort from the El-Bhat, to at least harass them as they journeyed through their country. "Where do you think the El-Bhat have gone?" he finally asked Fre-steel.

"Ghosts. They are like ghosts. They will show up soon enough."

About half way to the Mines of Tenleth, Ranoof saw for himself, what Fre-steel was talking about.

They had arrived at the next oasis, ready to restock their water supplies ... but the well had been sabotaged.

"A desperate measure for the El-Bhat," Fre-steel commented. "Wells are the lifeblood to this society and considered sacred. They would never do this unless they felt it was their only hope."

"It *is* the first time that the people of Storlenia have invaded their country," Ranoof commented. "That has *got* to mean something to these people."

"Yes, you are right. But there is also a *reason* why no one ever comes here to invade."

Ranoof looked out across the wilderness landscape and was sure they were already staring that reason in the face.

Eventually Braddock and The Commander arrived at the oasis and a Council was called.

"It looks like we have enough water to last us to the next oasis, but if it's in the same condition ..." The Commander offered as an opening statement.

Everyone looked to Fre-steel for advice.

"Well ... it seems that we have no choice but to split up," he recommended.

"Isn't that what they want us to do?" Braddock asked, obviously concerned about the suggestion.

"What do you mean split up? And why would we do that?" The Commander jumped in.

Fre-steel was nodding at their questions, ready to give them answers.

"Later today, we will come to a junction road, that heads west. But ... we will set up camp ten leagues before the junction, to remove any suspicion regarding my plan," he began.

He turned to Ranoof. "Once we've camped, I will give you instructions to lead the Trackers onward, down the shortest way to the Mines of Tenleth. It is what they are expecting us to do.

"After dark, I will take the Tinkers on the junction road towards an oasis that I know about. We will take most of the water wagons with us.

221

"We will meet you at the next oasis. It is sure to be sabotaged, so wait for us there. It will be the safest place to stop. They will assume that you are out of water, will have to dig a new well, and will surely die before you can get enough water for your men. It is why nobody ever comes here to attack. The desert always does the fighting for them."

The Commander was looking at Braddock.
Braddock was tugging on his gold earring. "Don't worry, we will bring him back alive ... with the water," the old Tinker said.

--------- <> ---------

During the night, the winds of northern Denlen never stopped.
The sound of moving wagons was snuffed out so thoroughly that not even the Tracker Guards heard the Tinkers leave. And by dawn, the shifting sands had buried every evidence of their passing.

The Commander had joined Ranoof in the lead wagon, as they prepared to head south to the next oasis.
The wind had brought a dusty haze to the firmament above, blotting out the guiding track of the sun as it moved across the sky.
And the well-travelled road ahead was beginning to disappear below the shifting sands. Ranoof snapped the reins, anxious to begin while there was still a road to follow.

"I am beginning to understand Braddock's concern of splitting our forces," The Commander said, after travelling for a while. "If this wind persists, we might never see each other again."
"But ..." Ranoof grinned, "the El-Bhat will never see us coming."

By mid-morning there was no sign that the winds would abate anytime soon.
"Do you think we should continue if the road totally disappears," The Commander asked.
Trackers were famous for their ability to know where they were, and how best to get where they were going. But that was back in Storlenia where they had access to the stars, the sun, and familiar landscape.
The soup they were travelling in, was something completely foreign to them. It was why The Commander had asked the question.
Ranoof kept driving, he didn't know how to answer the question. In fact, he wondered how Fre-steel was managing. Surely, *he* must have some

The Caves of Balhok

idea of how to follow the road in these conditions, considering that Fre-steel would be required to travel much further before they met again.

For that matter, what did the El-Bhat do? For it occurred to him that these winds were a steady affliction to travel, just like heavy rain was back in his home town.

'But at least with the rains' Ranoof thought, 'you didn't have to worry about leaving the road on a darkened night.' And that was because the rains softened the road, allowing the wheels from fellow travellers, to create ruts. Which always kept his wagon wheels where they were supposed to be on those black nights. Indeed, more than once, he fell asleep, knowing he *couldn't* leave the road.

"Guaranteed *these* roads have never seen a rut," he mumbled to himself.

"What was that?" his companion asked.

"Oh, I was just thinking ... about ruts."

A few heartbeats passed, and then they simultaneously looked at each other.

"Packed dirt ..." Ranoof began.

"... under the wagon wheels!" The Commander finished.

A cheerful Ranoof drove his wagon immediately off the road to test their idea.

They didn't go far before the wheels had sunk into the sand too far to allow the horses to pull the load.

The following day, shortly after the winds died away, they arrived at the next oasis.

Without getting out of the wagon, Ranoof and The Commander, could see the pile of rocks rising out of the well. Sabotaged as expected.

While other Trackers unleashed the horses, Ranoof walked over to the well.

It was typical for oasis wells to be as wide as a man was tall. The depth varied, depending on how far down the underground stream was. But even for the shallowest well, that meant removing a lot of rock.

He laid his hand on the boulder at the edge of the oasis. It would take four or five men just to move it ... never mind take one this large from the bottom to the top. And then there was the sand that was added to fill the spaces between the boulders.

As he contemplated the effort it was for the El-Bhat to plug this well, he heard the snort of a horse who had wandered unattended, over to his side.

"Sorry, no water today," he said to the anxious horse.

He reached to take hold of the reins, but the horse pulled away and snorted again, as he sniffed among the rocks.

When he tried again, the horse jumped away and went to the other side of the well, where he continued his search for the water.

Before Ranoof could move, one of the Trackers in charge of the horses, laid a hand on his shoulder. "It's strange that he can smell water from so far down."

Ranoof turned to see a studied look and a furrowed brow.

"What are you suggesting?"

"I am saying that this horse wouldn't be so persistent if he couldn't smell the water. But that must mean that these rocks, and sand, don't go down very far."

Ranoof was grinning as he ran to find The Commander.

"It makes sense. Especially on the *second* sabotaged well. They knew we were expecting the exact same thing here, as at the previous location," Ranoof said as they walked up to the edge of the well, where the horse was still trying to get to the water.

"We would die of thirst before we could dig another well, and ... after we leave, it's a simple matter to restore this one."

"Well done," The Commander said to the Ferrier Tracker. "And give the horse an extra ration of grain ... and water."

By nightfall, the men had restored the well, and filled the barrels of the few water wagons they had. Now they would wait for the Tinkers.

Chapter 43 - The abandoned mine shafts

Two days later, as the sun was peaking above the far horizon, The Commander found Ranoof at the southern edge of the oasis, staring down the road towards the foothills and the Mines of Tenleth beyond.

"Any idea why he isn't here yet ... did he say anything that might help?" The Commander asked.

"Nope," was the quiet reply.

"What about water supply in the foothills?"

"There are springs. The largest one, close to the Mines, is heavily guarded."

Ranoof looked at The Commander for a response. He knew Fre-steel was supposed to have caught up by nightfall the day before.

"We need to move on," The Commander declared, "and hope we find one of those springs before we run out."

"I left a coded message for Fre-steel at the well ... if they make it." Ranoof added.

The two Trackers headed back to the wagons.

"I will send out spies as soon as we get close to the foothills," The Commander said as he jumped up into the wagon. "And as soon as we are *in* the foothills, with the advantage of elevation, we can watch for the Tinkers."

The only constant on the journey south, were the roads.

After they left the hot grasslands of Border Pass, they journeyed through fertile fields of fruit trees and of grain.

Then further south, as they entered the windswept rocky lands, Fre-steel advised them, they were entering El-Bhat territory. Eventually the rugged terrain shifted into vast stretches of parched desert, frequently dotted with various sized oases.

Ranoof could now see foothills in the far distance. They were the northern link of the mountain chain that hid the Mines of Tenleth. This much Fre-steel had told him.

Occasionally he would stand and turn around to see if he could see any sign of the Tinkers.

He knew The Commander was right to insist they move on ... to complete the mission. But without Fre-steel, they were walking blind into the enemy camp.

But he hadn't given up hope.

Mostly because they needed Fre-steel ... and the Tinkers.

"You're worried," The Commander suggested, after Ranoof sat down on the bench.

"Well ... of course," a surprised Ranoof replied. "Shouldn't we be? If he doesn't show up ..."

"Ever thought about why *you* were chosen?" The Commander asked after a period of silence.

In fact, he hadn't ... not really.

His eyes looked down the desolate road, as the dawn cast shadows of light across the distant foothills. His hands held the reins to horses that needed no guidance.

'I suppose', he thought to himself, 'it began when my father first took me into the Woods of Lartenelle.'

His father wanted him to follow in his footsteps as a Tracker, so he took him there to advance his training. And it was there in that forest that he decided that he wanted to be a Tracker ... and never to drink wine.

Then Mitrock asked him to join the twelve Trackers who were assigned to escort Urshen to Border Pass. Apparently, this young man in a Robe, was somehow important, but to Ranoof, he was simply obeying orders.

Until the day, Urshen rose to his feet, in front of a small squad of El-Bhat, who had entered the prison with orders to cut off his hands. And he defeated them all, with impossible speed and fighting form.

Then Deema called Urshen the Chosen One.

Then Ranoof found himself linked to Urshen and the other Trackers in the Circle of Blood, as they defeated the El-Bhat at Border Pass.

Then he escaped the entrapment at Pechora Tracking Guild ... because he didn't drink wine.

And because he met Protas in a barn, he hurried to Qar-ana where he met Zephra, who gave him two Amulets, with the assignment to have them joined into one, and taken to Braddock.

And there in Tinker Village, after he passed on the glowing Amulet, he became part of a threesome, that were shown a dark future for Ankoletia ... unless they could complete their missions.

His mission was to assist Fre-steel. A Tracker whose ambition was to free, the women and children slaves, at the Mines of Tenleth.

He had assumed that he was there to simply assist Fre-steel ... who *was* the chosen one.

But looking back ...

Was *he* the one who was supposed to carry the weight of this mission?

Was it why he was here?

Was Fre-steel already dead?

"*Chosen* can mean so many things," Ranoof finally answered, not ready for the enormity of what The Commander was suggesting.

"Awareness ... can take time," The Commander offered. But hoping that it wouldn't take too much time. They couldn't afford it.

--------- <> ---------

The Head Band Leader waited, as one of the Personal Guards of the Next Quorum Leader, entered The Quorum Room, with his message.

Soon they re-appeared. "You may enter now."

The Head Band Leader touched the gold inlaid door, which led to the Quorum Room as he entered. Soon he was sitting on soft pillows, as he considered the eyes of the Quorum Leader.

"It was as you said," he began. "The enemy arrived soon after we took our position on the Mountain of Despair. They were there to open the Cave door ... as you said. But they have been vanquished."

The Quorum Leader showed no sign of surprise or acknowledgement. Only a look of smug superiority.

So, the El-Bhat Band Leader added, "... at a cost of many of my men."

Apparently, from the response of the Next Quorum Leader, that fact was not relevant. He simply continued.

"Now ... I want you to go to the Mines of Tenleth and gather more men on your way. I have already sent as many warriors as I can allow, who wait for your arrival. You will assist them to protect the slaves and the Mines."

The Next Quorum Leader reached for his goblet of chilled wine as he considered his next words.

"Many warriors from Storlenia already crowd the road to Tenleth. They are there to take away our slaves. But the Mines cannot be operated without slaves!" The Quorum Leader's green eyes glowed with anger.

"The Storlenians will arrive first. Then the El-Bhat, that Ou-Leesen has gathered, will arrive next ... again to free the slaves."

"How many Storlenians are coming? And are there any Trackers?" His memory of how his men were almost defeated by twenty Trackers, still burned like glowing coals in his mind.

"There are Tinkers ... and Trackers. But they can be defeated without losing a single warrior. My personal Guards will explain this to you."

"What about the El-Bhat that follow Ou-Leesen-el-Bra-ten?" the Band Leader asked. "They are misguided but they are still El-Bhat."

"Ou-Leesen is nothing without the Dagger of Truth. And because it does not belong to him, he grows weaker every time he uses it.

"*Force* him to use it, and soon you will be placing the Dagger of Truth in my hands."

"It will be done," the Band Leader bowed his head in submission, and then added, "These are strange times. The Mountain of Despair, the Mines of Tenleth, and the Dagger of Truth ... all in commotion."

"Yes ... you are right. But we *will* succeed. And then the El-Bhat will finally take their rightful place, as rulers of all Ankoletia."

The Quorum Leader extended his hand towards the gold-gilded door, signifying that their meeting was over.

The Band Leader paused as he considered the orders.

"My men are exhausted and many wounded. We have travelled far and fought much. We need a few days rest before we leave."

The Next Quorum Leader closed his eyes as he considered the response. After a few moments, he opened them. They glowed more brightly than ever.

"You may rest a day, but then you must leave if you are to arrive before they do. Remember ... our enemies *must* fail."

As the Head Band Leader left, The Next Quorum Leader smiled wickedly to himself. The Green Lady had prepared him well for this last battle. Soon he would be the Next Leader *of Ankoletia*!

Once they reached the foothills, it didn't take long for the Tracker spies to find the first spring. And soon the water barrels were once again full. And the journey continued.

At the next camp, Ranoof sought out the spies. He was curious about the emptiness of the land north of the Mines.

"The only thing we can figure ... is that they have been gathered," one of the spies offered.

So, his hunch was true. Not only could he see no El-Bhat from the wagon, but there were none to be found in the foothills either.

The next morning, as he jumped up onto the bench, and took the reins, he looked at The Commander. "When I asked Fre-steel about why there were no El-Bhat, he said they were ghosts. And that made sense before. We saw a few, south of Border Pass, and then we saw evidence of their passing at the sabotaged wells. But ... we are getting *close* to the Mines ... the *famous* Tenleth Mines. Why are there no El-Bhat harassing us ... trying to defeat us before we even make it to the Mines?"

"Perhaps it's easily defended," The Commander responded. "And ... making the enemy come this far ... through a land that is very hostile, has to be part of their strategy. But we probably won't know for sure until we get there."

Ranoof liked The Commander's logic, but the last part, about not knowing until they arrived, sounded bells of warning. These El-Bhat were cooking something up, that was sure. His concerns made him think back to the Butcher Block at Border Pass.

He wagged his head at the memory, knowing that the outcome would have been very different if Urshen hadn't been there. 'Yeah,' he thought, 'sure wish *he* was here right now.'

Later in the morning a Tracker spy came riding up to the Lead Wagon.

"Commander, we have spotted the Tinkers. South of here there is a junction. They were down that road about ten leagues."

"Finally, some good news," Ranoof commented, as the rider left to spread the news back down the Wagon Train.

"Yes. But undoubtedly, they have a story to tell," The Commander added.

A short time later, the two Lead Wagons sat at the junction, ready to share intelligence.

The four of them jumped down, but Braddock was the first to speak.

"Before we get into it, our men and horses could use whatever water you might have to spare."

"Of course. Barrels are mostly full. Springs are easy to find."

Braddock gave a whistle which emptied the wagons of his men, all carrying empty water buckets for the horses.

Ranoof jumped back up to retrieve their water bottles and then handed them to Braddock and Fre-steel.

The Commander watched the procession for a while and then asked Fre-steel, "What happened?"

"They anticipated our plan. The first oasis we came to, was also sabotaged. We had to keep moving until we found water.

"And when we did, those villagers allowed us to take whatever water we needed, but we had to agree that other oasis wells, would be for the villagers only."

"See any El-Bhat?" Ranoof asked.

"None," Braddock replied. "Remind you of the Butcher Block?" he asked The Commander.

He was nodding in agreement. "How far are the Mines from here?" he asked Fre-steel.

"A day to the next water source, and then another and we will be there."

Later that day, after filling the water barrels, the Trackers and Tinkers set up camp not far from the spring. They would leave the wagons at that point and travel the remaining distance on foot.

The Commander, Braddock, Ranoof and Fre-steel, gathered around the campfire to finalize their strategy.

After Fre-steel shared what he knew about the Mines and the region surrounding them, The Commander and Braddock agreed it was best to split up the men into four groups, being led by one of them.

Each group would approach the Mines from a different direction, thus creating flank support and confusion among the El-Bhat.

The plan made sense and soon the discussion drifted to silence as they contemplated what tomorrow would bring.

Ranoof pulled his collar up. The Desert night air was cooling fast. He decided that he had one last question for Fre-steel. "Before we met, you were coming here by yourself. What were you planning to do ... to rescue them?"

Fre-steel pushed the coals around for a while with his stick, as he thought about the question.

"In the beginning ... my plan to rescue the women and children, was driven by my need to feel redeemed. My path to redemption was built on successfully freeing the women and children from Tenleth.

"When I finally realized that my plan was reckless at best, I abandoned the idea. Ironically, when you entered my prison cell, I had already made up my mind to find some other way to pay back society, for my ... foolishness." Embarrassed by his confession, he returned his attention to the coals.

"You haven't answered my question ... how you were going to rescue them?"

He laid the stick down. "After the traitorous Guild Master transferred me to Border Pass, I was sick at heart. The El-Bhat picked up on that immediately, and so, instead of killing me, they lied to me, until I believed that *their* way was the way of enlightenment.

"As part of my recruitment, they sent me on a mission to transfer women and children from Toobor to the Mines. When I arrived, the Slave Masters tormented me with despicable assignments ... including dragging the dead slaves, to the Death Pit.

"When slaves collapsed, and couldn't be revived, the quickest way to the Death Pit, was using an abandoned mine shaft. I soon learned that there were other abandoned shafts. Shafts that could be used to escape to the foothills beyond the *active* shafts."

"What made you change your mind about using this plan?" The Commander asked.

"The smallest sound echoes through these shafts like thunder. If a child cried out, all would be lost."

Braddock caught the eye of The Commander, "I think what this plan needs is a diversion."

"Perhaps three diversions," Ranoof suggested.

"Agreed," The Commander said. "By the Fates, I believe we have hit on a very important element in our strategy. Fre-steel, tell us how you see your plan unfolding with the support of your group and a diversion created by the other three."

An enthusiastic Fre-steel threw his stick into the fire, as he led the discussion, of a plan he believed would work.

Eventually, satisfied that they were ready for anything the El-Bhat had prepared, they retired.

Chapter 44 - The Mines of Death

Ranoof silently led his group down the middle, while Braddock and The Commander, each took one of his flanks, until they were within the far perimeter of the Mining Area.

Fre-steel and his men, had left many hours earlier. They would descend from the foothills behind the Mines, into an abandoned mine shaft, where they would be able to rescue the slaves, while the El-Bhat focused on the diversion, the other three groups would create.

It was still dark. The slaves and most of the El-Bhat would be asleep.
With outstretched arm, Ranoof wagged his thumb, to test for enough light. Once he could see his thumb as it moved back and forth, it was time to move forward and engage the El-Bhat Guards.
Until then, he had more than enough time to worry about the emptiness. The same emptiness they had followed throughout the El-Bhat lands.
They had encountered nothing in the way of far-out perimeter Guards. This was impossible in view of his certainty that the El-Bhat knew of their coming. Where were they?

--------- <> ---------

With excitement, Fre-steel led his men down familiar shafts, that would eventually lead to the sleeping pens of the slaves.
The combined group of Tinkers and Trackers were so silent, that he occasionally found himself turning around, to reassure himself, that they were still following him along these abandoned tunnels.
At the end of the last tunnel, they waited for the test of light.
When he could see his thumb wagging, they silently moved out of the tunnel.

The closer they got to the sleeping pens, the more Fre-steel knew that something was wrong. Everything was too quiet.
His men crowded around him as he stared at the open doors. Beyond those doors, the pens were empty.

--------- <> ---------

Ranoof could see his thumb. Carefully he began to move forward ... until someone shouted from afar.

"Do not come forward ... or they will all die!"

He stopped and crouched down to minimize his exposure. His men followed his lead.

He reviewed the message in his mind. Surely 'they will all die' couldn't be Fre-steel and his group. There would have been a struggle ... and lots of noise.

'*They* ... must be ... the slaves!' he thought to himself.

He thought he could hear Braddock's men move to his left.

There was another shout. "Stop ... or they will die!"

There was a long pause as the morning light continued to illuminate the desolate landscape in front of them. And then there was another shout.

"See for yourselves. If you advance ... they will die!"

The ground in front of them, dipped downward towards the Mines. With the advancing rays of sunlight, Ranoof could see the Guard that had shouted the commands.

Past this Guard, he was beginning to see the outline of a large body of men. But that didn't make sense. That was in the direction of the Death Pit. Far to the right of the Mine entrances where they expected to find the El-Bhat.

Once the light had revealed the three groups of invaders, the Guard turned and pointed to the Death Pit. He shouted an invitation. "Send three men to see for yourselves."

The Commander was the first to come forward, then Braddock and Ranoof.

They walked a short distance past the Guard where the scene before them was terribly clear.

The El-Bhat had gathered all the slaves and positioned them around the Death Pit.

And around the perimeter of slaves, were the El-Bhat ready to use their swords to push the slaves into the pit, to their death. A thousand slaves surrounded by a thousand El-Bhat.

Now Ranoof could understand the emptiness of the land. Of course, there was no need to attack the advancing enemy. All they had to do was to watch and wait.

All the slaves were gagged. It explained the silence.

Ranoof looked over at The Commander and Braddock. He could see defeat written on their faces.

The Commander was the first to speak. If nothing else, he needed to buy Fre-steel enough time to discover the rout and hasten out of the tunnels.

"You need the slaves. You wouldn't do this," he shouted.

The Guard raised his sword and the screams of several slaves could be heard as they plummeted to their death.

"Do you surrender?" the Guard shouted.

"We will never surrender. But we will return to our lands," The Commander replied.

"Then you must surrender your weapons. You may keep your knives."

Braddock looked at The Commander and nodded in agreement to the terms.

"Very well … but we will leave our weapons *after* we have safely boarded our wagons."

"We will follow you to Border Pass to see if you keep your word," the El-Bhat threatened.

The Mines of Tenleth huddled in silence as the Guard watched the three return to their different groups. And then leave Tenleth forever.

The road back to the wagons was a long path for Ranoof.

There was no hurry. They needed to allow Fre-steel extra time to meet them at their departure point.

But he was full of questions.

Why did they come?

Why was he given the dream that instructed him to assist Fre-steel, in freeing the women and children?

How did the El-Bhat know exactly what their plan was?

Surely, they expected conquering invaders to want the wealth of the Mines ... not the slaves! But they knew exactly what they came for ... probably from the moment they entered Shaksbah. But how?

"They knew. But they couldn't have known!" an angry and determined Fre-steel shouted at the other three.

"Will we go back?" A disheartened Ranoof asked.

"Of course not," The Commander said to Ranoof. "When it comes to the El-Bhat, I say what I have to say to keep us alive. But we are not defeated. And they know it."

"I too was surprised that they knew," Braddock offered Fre-steel. "But obviously, the terms of this war have changed. We know things that we normally wouldn't know. And now, so do they."

"That makes sense. But what will we do now?" Fre-steel asked.

The Commander looked at Braddock who nodded in agreement. "We will find a place for the wagons. A place in the foothills, easily defended. And then, in small groups of fifty, we will watch the roads. And we will watch the El-Bhat.

"We will look for opportunities to harass them, to plunder their food supplies, to cut off communications. Until we see an opportunity to free the slaves. By the Fates above ... I did not come down here to turn around and go back."

Fre-steel was nodding enthusiastically. "I think I know a good place for the wagons."

Ranoof and his small group were assigned to watch the road to the east. They were high in the foothills when they spotted the dust cloud. It was massive. Whoever was coming, would arrive at the Mines within half a day. They hurried back.

"It must be the Militia that we have heard about," The Commander suggested. "And coming from the east, means that they have already defeated the Government forces at Kel-eetan."

"What will we do?" Ranoof asked.

"Spread the word to the men. Have them retreat to the wagons. We must not engage the Militia. Soon they will take control of the Mines. Meanwhile we will watch ... carefully.

"Eventually they will send most of their wagons back to Kel-eetan and Storlenia. Then we will find an opportunity to free the slaves."

--------- <> ---------

The Head Band Leader argued with the El-Bhat in charge of the Mines.

"The Storlenians come with weapons that fire brass balls ... like these," he pulled one from his silk pouch.

"I have seen what they can do. Our only hope is to force them to fight here in the Mines."

"Our only hope ... is to remember that we are El-Bhat," the large El-Bhat shouted back.

"Prepare the men. We will stall them until the darkness of night makes us invisible."

--------- <> ---------

Back in the foothills, The Commander and Braddock watched with their telescopes.

Hundreds and hundreds of wagons spread out as they approached from the east.

In response, the El-Bhat began to pour out of the Mines with their horses and catapults.

--------- <> ---------

As the main body of El-Bhat busied themselves with securing and preparing the long-range catapults, Bands of horse-riders rode forward to engage the enemy.

It would be a while until the advantage of darkness descended upon those desolate plains. They must hold the enemy until then.

But those riders never got close enough to fire an arrow. Soon brass balls were ripping into their flesh ... and their horses.

And the wagons kept coming.

The Head Band Leader stared in awe at the magnitude of the enemy that approached.

He thought back to his conversations with the Next Quorum Leader. The instructions regarding the Storlenians at the Mountain of Despair and those that came to free the slaves, was evidence that the Quorum Leader knew things that a mortal man could not. And the El-Bhat came off as conquerors ... both times!

But where was Ou-Leesen with the Dagger of Truth?

And why was there no mention of this advancing horde of Storlenians with wagons that covered the land like ants.

If they already had the Dagger of Truth, perhaps the tide of this battle could be turned in their favour.

But they didn't. And the dark power that had advised their Quorum Leader, had betrayed the El-Bhat!

"Fire," a voice behind him shouted. The Storlenian wagons were now in range of the catapults.

And for a while, the El-Bhat had their moment of glory. But there were just *too many* wagons.

The world had become a strange place of power and confusion, for the Head Band Leader, as he thought back to the Storlenians at the Mountain of Despair, and their Sticks of steel and brass.

They could have easily killed the El-Bhat, but they didn't. All they were interested in, was to keep the Trackers from opening the Cave door … exactly what the El-Bhat wanted.

And now, it was only a matter of time before those brass balls shredded him and the other El-Bhat, like the Trackers he left dead, back on the mountain slope.

--------- <> ---------

The Head Band Leader was now lying among the dead at the Mines of Tenleth as the Green Lady visited the Next Quorum Leader.

"It is only a matter of time now," she purred seductively. *"Within a few days, the Dagger of Truth will be yours, and you will be the Next Leader of Ankoletia. I will return to instruct you in the gathering of your people."*

He bowed his forehead to the rich carpet and smiled as she disappeared in a mist of green. He would soon realize what Shanteef and Arl-sheen only dreamt of.

Chapter 45 - The chain of remarkable events

The Trackers and Tinkers watched as the Militia busied themselves as the new operator of the Mines.
The spies reported that the slaves were immediately put to work throwing the dead El-Bhat into the Pit of Death.

Next, they shovelled a layer of lime dust over the El-Bhat bodies until the shining black surface was white as snow.

Ranoof watched the spies leave after giving their report. Life could be so ironic ... the *slaves* were busy throwing lime dust over the *El-Bhat*.

'These are definitely strange times,' thought Ranoof. He went to find Fre-steel, he needed someone to talk to. Someone that could make sense of what was going on.

A few days later, in the early morning, the spies from the far perimeter returned. Their assignment was to watch the roads, fifty leagues out. This was well beyond the range of the telescopes. Braddock and The Commander wanted to know everything that was happening in the area, as they waited for the main body of the Militia to leave.

"There is more El-Bhat coming ... from the south. Lots of them!"
"Do they have wagons and catapults?" The Commander asked.
"No catapults, only wagons."
Ranoof watched Braddock and The Commander exchange looks.
"They will be butchered," Braddock said quietly.

'A strange dilemma,' thought Ranoof as he watched to see what The Commander would do.
They thought they were only days away from the moment when the greater portion of the Militia would leave, allowing them a window of opportunity to rescue the slaves.
And then suddenly ... another enemy was about to arrive.

It was truly a frustration to their plans. But could they allow them to be slaughtered like the El-Bhat who had protected the Mines.

"Perhaps ... we should send a few spies with a message," The Commander said to the others.

"They will need a flag pole, with two strips of red cloth," Fre-steel interjected. "This is how the El-Bhat greet other El-Bhat. Also ... once our spies see the black warriors, they should stop and wait for *them* to come."

"I want to go with the spies," Ranoof suddenly jumped in.

"Too risky," The Commander replied.

"Maybe ... but I *need* to go."

The Commander looked at Braddock who shrugged in response, and said, "I would let him go."

"All right. Assign three to wait with the flagpole. And you hold back and watch with the other spies. We need to know how this goes ... and we need to keep you alive."

The wind was gently flapping the colourful Tinker scarves. Ranoof and the other two spies waited as the long line of wagons approached.

It seemed a shame to waste good water here in the desert, but he had no choice.

He threw the water as he did every morning.

Once Ou-Leesen-el-Bra-ten stopped sputtering and shouting, Stek said, "Today we arrive at the Gates of Tenleth. So, this was your last wake up call."

He grinned and left the tent.

By late morning they could see the foothills that harboured the Mines of Tenleth.

They stopped to eat. This would be the last meal before many of them would die.

Stek was in the front wagon with Ou-Leesen, as they travelled those last fifty leagues towards the Mines. Suddenly he stood up ... and pulled out his telescope.

There were men on the road ahead. Trackers to be specific.

"What do you see?" Ou-Leesen-el-Bra-ten asked.

"Something I didn't expect to see."

He sat down and passed the telescope to the El-Bhat Leader.

The black warrior was taping the scope on his thigh, as the wagon rolled onward.

"Advisor ... how is this possible? Especially since we are on the south road of Tenleth?"

"Don't know. But we won't have to wait long before we do know."

--------- <> ---------

"Do you see what I see," one of the spies asked.

"Yeah, the one on the left is not El-Bhat," the other spy replied.

Ranoof was wishing they had a scope between them, but they left the scopes with the spies waiting behind. So, he squinted until the Lead Wagon stopped.

Ranoof watched carefully as the one who wasn't El-Bhat, removed his black silk head scarf.

It was Stek! One of the original twelve Trackers, that escorted Urshen to Border Pass. The one who was sent to Seven Oaks, with the message that the Back Gate was unlocked. And then disappeared.

And here he was in Shaksbah ... sitting beside an El-Bhat ... with hundreds of wagons and thousands of black warriors behind.

'Strange times,' thought Ranoof, 'definitely strange times.'

They waited for the Lead Black Warrior and Stek to dismount and come forward. But only Stek jumped down.

--------- <> ---------

Stek recognized Ranoof right away.

"I know the Tracker holding the flag pole," he said to the black warrior as the wagon approached the three men. "The last time I saw him we were at Border Pass." Stek reflected to their experience with Urshen. "He knows something about ... *power*," Stek added.

That statement changed things for Ou-Leesen. All he thought about, since they left the deposit of clay covered gold bricks, was the power that he was trying to control. A Power that was trying to control him.

"Find out why they are here," he finally said, as Stek stopped the wagon at a safe distance.

Stek jumped down and with a grin walked slowly to the unarmed Trackers until he stood directly in front of Ranoof.

He wanted to fling his arms around his old friend, but instead, he shed the grin and said, "The El-Bhat Leader wants to know why you are here."

"We are here to warn you. The Guild Militia from Qar-ana, are now in possession of the Mines of Tenleth. They have already destroyed the El-Bhat who tried to protect it. If you proceed, you will die … like them." Ranoof knew the El-Bhat couldn't hear him, but he bowed towards him anyway, something Fre-steel had taught him.

Obviously Ranoof thought his message was finished, but Stek knew that Ou-Leesen-el-Bra-ten would want to know why they had come into Shaksbah … to the Mines. Not just why they were on the road now.

"But why are you here *in Shaksbah*?" Stek asked.

"We have come to free the slaves," Ranoof answered.

Surprised at his answer, Stek turned and looked at the black silk warrior and said, "Ranoof, you need to elaborate."

Ranoof studied Stek as he considered how he might do that.

"He likes direct answers," Stek quickly offered.

Ranoof took a moment to rock on his feet and then replied, "I had a dream … given to me from the Cave … that made it clear that I was to help Fre-steel, free the slaves."

Stek's eyebrows lifted in surprise. He remembered Fre-steel as a traitor.

"Behind us, are several thousand Trackers and Tinkers that have come to help. Our first attempt of using the abandoned tunnels to free them, failed. Somehow the El-Bhat knew what we had come for … and threatened to push the slaves into the Pit of Death if we didn't leave.

"Then … while we waited for another opportunity, the Guild Militia arrived and destroyed the El-Bhat. They came from the east, so we are sure they have already conquered the government of Shaksbah. We expect that within days, most of this Militia will return to centres of power. That is when we will make our second move to free the slaves." He bowed his head towards Ou-Leesen.

"Wait here," Stek advised.

Back up on the wagon bench, he began, "There are thousands of Trackers and Tinkers here to free the slaves. They are here because of … instructions from the Cave.

"The Government Militia from Storlenia have already arrived. They have possession of the Mines. Ranoof, the Tracker holding the flag pole, is here to warn us of the Militia."

Ou-Leesen-el-Bra-ten was watching Ranoof while Stek updated him. "You trust him?"

"As much as I trust you."

"Have my Personal Guards bring him to my wagon."

Ranoof bowed as he stood before the El-Bhat Leader.

"I have been told that you were at Border Pass," Ou-Leesen said, inviting Ranoof to elaborate.

Ranoof considered the Warrior's opening statement. "I was up on the East Plateau … with Urshen."

The El-Bhat Leader looked at Stek.

"Urshen is a man with talisman power," Stek offered, remembering how he defeated the group of El-Bhat Guards in their prison cell.

Returning to Ranoof, the warrior asked, "Did he cause the Wind that destroyed my people?"

"Yes … with the help of Tracker blood and a second talisman."

Ou-Leesen could still see in his mind the hurricane of death, as El-Bhat toppled to the Butcher Block below.

"Do you trust the power?" Ou-Leesen asked.

Ranoof paused. "I became a Tracker, because my father was one. I am a simple man. What matters to me, was how I felt when I was invited to experience the power. So yes … I trust the Cave."

Ou-Leesen stared north towards the Mines of Tenleth as he considered his situation.

"We are also here to free the slaves. And we have brought wagons full of supplies to assist them to leave this place.

"Are you more than a messenger?" he finally asked Ranoof.

Ranoof wasn't totally convinced that he had the authority to negotiate, so instead, he asked a question of his own. "Are we allies?"

When Ou-Leesen-el-Bra-ten turned to Stek, the Tracker was nodding yes … and then added, "The Trackers and Tinkers know of abandoned mine tunnels that can be used to free the slaves. I think they could be successful if they had our support to distract the Militia."

"Ranoof … do you agree with my Advisor?"

The Tracker looked down at his boots, as he considered the question.

"Well …," he started, as he looked up into those green eyes, "I guess it depends on the distraction. The Militia have a weapon that easily conquered the El-Bhat that guarded the Mines."

"We have a weapon of our own," the black silk warrior responded, as he rested his hand on the pommel of his Dagger, "and I am ready to lead my men *today*."

"Ok … but we are convinced that most of the Militia will leave within a few days. Giving us much better odds."

When Ou-Leesen did not respond to the suggestion, Stek was ready with a reply.

"To be effective … our weapon *must* be used today," Stek told Ranoof. "Tell the Trackers and Tinkers that our opportunity is *today* … not another day. Can we count on you?"

Ranoof turned to look at the thousands of black silk warriors that stretched south. It didn't seem right that so many El-Bhat should have to give their lives to free the slaves. There was so much that he didn't understand. But then again, what was *another* link in the chain of remarkable events.

"Yes … we will be ready when you face the Militia."

Stek and Ou-Leesen watched until the small group disappeared below the sandy horizon.

"Advisor … how will we face this new enemy. What is my plan?"

"I have an idea … but it needs to be tested using the Dagger."

"Unfortunately, the Dagger almost owns me. The next time I pull the Dagger from the Scabbard, it will have to be to defeat the Militia."

"Then *I* will have to do it," Stek said solemnly, "and you will have to be my Guard and watch for any signs of failure … as you did in the Keep."

The El-Bhat Leader removed the Scabbard and passed it to Stek.

Stek sighed as he prepared to remove the Dagger of Truth. Last time he held the Dagger, he was filled with confidence … that he knew himself well. But that had changed. And he knew that he was only free, because of the quick thinking El-Bhat at his side.

What enticements would he face this time … that were beyond his strength?

He sighed again.

The lives of five thousand El-Bhat depended on two men in the Lead Wagon.

And *they* were hanging by a thread of hope.

'Well,' he thought, 'there is only one thing to do.'

He pulled the ornate blade with the emerald pommel, from the Scabbard.

Chapter 46 - The Etchings of Knowledge

The sensation was familiar as Stek plunged into a pool of water, and quickly pushed his head above the surface.
He remembered the green mist bubbling off the water ... and the door set into a wall of filigree gold.

He headed for that door and quickly walked through it.

The next room was brighter with the same Green Light. And there standing behind a table, was ... *the* woman.

His heart immediately began to pound in his chest. She was so ... mysterious ... and fascinatingly beautiful!

"Hello Stek. I have waited a long time for you to return."

Her voice was so ... familiar. So soft ... so seductive. It was hard to think. She mentioned that he was returning. He felt confused.

"Why did you ever leave me?" Her eyes were pools of sadness. That yearned for his love.

"I ... don't remember," was all he could think to say.

Her eyes drifted downwards towards a gold cradle that held an extremely ornate dagger, with an emerald pommel.

"I wanted to give you this ... as a token of my love."

She picked up the Dagger and held it out to the Tracker.

"It's ... beautiful," Stek said, without taking his eyes from her perfect face.

She extended her arms, a small gesture, inviting him to take the Dagger.

He walked towards her. Slowly.
He knew she was offering him the Gift, but he couldn't stop looking at her eyes.

Instead of taking the Dagger, he extended his hand to touch her perfect face.

"Wait," she quickly said. The word was soft but impossible to ignore.

His hand was frozen, close to her skin.

"Many men have wanted my love. But they had no power. And my love will be given to a man with power."

He turned his eyes to the Gift she held.

"If you take this Gift ... you will have ... power."

He lifted the Dagger from her hands and began to run his fingers across the intricate etchings on the blade.

"*If you want the Dagger's power, you must kiss the emerald stone.*"

Stek didn't notice that her words began to fade, as his fingers *read* the etchings on the blade. It was incredible. Those small markings contained elements of the *key word* that, when spoken, opened doors to enormous knowledge. Knowledge of how to use the power of the blade!

But the *key word* was incomplete, so he quickly turned the blade over and repeated the exercise.

"*You must kiss the emerald stone!*" the Green Lady hastily reminded him, "*If you wish to have power ... and my love.*"

Stek spoke the *key word*, and immediately 'doors' to understanding of the Dagger's power, flew open everywhere in his mind ... and he remembered the question that he wanted to ask.

As those doors opened, alluring words danced on the fringe of his mind, desperately trying to convince him to do something. But a heartbeat later, it was too late. He already had the answer.

--------- <> ---------

"He's back," the Technician softly wailed in excitement. The Tracker was holding the Dagger of Truth again!

Luckily, he was already at the Queen of Gold's Power Console, when Stek took the blade.

His fingers flew across the Console as he reloaded the previous instructions.

Last time, the Green Lady had come very close to binding the Tracker, to the power of the Dagger. So, minor modifications were all he needed.

He followed the Tracker, as his mind entered the program through the pool of Pu-el-tal and walked through the door to her chambers.

He watched as the Tracker hypnotically moved towards the Queen of Gold.

Watched as he took the Dagger.

Waited for him to kiss the emerald.

Quickly added code to encourage him that he *must* kiss the emerald.

Nervously watched as his fingers glided across The Etchings of Knowledge.

Then listened, in horror, as he spoke words from The Book of Power. "This should be impossible!" he screamed.

Terrified, he immediately closed the session with Pu-el-tal, the Lady of Harleem.

The Technician buried his face in his trembling hands, horrified at what this could mean.

--------- <> ---------

Stek calmly lifted his head, still holding the Dagger with both hands. "Advisor ... do we have a plan?"

"Yes," he replied, his countenance more solemn than the warrior expected.

"Your test went well?" he queried.

Stek looked straight ahead as he responded. "Much better than I expected. I went in search for the gold coin and found the treasury."

"What does this mean?" Ou-Leesen asked, suspicious of what the Dagger might have done to Stek.

"It means that the plan is *secure*. With the Dagger and the words that I will give you, you will be able to create a Curtain of Defence that will stop all the terror the Militia can throw at it.

"But ... I must never be allowed access to the Dagger of Truth."

Ou-Leesen-el-Bra-ten studied Stek for a moment, seeing the contradiction of him still holding the Dagger and knowing he shouldn't.

"Stek," he said firmly, "put the Dagger of Truth into the Scabbard."

"Help me," was Stek's quiet reply.

Ou-Leesen slid the Scabbard over the blade while Stek continued to hold it ... with his eyes closed.

Holding the Scabbard, Ou-Leesen reminded Stek that he must open his eyes and "let go of the Dagger."

Stek opened his eyes, but the warrior could see hesitation ... reluctance. He ripped the Scabbard out of Stek's grip.

After a moment, Stek turned to his friend. "It is far more powerful than either of us have imagined. I know the *key word* that opens the treasury to the words of power. Words that can do anything."

"Do you have the words that I will need?" Ou-Leesen asked.

"Kel mal turet potu maknees," Stek responded. "These words of power will create the Curtain that we will need to defend our warriors.

"When this is over," Stek continued, "you must kill me ... because I know ... the *key word*."

Ou-Leesen-el-Bra-ten nodded in agreement.

"And now, we have an enemy to defeat," Stek reminded the warrior.

With heavy hearts, the two friends that bridged enemy lands, watched for the Militia as they urged the Lead Wagon forward.

They were within a league of the Mines of Tenleth when the might of the Militia could be seen, spread across the road. Wagons fitted with the dreaded Brass Slings, filled the landscape.

"Here is where we must all leave our wagons," Stek said as he jumped down.

Together they walked down the road as five thousand El-Bhat followed.

"*We* might never live to see the slaves walk away free ... but with the help of our new ally, I think they will," Stek offered as consolation.

"And today ... I will be free as well," Ou-Lessen said softly. "And I will see my father. He will be very surprised when I tell him that I stood strong against my enemies ... with a Tracker at my side." He grinned.

"I think this is far enough," Stek said. "Time to say those words."

As soon as he uttered the phrase, a Green Light burst out of the blade, forming a Wall that spread in either direction for a great distance.

Ou-Leesen-el-Bra-ten struggled against the enormity of the power ... and its pull against his life force. He started to walk forward but within moments, he had already dropped to one knee.

Stek knew immediately that they were in trouble.

He waved for the Personal Guards to rush forward as he wrapped his hands around those of the El-Bhat.

Stek grunted as he shared the burden.

With the support of the Personal Guards, the El-Bhat Leader was soon moving forward again.

The Militia spies returned, with the news that a very large force of El-Bhat were marching towards Tenleth, on the southern road, with wagons. But no Catapults.

The Militia Leadership had already assigned those wagons that would be left behind at the Mines. All the rest rumbled south to meet their new enemy.

With confidence, the massive group of War Wagons positioned themselves on the road. They spread far to the east and west, preventing the possibility of a flank attack.

The Militia Commander waited as the El-Bhat slowly moved towards them. The approach was not like El-Bhat. They were usually much more aggressive.

He sensed that something wasn't right. He turned and looked back towards the Mines.

True, there were enough War Wagons to defend against a significant force, but still, he felt uneasy. He called a spy and sent him back with the message, 'Something isn't right. Stay on active alert and keep the spies busy.'

The Militia spy had just left for the Mines when the Leaders in the El-Bhat front wagon disembarked and walked forward.

Suddenly a brilliant Green Light stretched across the land, like a blanket between the El-Bhat and the Militia.

Nusdek, Head Leader of all the Militia Guard, had once told him of such things. 'The power is great but the one who uses it, is still flesh and blood. So be patient and watch for the weakness'.

He called another spy to his side. "Once we know how this blanket of Green Light affects our firepower, take a message back to the Mines that describes our situation."

The spy nodded in obedience and waited to see what would happen.

A Militia warrior, in the Lead Wagon, held high the Militia flag, waiting for a signal from The Commander.

Then he dropped it and the War Wagons commenced firing on the unprotected El-Bhat ... with no effect. The Brass Balls fell to the earth the moment they hit the Curtain of Green Light. The spy rushed off to the Mines to report.

With another signal, the flag was raised, and the firing stopped.

The Militia Commander had watched carefully from the moment the wagons were in sight. Looking for that weakness that Nusdek had talked about.

And suddenly … there it was, as the Green Light began to flicker, like a candle in the wind. These El-Bhat would soon join their brothers, in the Pit of Death.

--------- <> ---------

Ou-Leesen could feel Stek's strong hands wrap around his. Immediately the drain on his life force stopped.

He could feel someone pull him upright.

They continued to advance.

As soon as he closed his eyes, the scenery changed.

Above, the sky was dark. In front, a menacing Wall. Its surface weeping drops of green blood.

On the other side of the Wall, he could see a Death Pit and he could hear the howl of a black desert wind that pounded against that Wall.

Ou-Leesen held the brace that kept the Wall strong, while behind him, Stek pushed against his shoulders, providing necessary support.

But even with Stek's help, the effort required to support the Wall, was beyond the limit of his endurance. He could feel it and knew that eventually the Wall would fall.

It wasn't long before that black wind began to pick up desert stones, and hurled them into the Wall, testing Ou-Leesen's resolve. The Wall held and soon the stones stopped.

But eventually their strength wasn't enough, and the Wall begin to tip against Ou-Leesen.

--------- <> ---------

From the moment Stek wrapped his hands around Ou-Leesen's hands, the real world disappeared.

He found himself kneeling opposite Ou-Leesen, his hands, on top of *his* hands, as he gripped a rod that vented mist like a boiling pot.

All around was a large dark field.

In front of him was a shimmering green Curtain.

Behind, he could see El-Bhat marching forward, their eyes glowing fiercely, as they followed Ou-Leesen-el-Bra-ten.

On the other side of the Curtain, warriors with death painted on their faces, stood beside large wagons.

Within the wagons stood huge Weapons, with large gaping jaws that spewed black burning skulls at the El-Bhat.

Stek watched as skulls crashed into the Green Curtain; the only thing that kept the El-Bhat alive.

He turned his attention to his El-Bhat friend, his face filled with pain. His garments soaked with sweat.

Stek could feel the searing heat of the rod, even through Ou-Leesen's hands.

The pounding sound of the black skulls hitting the Curtain stopped. Ou-Leesen relaxed his clenched jaw as he took deep gulps of air, trying to strengthen his body against the next onslaught.

The ground beneath them moved relentlessly towards the warriors with death painted on their faces. Eventually the green Curtain would engulf them and destroy them ... if they could hold on.

Stek looked through the green Curtain. They were about half way. He was beginning to think that they just might make it.

And then Ou-Leesen slumped into Stek's chest. He was barely conscious.

And the green Curtain started to flicker, like a campfire as it burned down.

The Militia Commander watched as the flickering spread from the middle to the ends of the Curtain. Then the flicker progressed to a rapid stutter. Soon the Curtain would fall. And he would vanquish his enemies.

As he prepared to raise his hand for the firing to commence, an Aide rushed to his side, shouting, "Commander ... Commander, look," as he pointed skyward.

The Tracker that had the advantage of the window, got up from the meal and walked to the open doorway and looked up.

"Everyone, you need to see this."

Bru-ell, Benton, Velinti and the rest of the Trackers, spilled out of the cabin and watched in awe as they stared at the sky above.

Chapter 47 - More than flesh and blood

Previously, Bernado announced to Craslin, that his powerful friend wanted Zephra. In an instant, Craslin knew that he had lost the game. Fearful for Zephra's life, he instructed the Master Spy, to rescue Zephra.

The instructions were brief and delivered by Craslin himself. She was to join him for the evening meal. He specified what she was to wear. That was all the note said.

Craslin opened the door. Zephra was dressed in her Tinker clothes as he had requested.

She smiled and entered.

"I have taken precautions that will allow us to speak freely during our last meal together," he advised her. His smile was inviting but his eyes were weary.

'Last meal?' she thought to herself. 'Of course ... he means I will be leaving tonight. It is why he asked me to dress in my Tinker clothes.'

The clothes felt both strange *and* familiar. It had been so long.

"I will need a wagon ... I gave mine to Yaneek," she advised him.

He stopped eating and stared at her for a while. "I'm afraid you will not be needing a wagon. Later this evening, Nusdek will transfer you to Bernado's home." He looked down. "And I will not be seeing you anymore."

She set her fork aside. The news was unexpected ... and troubling.

"Why are you doing this?" She asked him. "This cannot be your idea," she declared with great concern.

He looked up. "I'm afraid," he began, "I have underestimated Bernado. This turn of events is beyond my control ... except for one thing.

"I have made arrangements for someone to rescue you as soon as an opportunity presents itself. This man is ... always successful. He will take you somewhere beyond the reach of Bernado and keep you safe."

She had never seen Craslin so melancholy. "Will I ever see you again?"

Finally, he offered a weak smile, but it was the smile of irony. "I'm afraid not. I wish it were otherwise, but ..." his words trailed off into silence.

Those were his last words.

Neither of them could finish the meal.

While they waited for Nusdek, she remembered back to their last meeting when she faced her own hypocrisy ... and his kind response.

She had to say something before Nusdek arrived.

So, she expressed her gratitude. For the books. For the teaching. For his sacrifice in helping Benekee through the healing.

For his friendship.

He nodded in appreciation of her words. But he found it difficult to maintain eye contact and his silence continued.

Nusdek's arrival was heard as the echoes travelled easily through the empty Guild.

She tensed.

He laid a hand on her arm, to comfort her.

When the door opened, she quickly got up and left.

A few Militia brushed past her as they entered Craslin's office.

As Nusdek escorted her away, she heard the door close. She knew it was the end of Craslin.

--------- <> ---------

Aram-Dentee II watched, as Nusdek, and a large company of Militia, escorted the Tinker girl out of the Planning and Development Guild.

His hand drifted to the Amulet that he always wore under his shirt.

It was Far-fel's idea. He was convinced that it would protect Aram against the powerful reach of the Golden Necklace. Considering his success, as a spy, it was probably true.

Once he rescued Zephra, he would give *her* the Amulet. She could use it to better effect.

Like a shadow, he followed them to Bernado's House. Nusdek entered with the girl, then left. But the one hundred Militia were left behind.

'This is going to be more of a challenge than Craslin anticipated,' he thought, as he drifted further away into the night.

--------- <> ---------

Zephra was escorted into Bernado's luxurious office.

From the time she left Craslin's Guild, she had it in her mind to escape … despite his reassurance that someone would rescue her. But there must have been a hundred Militia escorting them to Bernado's House. She would have to wait.

As the horses pulled her to an uncertain future, she tried to work out why this was happening.

Craslin was probably dead. Somehow, he had lost the game to Bernado.

And she was heading for a different type of captivity. Filled with uncertainty in every possible way. And with no friends.

Her thoughts turned to Yaneek, Benekee, Urshen and Protas. Did *any* of them have a future? She wondered.

Bernado entered. She watched him like a Mountain Cat as he moved to his chair. Instead of sitting, he first removed his prized long knives from the drawer. Then he sat down.

"I wish you to be comfortable while you remain under my care," Bernado began. "Your well-being is my first concern, and my men are responsible to see that my concerns are obeyed … to the letter. Punishable by death if disobeyed.

"Anything you wish … that is reasonable, will be granted.

"Do you have any questions?"

She looked at his long knives. They would be useful at some point.

"Yes … why did you bring me here? With Craslin dead, you could have just moved in."

He gave her a small nod of acknowledgment. She was quick and discerning.

"Tomorrow, all of Qar-ana will know that Craslin is dead. The people will have their day to mourn. Then … the following day, a procession of five thousand Militia will escort me, along with my prisoners, to my throne of power."

"Why am I your prisoner?"

Again, he offered her a small nod. But rather than explain, he opened the box that contained the Golden Necklace, removed it, and wore it.

Then he placed the small green stone at the front of his desk, within her reach, and said, as he touched one of the Medallions, "Touch the green stone ... but for only a moment."

She hesitated, but then decided that knowledge was power, and reached forward and touched it.

Being *convinced* was a luxury that Bernado had abandoned long ago. Now, he always needed to *know*!

It was why he wanted her to touch the stone, while he watched carefully for the *Halo*.

And there it was! He went from being convinced, to knowing!

He never intended to trade Zephra. At least not right away. No, she would be held in reserve for a dark day when he needed a prize jewel to trade.

He quickly reached across the desk to wrench the stone from her grip of terror.

She gasped for air and her hands trembled while her eyes searched the room, trying to understand what had just happened.

He waited.

When she looked at him again, he began to explain.

"Urshen was the only one that had the power to defeat ... I stand corrected ... to resist the power of this Golden Necklace. But he has already left this world ... for a better." He smiled inside at the double meaning.

"Where did you find this Necklace?" she asked, with as much calm as she could muster.

"I like to think that it found me," he answered. "But that's not the question you want to ask ... is it?

"You are curious about its power and where it comes from.

"It comes from a powerful race, who live up there," he pointed to the ceiling. "They trade things," he added as he picked up one of his knives and removed it from its scabbard.

"But trading can be like a two-edged knife. It requires careful understanding of the needs of the person you are trading with." He nodded, more to himself than to her.

"You are trading *me*?" she suddenly realized.

"I prefer not to," he answered as he placed the knife back into its scabbard. "It will depend on you," he lied. Now she knew everything he wanted her to know.

That he had enormous power.

That there was a possibility he would trade her to these people from the stars.

But ... if she cooperated, she might live a long and healthy life.

"What have you already traded?" Zephra asked, thinking back to his comment about Urshen.

"*Nothing* compared to what I will trade, in a couple of days, when I, as Emperor of Ankoletia, sign the Harvesting Document with Kareen-del-Harleem."

"Emperor? ... of Ankoletia?" she asked in astonishment.

"Yes. Shaksbah, is now under my control. You must have seen the Militia leave Qar-ana."

Zephra's eyes narrowed. "To control all Ankoletia, you would need to conquer more than flesh and blood," she rebuffed him, as she thought of her grandmother.

"Oh ... you mean, the *Master Cave*?"

Her expression betrayed her thoughts.

"So, you know about Amulets, and possibly a Cave ... but the concept of a Master Cave is new to you," he grinned in triumph.

"*More than flesh and blood* ... well said, Zephra. And yes, Nusdek's return has confirmed that the Master Cave will *never* be opened. It was the last barrier of my ascendancy to the throne of Emperor."

Zephra was stunned by the intelligence he was sharing with her. What he said meant that Storlenia had fallen. Shaksbah had fallen. And the power of the Amulets ... was lost. It didn't seem possible.

"How is it that the entire country of Shaksbah, is now under your control?"

"It is possible, Zephra, because they allowed it. Yes, Shaksbah gave us the key to conquer the entire country."

"The key?" she asked, bewildered.

"Yes," he answered. "Their gold. They thought to use it to buy power from our Guilds. Then they would rule *us* without shedding a drop of blood. But instead, we used their gold to build our Militia. Without the gold, there is no Militia. Nor the means to build thousands of the new weapon we call the Brass Sling. A weapon capable of destroying any force pitted against us."

The surprise on her face continued to grow with every new revelation that he shared.

His plan to enslave her with his words, was working.

"The Brass Sling," he repeated, "is the invention of a clever young man. Someone you know ... called Benekee.

"And to be clear ... Shaksbah giving us the gold, wouldn't have happened except for Protas."

"Protas?" Zephra whispered, curious as to how he could have been involved in the gold.

"Yes. A young man I sent to the Quorum for their pleasure and entertainment. But he ended up somewhere else. He ended up with the El-Bhat building Ou-Leesen Pass. The Pass they used to bring the gold through. And I'm convinced that without Protas's skill and knowledge, the El-Bhat could never have brought the gold to the front steps of Qar-ana, and then bargain for shipping rights of Storlenia's two main shipping ports.

"For sure ... this was Protas's work. So, in a way, Protas brought down the country of Shaksbah. Well, with a little help from his friend ... Benekee."

"Benekee?" Zephra whispered again. Wondering if the development and production of the Brass Sling had extended that far. She had heard things, but never imagined ...

"Yes. It's quite amazing. Over a thousand rapid-firing Brass Slings mounted on War Wagons.

"And while we are passing out credits, let me also say that, some of the genius of bringing down Shaksbah should include the name of Urshen. Because Urshen, built a better War Wagon.

"Far superior to the previous War Wagons, in agility, speed and stability. Perfect for this new weapon we call the Brass Sling.

"You see ... the increased stability allowed the Brass Sling to fire with accuracy ... while moving! Simply an effort of a mastermind. Something the old War Wagons could never have done."

He studied those beautiful dark eyes with golden flecks. Curious to know if she appreciated the genius of events that had worked in his favor.

But her eyes reflected neither fire of contempt, nor appreciation for his enlightened analysis. Instead, she had the look of a captive.

"It's really a simple story, isn't it? A story that proves small means can bring about enormous changes. And you will soon see, that by the means of something very, very small, a Colossus will be toppled. Stripped of the power he has over me."

He smiled in anticipation of his chance to bargain.

"I hope you will be comfortable until you return with me to the Emperor's Palace."

Then he left the room.

Zephra was rooted to the chair. She couldn't escape even if the entire Militia left.

Bernado's words had stripped her of her will and her power.

It was hard to imagine that an entire country had been conquered … because of the skills and persistence of Urshen, Protas and Yaneek's brother Benekee. Could it be true? Could her world have conjured up irony of that magnitude? Were the Fates asleep?

She thought of her Amulet. Given to Ranoof so that her White Bauble would finally be enshrined within Benekee's shards.

All for nothing.

She closed her eyes as her fingers moved to hush her trembling lips.

As tears tumbled down her once-proud cheeks, she thought of her good friend Yaneek. And the time they talked, before she left the Planning Guild.

In her mind, she remembered that sunny day, and how Yaneek's beautiful green eyes sparkled with intensity as she said, 'What you say is not enough … I need to know more … I told you, I want to be strong like you, responsible like you.'

Yaneek always said that Zephra was such a woman of power.

She looked down at her hands resting in her lap.
She was powerless.
A prisoner in a chair with no ropes.
In a room with an open door.

Two days later, she was back in the Planning Guild.
Zephra never left her room.
She barely had the strength to eat.

The Caves of Balhok

She was staring out her window when the Guards arrived to escort her into Craslin's old office.

Bernado was at the terrace doorway.

Beyond him, she could see five thousand Militia, that had assembled at Bernado's request.

He heard her come in.

"I am expecting Kareen-del-Harleem to appear any day now. And I don't want him to see you. So," he turned around to face her, "I am sending you away with Nusdek ... and many Guards. He is waiting outside ... in *your* wagon."

As they left the Emperor's Palace, Zephra looked over at 'the Wall', the term Bernado had used to describe his own personal Militia. She dared not think about the misery they would bring upon Storlenia, after Bernado signed the contract.

It was odd that he asked Nusdek to transport Zephra away in her own wagon. 'He likes irony,' she thought.

That night she was tied to her wagon, surrounded by a hundred Guards from the Wall.

Later, as Nusdek and his men continued their journey down the wide-open country roads, she watched for signs of her *rescuer*. But there were none.

Her spirits were low. But at least it was a sunny day, and the sky above poured down her warmth upon her little wagon.

Suddenly Nusdek pulled hard on the reins and said, "*What* is that!" He was looking to the right, far away, into the very blue sky.

Zephra stood straight up as she gazed in wonder at the horizon.

Chapter 48 - The Cocoon Transporter

Sometime before Nusdek and his three hundred Militia were sent to Shaksbah

With hands clasped behind his back, Bernado surveyed the five thousand Militia that made up his Wall. His life would soon be *impregnable*. All that was left, was to deliver the hostages *and* his demands, to Kareen-del-Harleem ... and he would be, an immortal Emperor of Ankoletia.

All loose ends were in place. Yaneek, Protas and Urshen, were secured in the prison cells of the Planning Guild. And Zephra was safely out of sight.

Tomorrow, the Alien Visitor would come to collect Urshen and the missing Specialist Tracker.

By now, Bernado knew that Kareen-del-Harleem had given him an impossible task, considering the Tracker took the Amulet with him.

He had come to believe that this was part of Kareen's bargaining strategy. To place Bernado in an embarrassing position, giving the Visitor the upper hand.

But Bernado was ready to parry that thrust. He had a replacement ... Protas.

And then Kareen would hear about his demands ... as he placed Yaneek on the bargaining table.

But he expected that his demands would meet resistance.

Again, he would be ready. That's when he would bring Benekee into the bargain.

He often thought of how simple things worked together, to produce the miraculous result of placing him on an Emperor's Throne.

It didn't seem that long ago that a group of seven Trackers arrived at his Guild, looking for someone. And by the end of that day, he had an Amulet in his possession.

An Amulet that somehow attracted the attention of another Tracker ... that left behind the Necklace. A Golden Talisman that had changed his life beyond anything he could have imagined.

But he soon learned that there was a price to pay. The power was not really his. It was *on loan*.

From a Titan that wanted *things.*

But to his astonishment, he learned that this Alien was bound by an even greater power ... rules.

And he might have never understood how to bargain with his Visitor, if not for a Tinker's wagon, that sat outside his abandoned House. So simple ... people with the Halo effect.

And of course, he knew about *permission,* thanks to details Kareen unwittingly shared with him.

Bernado smiled. It was these secrets that made them equals. If Kareen was truly more powerful than Bernado, he would just take what he wanted.

Instead, he bargained for a trade. A manoeuvre that only took place among equals!

Bernado left the terrace and walked to the Necklace, lying on a velvet bed.

Here laid the strength of his ambition.

And the prize of living another ten thousand years, was possible, because a Referee governed the Colossus from Harleem.

Knowledge was a beautiful thing!

Finally, he learned that he had leverage over Kareen because he had the power to retain, or deliver, the prisoners to someone else! And as Emperor he would have authority over everyone. Ankoletia would be like *one very large prison cell* ... as far as the Alien was concerned.

And that authority would allow him to keep Goldenrod forever.

Morning had come.

As was his habit, Bernado retrieved his long knives, and practised.

When he was finished, he held them for a while, and then returned them to the drawer.

They used to be important as symbols of who he was, whenever he met Kareen-del-Harleem.

But no longer. As he faced the Visitor today, he would meet an equal.

He had barely finished the thought when Green Light started to gather behind him.

He smiled to reassure himself. Then he turned to face the Colossus.

---------- <> ----------

"I am ready," Kareen-hys-Tebeel-del-Harleem said firmly, as he walked towards the transporter.

He strode onto the platform and confirmed that the 'weapons' were already in place. He was pleased that today, he would be adding genetic assets to his gold.

As he waited for the Technicians to conduct the final security sweep of the target area, he reviewed in his mind, the papers he would need to smuggle the two off-worlders into Harleem.

Then he heard the familiar beep that told him, the transporter had started.

"Please examine the weapons," Kareen said as he pointed to the neat stack sitting on Bernado's desk. "I took the liberty of including ... scopes," he said, searching for the appropriate word.

Bernado hefted the slim barrel of steel and brass. There was a rest at the one end that seemed designed for his shoulder.

He held it at waist level as he searched for the release.

"Are they ..."

He heard a loud popping sound. "... loaded?" he asked.

The loud popping sound made him jump, but when he looked over at Kareen, the projectile had stopped, suspended in mid-air, a pace from the Alien.

"Whoops ... my error," apologized Bernado. He had been careless in where he had pointed the barrel.

"I would expect no less," Kareen stately matter-of-factly. "But perhaps it's time to stop trying," he added as he stared at Bernado.

Bernado thought back to the time he tried to kill him with his long knives. He gave him a nod of acknowledgement, rather than argue the point.

The suspended brass ball dropped to the floor.

"What is the range?" Bernado asked, pleased with the design.

Kareen raised his hand, to accept one of the scopes that flew across the room.

Holding it up for Bernado to see, he explained, "With this ... mostly limited by your skill."

Before Bernado could take it, the Visitor lowered his hand, and the scope flew back to its original resting place.

Bernado placed the Brass Sling barrel on the table. He glanced at the scopes, curious as to why the Alien had sent it flying before he could examine it. But it didn't matter, these scopes were not part of the trade anyway.

"Satisfied?"
"Yes. And I have the *two* prisoners ready. The one who escaped could never be found, but I have a replacement that I am sure will meet your demands."

Kareen tapped one of his gold bracelets.
"Check the two prisoners," he said as he turned away from Bernado.

After a moment, Kareen turned to face the Tracker. "Agreed. But you have another prisoner that interests me."
"You must mean ... the woman," Bernado offered, feigning surprise.
"I wish to take her with me today."
"Of course," Bernado agreed, with a brief nod. However, he didn't move a muscle. He was waiting for the Colossus to suggest an offer.

Kareen-hys-Tebeel-del-Harleem was staggered by the details of the most recent communication from his Technical officers. *Another* prisoner identified as Class Six genetic material!
And by the posturing of the Guild Master ... he knew it as well.
'Very well,' the man from Harleem thought. 'The bargaining has started.'

"What is it you want for this additional prisoner? More weapons?"
"I want three things," Bernado began.
"First, a guarantee that Goldenrod and its power will always be mine."
"Second ... a guarantee that your people will do everything they can, to ensure that I will remain Emperor of this planet for a minimum of ten thousand years."
"And third, I want to be granted citizenship of your world."

Kareen was both surprised and impressed that this off-worlder understood the true value of what Kareen had to offer. He was obviously more than a Leader of mindless slaves. He decided to consider the request.

He touched one of his gold bracelets, "Is it possible?" he asked his Team in the sky above.

There was a long pause while the Visitor waited, then listened.

"You ask great things. Greater than you realize."
Bernado wanted to say, 'I believe that what I am giving you, is also of much greater value, than I can ever realize.'
But instead he said, "I know why you want *these* captives, and I know where I can get you one more."
The Visitor tapped his golden bracelet one last time, as he asked, "What is the name ... and where can this person be found?"
"His name is Benekee and is currently at the Mechanical Guild, here in Qar-ana."
Bernado spoke clearly, knowing that others were listening to his words.

There was another long pause before Kareen finally said, "I will take the three with me now. When you give me the fourth prisoner, named Benekee, I will agree to all three conditions. Are you satisfied?"
"As I hope you are," the Guild Master nodded in the affirmative.

Without a word, Green Light gathered around Kareen-del-Harleem.

--------- <> ---------

Bernado rushed to the Prison below.
Protas, Urshen and Yaneek were gone!
Those empty cells were a reminder of the importance of *rules*.

--------- <> ---------

Urshen and Protas were pacing the floor.
They knew something was up. The Guild Master had been in to check them several times the day before. Highly unusual.
"I can hear someone running down the stairs," Urshen quickly said, as Protas rushed to the iron-grate window on their door.
But before he could make a report, a green mist enveloped them both.

The image of Protas began to fade, as the green air around Urshen swirled into an opaque cocoon.

He stretched forth his hand to touch it. It had the texture of slippery wood. There was a subtle flexibility to it.

Urshen pounded it with his fists. It was like woven steel.

The last thing he remembered, was a sensation of movement.

Sometime later, his eyes flickered, opened and the cocoon was gone.

He was laying on the floor of a strange place. The floor felt warm and the walls gave off a soft green light.

He knew where he was. He had moved from one prison cell to another.

As he stood, he became aware that, besides Protas, there was a young woman on the platform.

As soon as Protas recognized Yaneek, he gave her a quick look, which told her she mustn't reveal that they knew each other. Urshen saw the subtle interplay and simply let his eyes go to the floor as he waited for someone to come.

Chapter 49 - Lost in space

The door opened, and the Guard pushed a young lad into the room. He looked to be around twenty. His face was badly scarred and disfigured. Benekee stumbled into the nearest prisoner. "Sorry," he said with eyes cast downward.

He immediately looked for his own space. He wanted to be by himself. He noticed a thin bed in the corner. He sat down, his thoughts frozen in the past.

"What's your name?" Urshen asked.

The young lad was staring at the floor, unresponsive. As though the other two in the room didn't exist.

'Or perhaps it's because *he* doesn't exist anymore,' Urshen surmised.

"My name is Urshen ... his is Protas. We could be together for a very long time," Urshen suggested.

"Huh?" Benekee mumbled, pulled from his despair by the noise of someone talking.

"We were just wondering ... what your name was," Protas added, trying to encourage the lad to engage.

There was an uncomfortable pause, as they waited patiently for him to respond.

"You can call me ... 'Lost'," he finally said, without looking up.

"We are good with that," Protas said, feeling the young lad's misery. "Pretty much sums up how we feel right now," Protas added, as he offered a feeble grin to their new visitor.

Seeing that the new prisoner wasn't ready to engage, they picked up from where they left off before the door opened.

"It seems strange that he would take *us*," Urshen proposed to Protas. "In a war, wouldn't it make sense that the enemy would want to capture those in power. If anyone is powerless, it's us," he said sullenly. "May as well be buried under tons of rock with a forest planted on top."

"Perhaps to make us *Permanents*," Protas eventually suggested.

Benekee's head slowly came up, curious that he had never heard of this before. "What are Permanents?"

The other two prisoners shared a look, surprised at his interest.

Protas turned to Lost and continued.

"Before the Great War, wealthy merchants had begun to change 'temporary' work contracts to 'permanent' ones. Then, as corruption continued to increase, the wages dwindled to nothing. At that point, they were referred to as *Permanents*. They permanently belonged to someone else ... they had no rights." Protas waited for Lost to re-engage.

As Benekee listened to Protas, he felt something about the two men he shared his prison cell with.

For sure they shared a common hopelessness. But it was more than that. He could sense a common thread of experience.

All of this did not change his own state of hopelessness, but he felt a bit more comfortable.

So, he made a point. "Seems they would want to transport more than *a couple* of Permanents," Benekee argued.

Both nodded but neither said a word. They knew that *their* capture, was only the beginning.

But Benekee misinterpreted their silence to mean disinterest, in what he had brought up.

He was about to introduce his companions to the fact that, all three of them had handled Amulets. He knew that, because he knew that both men were Seers. He had just felt it. And that made three out of three. Not an insignificant fact.

Instead, Benekee closed his eyes. It was easier to live in his world of misery than to try to fight his way out of it.

The next morning, after the only meal of the day was pushed under the door, Protas quickly passed the three trays around. Benekee just sat there on his cot staring at the food.

"I know it doesn't look like much, but it tastes okay," Protas offered as consolation.

Both of his visitors had already started to eat the strange meal. But Benekee didn't move a muscle as he stared at his food.

He had become somewhat of a culinary expert due to his four years training at Borit Betoon, but he had never seen food that came close to resembling what he saw on the tray. It was like porridge, but green and ... unappealing.

Instead of eating, his mind drifted to the time when he was told that Yaneek was dead. Killed by one of his Brass Slings.

From that moment, his life ceased to have meaning. He just didn't care about anything. He hardly noticed things that happened around him. He had to be told to eat or sleep.

But occasionally his strong sense of curiosity would pull him out of his pit of despair. Like today as he looked past the food to the room itself. For the first time, he noticed the strangeness of his surroundings.

"Where are we?" he eventually asked.

Both of his cell-mates paused and looked at each other. They did that a lot.

"Are we in Shaksbah?" He offered as his first guess.

Protas resumed eating, meaning he wanted Urshen to handle this one.

"Uhh ... no. We are not in Shaksbah," Urshen started slowly. "Obviously, you have never been to Shaksbah," Urshen offered as a bridge to their conversation. Not that he had ever been there himself ... but he came close.

"But then ... where could we be?" Benekee asked as he looked at the food again.

Protas stopped eating. He was very curious to see how Urshen was going to handle this situation.

"Think you need to be ... direct," Protas suggested as he resumed eating.

"Okay," Urshen responded to Protas's suggestion.

"Lost, we think …. we have been captured by people who live on Harleem. This is a place ... totally outside our world."

"When you say *outside our world*, you mean ...?" Benekee asked, wanting clarification.

"I was thinking *more* direct," Protas jumped in again.

"Agreed," Urshen said.

"At night, the stars that stretch across the sky, are circled by inhabited worlds. Some friendly like Balhok, and some with ambitions of conquest, like Harleem. Fortunate for us, Balhok has power beyond Harleem, the world that wishes to enslave us."

Their visitor simply stared at Urshen for a while. It was understandable considering the content of Urshen's explanation.

Eventually, Benekee's eyes went back to his food. Speaking more to himself than anyone else in the room, he said, "The people of Harleem brought me to *this* place."

Urshen offered a "Yes," wanting to encourage Lost to stay with the conversation.

"So then ... why doesn't the friendly power protect us by crushing the dark power?"

'Here comes the good part,' Protas thought eagerly, as he set his empty tray aside.

"The friendly power has a great respect for life and choice," Urshen continued. "It is why they don't come here to force us to join them. Instead, they allow us to choose, while they constrain the activities of Harleem."

"But I am *here*," Benekee looked around at his prison cell, "and I didn't choose Harleem."

After a period of silence, Protas was the first one to speak. "Lost, you're right, it isn't fair, but you have also made a *very* good point. Urshen, what if Lost is here ... for us?"

The one speaking called the other *Urshen*. It ... sounded familiar? He sighed, it was too hard to remember. Besides, he quickly decided it didn't matter.

"That would suggest ... there is still hope?" Urshen responded, not convinced.

"Yes ... I think that could be right."

"Lost, what did you do before you were brought here?"

Like he had just snuffed out a candle, Lost's interest in the conversation was over.

He simply laid down on his cot, turned his back to his cell-mates, and slept.

The following day, it was Benekee who broke the silence.

"Have you ever been hunting?" Benekee suddenly asked.

"I used to hunt with a sling," Urshen responded. It was hard to imagine how the world had changed since the days when he was living in the Lithgate Wilderness, hunting for game to supplement his garden supplies.

"All Beelstop and I ever wanted to do," Benekee continued, as he stared at the ceiling, "was to build a better hunting weapon."

271

Protas had never heard of Beelstop before, but he wanted to keep Lost talking.

"So … how did you come to work with Beelstop?"

"He was an old man … an inventor at the Mechanical Guild. I was hired to be his assistant. I helped him to build a machine to wash clothes."

The accomplishment sounded odd … but who was Protas to judge. So, he responded with "Hmm, sounds interesting."

"Yes. The effort was quite successful. But then … as I mentioned, he decided we needed to build …"

Benekee couldn't finish the sentence, but Protas knew it was about the better hunting weapon he mentioned earlier.

There was something about that event that deeply troubled the young lad. But he knew that if he was too direct, he would turn over and go to sleep.

"You know, the idea about a better hunting weapon, sounds like a great idea. There was a time that I faced off with a Mountain Cat. I only had a rock and a knife. Could have used something better, that's for sure."

Urshen had never heard this story before, so he propped himself up on one arm, waiting for Protas to continue. But Protas thought he was finished.

"You can't stop there," Urshen insisted, wanting to keep Lost engaged. "We need to hear this tale."

"Well … some time ago, when I was trying to stay ahead of my El-Bhat pursuers, I crossed over a mountain range and headed south into Shaksbah. I had little food so when I spotted *the* Mountain Cat, I decided to follow him, hoping to share in the spoils.

"But … unfortunately, the prey that the Cat was tracking, was a boy and his sheep."

"And you attacked a Mountain Cat with a rock and a knife?" Urshen asked. "Makes me wonder how you survived to tell the story."

"Like I said, I could have used a better hunting weapon. What did you call this invention?" he said as he turned to Lost.

"Beelstop wanted to call it the Brass Sling," Lost said quietly. "He thought it sounded better than the Brass Bow."

"You helped design the Brass Sling?" Protas asked, suddenly very curious.

But he had asked the wrong question. Lost was already laying on his cot, staring at the wall, ignoring his cell-mates.

Later that night, Benekee turned over to stare at the ceiling.

To the young Seer, the battle was lost ... the world was lost.
He had failed in everything he had ever attempted to do.

Chapter 50 - So many Caves

In the days that followed, Lost spent most of his time in his silent world.
Once, he returned to the question of where he was.
Now he knew he was sitting above the clouds in a Flying Boat from Harleem.

Protas tried many times to re-engage him in conversation. He felt that he was their 'hope'. Unfortunately, whatever useful knowledge the young man possessed, was buried too deep.

Protas looked up and saw Urshen sitting in the corner, sullen and more despondent than he had ever seen him.
"I know that look," Protas began the conversation.
Urshen raised his head enough to make eye contact and then looked down again.
"Despair … is the mother of that look," Protas continued, knowing they needed to talk. If he had his knife and a stick, he would have started whittling.
"And perhaps well-bred when you consider our circumstance," he added as he looked over at Lost, who was watching Urshen. Returning his gaze to Urshen, Protas tried to empathize as he began a litany of grievances.
"Inescapable prison … in a boat that floats around in space. Bound by captors that possess weapons we know nothing about. And it appears that our destiny lies on the planet of Harleem, rather than Ankoletia. And that *can't* be good!" He paused, waiting for Urshen to respond.

Eventually there was a response. Urshen raised his head, but in the direction of Lost, as he considered the terrible luck that had swept up the young lad into the same net, that had caught Protas and himself.

For Urshen to direct his attention to Lost, while Protas was trying to get Urshen to talk about his troubles, suggested to Benekee that somehow, he was part of what was bothering Urshen. That made him curious as to what was missing on Protas's grievance list.
"It's something else, isn't it?" Benekee said, as one who understood grief.
'Ahh, we've got him talking again,' Protas observed, anxious to see what Urshen would say.

There was a small nod, a brief sigh and then Urshen began.

"After I killed some El-Bhat Guards inside a prison cell at Border Pass, I looked up to see a man with his bow trained on my chest. It seemed like it was my turn to die. But to my surprise, the man with the bow, told me that he was convinced that I was 'the one'.

"Apparently, his father had a dream about someone who would come and save the Storlenians in Shaksbah."

Benekee, who was no stranger to dreams of significance, understood why this would mean a lot to Urshen. "You believe in dreams, don't you?"

Urshen was surprised at the lad's insight.

"Yes," he answered Lost. "And because of that ... I know they are supposed to *mean* something." Urshen turned his attention to Protas, daring his friend to disagree.

"You think that somehow you have failed?" Protas offered.

Urshen didn't respond. He simply went back to staring at the floor.

Soon, all three prisoners were silently studying the patterns under their feet.

Eventually it was Lost who spoke first.

"But ... what does it mean to be 'the one'?"

Urshen looked up ... intrigued that is was Lost who asked the question.

Encouraged by Urshen's interest, Benekee continued.

"The way I see it, being 'the one', doesn't mean there has to be only one person who accomplishes what needs to be done. Could it also mean that 'the one' is more like a Gatherer of others, who will do what one person cannot?" Benekee suggested to Urshen.

Protas was nodding his head, impressed by what Lost was suggesting. "You gathered me," Protas pointed out, supporting Lost's comment.

Urshen saw the invitation to temporarily escape his prison of despair. "Destined to be the *other* Seer," Urshen agreed, trying to sound cheerful. "You know you never did tell me about that dog, and where your Amulet came from," Urshen said, inviting further comment.

Protas gave a quick grin to Lost before he returned to Urshen.

"Remember the time you almost drowned in the river, and then afterwards you told me about the locations of the other Caves, that I was to remember if something ever happened to you?"

Urshen nodded. He offered a weak grin, at the memory and the irony, of them *both* sitting helpless, in a prison, high in the sky.

"Well, remember my journey to Aqabah with a group of El-Bhat warriors? It was on that journey, that I recognized the description of one of the Cave locations. So, I left the group and went in search of the Cave."

"You travelled with El-Bhat warriors?" Benekee interjected.

"With anyone else in the story, it wouldn't make sense," Urshen agreed, "But with Protas ... *anything's* possible," he clarified as he looked over at Lost.

Protas waited for Urshen to finish, and then continued.

"Yes, well, I found the Cave but not before I partnered up with Sausage, a dog that helped me find it. And ... he followed me *inside* the Cave, where he was given a very special collar, designed to hide the Amulet. After all, I was sort of a prisoner at the time, and wanted the Amulet to stay hidden ... but available. So, I trained the dog to come whenever I whistled."

Urshen grunted softly. "So that's the story behind our escape from Bernado's house."

Benekee wasn't surprised to hear the reference to Amulets. He already knew that Urshen and Protas were Seers. "How many Caves do you think there are?" Benekee asked.

"Many," Urshen replied.

Benekee turned to Protas. "Why do *you* think there are so many Caves?"

There was something about the innocent curiosity of the question, that stirred the wheels of Protas's mind. He had always thought that the answer, was simply to allow the people on Ankoletia, to have ample opportunity to find *at least* one Cave. But now he sensed that there was another purpose. He stared at Lost for a while, as he considered that question from a fresh perspective.

"You know Urshen, in light of our present circumstances, it seems to me that the lad is asking a *great* question."

Urshen looked over at Protas and immediately recognized 'the look'. It was one of those times when his friend was about to pull back the curtain of knowledge. Like the time, he told Urshen he was sure that there was an infiltration of El-Bhat into Storlenia, or the time he knew that the Tinker Train coming down the road, was the solution to their problem.

Urshen sat up straight, intent on hearing whatever Protas had to say.

"The people who *planted* the Caves on Ankoletia, would have certainly considered the entire landscape of our future ... including these Visitors," Protas said as he waved a hand towards the door that separated them from their captors.

"Interesting," Urshen added as he considered his early history with the Cave. He was about to say more but instead looked over at Lost.

"I say we trust him," Protas suggested.

Urshen decided to agree with Protas's judgement. He had never been wrong when it came to people.

So Urshen continued.

"At the beginning, I thought the purpose of the Cave, was to teach me how to heal others."

The mention of healing brought back a flood of memories to Benekee. He settled his chin into his hands. He was interested in what Urshen was saying.

"And at the time, in my small world, I was content and excited with that interpretation of why the Cave had called me. And secondly, I knew that the power of the Garden had come from another world, far from Ankoletia.

"But over time," Urshen continued, "my understanding of its purpose expanded to include the *preservation* of our race. And so, I assumed this path of protection, would follow a course that would allow us to see our enemies clearly, and that through *knowledge*, technical and otherwise, we would be prepared to defeat our enemies. But that was when our enemies were few and *born on Ankoletia*."

"And now?" Protas encouraged Urshen to pursue his train of thought.

Urshen turned to Lost again, beginning to see that maybe, their hope *was* buried inside his curious mind.

"*Now*, I would say that there must be a way to use the power of the Caves against our aggressors. But how to do that ... from up here ... escapes me," he said, waiting for Lost to say something.

But he didn't.

Chapter 51 - Back from the dead

Benekee once had the power that Urshen was talking about. But now ... all he had was despair ... for creating the death machine that took his sister's life.

Everyone was quiet for a while, and then Protas got up and started to pace.

"What about the water ... do you think that's important ... I mean how they connect?" Protas finally said.

With every new question that his cell mates asked, Benekee's curiosity grew stronger.

"Water?" Lost asked.

"The time Urshen almost drowned, he discovered that the rivers and underground systems of water, connect the Caves. It's how he knew their locations."

"I've overlooked so much," Urshen said to himself, "Never questioning why things were the way they were." He looked back to Protas, "It cannot be a coincidence. They were meant to communicate with each other. But why?"

"What do you know about the Caves?" Benekee asked, trying to be helpful.

"Good place to start," Urshen agreed, looking at his friend. "And since Protas has been inside more Caves than anyone else I know ..."

"On the outside, they are covered by a mountain," Protas began. "Entrance is possible through a large Quartz Door, using an Amulet. Inside there is a Garden made of crystal. In the middle of the Garden is a large Tree. The light is supplied by the Cave walls that glow, and there are crystal paths that allow the visitor to wander among the Garden. If you touch one of these plants, they transfer knowledge or power. But ... not everyone can enter. If you are not allowed, you will die a horrible death," Protas added.

"So, the locked door," Benekee was thinking aloud, "is to protect us."

"Yes," Urshen answered. "But ... imagine if the door was *always* open."

"Which way do the doors face?" Benekee asked Protas.

"Different directions ..." he responded slowly. "But hard to know without more locations," he finished, and then sat down.

"I am sure we have discovered something extremely important," Urshen shared with the other prisoners. "Despite the power of Harleem, there has to be a way to defeat them."

"I agree," Lost jumped in.

Both Urshen and Protas heard him but gave his comment no regard. They thought he was only being agreeable.

"So how do we accomplish this seemingly impossible feat?" Urshen asked, looking at Protas, who was staring at the prison cell door. "Wish you could get through that door?" He asked, wondering if Protas had a plan.

"No, just thinking about ... the other prison cell."

"I wonder how she is doing," Urshen said to his friend. "Prison is one thing ... but to be alone ..."

Protas shook his head at the irony. In Bernado's prison cell, he constantly thought of Yaneek, hoping that one day they could be together. And now, they were never so close ... yet it meant nothing.

He hoped that Urshen was wrong about Yaneek's suffering. He hoped that her delightful way of looking at life, was burning brightly.

That thought was so comforting, he decided to share it with Urshen.

"She certainly has it worse than we do," he began, "but one thing I've learned about Yaneek. She has a very positive way of ..."

"Yaneek?" Benekee quickly interrupted, as he slowly stood up. "Did you say ... Yaneek?"

"Yeah," Protas replied, curious as to why the young lad had suddenly become so animated at the mention of her name.

"But it cannot be .... *she* is dead!" Benekee insisted.

Then he saw his error. "I'm sorry. I'm sorry, my mistake. It must be a different Yaneek," he sadly said to Protas.

Suddenly Protas understood.

"Your real name is ... Benekee! Yaneek is your sister."

Protas grinned at the recognition. "Because of you ... I met Yaneek!" he excitedly added and laughed heartily. "You used to wear a Robe ... correct?"

He nodded 'yes' but still didn't understand and was afraid to believe what his cell mate was saying.

But he seemed to be overwhelmingly sure that his sister was in a cell close by. He could see it in his eyes. Eyes that invited him to believe.

His hands began to sweat. His breathing was rapid. He opened his mouth, wanting to believe. But he was so afraid.

Finally, the words tumbled out, as his hands fidgeted together, "Are you sure ... she is alive," he took a deep breath, "on board this vessel?"

Benekee stared at Protas, as he remembered something his sister had said, before she left the Guild.

'I am sort of in a relationship ... and I need to figure things out'

"She was brought here with us," Urshen jumped in, to add authenticity to Protas's statement. Now everyone in the room were on their feet, anxious to see where this new revelation was going to take them.

"He *lied* to me," Benekee suddenly hissed angrily. He wasn't sure why. But it probably had something to do with Yaneek, being a prisoner on this Flying Boat. And that was enough to feel a rage, greater than anything he had ever felt in his life before.

He closed his eyes and clenched his fists against the anger. The anger that threatened to overcome him. That lusted to pull power from the Garden below and punish Bernado ... immediately!

"Everything all right?" The voice came from the direction of the Robe. "I know it doesn't look so good right now ... but at least she's alive ... like the rest of us."

The voice broke the grip of the anger. He sunk his face into his hands. He realized, how close to the edge of darkness he had been.

'The Garden trusts you' were the words that always came to his mind, at times like these ... times when he despaired at his lack.

A quick sigh and Benekee opened his eyes. He wanted to look at his cell-mates. They had just given him the best news possible!

But he couldn't. The taint of darkness was still flickering at the edge of his mind.

So instead his eyes went back to the floor. "Yes ... everything is all right." It had to be, Yaneek was back from the dead.

Urshen realized that it was probably best to come back to the subject of his sister later. Benekee needed time to adjust to the astonishing news.

"We were talking about the Caves," Urshen reminded everyone. "And why there were so many of them, and what would happen if those doors were *always* open." He looked to Protas to continue the train of thought.

Hesitantly, Protas looked at Benekee, as he continued to stare at the floor, unable to regain eye contact.

Unsure if they should return to their previous discussion ... while Benekee was in so much pain, he looked over at Urshen who gave him the nod to continue.

"On the one hand," Protas began slowly, "as I mentioned, every Cave is encased inside a *mountain*. That's a lot of protection! But what still puzzles me, is that everyone who has ever died from being exposed to the inside of a Cave, has died *inside* the Cave. Even when the door was open."

"Kind of suggests that the range of that power is constrained like an Amulet," Urshen picked up the train of thought. "But then again, by linking the Amulet to twelve Trackers, I could extend the range of the Amulet's power significantly, at Border Pass."

"I have to believe there's a difference," Protas argued. "You were constrained because the Caves wanted you to be. If the Caves are constrained, surely it is self-imposed and can be removed anytime they choose."

"Ok," agreed Urshen. "But what if those doors were open and the Caves removed their constraint. Wouldn't that purge the planet of every incompatible life force ... including the Harleem Visitors?"

Benekee was deep in thought, his head still down. He was concerned that Yaneek was on the Flying Boat.

The fact that she was there at all, was *very* unexpected.

At least for the three of them, he was sure it was because they had handled Amulets. It made sense of *why* they were the first, and so far, the only ones captured. But why would they want Yaneek? It might be important.

His head came up, curious to study Protas, considering Yaneek's need 'to figure things out.'

Was he the reason she was here?

Looking straight at Protas he interrupted, "Why did they take Yaneek as a prisoner?"

As Protas exercised a cautious pause, Urshen jumped in. "Benekee, it is certainly unfortunate that your sister has been captured.

"I was in that identical situation a few years ago. Maybe it was just bad luck ... being at the wrong place at the wrong time."

"I disagree. I think it's important," Benekee protested, still staring at Protas.

"But we don't even understand, why the three of *us* are here," Protas added, inviting Benekee to say more.

"I think we do," Benekee suggested. "I suspect it has something to do with ... us being Seers," he whispered the last words.

Again, his two cell-mates shared a look. What they had just learned, explained a lot about *Lost*.

"Where did you get your Amulet?" Protas asked without tone or challenge.

"I discovered it at the Redemption Guild of Borit Betoon." The way he folded his arms, suggested that this was all Benekee was going to offer, in way of explanation.

Urshen looked over at Protas, "Did Yaneek ever mention having access to, or even knowledge of an Amulet?"

"Nope, it never came up."

"What about your dog," Benekee thought he saw a connection, "did she know about Sausage?"

"Well ... I did tell her about Sausage ... even taught her the whistle that would bring him if she was ever in need."

Benekee and Urshen were already nodding their heads in agreement.

"I suppose ... you might be right. After she left my prison cell, I thought I heard a whistle," Protas continued.

He looked at Urshen, "And since our re-capture, Sausage would know to stay with her.

"And ... living together, she would be exposed to the Amulet all the time," he said, continuing to nod in agreement with himself.

"Might be enough to qualify her. Assuming Benekee is right."

But Benekee was sure he was right. And had already settled into his bed in the corner. Now that the mystery surrounding Yaneek's imprisonment was settled, he wanted to think some more about his next step.

"Yeah, me too," Protas said as he headed for his cot. "Time to think some more."

Urshen, being the last man standing, quickly decided to do the same.

---------- <> ----------

Lying on his cot, Protas's thoughts drifted to Yaneek. Since he met her, he had always been in prison somewhere, with lots of time to think and dream. And his favourite subject was Yaneek.

'Imagine, meeting Yaneek's brother up here … in space, and finding out he is a Seer,' he mused to himself. What were the chances? This had to be good news.

Maybe they didn't have the ball yet, but they were back in the game!

Tomorrow, he intended to continue their discussion about the Caves and the doors.

Benekee had already proved to be a very useful team player. He had suggested great questions and insights.

And yet … it appeared, he was still holding back.

There was something he knew but didn't want to say.

Protas was sure of it.

---------- <> ----------

Urshen thought of Yaneek. Wishing he had a way to let her know, that her brother Benekee was here with them. It made him think of Zephra.

It seemed a lifetime ago, that they were walking along the river in Tinker Village, hand in hand.

If he concentrated, he could see those golden flecked eyes as they stared up at him, listening to him propose. They had talked about children and had even picked out the spot where they would build their new home.

He wondered if Braddock had already finished it … while he patiently waited for the two of them to return.

He hoped that Zephra was still safe. He knew from Protas, that she had hung her lariat at the Planning and Development Guild in Qar-ana.

Because of Craslin's schemes, the shipment of gold, the Guild Militia and Bernado assisting from the side-lines, he knew that she was right in the middle of all that was wrong on the planet below.

Knowing her, she probably had lots of opportunity to return to her father but preferred to stay. He smiled, as he remembered a few words that Braddock had shared with him, shortly before he left the Tinker Village. *'Lad, do you know who you're marrying?'*

'She was definitely full of fire,' he smiled. He only hoped that she had been more careful than he had been.

He laughed inside as he thought about how they would eventually compare stories. His story would be embarrassingly short!

--------- <> ---------

The following morning, while Benekee was still asleep, Urshen decided to ask Protas something he had always been curious about.

Looking at the ceiling, he began. "Protas," he whispered, "remember the time I took you to the Cave … and you walked down the path and stopped at a plant to touch it. I knew you had learned something important, but when I asked you about it, all you would say was, '*Something the Cave wanted me to know about you.*'

"You ready to talk about it?"

A soft laugh came from Protas's side of the room.

"Well … first, I was informed that you were the first Seer in over a thousand years.

"And that it was *destiny* that I would find you. And that destiny, would help you rescue me from myself.

"And that one day, I would know what you would know.

"Didn't realize at the time, that this meant … *what it was like to live inside four prison walls.*" Protas laughed again.

Chapter 52 - The return of the Old Woman

The pieces of the puzzle had fallen into place for Benekee.
Bernado had deceived him.
Yaneek was prisoner because she had also been exposed to an Amulet.
Somehow, that condition made them, more desirable to the citizens of Harleem.
And if he didn't do something about their captivity, they would soon be heading for Harleem ... never to come back!
But ... he still held one puzzle piece in his hand. And he wasn't sure if he had permission to lay it down ... to complete the picture.
He wanted desperately to use the power of the Cave. But could he? Was he *allowed*?

He remembered so clearly those words spoken by the Old Woman. How she was so proud of him, and how the Cave trusted him.
But ... he hadn't done so well lately. He wasn't sure if he even had the right.

His cell mates were sleeping.
He swung his feet over the side of his bed, and with head bowed, he closed his eyes.
He spoke to the Old Woman in his mind.

His words were hesitant. Self-incriminating. Sorrowful.
Finally, he said, 'I am willing to stay in this prison ... but ... if you will allow me one last opportunity to use the Cave's power ... to free Yaneek ... that is all I ask.'

'Benekee ...'
He recognized the voice ... and her cheerful tone.
With eyes still closed, he sat up a bit straighter. He was ready to accept anything she demanded.

'Benekee, the time has come for you to use the power. But first I want to show you something.'

As she spoke those words, his mind searched for her kind face in the smoky room he suddenly found himself in.

She wasn't there, but there was a door.
He moved quickly towards it and stepped through it.
And there in the middle of another room was a table and chair. On the table was some sort of device. It looked like two short telescopes fastened together.

He sat down and picked up the device and studied it for a moment. He noticed an adjustment ring, like any scope he was familiar with. With his fingers, he turned it with ease. The workmanship was obviously <u>very</u> fine. On the viewing end of each scope was a soft cup, designed to touch his face as he looked into those two lenses.

With both hands, he lifted the instrument to his eyes.

From his position high in the sky, he could see a small group of Trackers climbing down a mountain. He sensed an Amulet.
Following the scent of the talisman, he turned the adjustment ring to allow him to see closer.
'Wow,' he said softly to himself, as the image zoomed in until he could see the the leather pouch that contained the Amulet. The device was ... incredible.

He watched them as they descended and then changed direction.

Soon they were crawling through tall grasses … while a much larger group of men pursued them … carrying <u>hand-held</u> versions of the Brass Sling!

He thought of the Amulet and immediately shouted out a warning.

But of course … they couldn't hear him.

They suddenly jumped to their feet and ran towards a mountain in the distance, as brass balls pummelled them until two of them died. Benekee winced. But he knew more would die before this vision was over.

As they arrived at the mountain base, it was obvious that they intended on climbing that slope. But they had barely arrived, when arrows began raining down upon them.

He scanned further up the mountain until he spotted a large group of men dressed in black silk garb.

By the time the arrows were depleted, another Tracker had fallen.

Benekee turned his scopes back towards the large group pursuing them across the grasslands. The Trackers only had a short time before they would be facing enemies behind and in front.

There were so few Trackers compared to the army of men that wanted them dead.

He swung the device back to the Trackers.

They were still at the bottom of the mountain. They were waiting for the Black Silk Warriors to descend upon them.

Benekee held his breath as he watched <u>part</u> of the Black Silk Warriors rush down the slope, their voices shouting a message of assured destruction.

He zoomed into the wall of Trackers. They stood firm … quietly prepared to meet this new enemy as the previous enemy raced towards them from their rear.

'Who are these men?' Benekee questioned with unbounded admiration.

'And why do they carry an Amulet?'

He wanted so much to help them.

But it was no use.

They would die where they stood.

'But maybe not,' he thought as he quickly zoomed out.

Was there a chance they could escape the Black Silk Warriors before the men with the Brass Slings arrived?

'Yes,' he answered, realizing that the larger group was still a significant distance away.

Then the Black Silk Warriors crashed into the wall of Trackers.

The wall looked so small from his viewpoint high in the sky. So insignificant compared to the numbers that were being thrown at it.

And yet ... the Trackers were holding the line!
He zoomed in for a better look.
It was <u>incredible</u> to watch.
He saw it but was having a hard time believing it.
It was like ... they fought with the strength and speed of the Fates.
Or perhaps ... the strength of the Cave!

The wall of Trackers sped up the mountain side, leaving behind two dead Trackers ... and a blanket of unmoving black warriors. 'Amazing,' whispered Benekee.

The Black Silk Warriors that watched from the treeline slipped into the forest.

Moments later, as the Trackers themselves entered the forest, further to the west, the Brass Sling warriors had begun their ascent.

For the first time, Benekee saw hope of escape for these Trackers. The forest was their domain.

'Or maybe ... they are not trying to escape,' Benekee suddenly realized.

Benekee turned his device in the direction of their climb.

'Oh my,' he exclaimed.

There was a Quartz Door behind a ledge. He had never been inside a Cave, but he knew instinctively that behind that door was a Cave.

'That's why the Trackers are here ... with an Amulet. They want to open that door!'

'Interesting,' he said to himself as he turned his scopes back to the Trackers.

By now, they had separated into two groups. The larger one was left behind to protect the rear of those dashing upwards to The Ledge.

He zoomed in on the group left behind. If they could hold the men with the Brass Sling weapons long enough ...

Meanwhile, as two hundred men with swords and knives charged into the woods, another fifty followed behind to provide brass ball support.

The Trackers emptied their quivers as they slowly moved higher, keeping the enemy between them and the weapons below that fired upon them with abandon.

'It's working,' he exclaimed with surprise.

He swung his scopes to find the smaller group.

They were unsuccessfully pushing towards the Cave. There were more men above, with Brass Sling weapons firing upon them.

Next, they rushed to the west and disappeared into a ravine.

Switching back to the larger group of Trackers, he saw them storm The Ledge, defended by the Black Silk Warriors.

Despite the headwind of El-Bhat that poured onto that Ledge to replace the dead, the Trackers managed to gain a foothold, until the smaller group of Trackers leapt from above.

A hopeful Benekee kept his scopes fixed on the Tracker with the Amulet. This was the moment that had to happen.

The accomplishment of the impossible, by an impossibly small group of committed warriors.

He wasn't sure why that Door had to open, but everything in his being told him that it <u>must</u> happen.

And everyone on that ledge seemed to understand the same thing.

The fighting was unbelievably frantic as the Head Tracker made room for the Tracker with the Amulet.

The talisman was now in plain sight, held tightly, as the hope of the world. Quickly, the Head Tracker snatched the Amulet as the other Tracker fell dead.

And then … within hand reach of the keyhole … a shout could be heard.

A shout that ignited the boiling cauldron as a mass of Black Silk Warriors ignored the blades of the enemy and <u>pushed</u> everyone off The Ledge!

'Oh no …' a devastated Benekee whispered.

The struggle continued for a while as Trackers fought to regain the battlefield.
Fought to push their Leader free from the mass of bodies.
But on both accounts, their efforts were in vain.
In the end, all the Trackers were dead … and the Cave door was still closed.

The Leader of the warriors with the Brass Slings, slipped his barrel inside the chain and removed the Amulet from the grip of the dead Tracker.

He took it to the rock Ledge and laid it down.

Benekee's body tensed as he watched the steel barrel smash into the Crystal Amulet, breaking it into pieces.
He watched for a while, numb with grief, as the El-Bhat and the warriors with the Brass Slings, abandoned the mountain slopes.

He placed the scopes on the table and then laid his head into his arms and wept.

He wept because of the valiant sacrifice of lost lives.
And the tragedy of courage unfulfilled.
And the anguish of his dashed confidence, that <u>their</u> sacrifice was somehow meant to defeat the hordes from Harleem.

Eventually, his grief was spent.
He was ready to be taught.

His head came up as a thought flooded his mind.

'I was shown this to clarify what was left to be done!'

His head sank into his arms again. There was no comfort in that thought. It terrified him.

"I cannot do this," *he moaned.* "If I fail ... these men will have died for nothing."

But the pain of his words was eclipsed by the next thought that invaded his mind.

'What if ... there are no other options for the people of Ankoletia?'

His head came up, angry that life was so unfair.

And there on the other side of the table, was the Old Woman.

He looked down. She had always been so kind. And he was being ...

"Do you doubt your link with the Garden's power?"

"Maybe," *he offered, unable to meet her eyes.*

"Then why don't you test your concern. Heal yourself completely."

He looked up. He knew she was right.

She offered him her smile of encouragement.

"... Okay," *he hesitated.*

"When?" *she persisted.*

"Right away," *he agreed.*

Pleased, she patted his hand. And then disappeared in a swirl of smoke.

When the smoke cleared, he found himself back in his cell, sitting on his cot.

He laid down and rested his arms across his chest.
For sure, he had made the commitment.
But he needed a little time to let that commitment become part of him.

He could hear his cell mates move in their sleep, for quite a while, before he finally had the courage to invoke the power.
When it was done, he turned over and fell asleep.

Chapter 53 - The best laid plans

Voices from far away were breaking the grip of his slumber.
Voices that were getting stronger and clearer.
Eventually he could make out the words, '... *to live inside four prison walls,*' and then he heard laughter.

He sat up.
His cell mates had been talking.
He turned towards them and waited ... until they looked at him.

They were dumbfounded and speechless.

He asked, "It's my face, isn't it?"
They were still staring. They had seen the impossible.

The strangest thing to Urshen was not the healing, he knew the power of the Cave. The strangest thing to him was that it occurred on the Harleem Flying Ship, far from Ankoletia ... without an Amulet.

The strangest thing to Protas was not that Benekee's face was repaired, but rather, that Benekee *knew* that it was repaired as soon as he awoke.

It suggested to Protas, that Benekee was not only the recipient of the healing, but that he was *in control* of it!

"Yes ... it's your face," Urshen answered Benekee's question.

There was another pause in the room as everyone considered what had just happened.
"You told us you were a Seer ... but you didn't tell us everything ... that's for sure," Protas said slowly, inviting Benekee to say more.

The young lad looked around the room and then asked, "Do you think they can hear us?"
Protas glanced at his blanket. "Don't think that's gonna work. Can you provide us with a ... room within a room?" He suggested.

They sat on the floor, while Benekee invoked the power of the Garden to create a bubble, large enough to surround them.

"No one outside of this bubble can hear anything we say," he assured them.

"I'm convinced," Protas offered enthusiastically, "that the tides of victory have begun to move in our direction. It's now clear that Yaneek was captured and transported with us, as a gift from the Garden. And then there's you, Benekee. A Seer that doesn't need an Amulet close by …"

Benekee was nodding in agreement. It was time to invite these two Seers to work with him, to finish what the Trackers couldn't.

"I was shown things as you slept," he began. "The best our world had to offer, have already given their lives trying to open the Door of a Cave. But they failed. They made it to the Door, but they were killed, and the Amulet was broken."

"Is that what we need to do?" Urshen asked, "Open the Door to this Cave?"

"I don't know why … but it's very important."

"I knew it," Urshen eagerly exclaimed.

"And somehow," Benekee continued, "the forces controlled by Harleem, knew these men would be sent to open the Cave. Hundreds of warriors were sent … many with hand-held Brass Slings … to defeat twenty."

"So few," Protas said in amazement.

"It's about sacrifice … not numbers," Benekee suggested.

The thought was sobering.

"Back to the Door," Protas reminded everyone. "Based on what you have already said, it appears that you have to open the Door, of a *particular* Cave. Do you know where this Cave is?"

"I have seen its location. With the power of the Garden, I am sure I can find it."

"What about the Amulet?" Urshen asked.

"The fragments lie on The Ledge in front of the Door. I will mend the Amulet and slide it into the Keyhole."

"You are sure you can do all of this … from up here?" Protas asked.

"Yes," Benekee assured them with a whisper. Then his eyes dropped to the floor as he sighed. "I don't really know why … but the Garden trusts me."

Urshen smiled as he shook his head in disbelief. "Benekee … I would have never guessed. But my time in prison was a small price to pay for this moment."

"I have to agree." Protas grinned at Benekee. "Wait till Harleem finds out that they lost *everything* because of a young lad." He laid a hand on his arm. "Yaneek will be so ..."

Before that word left his lips, their prison cell door opened, revealing a Guard pointing a noiseless weapon towards Benekee.

The young lad fell, and the bubble collapsed.

Before Urshen or Protas could react, two Guards rushed in and dragged Benekee from the room.

'Impossible,' thought Protas, as he cast a quick glance at Urshen. 'This shouldn't be happening!'

As soon as the Guards and the body of Benekee disappeared, a tall man, with long hair and a perfectly white face, entered the room. His expression was like stone.

They both retreated to their cots and waited for the unpleasantness to start.

"My name is Kareen-hys-Tebeel-del-Harleem. I am the ... *Captain* of this Ship. Soon we will be leaving for Harleem. I want you to be comfortable and healthy on this voyage. Let me know if there is anything you lack."

It wasn't what either of them expected. Protas decided to push the envelope.

"We want better food," Protas demanded.

Urshen watched Kareen carefully to see how he would respond.

"The food we serve you is *engineered*, perfect for what your bodies require," the Captain explained.

"You're right about that," Protas agreed. "Never felt better. But it tastes ... boring."

"Unfortunately ... a pleasure you will have to do without."

Urshen decided to do a little pushing of his own. "We don't do well without our pleasures."

There was a pause as the Captain considered the complaint. His prisoners were beginning to misunderstand his offer to be helpful. It was time to remove that misunderstanding.

"When you have lived as long as I have," he began, "you come to appreciate that the greatest pleasures in life, are the oddities. Like irony.

"Something you do not know, is that your prison cell was never built for security. Except for the locked door of course. You see, you have no idea how valuable you are to the citizens of Harleem.

"Which is why your room, was designed to keep you free from disease and otherwise at the peak of health. And how do we know exactly what you need? We collect data from ... *sensors*. And that data is used by our Medical Officer ... not Head of Security."

Kareen's eyes wandered around the room as he continued, "These sensors are in the ceiling, the walls ... and the floor."

Protas was slowly shaking his head. He could see the irony coming.

"Had ... Benekee, not created the ingenious bubble of silence, we would have never known of your *little secret*. But because he did, alarms went off, warning us of a problem with the sensors."

Protas and Urshen looked at each other. They had underestimated the enemy.

"Irony is such a splendid thing. Don't you agree?"

Without a further word, Kareen-hys-Tebeel-del-Harleem left the room.

Back in the Control Room, Kareen spoke to The Technician.

"Let the Medical Officer know he is to keep the young lad permanently sedated. As soon as we have the contract for the planet, we will begin to extract his genetics. He is too dangerous."

Chapter 54 - Prisons within prisons

"Benekee ... Benekee.
Benekee you must open your eyes."
His eyelids were as heavy as lead. But there was something familiar with that voice. A compelling memory that he could not ignore.

"Oh ... it's you," he said, his tongue thick with weariness.

"Yes ... it's me. I have been given permission to visit you one last time ... to give you a gift. And then I must leave ... forever."

Benekee tried to stand in protest. He was stricken with the thought of never seeing her again. But the ropes that bound him to his chair defeated him.

"Why do these ropes hold me to this chair?"

"Benekee, you are bound by many ropes," she tried to explain. "Prisons within prisons."

"Will your gift free me from these prisons?" he asked, as he continued to struggle in vain against the ropes.

"It will ... but it is not the purpose of the gift. This gift is in answer to a plea from a man named Finn ... before he died. His hope was to free all of the people of Ankoletia, not just you."

"What did he ask for?"

"I think you should see for yourself," she said as she laid her hand on his.

--------- <> ---------

As soon as the smoke cleared, Benekee found himself standing on a forested mountain, and below was The Ledge ... filled with warriors and the sounds of clanging swords and of men dying.

He searched among the familiar Trackers for the Leader. He expected that the Leader, and Finn, would be one in the same. And when he spotted him, he knew he was.

Because he could feel it.

And he could feel what Finn was feeling.

The excruciating pain from his wounds.

The exhaustion that filled every fibre of his being.

The terrible darkness of defeat that threatened to overcome him.

And ... the strength of his mental willpower that pushed those things away.

Refusing to give up until he was finished.

Benekee watched and marvelled at the warrior's suffering, and his determination to succeed.

But then ... the weight of that experience increased, and Benekee realized, that initially, the doorway into the warrior's soul, had only opened a crack.

In agony Benekee clenched his fists, and trembling, dropped to his knees.

He could hardly breathe.

And still the door continued to open wider.

Sweat covered his entire body. The door was now fully open.

Inside, he wept for the suffering of this man.

It was unbelievable. It was terrible!

He gasped as he fought for another breath of air.

He fell forward onto his hands.

Amid the flying knives and swords, Finn occasionally glanced anxiously at another Tracker who was making his way to him, with an Amulet in his hand.

Finn knew that the talisman, would have to be pushed into the Keyhole very soon, or all would be lost.

Because of Finn, Far-fel managed to move close to the Keyhole, but the continuous volley of brass against the Tracker with the Amulet, was beyond the limits of physical endurance.

Finn could see it in Far-fel's pained eyes. He snatched the Amulet from his hand as his friend crumpled, dead to the stone floor.

With the swiftness of a snake, Finn shoved the talisman towards the keyhole.

But he missed the mark by a finger width as the battering ram of human flesh threw him off The Ledge with everyone else.

In the scramble of writhing bodies that followed, Finn could feel the Trackers who were still alive. Some were close enough to help.

"I have the Amulet," he shouted, "Push me up."

Arms and legs pummeled like battering rams to push Finn through the tangle.

Within moments, he was at the top, ready to jump back onto The Ledge.

But many Brass Slings were waiting for his exit as they fired in unison.

So much brass hit Finn all at once, the momentum literally pushed him off his feet.

He made a desperate attempt to jump back up, but his body wouldn't respond.

In the next few moments, before the brass weapons finished the job, Benekee heard Finn's plea to the Fates.

'Remember us ... send someone to finish ... what I couldn't.'

And then the heart of the greatest warrior, that Benekee could imagine, stopped beating.

Benekee's body, previously trembling from head to foot, collapsed, unconscious on that mountain slope.

"So now you know," the Old Woman said, "what plea I refer to ... and the *strength* of that plea."

She held his face between her two hands and with pleading eyes, she charged him with her final words.

"Embrace that strength Benekee ... and you *will be* the one to finish what Finn could not."

The kindest face, that he ever knew, began to fade.

He knew he would never see her again.

He looked down at the ropes ... and he thought of Finn.

Instantly, he could remember clearly, the full load of physical and mental pain ... and the darkness of defeat.

And the willpower that fought against that load, unwilling to succumb until he was finished.

It was horrific!

With eyes closed, his mind screamed in terror, hoping to rid himself of the memory.

Eventually the trembling stopped.

He thought he could feel the warm hand of the Old Woman, on his shoulder.

She had always been there for him in his time of need.

And she had said he would never *see* her again.

He wished he had told her how grateful he was ... for her touch and her words.

They were the greatest things in his life.

The Caves of Balhok

He thought about her most recent words ... and her desire for him to understand Finn's plea.

Suddenly he realized what the Old Woman meant, when she said, 'Embrace that strength Benekee'.

Now he knew. He had a decision to make. Either he would cast off that horrific load, forget that it ever happened, or ... he would embrace it, accept it, and then, it would forever be, *his* crushing load.

Every muscle in his body tensed as he pushed against the ropes.

A natural reflex as he considered carrying that crushing load, every day for the rest of his life.

Just the thought of it agonized him, terrorized him.

He was only Benekee, a young lad from Breckenden.

He wanted to please the Old Woman. But how was he supposed to do that.

He wasn't Finn!

No ... he surely wasn't.

And that thought echoed within his soul, until he thought he could hear the Old Woman say to him, 'No Benekee, you're not ... but wouldn't you want to be ... just like him?'

As he embraced *that* thought, the echoes that haunted him, died.

Until there was only silence ... and those ropes.

In the solitude of that silence, he returned to his experience with Finn.

And he realized something else.

He didn't just admire Finn ... he loved him. He loved everything about him.

And ... he hated those ropes.

And ... he knew ... he had just made his decision.

He truly wanted to be, *just like* Finn.

The fear was gone.

He took his last breath of life as 'Benekee from Breckenden'.

And embraced the crushing load.

The Medical Officer was preparing another dose of sedative when suddenly the lights went out.

There was a moment of dead silence before the auxiliary power came on, during which he thought he could hear the rustling of a bed sheet.

But before the auxiliary lights came on, he had already collapsed to the floor.

--------- <> ---------

For quite a while they said nothing as they lay on their cots, staring at the ceiling.

A ceiling full of *sensors*.

Their quick and easy defeat was so devastating.

Finally, Urshen opened a conversation.

"Do you think he's dead?"

"He *is* the greatest, and probably the only remaining threat, to their invasion," Protas lamented. "If he's not ... it's only because they still want him alive for a very special reason."

There were so many other questions that Urshen wanted to talk about. Very hard questions without an obvious answer. Questions that just might shred the shadow of faith, that he was clinging to.

He wanted to believe that Ankoletia would still survive ... but he was afraid he had just witnessed the promised death of their last and only hope.

It was truly his darkest hour. So those questions remained in the prison of his mind, behind bars of fear and anguish.

He wished Protas would say something. Finally, he turned towards the wall and tried to sleep.

Some time later, the lights went out. That usually signalled their scheduled sleep time, but it was way too early. And the soft whisper of the wind that entered from the ceiling above, went silent.

"Strange," he could hear Protas say.

Then dim lights came on to replace the normal lights.

"Something's happening," Urshen said as he sat up.

Protas was trying to puzzle it out. "My guess is that something happened to their power."

After a while, he got up and checked the door. "Still locked."

He had barely sat back on his cot when the door opened.
And there stood ... Benekee.

Chapter 55 - The Offer

In the dim green light, Urshen looked closer at the young lad that used to call himself Lost. There was something different about him. His face looked ... tortured.
"What have they done to you?" was all Urshen could think to say.
"And how is it, you are free? And what about the power?" Protas asked, hoping he saw a connection between the loss of power and the appearance of Benekee.

Benekee entered the prison cell and offered a weak smile.
"I am fine," he answered Urshen.
He looked at Protas and said, "Free? Not yet. We have been living in prisons within prisons. But with this open door, we only have one more to go."

Urshen approached the open door and looked down the hallway. There were several bodies, lying on the floor.
"Shouldn't we talk about this," Urshen whispered loudly.
Before the young Seer could answer, Protas asked again, "The power going off was you, wasn't it?" He said quietly.
"Yes."
"Do you have a plan?" Urshen asked eagerly.
"Yes. And this time ... I checked it out with the Garden."
"Wish *I* would have done that more often," Urshen whispered to them both.
"Why are you both whispering?" Benekee finally asked. "There is only one person on this vessel that can hear you, and he is in ... the Command Room. Waiting for me."

Protas was sure, that one person, was Kareen-hys-Tebeel-del-Harleem. And that was worrisome. He couldn't help himself. His hands wanted to whittle so badly, he had to clasp them behind his back, out of sight.
"I don't mean to be a sceptic, but Kareen didn't get to be Captain of this Ship, with authority to conquer our world, without being extremely clever and ruthless."
"And don't forget experience. He is many hundreds of years old," Benekee added as he watched Protas pace.

Those words of agreement were meant to bring comfort ... that Benekee understood his concern. But it only elevated Protas's need to whittle.

"Do we even have to confront him? Can't you just use the Amulet ... now?"

"Meeting him is a suggestion from the Garden. I'm inclined to follow it."

While Protas engaged the young Seer with his lingering concerns, Urshen had been considering why Benekee had come to their cell. "What do you want us to do?"

"Witness. And watch my back."

And with those succinct instructions, Benekee left the cell, leading the way.

A few corridors later, the three Seers congregated at the locked Command Room door. Benekee turned to the other two. "By the way, I have disabled his weapons."

With eyes closed, Benekee placed his hand on the door. With barely a whisper of sound, the door opened.

It was a repeat scene of the corridors. Bodies everywhere.

Benekee walked slowly towards the only man, still standing in the Control Room.

Before he got too close, Protas extended an arm to stop Benekee.

Kareen was listening to their approach, but his eyes were on a picture of light. The picture was beautiful. Forests and mountains.

"It usually doesn't get this far," the Alien said to his visitors.

Benekee recognized the scene from the planet below. "The Mountain of Hope," he said for the benefit of Urshen and Protas.

"Hope? Depends on your point of view," Kareen protested.

"It can be *your* point of view," Benekee countered.

"If you mean surrender? Then you don't understand the ... *relationship* ... between us and the Sons of Balhok."

A few paces away, there was a chair. While he listened to Kareen, Benekee headed for it and sat down.

"I am sure there is history between your two races. But I am here to extend you the offer of life, to you and your crew."

"You are only a lad, who doesn't understand anything," the Alien said, still refusing to turn around and face his captors.

"Do you think it was my idea … that brings me to you, with this offer?" Benekee asked the proud Visitor. "If you do, then you do not understand the generosity of … *the Sons of Balhok*."

Protas began to fidget with his hands. He didn't trust the Alien for a moment, and Benekee's dialogue was making him *very* nervous. He looked at Urshen who was busy studying the bodies hanging over chairs, tables or lying on the floor.

"You think to offer me life … but I cannot go back to Harleem. And I will not live on this backward planet as a slave."

"Ankoletia is about to enter a golden age. Your skills would be … extremely useful. And … you can keep your gold."

From the moment they began the dialogue, Kareen noticed that the lad's voice betrayed an increasing weariness. He certainly held the power of the Cave, but it appeared that it was too much for him. If he could keep him talking long enough …

"On Harleem, with that gold … I have the power of immortality. What you offer me is chaff by comparison."

For Protas, that was the last straw. If it was up to him, this pompous Alien would already be dead!

But he respected Benekee … and the Garden. So, with clenched fists he began with words that were quiet and slow.

"Is it your pride, that prevents you from accepting this offer … or is it … *irony*?

"The irony of a young lad, the conqueror of Harleem's invasion, sitting in your Captain's chair, while he dictates the terms, of your freedom?"

There was a brief flicker of Green Light around the edges of the Alien. Protas knew that things were about to change! With one hand clutching his Robe, he was already on the balls of his feet, ready.

Kareen recognized the voice of the one with the Robe. He thought to mock him with his own words. He turned around slowly and faced the three weaklings. Perhaps it was already time to make his move.

As Benekee listened to Protas's logic, his ability to hold up his head to face Kareen, failed him.

But he didn't need to see the eyes of the Alien to know that he was in a rage.

Benekee knew he must say his last words quickly.

"So you ... and your crew ... would rather die?"

The Alien knew that the boy was close to collapsing.

Kareen-hys-Tebeel-del-Harleem decided to wait no longer and rushed the young lad.

A long time ago, Bru-ell taught Protas that his Robe was his best asset ... and how to use it.

As expected, Kareen ignored him as he charged towards Benekee, but he shouldn't have, because the Robe flew in his face blinding him, and a strong kick from Protas threw the Alien off his feet.

With his Robe and his Tinker fighting skills, Protas kept the large and powerful Alien on the floor for a couple of heartbeats.

But then, just as quick, it was over. Urshen heard a broken bone as his friend flew across the floor.

In an instant, the Warrior inside of Urshen, surfaced ... angry and ready for battle.

Running towards Kareen, he grabbed a metal flask from a nearby table and with fighting skills that the Alien did not expect, he beat him backwards a pace.

But Kareen was far too strong and experienced for this off-worlder, and with minimal effort he too was soon flying across the room. Now it was time to destroy the young lad!

Benekee could hear the desperate attempts, of the other two Seers, as they did their best to defend him.

He was now so weak, he was hanging on the side of the chair.

He could hear Kareen rush towards him ... and then slam into an invisible wall.

The Alien was not to be deterred and quickly got up and starting pounding at that wall with his Gold Wristbands.

"It doesn't appear ... that he wants ... to accept the offer," he whispered to the Garden through tired lips.

Benekee nodded weakly at the Garden's reply and soon had Kareen suspended in mid-air, hanging upside down.

Next, Benekee extended his power to Protas and Urshen, and healed them.

The two Seers were soon by his side, lifting him out of the chair and helping him to stand.

"Are you okay?" Protas asked, as he looked at the Alien, hanging from an invisible meat hook.

The two Seers heard a barely audible whisper, "Yes."

"I think he needs to lay down and rest," Urshen suggested.

Soon they had a table cleared and laid him on it.

They waited and hovered anxiously, above the almost unconscious Benekee.

Finally, Benekee could whisper a few words, "It's the load. I am still getting used to it."

Protas looked at Urshen with a look that said, 'The load?'

Urshen remembered the tortured look when the young lad first appeared at their cell door.

"I think the load, was from the Garden," he suggested.

Protas gave an understanding nod.

Under the soft glow of green lights, they continued to wait.

Later, Protas asked Benekee, "Is there something we can do?"

"Yes ... please sit down."

Chapter 56 - The Blanket of White Light

Eventually Benekee stirred. The two Seers were immediately at his side. "Can you bring me some food? You will find the kitchen, if you head back to our cell, and keep walking. And bring Yaneek with you ... her door is now open."

'Finally,' thought Protas, as the two raced towards her cell.

Soon they were back, with the food and a very surprised Yaneek.

Protas and Urshen propped up Benekee while his sister fed him with a spoon.

"Hi sis," Benekee croaked between spoonful's. "You have no idea ... how glad I am to see you."

She smiled as she shoved another spoonful into his mouth. "I know ... who else would have the patience to feed you like a baby."

"Never thought ... I would say this ... but thanks for the food." Benekee could already feel strength pour into his body.

"Protas tells me that you are responsible for getting us out of our prison cells."

"I guess I played a part."

"And soon," Urshen jumped in, "he will be the one, to free the entire planet from these *Visitors*."

Protas had been anxiously watching Kareen, as he continued to pull himself up, to attack the invisible meat hook.

"Benekee ... I got to tell you. I wish *soon* was now. This waiting is killing me!"

"There ..." Yaneek said. "Last spoonful."

"You feel okay now?" Protas was quick to ask, casting another glance towards Kareen.

With a little help from his friends, Benekee was up, his feet dangling over the side.

"Sis ... see that picture of light ... over there. That ... is the Mountain of Hope."

Benekee motioned for the two Seers to help him off the table.

"And now ... if Urshen and Protas ... will take me closer to that picture ... I can start ... and they will witness."

Kareen watched as the four prisoners walked to the display screen. He had given up struggling. Now he would wait.

And hope that the young lad was incapable of using the amount of power, it would take, to ignite the Mountain of Despair, from out in space.

If he failed, it might kill him. And then he and his Ship would be free. And Ankoletia would still be his!

Standing together, facing the marvellous picture of light, Benekee began.

"My Seer Brothers. First … I will repair the Amulet. But for you to witness … we will need to change the picture … like using a scope. Take me to that table with all the lights."

As they assisted the young lad forward, Protas thought to ask, "Will the people of Balhok open the Door of this Master Cave … if we fail?"

"They cannot," Benekee replied. "They are … the author of the *power* … that will strengthen us … against the enemy from Harleem.

"But we are … and must always be … the author of our *destiny*."

Kareen watched the young lad touch the control panel. A moment later, he could see the broken fragments of an Amulet on the monitor. His hanging body tensed as he waited to see what would happen.

Benekee closed his eyes as he reached across space, to that image of shards lying on a remote mountain ledge, in Shaksbah.

Yaneek gasped as she saw the broken pieces of crystal come to life, and form into a complete Amulet … that hung in mid-air. Then the talisman glided towards the Quartz Door.

Protas could hear his heartbeat it was so quiet, as everyone watched the Amulet enter the Keyhole … and disappear, as it completed its passage.

He held his breath as he waited for the door to open. And waited some more.

"The door didn't open," a surprised Urshen finally said.

Protas and Urshen looked at Benekee, who was now slumping against their support, head hanging down, eyes closed. There was no response.

They looked at each other, feeling helpless. Like two bookends, whose only purpose was to help a Seer, keep standing.

"Why is *nothing* happening?" a very impatient Protas said to everyone in the room.

There was another period of silence, before Benekee finally raised his head and said, "Patience ... my Seer Brothers. And witness ... the *power* of the Garden."

With his hand, still on the control panel, Benekee adjusted the image so that the picture of light showed the Mountain of Hope from The Ledge to its summit.

Yaneek was standing in front of the picture of light, her eyes going back and forth between her brother and the monitor as he moved towards the table with all the lights.

She stood in awe as he healed the Amulet and carefully moved it into the small hole beside the Quartz Door.

But he was also losing his strength.

For every moment that passed, he looked more and more depleted.

Then there was confused silence when the door didn't open.

It was terrifying. She knew he had to succeed. Protas had told her, he was their *only* chance at rescuing the future of their planet.

She was biting her nails as she heard Benekee say, '...witness the *power* of the Garden'

Like everyone else, her eyes were riveted on the picture of light.

She took a step closer. Did she see something?
"I see it ... it is *happening*!" Yaneek whispered through tears of joy.

Protas strained to see what she was seeing.

And then it was clear.

Rocks were tumbling from the sides of the mountain, as though it was shedding its skin.

At first it was only small, random pieces.

But soon, rocks from the top to The Ledge, joined the avalanche of material that slid downwards, past the Quartz Door.

Kareen looked on in horror as the Mountain of Despair shed its rocky shroud to the foothills below, to reveal the inner chambers of power. The mechanism that would purge the planet … including his ship!

Sweat began to trickle down his back. He knew that everything was lost.

Urshen looked at a very exhausted Benekee. "I think we should put him back on the table."

Protas nodded but couldn't take his eyes off the picture of light, as they moved the Seer.

Yaneek followed them and stayed with Benekee.

The two Seers returned to finish witnessing the event.

Now that all the mountain above The Ledge had sloughed off to the base below, a clear view of the inside of the 'Cave' was on the monitor.

Protas could see a labyrinth of … metal and crystal … as it spiralled to the sky above. He was shaking his head in disbelief. "Imagine … all of this, was inside of the Mountain of Hope."

"And only moments ago, the Talisman lay broken on The Ledge," Urshen added.

Out of habit, Protas turned to check on Kareen, who had resumed pounding at the invisible meat hook.

"You should have taken the offer … irony or not," Protas said to the defeated Captain.

Urshen, anxious that Protas not miss anything, tugged on his friend's sleeve and said, "Look."

In the middle of the mountainous structure, there was a massive column that extended to the summit.

Spheres of crystal could be seen leaving that column, and ascending upwards until they reached an altitude, high above the clouds. Then, as if guided by an invisible force, the spheres headed outward across the sky, each one, travelling toward a unique destination.

The crystal globes continued to pour out of the column, until there were thousands of them moving across the sky.

"Benekee, I wish you could see this," Protas shouted with enthusiasm. "Thousands of crystal orbs have been ejected from the Cave into the sky above. But our view in the picture of light, does not allow us to witness what is happening, as they move away from the Mountain. Can you adjust the view?"

Without a sound from the young Seer, the view changed, until the surface of the planet and the sky above filled the glass screen.

For hundreds of leagues, the moving orbs could be seen expanding across the sky, forming a pattern, like a crystal doily, that draped the planet below.

The two Seers watched as the globes continued to expand out of their view, sparkling under the morning sun.

"Benekee ... the view below us, is filled with a pattern of these crystal spheres," Urshen observed. "And, it continues to expand. We can only assume that they will eventually surround our entire planet."

"What is their purpose?" Protas turned to ask.

Yaneek had already propped her brother up, so he could see the picture for himself.

"Once they are all in place," Benekee began, "they will be connected to each other ... by the power from the Master Cave. This *Blanket of White Light* ... will serve two purposes.

"First, it will form a protective barrier ... to keep out our enemies. Harleem will never ... visit us again.

"Secondly, because this immense ... crystal umbrella ... surrounds all Ankoletia ... our planet will become ... one *very large* Cave. The purge of darkness will be followed ... by a golden age of learning and growth."

"What do you mean ... purge?" Yaneek queried.

"The Power of the Garden requires ... a minimum standard," Benekee answered. "Those who are out of harmony ... no, a better way to say it is ... those who have adopted the ways ... of darkness ... and indeed have become slaves to it ..."

Benekee turned and looked at Kareen. "... will be destroyed."

Kareen-hys-Tebeel-del-Harleem, still hanging upside down, scowled at Benekee's words.

"This is no fitting way to die!"

It was the first time, that the three Seers had heard Kareen raise his voice.

"At least allow me to stand as a free man ... a warrior of Harleem, when I meet the Light of Death."

Protas kept one eye on the young Seer, and the other, on the man from Harleem. He saw too much of his old self in this cunning warrior from the other side of the Galaxy, to feel relaxed ... even when it seemed impossible for Kareen to accomplish anything.

He knew what *he* would do if he was on the brink of destruction. And that made him *very* nervous.

"Don't do it Benekee ... not yet ... not until he is bound by an oath to the Amulet."

But before the young Seer could respond, Urshen interrupted.

"The Globes are not moving."

Everyone stopped what they were doing as they all watched intently for the burst of Light to surge up the Column and across the sky ... connecting all the spheres as one Barrier of Light.

As he held his breath, waiting for the event, Urshen thought about the change on people everywhere that this Dome of Light would create.

He wondered if this Planetary Cave, that Benekee talked about, would affect the Circle of Blood ... that had once united Urshen with the twelve Trackers.

It was hard to imagine a future with so many possibilities!

Once it started, it happened faster than Protas had imagined.

A pillar of White Light shot upward from the column, hit the first crystal globe, and then spread outward, in all directions, lighting each sphere across the sky.

Until an entire Blanket of Light was formed ... between them and the surface of the planet.

"How ... will we return to the planet?" Protas asked everyone.

"We will ... use this Flying Ship," the exhausted young Seer answered.

The Caves of Balhok

He had barely finished the sentence, when the power of the Flying Ship returned.

Lights came on and quiet noises of every description, announced that all operations had returned.

"Will we not need a 'hole' in the Dome to sail through?" Urshen asked. "And does the young Seer know how to fly this Ship?"

"I think we might need to wait on those questions," an anxious Yaneek said, as she laid her exhausted brother back on the improvised bed.

"He's done well hasn't he," Protas said as he walked towards Yaneek, hoping to comfort her concerns.

At the 'bedside' he gazed down at the youthful but very tired face. "You have quite a remarkable brother."

When she turned her attention towards Protas, he added, "of course ... it runs in the family."

After the main lights came back on, Urshen noticed a window appear, as a panel in the far wall slid upwards. As soon as Protas joined Yaneek, he walked to the window.

And there below him, a Curtain of White Light stretched across the sky, like a holy veil, covering his world.

He stared down at Ankoletia ... his home. A beautiful blue and white orb, floating in space.

Urshen reached out as if to touch it.

With his hand on the glass, he thought of a lady with long black hair, that he was yearning to see.

It wasn't that long ago, that Bernado brought him to Qar-ana. The city where Zephra lived. They were finally so close and yet so far apart.

He thought back to the day, he awoke in his cell room and saw Protas, staring at him through iron bars. He would always remember those bold words, spoken by his friend.

Breaking the silence, he said, *"They should have never put us together in the same place, it will be their ruin."*

"I don't know about you," he continued, his hand still pressed against the glass, "but I never imagined a triumph like this.

"Protas ... it appears that you were right. It truly was their mistake, to place us together.

"But little did I suspect, that our role in all of this, would be to prop up a young lad, who was destined to conquer ... the conquerors from Harleem."

Urshen turned to Protas, who was grinning from the memory ... and the irony.

Then he left the window to join Protas and Yaneek, hovering over a resting Benekee.

Looking down into his face, it was still hard to believe, that the young lad resting on the improvised bed, was the key to stopping the invasion from Harleem.

Suddenly Benekee opened his eyes, and looking up into those three faces, he croaked, "I have the answer!"

As usual, Urshen and Protas gave each other that questioning look.

"I was curious to know ... if we can keep this Flying Boat," Benekee explained.

"We are!

"Imagine ... what life will look like in twenty years ... with the advantage ... of Harleem technology!"

Rick AW Smith hopes that you enjoyed the experience of reading *The Caves of Balhok*,
The third book of the *Seeds of Balhok* series.

The artwork for the cover of *The Caves of Balhok* was done by Blake E Davis.

ABOUT THE AUTHOR

Rick AW Smith, a fan of fantasy, decided it was time to contribute ... while working in the cold dark reaches of northern Russia.

Rick has recently returned to live in Canada after touring the world for fifteen years (through work), where he finished book three of the trilogy 'Seeds of Balhok'.

His ambition to write began many years ago when he was asked to stand in front of his literature class to read a couple of short stories that he had written. But like many youthful ambitions, this one needed to incubate for decades.

He always enjoyed heroes that were as mortal as anyone, but not overly reluctant. Adventure with a bit of romance that kept him turning pages well after midnight, and an ending that not only left him begging for the next book but explained the mysteries that were carefully woven through the plot.

Manufactured by Amazon.ca
Bolton, ON